WHISPERING WAVES

WHISPERING WAVES

Jamie Berris

Whispering Waves

Jamie Berris

Edited by Theresa Wegand

Cover by Sarah Hansen at Okay Creations

To Jason, Alex, Tori, Cole, and Miya, my everything.

To Grandpa Norm, my mourning dove.

To Grandma Barbie, my comfort.

CHAPTER 1

Lydia's Last Day

Sadie

Nicholas was down the road at the neighbor's house for the day, playing with his friend Gabriella. Lydia had already said her good-byes to him, and now it was time for her to do the same with Sadie and Jayna. Sadie's mom was in the guest bedroom, the room set up for Grandma Rose and Grandpop when they came home for visits from their winters in Florida and summers up north on Torch Lake.

Even though they had almost seven months to digest their mother's fate, it still seemed surreal, so unfair. Sadie couldn't help but wish for some miracle to happen. She had prayed and prayed—the thought of life without a mother was too hard to comprehend.

As Lydia's breaths became shallow and further apart, Sadie knew no miracle was taking place, no extra time, no more family vacations, no more Friday family date nights eating out or trips to the mall together.

Sadie and Jayna were on either side of the bed, each hanging on to one of their mother's hands. Sadie was stroking the back of Lydia's hand. Lydia's breathing had become labored, but occasionally she would gently squeeze her daughters' fingers. Sadie didn't know if she was doing it on purpose or if it was a reflex.

Grandma Rose, Grandpop, Aunt Josie, Aunt Nevie, and Dad all sat in the chairs sprawled around the bed. The silence in the room was only broken by the sound of a mourning dove sitting on the roof, cooing.

With everyone in the room, Sadie felt like she was suffocating and was overwhelmed and overcome with tears. Her tears set off Jayna's, and then, like a ripple effect, everyone's in the room. One by one they all moved in closer and huddled on the bed, scooting close to make room for one another.

Grandma Rose was the first to speak up. "This isn't what our Lydia wanted. She wanted us to be by her side and talk about all the wonderful memories we've created with her."

"Hold hands," said Grandma Rose.

Sadie had her mom's hand in one and grabbed her Aunt Josie's in the other.

Grandma Rose started praying, "Lord, you have chosen to take our dear Lydia to live in your Heavenly Kingdom where she will await each of us. Let us carry her in our hearts and know she will be at peace with you and we will be reunited with her when you have declared us to do so. Comfort us in our time of grief and help us to treasure the memories she is leaving behind. Take her with your grace and touch us with your healing hands. In your name, we pray."

"Amen," they all said together.

Just like that, they all looked to one another with drier eyes. It was always like Grandma Rose to take control.

Sadie stroked her mother's forehead with one hand and rubbed her thumb across her other hand as she held it. Jayna had both of her hands cupped around Lydia's, and Kurt placed his hands on his wife's leg. Aunt Josie was sitting cross legged at the end of the bed, massaging her sister's feet, and Aunt Nevie had come to the top of the bed where she could rest a hand on her sister's head. Grandma Rose and Grandpop were on the other side of the bed, stroking their daughter's leg and arm.

"She can feel it," Aunt Josie said. "She can feel us, our touch and our love."

Lydia May Booker took her last breath and passed away, knowing her family had each other.

May 6, 2013

As Sadie glanced around the cemetery, she noted the signs of new life everywhere. The trees were heavy with buds just about to bloom. The daffodils, a beautiful canary yellow, and tulips, in every shade of color, opened toward the sun. Somehow, with all this beauty, Sadie still felt engulfed by death and its ugliness.

While singing "Amazing Grace," Dylan took her hand in his and kissed it. She turned to him and saw his eyes were welled up with tears. The sight nearly made her break down again.

She and Dylan had been going out for six months and she thanked her lucky stars every day for him. Losing her mother would have been ten times worse without him by her side.

Her grandmother grasped her other hand and eyed her to see if she was okay. Grandma Rose looked stunning, as usual, in her tailored cream suit and pink wool coat. Sadie saw many of her mother's features when she looked at her grandmother. Her mother and grandmother had often been told they looked like sisters.

Lydia had always kept her sandy blond hair long and loose. Her large, almond-shaped, brown eyes had rarely sported anything more than a coat of mascara, but her full lips were always played up with different colors of lipstick. Her mom had been a head turner, and frankly, Sadie was proud of that.

Sadie resembled her mother more in mannerisms and personality than anything. With dark hair, pale blue eyes, and fair clear skin, she was definitely her father's child when it came to looks, but that was okay with Sadie since she always received compliments about the contrast between her dark hair and light eyes.

Jayna, Sadie's younger sister, who would someday pass for their mother's twin, had her head buried in their grandpop's chest. Their dad held three-year-old Nicholas, who looked a touch like their mom, but nothing like Sadie or their dad.

Sadie heard the sniffing of both her Aunt Nevie and Aunt Josie behind her and contemplated taking them up on their offer to fly back to NYC with them after the funeral.

They dually owned an upscale boutique and were constantly calling with news of celebrities shopping in their store. It was tempting, but Sadie couldn't imagine leaving her family right now.

As "Amazing Grace" echoed to a close, the minister said one last prayer. One by one, mourners placed pink, yellow, and purple tulips on her mother's casket before meandering to their cars, cars which filled every road and crevice of the cemetery and beyond.

The cemetery had emptied out and fallen quiet except for a single mourning dove perched on the fence nearest Lydia's gravesite. As they individually said their good-byes, the bird broke out in song, "*Whoo-ahh-whoo-whoo-whoo*." Sadie didn't speak it out loud, but she felt her mother's spirit watching over them.

The luncheon following the funeral was tolerable, thanks to the Valium Sadie's grandmother slipped her. If Sadie's dad had known, he would have strangled his mother-in-law. He was still irked about the belly-button ring Grandma Rose had paid for and had driven Sadie to get last month.

Sadie had explained to her dad a thousand times that both she and her Grandma Rose had okayed it with Mom.

Kurt had only glared at Sadie. They both knew that, with only weeks to live, Lydia was not going to deny her daughter anything. Sadie had no argument; she was fully aware that she'd taken total advantage of her mother's illness, but sometimes that's just what fifteen-year-olds do.

"Say-dee," Nicholas whined, squeezing her leg, pulling and grabbing at her as he begged her to pick him up.

She looked down at his face smeared with frosting and lifted him to her chest where he laid his tired head on his big sister's shoulder. Sadie wiped the sweet lavender icing from his cheek and let him lick it off her finger, thinking it would have been more appropriate to serve dirt dessert at a funeral rather than cake.

The luncheon turned into a two-hour celebration of Lydia's life, with a video and countless pictures. Hundreds of people crammed into the ballroom at the country club for turkey and avocado pesto wraps, chopped chicken salad, and seafood chowder—Lydia's favorite lunch items on the menu.

Sadie wanted nothing more than to get out of the confining room and away from all the old people smothering her with kisses and hugs and telling her it was going to be *alright*.

Alright? *Alright* going home to a house without the glue that held the family together? *Alright* having to be the one to do the laundry for a family of four? *Alright* trying to comfort three-year-old Nicholas as he cried for his mommy at breakfast, lunch, nap time, bedtime, and countless times in between?

Alright trying to do homework or make it to tennis practice when Sadie felt obligated to spend every second reading or playing trains with Nicholas, trying to soothe his sadness? *Alright* trying to act like everything was *alright* when her mother was dead and she was only fifteen, suddenly thrown into her role?

Why was it so hard, even for adults, to understand that, sometimes, saying nothing at all spoke louder and clearer than a bunch of nervous garbage? Sadie's mother always told her she was wise beyond her years. Maybe this was one of those moments, or maybe she was just sick of people telling her she was going to be *alright*. Everything felt completely *all wrong*.

Annoying Sadie further was the fact that Marissa, her mother's worst enemy, not only attended the funeral but hugged her dad thirty seconds too long and talked privately with him for almost five minutes.

Sadie wasn't the only one to notice either. She caught her mother's longtime friend, Andrea glancing their way suspiciously several times.

After stepping away from her dad, Marissa moved in on Jayna. She hugged her, stepped back, and spoke to her while resting her hands on both of Jayna's shoulders, and then hugged her a second time.

Why Sadie thought Marissa wouldn't seek her out as well was silly. When Marissa approached Sadie, with Nicholas still clinging to her chest, Marissa's bottom lip trembled. She held out her arms, and to Sadie's surprise, Nicholas went right to her.

What? He doesn't even know her! Who does she think she is waltzing over here and taking Nicholas from her?

Marissa proceeded to hug and kiss Nicholas's cheeks and forehead while resting a hand on Sadie's shoulder telling her to call her if she ever needed help with anything. She offered to give Sadie rides to tennis, help with babysitting Nicholas, deliver meals, grocery shop, or take the girls shopping.

Marissa must have sensed both the confusion and anger on Sadie's face. She quickly handed Nicholas back over to Sadie and said how sorry she was. Sadie wasn't sure if Marissa meant sorry for her loss or sorry for overstepping her boundaries and being inappropriate.

Marissa's eyes were filled with tears as she walked away, grabbing Paige's arm as she stood talking with Sadie's friends, and left the country club.

Sadie wished she knew what had caused the rift between her mom and Marissa in the first place. Her mother was extremely tight-lipped whenever Sadie asked her about it.

Marissa and Lydia had been best friends since college. Marissa had been the maid of honor at Kurt and Lydia's wedding. She'd held their children as infants, and there was a time when Sadie and Jayna called her Aunt Rissy.

The two families had countless barbecues and many vacations together. Marissa and her husband Marcus started having problems about five years ago, and Lydia was there helping Marissa through many brutal fights. Then, a year later, all hell broke loose, Marissa and Marcus divorced, and Lydia and Marissa's friendship was shattered.

For the first year or two, both Sadie and Jayna asked about Aunt Rissy and Paige. Lydia had skirted around with excuses about being too sick to do anything social when she was pregnant with Nicholas, and then too busy with Nicholas when he was a baby. Lydia also explained that Marissa was going through a rough time with her divorce and she needed alone time.

Finally, the girls were old enough to understand that the friendship was broken, to say the least. Sadie knew something big went down, so much so that, when their mothers were at school functions and ran into each other, they both looked the other way; not even the slightest nod was shared.

Finally, in the safety of the car, Sadie turned around to see that Nicholas had fallen asleep in the backseat next to Jayna. Jayna's ear buds were stuffed in her ears and were turned up so loud that Sadie could sing along with her from the front seat. Normally, their mom would have told her to turn it down before she went deaf. Dad didn't have the energy or guts to say anything to her, and Sadie liked the fact that it kept Jayna quiet. Things were definitely going to be different without a mom.

Sitting in the front seat with her dad, Sadie was instructed to pick a radio station. Kurt stared straight ahead, eyes on the road. His features looked softer today than they had in as long as Sadie could remember. She couldn't quite tell if it was sadness or relief.

"Sadie, we're still a family," he said.

She waited, expecting him to go on. He didn't, and they sat in silence the rest of the way home. Beyoncé was singing "Irreplaceable" on the radio. Sadie wondered if her dad would ever date again. She wondered if he would replace her mom; she hoped he realized that Mom was *irreplaceable*.

Dear Sadie,

As you know, I have written you many little notes to read from time to time. Some I have dated for you to open on specific days or events; others are just general garbage that you can grab and read whenever you want to hear my "rambling" as you call it, or maybe it's nagging, whatever.

I'm sure you recognize the decorative box as you were the one who picked it out at the craft store (for Jayna's dance certificates). At the time, I couldn't tell you that it was actually for these letters because it was too hard to accept.

Obviously, the dated ones are meant for specific events, but you have my blessing to tear through the entire box at once if you wish. I can only hope they guide you through many stages of your life—just as I would have.

This one was to be opened on the day of my funeral, a day I know you will never forget. I'm hoping for a beautiful spring day, but if we get a raging thunderstorm, I guess that would be okay too. How many thunderstorms have we sat and watched in the screened porch together, Sadie? Too many to count, that's for sure. Not many two-year-olds are obsessed with thunderstorms. Most are scared to death, but you always found them fascinating. I've always found you fascinating. I love and admire your fearlessness, curiosity, and drive for adventure.

I hope you remembered to spread the word that I didn't want everyone wearing black to my funeral. I want color, but since you weren't supposed to open this up until after the funeral, it's okay if you forgot. At least I don't have to worry about Grandma; we know black is not her color. She will either wear cream or pale pink, lilac, or possibly a pale yellow if the sun is out. Was I right? Laugh, Sadie, please.

I want people telling jokes, funny stories, and remembering me for the life I was so fortunate to live. Oh, I just thought of something. Remember Lila Briggs from our old church? She has to be about 110 by now. Anyhow, to every funeral she attends, she wears a hat that looks as if a cockatiel has been strangled and pinned to her head. I'm not sure if it represents something, but it's bright orange with blue, green, yellow, red, and purple feathers mangled on it. I hope it makes you smile when you see her. I know Nicholas will probably blurt something out about it, which is okay. Let him—it will get a laugh out of people.

Sadie, I know today is going to be rough, especially for you because you're the one in the family who has always been worried about everyone else. Jayna and Nicholas are in good hands, and I know you want to be strong for them, but honey, don't forget to take care of yourself. Dad, well, we all know how Dad deals with curve balls. He ducks, so bring him back to reality every now and then.

Keep your chin up, sweetie, and stay strong. You've always been a fighter—don't quit on me.

Lots of hugs and kisses, love ya,

Mom

P.S. Maybe you could talk Grandma into making a big pot of chicken and dumplings for you. It always made you feel better when you were upset about something. And since you're the only one in the house that can stomach it, you'll get it all to yourself.

P.P.S. When I was eleven, I threw up for three days after eating those dumplings. Haven't eaten them since! I know. I know. You've heard that story a thousand times. Now you've heard it a thousand and one times.

P.P.P.S. Is there such a thing? I mean as P.P.P.S?

Luckily, Sadie had opened the letter from her mom the morning of the funeral. She quickly sent out a mass email asking people to wear color and most did. Yes, Mrs. Briggs had that horrific feather thing on her head. Nicholas didn't blurt out anything embarrassing, but he begged to touch it, and Mrs. Briggs was delighted.

CHAPTER 2

Dear Sadie,

I know you are hurting deeply, but guess what? I'm free of pain now—no more suffering, no more worrying, no more questioning, no more tears. I've been set free of all that, and I'm playing tennis in Heaven. My, how I've improved since I've gotten here! Please laugh and wipe away that tear.

Sadie, it's okay to cry, it's okay to be a little angry and sad, but please don't let my death consume you—don't be bitter, baby girl. When you miss the sound of my voice, watch our family videos. When you want to see my face, look to all the pictures. When you want to feel my love for you, stop and close your eyes, quiet yourself, and feel me with you.

The first year without me will be tough, really tough. As the days go by, it will get easier, I promise. You have to allow it. I want you to go on living, not sulking. Hang out with your friends and Dylan, play tennis, watch funny movies, and laugh. Spend endless hours texting nonsense, Snapchatting, and doing whatever you do on Instagram. Crank the music in your bedroom as loud as ever and sing. Find happiness, Sadie—it's all around you to embrace, if you let yourself.

Without a doubt, I know you'll be a great role model and big sister to Nicholas. Keep my memory alive for him. Smother him with hugs, kisses, and love. Most of all, teach him to be a gentleman and use his manners.

Please have patience with Jayna. God knows you'll need it with her! You two share such a special, deep bond of friendship, but you are a typical set of sisters and you will have your occasional blowouts. Don't sweat the small stuff, Sadie; treasure the closeness you two share. Having two sisters of my own, I know what amazing friends they are; I want you two to also have that.

Go easy on Dad, Sadie. He's new at this single father stuff, and it's my fault for not allowing him in the laundry room . . . or the kitchen really. At least he can grill!

Oh, Sadie, I feel like I've left you with so much responsibility. I wish I could just tell you to remain a kid and not grow up too fast, but who am I kidding? That's impossible. So I guess I'll leave you with this today: Stay true to yourself. I couldn't be prouder of the young woman you've become.

I love you, Sadie.

Mom

Her dad was at work, and Sadie was stuck home with Jayna and Nicholas. At twelve, almost thirteen, Jayna was old enough to babysit Nicholas by herself, but the last couple of weeks he'd been acting out, throwing tantrums, and wetting the bed, obviously missing his mommy.

Sadie was far more sympathetic toward Nicholas than Jayna was, and she also had the patience that Jayna lacked. So even though she hated that she felt like a prisoner at home while all her friends, including Dylan, were at the beach, she knew Nicholas needed her, and he meant the world to Sadie.

Sadie had made a promise to her mom that she would be there for her brother, and she was not going to break it. Never did she realize how tough and tiring it was going to be.

Jayna and her friend Chrissie were doing handstands in the pool and asked Sadie to judge them on a scale of one to ten. Sadie sighed; all she really wanted to do was be alone with her magazines. Hadn't she entertained enough today already? And really, how old were they?

Ignoring Jayna and Chrissie, she checked her phone and noticed she had several text messages. The first was from Dylan.

Hey sexy, what r u doin? Wish u were here. Miss u, luv, D.

The next was from Myla.

I'm spending the night. Have so much to tell you.

The last was from Kyla.

The parents are making me go to my brother's stupid All Star baseball game tonight. I'm going to miss my besties, but I'll be over first thing in the morning. *Ciao*.

After replying to her texts, Sadie closed her eyes and relaxed, feeling the sun on her face. Just as she started to doze off, Nicholas came running outside, crying, his shorts and bottom half of his T-shirt soaked from another accident.

Nicholas dove into Sadie's arms.

"I want Mommy," he screamed.

"I know, bud. I know," said Sadie as she cuddled him and kissed his teary cheeks. They'd told Nicholas that mom was living in Heaven with Jesus, but lately when Sadie brought it up, he'd cover his ears and yell at her to be quiet.

Last week he sat in the car for over an hour while he pleaded for his dad to drive him to Heaven to visit his mommy.

Chrissie bounded out of the pool. Wrapping herself in a towel, she offered to go strip the bed and throw the sheets in the wash for Sadie. Jayna, on the other hand, acted oblivious to what was going on and continued fetching diving sticks. Sadie wondered for the millionth time if it was immaturity, denial, anger, or just plain selfishness. Whatever Jayna's problem was, Sadie didn't have the energy to deal with her sister.

She thanked Chrissie for the help and took Nicholas inside to change him into his swimsuit. *Why bathe him when she could put some swimmies on him and let him paddle around for an hour?*

On their way back outside, Sadie stopped in the kitchen for a glass of iced tea. She was going to crash if she didn't get some caffeine in her system, and Jayna had drained the last of her Cherry Coke Zero that was clearly labeled with Sadie's name. "I want ice cream," Nicholas said as Sadie opened the freezer for ice cubes.

About to say "no" to the second bowl today—the first was at 9:30 this morning—Sadie caved, avoiding the controversy. "Sprinkles and whipped cream too?" she asked.

CHAPTER 3

Sadie

Sadie played with the charm bracelet on her wrist as she waited for Dylan to pick her up. Dylan had bought her the charm bracelet for Christmas with a charm shaped like a heart that said *love*. For her fifteenth birthday, he added a charm that said *always*. After her mother died, he gave her a charm that had a dove on it and said *peace*.

The air was already balmy and thick with humidity at eleven in the morning as she sat on the front steps. She couldn't handle listening to any more of her dad's rules. She wanted to hop in Dylan's getaway car as soon as the Mustang pulled in the driveway.

"I don't like you alone in the car with him," Kurt said regularly.

"How else are we supposed to go to the movies or meet up with friends?" Sadie always replied.

Sadie knew he was only trying to protect her, but it felt more like smothering. She and Dylan were meeting up with a big group at the beach for the 4th of July.

She had packed her overnight bag because she was staying the night at Kyla's cottage. Her dad hadn't asked whether or not Kyla's parents were going to be there, and Sadie didn't mention that they were in Chicago.

Sadie was excited about the night ahead and nervous too. She was still a virgin. She and Dylan had talked about having sex, but they hadn't yet. Tucked deep in her overnight bag was the package of pills she had started taking a few weeks ago.

Last night on the phone, Dylan mentioned how excited he was to spend an entire day and night with Sadie. A ripple ran through her from head to toe. She took that as a sign that she was ready. She was basically in tenth grade! She was still only fifteen, her conscience told her. She should wait until she was married or at least in college. At the very least it should be with someone she was totally in love with. Hmm, she *was* totally in love with Dylan, wasn't she?

Sadie had talked to her two best friends, Myla and Kyla, about having sex. Myla was a virgin and claimed she would be until her wedding night. Kyla had already had sex with her then boyfriend over spring break. Sadie was still torn.

Dylan's hand was resting on Sadie's thigh as they drove to the beach. The windows were rolled down and the music was turned up loud. The sweltering heat caused Sadie to stick to the leather seats, and yet she had goose bumps.

At the beach, their Beats Pill was blaring tunes from Megan Trainor, Katy Perry, Taylor Swift, The Chainsmokers, and Pit Bull. Sadie joined the girls stretched out on their beach towels, chatting, while the guys played catch with a football and surfed the shoreline on their skim boards. Without a second to run, Dylan, Riley, and Zack scooped up Sadie, Myla, and Kyla from their towels. The girls were kicking and screaming as the boys ran them full force into the cool waters of Lake Michigan.

Lucky for Sadie, her top was tied; Kyla, well, she wasn't quite as lucky. It took Zack ten minutes to find it in the water since the current was strong and quickly carried it away. If Zack planned on staying at Kyla's cottage tonight, he had some serious sucking up to do.

Once Sadie got used to the water, it wasn't so bad. She clung to Dylan, her arms and legs wrapped tightly around him. His body was warm, muscled, and tan. They were kissing and floating around in the water as their friends splashed and dunked each other around them.

Dylan's nose was pressed to Sadie's as he looked deep in her eyes. "Is tonight the night?"

"I think there could be some serious fireworks in the air tonight," she said and kissed him because she didn't know what else to say.

The previous winter Lydia had taken Sadie to her first OB-GYN appointment. Thank God it was quick, but it was embarrassing all the same. Since Lydia knew she would not be alive for the next appointment and she knew Dylan and Sadie were serious, she had suggested Sadie start taking birth control pills.

Sadie had acted offended, telling her mother she had no intention of having sex with Dylan. Of course, the first part of that was true, but the second part she was uncertain of.

That was all everyone talked about at school: who was doing it, where they were doing it, and if they were on the pill or they used condoms.

Everyone knew Dylan and Sadie hadn't done it yet, and she was feeling some pressure. Sadie caved and told her mom how she felt about Dylan and that she was considering having sex with him. She couldn't believe in a million years she was having this conversation with her mother! Lydia reminded Sadie that this was their only chance, and it was a hurdle that she dreaded, but didn't dare leave it up to dad.

Lydia told Sadie they were getting a supply of pills no matter what. In the end, Lydia had said it was Sadie's choice whether to take them or not, and she made it very clear that Sadie not misunderstand her intentions.

Lydia firmly sided against Sadie having sex, told her she would be disappointed, but she felt it was her duty to take this next step with her daughter before she died. It was the responsible parental thing to do.

Her mom's voice still echoed in Sadie's head. Lydia had been halfway out the door when she turned around with the strangest look on her face. "Sadie, sex doesn't mean love, and you can be in love and not have sex. And sex can hurt, really hurt, the people you love if you're not careful." Lydia started to walk out again and stopped one more time. "And, Sadie, babies can come from anything. They aren't always produced out of love or with the person you want to spend the rest of your life with."

With that, she said dinner would be ready in a half hour, and she walked out of Sadie's bedroom.

CHAPTER 4

Sadie

"Ouch, not so hard, Jayna. I have a sunburn, remember!"

Sadie had given Jayna the duty of putting sunscreen on her back, and she failed miserably. After floating in the pool face down on a raft half the afternoon, Sadie was more than pink; her back was burnt to a crisp.

"I'm barely touching you. Jeez, relax," said Jayna, squirting more aloe on her sister's back.

"You just squirted it in the shape of a heart. Does that mean you're asking for forgiveness?" snickered Sadie.

Jayna ignored Sadie and closed the lid. Sadie's back was so hot that the gel quickly turned to liquid. "Do you think she watches us all the time?"

Jayna didn't have to specify. Sadie knew she was talking about their mom. "I don't know. Sometimes I feel like she's an angel flying above, looking down on us, just observing, and maybe putting thoughts in our heads. Other times I feel like maybe her spirit is housed inside of us and she is along for the ride and sees things and feels things as we do."

Sadie was lying face down on her bed, and Jayna was sitting next to her, rubbing the aloe in. Jayna started drawing letters, something they had done since they were little to help them fall asleep at night. Knowing the drill, Sadie instantly started calling the letters out as Jayna wrote them. *I miss Mom* was her first message. *I love you* was her second message, which took Sadie by surprise; they had been extra catty to each other these past few weeks. Sadie knew Jayna was hurting badly, she hadn't said *I love you* in as long as Sadie could remember.

She turned to stare at her sister. She hadn't gotten a haircut all summer, so it hung more than halfway down her back, and the bottom three inches were bleached a blondish green from the pool, while the top was full of light caramel streaks. Jayna had lost about five pounds, which wasn't much for the average person, but Jayna was skin and bones to begin with. She simply hadn't developed any curves yet.

"Jayna, this is the worst it can get. It will get better as time goes on. I mean it's only been three months." Sadie didn't know what else to say and wasn't even sure she believed herself.

"How can it get better?" Jayna whispered, on the verge of tears. "Nothing is going to bring her back. I think about her from the second I wake up to the second I go to bed. I want to wake up and feel happy, and without Mom, I don't see how that will ever happen."

Sadie took Jayna's hand. It was warm and sticky from the aloe. "Want to ask Dad if we can ride our bikes into town and get ice cream? C'mon, it will be fun, just the two of us. We'll have to hurry; it'll be dark soon.

"I spent my allowance already." Jayna smirked.

"I doubt that's true, but I'll buy anyway."

"A large peanut butter cup flurry with extra whipped cream does sound good."

"Mooo, mooo," Sadie teased, but wished her sister would eat about four of them.

They both giggled and Sadie hugged her little sister.

CHAPTER 5

Kurt

Kurt took Lydia's diary out of his nightstand drawer. Lydia had kept a personal diary since she was seven years old. She documented her daily life over 13,000 times, rarely missing a day. Once Lydia finished a diary, she put it in a plastic tub in the basement. Dozens of full tubs took up an entire wall of floor-to-ceiling shelves that Kurt had built her in the storage room.

Kurt had suggested she go digital and start writing on her laptop. "SanDisk's take up way less space," he'd argued. Lydia told Kurt that was the most ludicrous thing that had ever come out of his mouth.

He had never read a single entry until after his wife died. Lydia had asked Kurt early on in their relationship to respect her privacy and keep his hands and eyes off. Even though he was always curious, Kurt didn't want to break his promise and told Lydia she could trust him.

While they were dating, he was very intrigued, and even still when they were first married. From time to time, he would peek over her shoulder or read a couple of lines when she left it open on the nightstand or in the chair on the front porch. As the years went on, the diaries lost their appeal. Kurt had about as much interest in reading his wife's diary as he had reading the *National Enquirer* from the supermarket check-out lane.

Now that his wife was gone, besides his children, her diaries were the best gifts she'd left him. They were the keys to the memories of their past together. The diaries also held the answers to so many questions that still plagued his mind from an extremely difficult time in their marriage, a time that he was glad he didn't walk away from, because even though he acted strong, inside he often felt like giving up, becoming another statistic of divorce.

When Kurt opened the container dated back five years ago, he felt an overwhelming ache for his wife. He could smell Lydia on the pages. The neat, right slant of her handwriting was one of those simple things that he never imagined he'd miss.

Once Kurt found the bundle of diaries he was specifically looking for, he took them upstairs and sat in the dark living room with the truth resting on his lap.

February 4, 2009

Marissa and I went shopping and out to lunch today. I got the cutest boots—nothing like retail therapy! Anyway, Marissa and I had another long talk about her and Marcus. Their marriage is extremely strained.

She complained that he was never around. If he wasn't working, he was in whatever seasonal league or sport he could be in—golf, poker night, hunting, the cigar club—it was basketball at the moment.

Marcus has been traveling more than ever for work, and Marissa feels like some of it may not be necessary, that it is just to get away, and possibly get away to someone else. She is sick of feeling like a single mother to Paige, selling real estate, and taking care of the house by herself.

To comfort herself, she shops. Oops, I talked her into a new Armani Collezioni suit for work today. Marcus yells at her to stop spending so much money. He says the reason he travels and works such long hours is because she's *constantly spending. She says she spends out of spite because he's never around . . . blah, blah, blah. It's not good!*

Marissa is totally stuck on the cheating thing. When she asks him about it, it turns into a nasty fight, so now she feels like the dumb wife who lets her husband get away with adultery.

She suggested a vacation to Marcus, and he said he'd think about it. Marissa asked if Kurt and I would want to go along and be a buffer. She thinks it will help them to both be on good behavior and could possibly help for Marcus to see how good Kurt is to me. I didn't bring it up to Kurt tonight. I guess I'll have to think about this one carefully. I'm not so sure I want to deal with the tension.

Kurt always tells me I get too involved in Marissa's marriage. What he doesn't understand is that Marissa is like another sister to me. Nothing between us is off limits. When she hurts, I hurt. I guess that's his point.

Nope! He wasn't ready, not yet. He would get to that time period eventually. He was still too raw emotionally to read anything from 2009 to 2010.

Kurt put the diaries from those critical months in his nightstand and went back to the basement and dug out one dated back to 1996, the year they were married. He read entries that put him back to their wedding night, their honeymoon in Jamaica.

Settling into the diary, Kurt took a swig from his beer and decided this was a good place to start. The early years brought back such good memories. Life was so simple; with only the two of them to think about, their lives were carefree. The most stressful it got was deciding what to eat for dinner or where to take the boat for the weekend. He would read about the rocky time of their marriage . . . eventually.

October 6, 1996

Jamaica is awesome and so is my husband. Married life is bliss. Today we climbed the Dunn's River Falls. The water was freezing! It was also very beautiful and romantic. The guides made us kiss a thousand times and never stopped snapping Polaroid pictures. We lay lazily by the pool with cocktails and talked about our next vacation; we're thinking St. Thomas. Ah, married life is good.

Kurt just turned off the shower. Room service delivered champagne and chocolate-covered strawberries. Tonight's lingerie is pink satin.

Kurt closed his eyes and remembered the day, crystal clear. He'd held Lydia's waist as they tumbled backward, lips locked, into the "plunge pool" at the falls. The guide had taken a Polaroid picture, and it was one of Kurt's favorites to this day. It was stuck in the scrapbook Lydia had made with their wedding and honeymoon photos and memorabilia.

Lydia had at least twenty different pieces of lingerie that her girlfriends had given her for the honeymoon, but that pink one was her favorite. She was ecstatic the week after she gave birth to Sadie that she could fit into it again. Kurt didn't have the heart to tell her it was busting at the seams.

Two weeks after Jayna was born Lydia fit into it once again. A small hole developed in the side stitching, and Lydia had tried to sew it back up. She wasn't much of a seamstress, and it ended up lopsided, not to mention she used orange thread.

Kurt wondered what happened to the pink lingerie. The last time he remembered seeing it on Lydia was just before Lydia got pregnant with Nicholas.

At 12:30 a.m., Kurt put the diary away and went to check on his sleeping children. Tonight Sadie was sleeping with Nicholas in his bed, and Jayna was sleeping by herself in Sadie's bed. He watched them all sleep and prayed he could at least be an average dad. He knew he wasn't in the running for any gold medals, but he also knew he never fell short when it came to loving them. And he did love them, all three of them.

CHAPTER 6

Sadie

On April 10, 2014, Sadie's sixteenth birthday, "Teenage Dream," by Katy Perry, was playing on her alarm. Opening her eyes, Sadie was happy to see the sun peeking through the blinds.

"Sweet sixteen," she murmured to herself, ecstatic about getting her driver's license after school.

Before Lydia died, she'd told Sadie she could have her black Infiniti QX80 for her sixteenth birthday. Having driven it with her permit, Sadie felt like an old pro, but to have it officially be hers, and to drive anywhere at any time, alone, gave Sadie goose bumps.

She knew if her mom were alive she would be driving a used something or other at a fraction of the cost and style of the Infiniti. Her dad hadn't argued that night at the dinner table when Lydia declared that Sadie would become the proud owner.

Sadie knew it was a flashy and expensive car for a teenager with a brand new license, but given the circumstances in which she received it, well, she wasn't going to put up with anyone criticizing her for being spoiled.

In the kitchen, Kurt sat with a cup of coffee, staring out the window. *The Today Show* was on the TV mounted to the wall, but the volume was turned down low. Sadie poured herself a cup of coffee—she'd been hooked since she was twelve—and sat down next to her dad at the table.

"It's my birthday, Dad."

A smile crept across his face. “How could I forget, Sadie? Happy sweet sixteen, sweetheart,” he said as he looked at the *Bon Appétit* chalkboard propped on a stand in the corner of the kitchen. Sadie had been counting down the days to her birthday since January. Every morning she erased and rewrote a lesser number. Today Sadie wiped the board clean and wrote *HAPPY SWEET SIXTEEN, SADIE* in giant bubble letters.

Kurt handed his daughter a small box wrapped in lilac paper with a tiny iridescent bow. “From Mom and me,” he said in a voice with more sadness than Sadie needed on her birthday.

She hadn’t wanted to cry today, but Sadie could already feel the tears welling up in her eyes and choking her throat.

“Did Mom wrap it?”

Kurt nodded. “When have you known me to wrap a present, sweetheart?”

“Are you going to call me ‘sweetheart’ all day?”

Kurt smiled wide and the corners of his eyes creased. “I’m sure you’ll give me a reason not to at some point.”

“Funny, Dad.” Sadie unwrapped the box and discovered Lydia’s princess-cut diamond earrings sparkling up at her. She was ten when her dad gave them to her mom on their anniversary.

Sadie put them in her ears and turned towards her dad. “May I wear them to school?”

“Take them out at tennis.”

Sadie knew he’d let her. Ever since her mom died, he was all about living in the present and not waiting until tomorrow to do what you could today. She wiped a tear that had crept down her cheek and gave her dad a hug, thanking him. He knuckled the back of her head, as he had since she was little, and told her he loved her.

“She also left you this,” he said, handing her a card. “Maybe you want to wait until after school to open it.”

Nodding, Sadie grabbed the box and card and took the stairs two at a time to wake up Jayna and Nicholas; she still had to get on with the morning routine.

Dylan came up from behind Sadie and rested his chin on her shoulder as she was reaching into her locker.

"Could I make your life any sweeter, birthday girl?" he asked.

Sadie whipped around, nearly eye to eye with Dylan, thanks to the wedges she wore today. He grabbed her chin and kissed her lips. A flutter of emotion washed through her, and she hoped no teachers were near.

Even though Dylan and Sadie had been together for a year and a half now, she was still shy about kissing in public, especially terrified of a teacher witnessing.

Dylan could have had any girl in the entire high school, and Sadie still wondered, *Why her?* She considered herself pretty, but definitely not the prettiest girl in school, or even in the sophomore class. Sadie wasn't a cheerleader or on the girls' rugby, volleyball, or soccer teams with the ultra-popular girls.

She knew what she was doing on the tennis court and had as many friends as she needed, but she wasn't the most popular and certainly not the life of the party. Guys like Dylan were supposed to date *those* kinds of girls, so she really didn't get it, and neither did *those* girls.

Sadie pushed Dylan's sideswept dark blond hair out of his eyes to reveal the light green hue hidden behind. "That depends," she whispered close to his mouth, thankful she just popped a mint.

"Depends on what?" he asked with a flirtatious grin.

"Depends on whether you let me take you for a spin in my new wheels."

"Where to?"

"Anywhere or nowhere."

Dylan pressed against Sadie, pushing her back into the locker. Over Dylan's shoulder, Sadie saw Allison walking by, darts shooting from her eyes. Once she caught Sadie's glance, she quickly said something to her friend Sami and they both laughed.

"Bitch," Sadie mumbled.

"What?" asked Dylan.

"Nothing." Sadie gave Dylan's chin a peck to show Allison that he was hers.

Sadie had asked Dylan countless times why he dumped Allison to date her. "She's not you" was always his response.

Sadie so wanted to blow off tennis practice and go straight to the Secretary of State after school to get her license, but her dad gave her some lame lecture about having to be responsible, saying only responsible people were given the privilege to drive.

She knew this was bull because her dad couldn't wait for her to get her license so she could help with picking up Nicholas from preschool and carting Jayna to and from dance. Not to mention getting groceries and picking up his dry cleaning.

Kurt managed to make it to the last half of Sadie's tennis practice. Unfortunately, he spent most of the time chatting with Marissa. Sadie felt she was being loyal to her mother by still considering her the enemy.

Marissa's daughter Paige and Sadie were still friends, but they didn't hang out as they did when they were younger. It was sort of an unspoken rule to never talk about Marissa and Paige around their house.

Most of the time Kurt rushed to tennis to pick Sadie up just as it ended. Lately, he somehow managed to get out of work early to be there for the last half, and he never missed a match, no matter if it was an away game. Every time Sadie looked his way, he and Marissa were talking and laughing. It was rubbing her the wrong way, but she had yet to bring the topic up to her dad.

Sadie wasn't the only one who noticed her dad and Marissa being overly friendly to each other. The other moms were whispering about the two of them sitting together, spending more time gazing into each other's eyes than watching their daughters play tennis.

The fact that she knew people were gossiping only angered Sadie more. What a disgrace her father was! In Sadie's eyes, he was being unfaithful to both their mother and his children.

Sadie wondered if the entire posse of mothers knew what despicable thing Marissa did to Lydia to break apart a twenty-year friendship. With the sight before her, Sadie was more determined than ever to find out.

Dear Sadie,

Happy Sweet Sixteen!!! My first born baby, sixteen years old, wow! Take a moment today to stop and feel me kiss and hug you sixteen times. I am with you, Sadie, always, and so is God. Talk to Him. Talk to me. We are listening. God hears your prayers. Go to Him with all your dreams, worries, wishes, fears, hopes, anxieties, and sorrows, and most of all, thank Him for all that He has given you.

Okay, I won't preach anymore today. I know you hate it when I do that, but come on, Sadie. As you get older, you have to admit that Mom occasionally knows what she is talking about and has some so-so advice. ☺

So, take care of my Infiniti and have fun cruising around town. Do me a favor and go get us an ice cream sundae to split. How about Hudsonville's triple peanut butter cup, smothered in caramel, whipped cream, and a maraschino cherry? (Still don't know how you can eat those fake cherries, yuck.) Think of me with each bite, knowing I'm right beside you celebrating your special day. Oh, you can have the last bite. I eat it day and night up here in Heaven!

I remember the day I got my license. I didn't have any particular place to go, so I decided to get my dad a Father's Day card, a month ahead of time, and I stopped by a friend's house to say hi. It wasn't anything important, but I remember feeling such freedom to be truly out on my own, alone, without a family member or another adult.

I realized that I could drive clear across the country to California if I wanted. I could take myself to the mountains, the ocean, or just shopping if I felt like it. It was an amazing feeling.

The point is, Sadie, you are embarking on a new adventure in life, giving you freedom and independence. Be wise in your decisions, be responsible, and be cautious, but also courageous. Have fun with your new set of wheels and your newfound freedom.

Happy Birthday, Sadie. I love you,

Mom

P.S. Take good care of my earrings. Dad was very nervous about giving them to you this young. He wanted to wait until you were eighteen or until you graduated from college, but I didn't see the point in having them sit in my drawer. Enjoy!

CHAPTER 7

Kurt

Kurt was oblivious to the drinking going on right before his eyes. Or that was what he kept telling himself. Every half hour or so he would check on the growing number of kids in his garage to make sure there were no visible signs of alcohol or drugs. At this point, he figured if he didn't outright see it then he was going to assume it wasn't there.

He never imagined his stress level would creep so high with all these kids under his roof. Why did he allow this party? He knew there was probably more going on than he could imagine.

When Marissa pulled in the driveway, Kurt's heart fluttered—heck everything did. It had been so long since he had been touched, needed. Marissa seemed to feel the same way about Kurt, but they were treading on thin ice when it came to exposing their feelings. Kurt knew his kids would have a hard time with him dating, especially since in a few weeks it would be the first anniversary of Lydia's passing. Sadie, he knew, would be furious.

Kurt took Marissa into the house and mixed her a vodka tonic. He had already put Nicholas to bed, and Jayna was staying at Chrissie's house. He didn't want his thirteen-year-old sneaking into the garage and some high school horn dog hitting on her. Worrying about one daughter was enough tonight.

Sadie

When Sadie and her two best friends barged through the door and saw Kurt and Marissa sitting together in the screened porch, she glared at the two of them and tugged Myla and Kyla upstairs without saying a word. Sadie was seething as she and her friend's smoothed their hair and applied lip gloss. What the heck was that woman doing in *her* house? Was her father trying to ruin her birthday party? Or did Marissa show up uninvited? Was she seriously trying to move in on her dad? Sadie's mind was swirling with accusations.

When the girls came back downstairs, Myla and Kyla were both laughing at the way Noah kept doing the sprinkler, oblivious to Sadie's angst. Sadie once again snubbed Marissa with a nasty look and an added humph as she trailed behind her friends.

She wasn't two steps out the door when she heard her dad apologize to Marissa on Sadie's behalf.

Sadie flew back in the garage and headed straight for her can of Sprite, which she had mixed with vodka. She cringed as she swallowed and felt the alcohol burn as it slid down her throat and into the pit of her stomach. She was on the verge of tears when Dylan spun her around.

His lips pressed to hers as he began to dance with her. She couldn't tell if the alcohol she tasted was on her tongue or his. Dylan placed his hands on her hips and she sank into him.

"Sadie," she heard her dad's voice call out over the thumping of the song, "Bang, Bang."

Normally, Sadie would have escaped out of Dylan's embrace if her father was in eyesight, but this time she slowly peeled her lips away and turned to face her father. Marissa was standing next to him but peering around the garage with disbelief across her face—probably scanning for her own daughter. Paige was most likely somewhere in the crowd with the rest of the high school.

"Sadie, can I talk to you outside for a second."

She turned away from Dylan and brushed shoulders with her dad as she walked past him and Marissa and out the garage door. Sadie folded her arms in front of herself, partly because the night was cold and partly because she was already on the defense and ready for a lecture on how disrespectful she was.

"There isn't anything going on in there that I should know about, is there? I feel like this party is getting a little out of control."

Kurt was trying to look Sadie in the eyes, and she was doing everything to avoid eye contact, even though Sadie knew that was a dead giveaway to lying. "No, nothing you should *know* about," she said, looking past him.

"Don't get snotty with me, Sadie. I'll end this party now. Every single person in there is technically my responsibility, and if anything were to happen to one of them, I would be held liable."

"Everything is cool, Dad. I promise." It was, right? No one was puking drunk, and there were no serious drugs that she knew of.

"Okay, let's just keep things cool."

Sadie shook her head. "Is that it?"

"Two more things."

Shit, here we go.

"I ordered pizzas, and they should be here any minute. It's probably a good idea for you kids to eat," Kurt said with a nasty smirk.

Sadie panicked, wondering if he could smell the alcohol on her breath. She remembered the piece of gum in her pocket and wished she'd remembered to pop it in her mouth.

"Also, Marissa came by to help me chaperone. I'd appreciate it if you could be polite to *all* the guests here. A simple hello would do."

Hearing Marissa’s name on her dad’s lips made Sadie’s gut churn. Call it woman’s intuition or whatever, but Sadie could see the writing on the wall—this was the beginning of the end. Her intuition was right—something was going on between her dad and her mom’s ex-best friend.

CHAPTER 8

Sadie

Tomorrow, May 2nd, would be the one-year anniversary of Lydia's death. Emotions had been up and down throughout the last year; to say they lived on a roller coaster wasn't far from the truth.

They had come a long way in the past year. Since getting her license, Sadie had the freedom to come and go as she pleased, driving herself to and from school, tennis practice, and to her friends' and Dylan's houses. She and Jayna were also getting along better.

Jayna was kissing up to Sadie so she would cart her and her friends around, dropping them off at the mall or the movies. Sadie had been letting go of the reins around the house. Jayna had had no choice but to step up to the plate and watch Nicholas more often and help out with more chores, mainly doing some of her own laundry instead of expecting Sadie to do it for her.

Nicholas seemed to be steadily improving as well these last couple of months. He hadn't cried as much for his mommy. Lydia was most likely slipping from Nicholas's memory, even though she was still a part of the family through videos, pictures, and letters that Sadie and Jayna read to him.

Thanks to Sadie, Nicholas still had a mother figure. Kurt told Sadie he was grateful for his daughter's devotion and couldn't imagine how he would keep his family on track if it weren't for her running the show.

Sadie suspected that Kurt and Marissa had been more or less seeing each other for the past few months but had kept it mostly private. Marissa hadn't been back to their house since Sadie's birthday party, but Sadie knew they were secretly seeing each other. Kurt had been having dinner with "clients" on a weekly basis instead of his usual monthly outing.

The spring night was warm and Sadie had finally finished her homework. She went downstairs to tell her dad goodnight and heard him outside on the phone.

As she got closer, she could see him sitting in the chair by the grill, illuminated by the full moon and a clear starry night.

"I can't wait to see you again," he said before hanging up.

Sadie was standing on the other side of the screened door as he went to walk inside.

"Who can't you wait to see?"

CHAPTER 9

Dear Sadie,

It's been 365 days since I've been without you, physically. But, Sadie, we both know I'm always with you in your heart. I know today must be difficult, but I can only hope that things are getting better. You made it through an entire year: four seasons, all the holidays, birthdays, sad days, and happy days.

Treasure life, Sadie. I mean stop and listen to the birds sing, pluck a bunch of wild flowers and stick them in a vase on the kitchen table. More importantly, take the time to stop and smell them when you walk by. Watch the sun rise and set now and then, gaze at the stars, and really enjoy and appreciate the color of the trees in the spring and fall. Feel the sun on your face and the harsh winter wind slap at your cheeks.

Laugh as often as you can, at yourself and with your family and friends. Don't hold grudges; it's such a waste of time and energy. Be quick to forgive and quicker to forget. Admit your mistakes and learn from them, but don't hold them against yourself. Dream big and never give up.

Believe ~ In ~ Yourself.

Today may be the anniversary of the day that I died, but I don't want it to be a day of sadness. Let it be a day for remembering our good times. I'll start. Remember when we were at the deli at the grocery store and you walked up to a hunched-over, little old lady and started pulling on the hairs growing out of her chin? I was beyond mortified!

You were probably just three and Jayna was a baby. I was ordering lunch meat, and out of the corner of my eye, I saw you being so cute talking with this elderly woman. In reality, you were just intrigued with her inch-long chin hairs. Next thing I know, I see her chin nudge forward and she yelps. You had grabbed onto one little whisker and started pulling it! There were at least five other mothers waiting at the deli, looking at me like I had just allowed you to beat her with her cane.

The sweet old lady looked at me and asked me if she had something on her chin. I didn't have the heart to tell her, but you did. As the words started coming out of your mouth, my hand flew across it to try and silence you. I had never wanted to disappear more in my entire life!

I was so embarrassed, but I wasn't sure whether to abandon my cart and run out of the store or to laugh and make a joke out of it.

I threw my turkey in the cart, grabbed your hand, and proceeded to walk away with a smile on my face as you continued to yell, "But Mom, she had long hairs sticking out of her chin."

Now how can you not laugh at that story?

Remember when I was pregnant with Nicholas and Jayna announced to our waitress that the doctor was going to stick his hand in my privates to get the baby out? I was in mid-drink, and I snorted my lemonade out my nose and clear across our table of food. Our poor waitress, the look on her face!

What about the time we were in Pentwater and I was playing on the monkey bars with you and Jayna and I fell off and I knocked myself out cold? Ranger Rick had to come to my rescue because Dad was off fishing . . . seriously!

Which reminds me of last summer when we were all fishing off the pier and Dad reached back to cast his pole and caught his hook, worm included, on Jayna's braces. She went ballistic as the worm wiggled on her tongue and Dad kept tugging her head before he realized he'd hooked her wire! Ha! Hilarious!

We've had gazillions of laughs together, Sadie. Remember the fun times, keep making them, and keep laughing.

I love you,

Mom

Sadie welcomed the raging thunderstorm; it was fitting for the day. She felt like she had a thunderstorm brewing inside her chest. Every time she looked at the clock, she thought back to the events of her mom's last day: when they all said their good-byes, when they sat by her bedside and prayed, when Lydia took her last breath, and even when the coroner came and took Lydia from her home.

That had to be the hardest. Knowing her mom would never physically walk through the house again had been, and still was, hard to bear. A year later Sadie could still see her moving around the kitchen, cooking meals, and emptying the dishwasher. She had packed the most amazing lunches: fancy wraps with provolone or goat cheese, marinated mushrooms, and stuffed peppers.

Sadie remembered getting teased about her lunches when she was little, but as she entered middle school, everyone was asking to trade sandwiches. Lydia loved to cook gourmet, and she taught Sadie to appreciate good food.

Lydia had a thing for brownies. She did not make the quick and easy kind out of the box. Ever. Desserts in the Booker house were made from scratch. Her brownies were thick, gooey, and rich, and she always put something in them, whether it was caramel, chunks of chocolate or candy bars, M&Ms, or peanut butter cups.

Sadie had a brownie in her lunch every day since she started kindergarten. Sadie's grandmother Rose had started the tradition and Lydia had carried it on. Plenty of days Sadie gave them away to her friends; no one could eat a brownie every single day of her life. Sadie hadn't eaten a brownie in a year; she wasn't sure if she would ever let another pass her lips.

The one-year anniversary landed on a Friday, so Kurt said they could skip school. At eleven in the morning, they were all moping around in their pajamas. Sadie heard the buzzer on the dryer and went into the laundry room to fold the clothes. Usually she folded the clothes on the counter in the laundry room as she took each piece out of the dryer. Today she filled the laundry basket with the clean clothes and took it out into the kitchen to fold the clothes on the countertop. That was where Lydia had folded laundry.

Nicholas was watching his *Cars* DVD, and Jayna had the music in her room upstairs cranked. Kurt was in the basement, lifting weights. He dealt with stress by lifting weights and boxing. Sadie could measure his stress level by how long and fiercely her dad pounded the bag. She was hoping he would come get Nicholas and include him in the boxing. She probably should have been playing a game with Nicholas or reading a book to him, but she didn't have the energy and felt like being alone. So there he sat, comatose in front of a movie.

As Sadie folded the laundry, she thought about the events of the last year. They made it through the holidays and the first day of school. Jayna got her period, and Sadie had to show her how to use a tampon. Last week she took Nicholas's training wheels off and taught him how to ride a two-wheel bike, and they had all blown out candles on a birthday cake not made by their mother's hands. Sadie welcomed sweet sixteen, Jayna thirteen, and Nicholas four. Kurt was a forty-four-year-old widower.

Lydia was absent for Jayna's dance recital, Nicholas started indoor soccer over the winter, and Sadie just made it to the state finals for tennis. Lydia had given Sadie her first racket at age four and taught her how to play. The two of them played tennis together all summer long while Sadie was growing up. She remembered riding their bikes to the high school courts several times a week and, more often than not, stopping for ice cream on their ride back.

Lydia was good about spending individual time with her kids. She and Jayna would dance together in the living room for hours. Jayna was a dancer and took hip hop, ballet, and tap. Lydia also had been a dancer while she was in school. She had one daughter for each of her hobbies.

Sadie felt like Nicholas was really cheated of the special time that his mother would have devoted to him. That was probably why Sadie felt guilty that he was sitting in front of a movie right now. Their mom would have been doing something fun with him.

Kurt was a loving father, but when it came to spending quality time with Nicholas, he sometimes needed a little push. If Sadie suggested something for the two of them to do together, Kurt was always willing, but it didn't always come naturally.

Sadie put the laundry away and cleaned the bathroom on the main floor. It was a perfect day to go crawl back in bed and sleep the storm and sorrow away, but looking at Nicholas still vegged out in front of the TV made her cringe.

She sat down next to him, and he immediately snuggled up to his big sister. He had always been a little cuddle bug, even still at four. Sadie kissed his forehead, and suddenly tears were streaming down her cheeks. She missed her mom for herself and for him.

Kurt came upstairs and she quickly wiped her tears away. "Go get dressed, you two. We have plans. It's a surprise. Tell Jayna to get ready too. I'm headed for the shower."

Nicholas showered with Sadie, and per his request, she gelled his hair. Nicholas was adorable now, but she knew he was going to be even more of a looker when he got older. He had a very unique look to him. Whereas Sadie looked like her dad and Jayna looked like their mom, Nicholas was a mixture at most, but even that was hard to see sometimes.

Sadie caught herself staring at the nose that was definitely his mother's. He was puckering his lips ever so slightly just as their mom did when she was deep in thought or concentrating on something. Nicholas's eyes were mesmerizing. They were deep blue, sometimes almost gray-looking, nothing like anyone's in the family.

Without any idea where their dad was taking them, Sadie dressed Nicholas in a decent pair of cords and a white shirt with dark and light blue stripes. She figured they could at least honor their mom by dressing nicely for the day.

Sadie put on a pair of white skinny jeans that Dylan had drooled over. Even though it was pouring out, it was still spring, and the weather was supposed to do a one eighty this afternoon. She picked out a lavender top she had just bought from Hollister, pulled her hair back in a messy bun, and added her mom's diamond earrings.

Kurt was waiting for them in the kitchen. He was eating a banana and watching the rain fall outside the window, no doubt thinking of Lydia. Of course, Jayna was still getting ready; it was always a process for her.

"Let's go, Jay," Kurt yelled for the fourth time before Jayna walked downstairs.

When Sadie first saw Jayna appear in the kitchen, her gaze quickly turned towards her dad. He, too, recognized the sweater she was wearing. It was Lydia's favorite Michael Kors cream cashmere sweater that she had worn in the family portraits they had taken soon after she was diagnosed with cancer.

Jayna and Sadie had worn a few of their mother's things—her everyday jewelry, shoes, some of her tops, things they always did—but this was different. It had meaning. It was like . . . *the sweater*.

Jayna knew all eyes were on her. Nicholas was oblivious, but Kurt and Sadie were both thinking the same thing—how much Jayna resembled Lydia. She had their mom's long straight hair, mascara swept her lashes playing her eyes up to an almost exact match of Lydia's, and she was wearing lipstick, which had to have been their mom's.

Sadie also noticed how much Jayna had developed. *When did that happen?* It seemed only yesterday she was flat-chested and gangly. Today she filled out the bust in the sweater almost as much as Lydia had, and when had her legs gotten so long?

Looking past her family, Jayna grabbed a bottle of water from the fridge and headed for the door.

"I guess we're ready?" Kurt said as they filed out.

Kurt backed the car out of the garage and paused before putting it in drive. "You girls look nice. Mom would have been proud."

They pulled into Frederik Meijer Gardens, and Sadie felt her heart flutter just like the butterflies they were about to see. Lydia was diligent about always taking trips to the same places every year at the appropriate time or season.

In the spring, they saw the butterflies blooming at the Gardens. Summer meant, of course, the beach, bike rides and picnics, and berry picking at a local farm. They visited their favorite orchard to go on hayrides, pick apples, eat donuts, and drink cider at in the fall. They visited the same pumpkin patch year after year to pick out Halloween pumpkins and gourds.

The last Saturday before Christmas they would bundle up and ride in the horse-drawn carriage through town to look at Christmas lights. Afterward, they would always go out for hot chocolate and dessert. St. Patrick's Day breakfast always meant green scrambled eggs. Valentine's dinner included red and white heart-shaped cheese and lobster ravioli. Lydia liked traditions; she was a creature of habit.

Sadie was trying hard to take on some of the smaller rituals that her mother had, such as making green scrambled eggs for breakfast on St. Patrick's Day and heart-shaped pancakes with red M&Ms for Valentine's Day. But since their mom died, they had only made it to the pumpkin patch last fall—no carriage rides, no apple picking at the orchard, and no family picnics.

It wasn't that Kurt didn't do special things with his kids, because he certainly did, but he was more spontaneous and did things by the seat of his pants, and they weren't the predictable things his wife had done.

The Booker Family albums contained almost the same pictures and events at the same places year after year. Everyone was just another year older, with different clothes and hairstyles.

As they circled the parking lot, trying to find an empty space, Sadie couldn't believe that her dad had thought of this adventure on his own. The rain had slowed to a heavy mist, and it was warming up to feel humid. Nicholas insisted that everyone carry umbrellas, so they popped them up and dodged the puddles as they made their way to the door.

Inside, it was a tropical paradise. The glass walls and cathedral ceilings let in plenty of natural light. Everywhere they looked, lush green plants and palm trees flourished.

Exotic flowers sprinkled bright red, purple, orange, pink, and yellow colors ubiquitously.

As they walked through the warm garden heaven, butterflies of all colors and patterns swarmed their bodies. Some would land on their arms or heads; others were more timid. Many butterflies were sucking the nectar from the flowers or oranges, and as they did, they ever so slightly fluttered their wings. It was beautiful and peaceful.

Sadie imagined her mother in heaven—peaceful, warm, in a tropical paradise with no pain. She also thought of what she was missing on earth: simple moments like this with her family.

Nicholas was on Kurt's shoulders and Jayna at his side. They were looking in a big glass cage filled with cocoons about ready to hatch into butterflies. As Sadie stared at their backs, the sadness suddenly felt excruciating. She didn't know where she belonged anymore. Was she a kid in this family, or was she her mother's replacement? Sometimes the burden was overwhelming and it felt sickening.

Kurt turned around and saw Sadie's blank stare and watery eyes and his face fell. "Should we go?"

"No, I'm okay. I miss her so much, and I can't help but imagine what our life would be like if she were still alive. Mom loved doing this kind of stuff. It's just not the same."

Kurt shook his head and wrapped his arms around his daughter. Jayna turned and walked the other way, as if Sadie was overreacting and embarrassing her.

After the butterfly gardens, they went to Lydia's favorite French bistro. For dessert, they ordered their mom's favorite coffee-infused crème brulée, chocolate-filled crêpes, and cream-filled éclairs.

Nicholas kept mentioning that he missed his mom, but these days he clung to Sadie so much that she doubted he really understood the words he said and simply repeated what he was hearing. The deep-hearted longing he felt for her was fading, and Sadie knew that she was everything to him, sister and mom all rolled up in one. Sometimes it was comforting; other times she hated and resented the responsibility.

On the way home, Sadie was busy texting Dylan when Kurt's cell rang. She sensed his demeanor change as he looked at the number on the screen. He let it go to voicemail and tucked the phone back in his pocket. Sadie didn't bother to ask who it was. She knew.

Later that evening, Dylan and Sadie were going to the movies. She told her dad good-bye, and as she was walking through the mudroom, she saw his cell lying on the counter.

She couldn't help herself. She pressed the recent calls button and, sure enough, saw a seven-digit number with Marissa's name underneath it. Rage raced through Sadie's veins as she chucked the phone back on the counter and followed Dylan out, slamming the door behind her.

CHAPTER 10

Sadie

Sadie found herself daydreaming out the window during Psychology, oblivious to the fact that Mrs. Lawson was calling on her. She was thinking about Dylan.

Sadie shifted in her seat and focused her attention on Mrs. Lawson. "I'm sorry, what did you ask?"

The room was silent, and Sadie wondered if everyone thought she was brain dead.

"I just asked for your input on last night's reading assignment," said Mrs. Lawson.

Sadie rambled her way through some sort of response, using words she knew Mrs. Lawson would approve of, and then let her mind wander again, this time to her tennis match after school. Dylan had a lacrosse game at the same time, so neither one of them could watch the other. He had promised to come over tonight after his game so they could go for a walk.

Sadie's thoughts then drifted to Marissa's phone call to her dad's cell on Friday, and she wondered if Marissa would be at the tennis match. Of course she would; she was always there to watch Paige *and* see Sadie's dad.

Sadie and Paige had been so close growing up—until their mothers stopped speaking. They were still friends, but they kind of hung out with different crowds now. Sadie wondered if Paige suspected anything between their parents or if she even cared.

She was tense just thinking about it. She imagined smacking Marissa with her racket if she dared sit next to her dad at the match. Wouldn't that be a show? It still upset her that Marissa came to her mom's funeral. For all Sadie knew, Marissa was probably glad her mom was dead, especially now that she had moved in on her husband.

After school, Sadie changed in the locker room and tied her hair up. She felt strong today, was sure she would win. She had to, for her mom. Because of her, Sadie fell in love with the sport when she was little.

Ten minutes into her first match she was ahead thirty love. There was still no sign of her dad, but Sadie knew exactly where Marissa was sitting, and she kept glancing that way, making sure he hadn't slipped in next to her. Honestly, Sadie would have rather had her dad miss her match than be there sitting next to Marissa. Petty? Yes.

After winning her first match, Sadie was talking to her coach when Kurt walked across the parking lot toward the courts. Sadie followed him out of the corner of her eye. As he approached the bleachers, she saw him scanning the crowd, which consisted mostly of parents and younger siblings. Marissa and Kurt spotted each other simultaneously. Marissa waved and Kurt climbed the bleachers to her.

Sadie outright glared at her father, and she was sure he and Marissa had both picked up on it. Good, she thought. A sinking feeling settled in her stomach as the reality was becoming more apparent that they were becoming a couple.

Back on the court, Sadie was on fire, and it worked to her advantage. She won every match and felt like she still had energy, or maybe anger, to burn off.

Every time she glanced towards her father and Marissa, they were talking and laughing. Sadie sought out Paige to congratulate her on a win, but more or less was feeling her out to see if she knew what was going on. "Looks like our parents are a cheer team."

Paige looked to the bleachers and smiled. "Your dad looks good. You know . . . he's looking better . . ."

Sadie knew Paige meant since her mom died; she also knew Paige hadn't caught the sarcasm in her voice and was clueless as to what Sadie was really referring.

Paige congratulated Sadie on her wins, and Sadie was equally as polite, dishing out compliments to Paige before they parted ways.

Dylan had picked Sadie up for school this morning, so she had no choice but to ride home with her dad. Why hadn't she thought this through? As she began walking toward the bleachers, Kurt shot up from his seat and quickly said goodbye to Marissa. Good, thought Sadie. She liked the fact that he was scrambling because of her, even though he put his hand on Marissa's arm and gave her sort of a half hug.

Sadie turned and started walking towards the car, her dad following behind. She threw her racket and backpack in the backseat and slammed the door before climbing in the front. Her dad looked at her, almost scared.

"Way to go, Sadie! You were amazing out there," he said, patting her leg.

"You noticed?"

"Of course I noticed. Everyone there noticed. Didn't you hear everyone cheering and yelling your name?"

"Not really." She really hadn't; she was so focused on how her father could be attracted to someone, Marissa of all people, so soon after her mother's death, that she barely even remembered the match. It was actually a miracle that she did so well.

She could tell Kurt knew she was pissed, but they sat there in silence, neither of them daring to say what was really on their minds. Every second of it was awkward, and Sadie knew she was acting like an immature brat, but she couldn't help it.

"What's for dinner?" Kurt asked.

"I don't know. Do I always have to be the one to figure it out for everyone else? I don't feel like cooking anything, I have homework, and Dylan is coming over in a while. Eat toast." She huffed, and the dam broke and the tears spilled.

"Sadie, I didn't mean what are you cooking for dinner. I was asking what sounded good to you. I thought maybe we would get takeout from that Mexican place you like to celebrate your win."

Kurt's voice remained even and calm as he spoke. Sadie looked out the window to avoid his gaze. She didn't care about food. She cared about what was going to happen to their family if her dad started dating Marissa.

"Are you in love with her?" she blurted.

"Are you talking about Marissa?"

"She's the one calling your cell, coming to my birthday party, and the one you come to see at my tennis matches."

"Sadie, I'm at your matches to see you." Kurt paused and inhaled deeply.

"Well, are you?" she asked again.

"It's complicated, Sadie. I enjoy sitting next to her at your tennis matches, and I was appreciative of her help at your birthday party. I like her company."

"So you like her—you have feelings for her?"

Kurt took a second to choose his words carefully, but then settled. "Yeah, I guess I do."

"How could you? I mean Mom and Marissa were best friends. Even worse, they had a fight and didn't speak for, like, four years. You're betraying Mom, humiliating her! She's only been dead a year! You're, like, dating her worst enemy!"

"Sadie, Marissa and I aren't a couple."

Kurt pulled into the Mexican restaurant and found a parking spot. He turned to face Sadie. "I would give anything to have your mother alive and well, but she's not, and I have to move forward. Mom and I talked about me being in a relationship before she died. She wanted nothing more than for me to find companionship and one day have a relationship with another woman."

"It's too soon, and why Marissa?"

"I can't say why Marissa. Maybe because she's a woman I've known for years and I feel comfortable talking to her. Maybe because we share so much history and she knows and adores my children as if they were her own. Possibly because she and Mom shared similar qualities and I feel close to your mom when I'm around Marissa.

"When I look at Marissa, I'm reminded of so many good memories our families had together laughing and playing, and those are the memories of Mom I don't ever want to fade."

Sadie had quieted her tears a little, but the hurt was still there, even if what her dad was saying made some sense. It was still Marissa. As if her dad was reading her mind, he began talking again.

"Your mom never brought it up because she wanted her last few months to be about nothing more than our family, but she and Marissa had talked through their problems. They had reconciled and Marissa had forgiven your—" Kurt quickly diverted, making Sadie wonder what he left out. "They had forgiven each other, Sadie."

Sadie had no idea that her mom and Marissa had reconciled. Why hadn't her mom told her? Did they really? She didn't want her dad dating a woman that her mom didn't get along with because the thought of anyone having ill feelings towards her mother, who was now nothing more than an angel, bothered her. To think that anyone who knew her was indifferent to her death hurt Sadie. In an odd sense, she wanted people to feel sad as a sign that they loved her.

"Marissa was at the funeral," Sadie remembered, but then again, who wasn't?

"Of course she was. Mom and Marissa had worked through their issues. Marissa and Mom were together nearly every day in her final months while you kids were at school. I guess you could say they kinda became sisters again."

Sadie couldn't help but laugh. "Ew, that would be wrong of you, Dad, really twisted."

Kurt laughed too. "Stop it, Sadie. You're sick. You know what I mean."

Sadie dried her eyes, but she couldn't say she felt settled inside or that she was even close to being okay with her dad and Marissa. She wasn't stupid; she knew they were more than what her dad was leading her to believe, and it hurt, really hurt. How could he just move on—and with Marissa of all people? There was no way her mom would have been okay with the two of them dating, reconciliation or not!

Kurt cleared his throat. "I know Mom's death has been especially tough on you. You've taken on a huge role at home, and I appreciate and hate it every single day."

"I love seeing how Nicholas has fallen in love with you in more than a sisterly way. We both know he views you as his mommy. I also hate the fact that you have all the responsibilities you have. You're sixteen and shouldn't have to worry about things like dinner, housework, and caring for Nicholas, well, Jayna, too. I don't know what to say, Sadie. Mom took care of everything, you know that. I've never had to juggle work, meals, grocery shopping, running kids here and there, and you know what the laundry looks like when I do it."

Sadie didn't say anything. She wanted her dad to go on. She was definitely feeling trapped at home, and the resentment was building. She was hoping this would be the start of something.

He smiled and continued. "I get stressed and I pull away more. I'm sorry. I don't mean to. Honestly, Sadie, it's one of the things I've been talking with Marissa about: how I can be more hands on and . . . not fail you as your only parent."

"So, good, Marissa is only going to be a friend to help you out with domestic and child-rearing tips?"

"Sadie, I am human and I do have feelings."

"I still don't like the idea of Marissa, or anyone for that matter. It's just that I can still see Mom at home. I can glance in the kitchen and see her at the sink. I walk into your bathroom and can picture her dressed in her robe, drying her hair or curling her eye lashes.

"When I look out back into the overgrown garden of weeds, I can still see her tending to the vegetables and flowers. I see her reading a book, sprawled out in a chair on the porch, and sometimes I can still hear her singing along to her iPod while she vacuums. I can feel her presence, and I don't want someone else coming in and taking that away. I don't want anyone messing up her way of doing things and taking away those memories."

"Oh, Sadie." Kurt hugged his daughter.

"Can you just wait? I mean another year or two and things will be different. It's too soon. I know you say Mom and Marissa worked through their issues, but what did Marissa do to Mom anyway? Whatever it was, it hurt Mom really bad, for years."

Kurt's face twisted and Sadie definitely caught it. "Let it go, honey. It was between them."

"Well, it bugs me that it took Mom dying for Marissa to finally ask for forgiveness. And now she's moving in on you. I can't let that go."

"It wasn't like that."

"Then what happened? Dad, I have a right to know!"

"No, you really don't, and this is the end of the discussion."

Sadie could see that Kurt was getting upset.

"Sadie, you kids are the most important thing in my life and I love each and every one of you . . ."

"To the moon and back," they said together.

"So don't, don't date her, Dad, please," Sadie begged.

"But that's a pretty selfish request. It's not fair."

"It hurts, Dad."

"It hurts me too."

Dear Sadie,

Okay, this is a tough one, kiddo. One of these days, Dad will start dating again. Shocker, I know, but life goes on, honey. I don't really know what to say except try and be open-minded. I know no woman will ever live up to me (hee-hee), but you can't expect Dad to be alone the rest of his life.

I can only pray she sees what treasures you kids are and loves you dearly. You have my permission to love her back. Who knows? You could inherit stepsiblings! She could be a wonderful grandma to your children someday, Sadie.

I just want you to know that I gave Dad my blessing to give his heart to another woman once I was gone. And, Sadie, I want you to know it's okay too. You are going to need that mother figure as you go through the stages of life. I know you've got Grandma, but we both know she's, well, Grandma, and she won't be around forever. And Aunt Josie and Aunt Nevie are always a phone call away, but honey, Aunt Josie and Aunt Nevie live the New York life. Frankly, their morals and advice scare me, but they are my sisters, and I know they love you like a daughter and will be there whenever you need them.

Anyhow, I'm rambling as usual. Just please understand that, at some point, Dad is going to have to move on, all of you will, and it's okay. It's okay, Sadie.

I love you,

Mom

CHAPTER 11

Kurt

Kurt sprayed some cologne on and took a closer look in the mirror, making sure there were no nose hairs sticking out or unruly eyebrow hairs. He felt nervous about going out to dinner with Marissa, which was stupid, really. Something was different about tonight; it felt very official and Kurt had the jitters.

Kurt was feeling the pressure. The pressure from what? He couldn't quite figure it out. Was he worried about keeping the conversation flowing? Not really. Was he nervous about kissing Marissa? He had done so plenty of times already. Was Sadie right? Was this all too soon? Was he making a bad choice by dating Marissa?

Sadie was spending the night at Myla's, and Jayna was spending the night at Chrissie's. Kurt didn't mention to either of his girls that he was going out, and he was hoping that tomorrow morning Nicholas wouldn't bring up the fact that Dad left him home with a sitter. He had asked a co-worker's daughter to babysit instead of one of their usual sitters, which were mostly young tweens from their neighborhood.

Marissa looked stunning when she opened the door, and Kurt almost felt guilty for noticing. Marissa was Lydia's opposite, which was good in more ways than one. Lydia had been tall and thin with long sandy hair. Marissa was petite with shoulder length blond hair. She had big pale green eyes and small soft features. When she smiled, she had girlish dimples that made her appear ten years younger than she actually was, and Kurt couldn't help but be attracted to her kindness.

Marissa wore a sleeveless white dress with lime green piping around the hem and across the chest. The dress was classy and flirty all rolled into one. When she opened the door, she grabbed a matching lime green purse and white shawl off the entry table and quickly closed the door behind her.

"Paige home?" asked Kurt.

Marissa giggled. "Yes, she has two friends over. When I stuck my head in her bedroom door to tell her I was going out with a friend, she didn't ask who, and I didn't mention names. Kurt was a step behind Marissa as they walked to the car, and he couldn't help but admire how strong her calves appeared in her heels. Both Lydia and Marissa had incredible legs from all the tennis they played over the years.

As he opened the car door for Marissa, he put his hand on her arm, stopping her before she got in. "You look beautiful," Kurt said with a quiver in his throat. He took a small step back, realizing how close they were standing.

Marissa's dimples shone brightly as she smiled, looking completely at ease. "How nice of you to notice, thanks," she said playfully.

As Kurt walked around the car to the driver's side, Marissa couldn't help but chuckle to herself at his nervousness; it was completely non-Kurt, and it was perfectly cute.

Kurt wasn't surprised when Marissa ordered a pomegranate martini. She had always been a fan of martinis and had been known to bring her shaker and concoctions whenever they used to get together. Kurt had his usual beer, and they ordered *calamari friti* and seared scallops as an appetizer.

They sat outside and enjoyed the warm spring breeze rolling off the water. The seagulls and waves filled the air with sounds of the summer that was fast approaching. Marissa raised her glass for a toast.

"Here's to good company and"—Marissa looked into Kurt's eyes— "thankfulness for the past, enjoying the present, and looking forward to the future."

"Nicely put," agreed Kurt as they clinked glasses and drank.

Kurt ordered the filet with béarnaise sauce and lump crab, and Marissa the grilled Thai Salmon. As soon as Kurt spotted the salmon on the menu, he knew that would be Marissa's pick. He also knew the lobster risotto would have been Lydia's.

"Do you remember the trolley ride after Blake and Kara's wedding? We stopped at Rose's restaurant on Reeds Lake to use the bathroom, and the best man, Chris, took off his tuxedo pants and coat and jumped in the lake in his boxers," remembered Marissa. "We were the wedding party from hell!"

"Yeah, and he held on to his can of beer the entire time."

Their laughter filled the air.

"We had some crazy fun times," said Marissa, taking a sip, looking deep in Kurt's eyes.

"Most of the crazy moments were before kids, but we always had fun, didn't we?"

Marissa sighed, remembering back when things were simple and she thought the four of them would be the friends that retired together somewhere tropical. "Absolutely, I wouldn't trade those years for anything."

"Me either," agreed Kurt.

For the first time, there was a lack of words between Kurt and Marissa, and they each took a bite. Marissa swallowed and put her hands in her lap.

"I'm not angry anymore, Kurt, about any of it. I mean it's the past. What good is it going to do me to sit around and stew?"

Kurt shook his head. They really hadn't talked much about Marcus and Marissa's divorce and the fallout between Lydia and Marissa. "You were hurt badly, Marissa."

"And you," she pointed out.

Kurt nodded.

"I wish it hadn't taken Lydia's cancer for us to reconcile. I feel like we were cheated of four years of friendship because we were both so stubborn and proud. I guess I learned my lesson the hard way."

"And what lesson was that exactly?"

"To simply be more forgiving and loving, less bitter and resentful. Life is too short."

"You hold no grudges?" inquired Kurt.

"None. You?" asked Marissa.

"No grudges, but sometimes questions, okay, maybe sometimes a touch of resentment."

"Ah, I went through that too, but I knew it was pointless and wouldn't change what happened. I always admired your marriage. In fact, I spent too much time comparing the way Marcus treated me to how you treated Lydia. I did a lot of griping to Lydia those last few years Marcus and I were married. Lydia was such a good listener . . . an amazing friend."

Kurt shifted in his seat uncomfortably. He felt like he needed to apologize for Lydia, even though he knew that was ridiculous. Instead, he pointed out to Lake Michigan. The sun looked as if it were riding steadily along the waves, glowing a magnificent shade of orange, casting out thousands of shimmering diamonds. A thin blanket of pinkish purple clouds hovered in the sky to complete the picture.

"I could watch the sun set every night for the rest of my life and never get sick of it," said Kurt.

Marissa laughed. "It would be pretty hard to get sick of a sunset in Michigan, especially when it's rare to get a glimpse of it from November through March."

Marissa pushed her chair back and suggested a walk on the beach.

The sky was clear and the stars shone bright. Kurt and Marissa walked beneath the Big Dipper and an almost full moon. They walked barefoot, carrying their shoes, and Marissa took hold of Kurt's warm hand. The water was still frigid, as expected in late May, but the sand still held the warmth of the sunny day.

"Ironic, isn't it?" said Marissa, "How things work out. Or not work out, but, well, happen." Marissa fumbled with her words. "I mean how unexpected things unfold throughout life. I never imagined I'd be walking hand in hand with you on the beach. I don't know what to make of it. May I ask your thoughts?"

"You mean was it meant to be? Or are we just two lonely devastated people leaning on each other? Maybe it's easy because there is no history or past to explain. Possibly we're both taking a little revenge? Does it matter? Does it make a difference right now, right here tonight?"

Stunned, Marissa walked a few steps before responding. Kurt had been thinking about the two of them more than she thought. "Do you think in the slightest this is wrong?"

"If I did, I wouldn't be here."

"But you have considered it?"

"Sure, especially after being condemned by Sadie."

"Okay, I'll rephrase. Do you think this, us, is worth it, worth trying?"

Kurt was silent for what seemed like two minutes, but was probably only ten seconds. "You're too stuck on hurting the kids and what other people might say or think about us."

"Aren't you?"

"Of course, I don't want to hurt the kids, but it would be hard for them to accept anyone at this point. Kurt squeezed Marissa's hand. "So to answer your question, yeah, I think it's worth it."

CHAPTER 12

Sadie

Here it was, an early summer Friday night, and Sadie was at home, washing window screens—lame. Dylan was two hours away, coaching a youth football camp, Myla was on vacation with her family, and Kyla was out on a date with a guy she met two weeks ago at the beach.

Nicholas and Sadie had the screens lined up across the back of the house. She gave Nicholas the scrub brush and a bottle of dish soap. After he lathered the screens, Sadie sprayed away the suds with the hose.

Every winter Lydia had taken the screens out of the window casings, and the following spring she lined them up and washed them before fitting them back in the windows. It felt good to Sadie to be productive. She had been doing all sorts of odd jobs around the house lately, in part to keep her occupied since Dylan was going to be working a lot this summer, but more so for Nicholas. He needed to learn how to do these simple chores. Lydia had always taken the time to teach her children how to fix things, clean things, and be handy. She was big on creating independent children.

As usual, Jayna wasn't helping and was in a foul mood. Jayna was currently locked in her room. She had been mean to Nicholas all day, shooing him away if he came near her and yelling at him for bothering her by asking for a Popsicle while she was relaxing in the hammock, watching YouTube videos on her phone.

Her new thing was to disappear for an entire afternoon on her bike without bothering to let Sadie know she was leaving the house. Kurt, being at work, never knew she did this and would have freaked out if he caught wind of it. Sadie knew that her dad would leave it up to Sadie to make her stay put, or at least let someone know when she was leaving. But after all, Sadie was Jayna's sister, not her mother.

Next week was supposed to be their annual trip to Pentwater. Every year, except last summer right after mom died, they rented the same cottage and spent two weeks loafing on the shores of Lake Michigan.

Their days in Pentwater consisted of basking in the sun, swimming, making sandcastles, riding bikes to town to shop, climbing Old Baldy, fishing, playing mini golf, eating ice cream, and making s'mores and dough boys over the campfire.

When Sadie was young, they went with Marissa, Marcus, and Paige, and of course the Sutherlands—Benton, Andrea, Bella, and Travis—were always there too. Since Lydia and Marissa's fight, it had been just Sadie's family and the Sutherlands.

Up until two summers ago, Sadie hadn't paid much attention to Travis Sutherland in any way except someone to play in the sand with and climb the dunes next to. Somehow over the years though, he had gone from geeky family friend to smokin' hot, and they had a two-week long summer fling the summer before their ninth grade year. They'd held hands in the sand dunes every chance they got, and they even kissed a few times.

Man, how Sadie's life had changed over the past two summers. Her mom hadn't yet been diagnosed with cancer, and she had only kissed one other boy besides Travis.

Travis and Sadie kept in touch the rest of August and September of that year, but then his phone calls and emails were fewer and farther between and stopped completely by mid-October. Once she met Dylan a couple of weeks later, she rarely thought of Travis, until recently.

Sadie was still completely in love with Dylan, but for some reason, the past couple of weeks she couldn't help but wonder if she would soon be hanging out with Travis. Sadie would never admit it out loud to anyone, not even Myla or Kyla, but she really wanted to see him.

Maybe it wasn't simply Travis; possibly it was his whole family that she missed. They brought back memories of endless summer vacations when life was simple. Whatever it was, she had a longing to go on their annual vacation to Pentwater.

The last time she saw Travis (besides their family Christmas card picture) was briefly at her mom's funeral. He was there along with his family and gave Sadie an awkward hug and told her he was sorry. Sadie thanked him and was quickly swept up in someone else's arms. By the time she could escape all the agonizing condolences, Travis was gone. Sadie wondered if he saw Dylan by her side, giving her a kiss before leaving that day.

Kurt hadn't mentioned anything about Pentwater all summer, and neither Sadie nor Jayna had brought it up to him. Last year it came and went without a thought, but now that it had been over a year since her mom died, Sadie knew she was ready to go back. Lately it was all she could think about. So how was she going to bring it up to her dad?

Suddenly, out of nowhere, Jayna ran up behind Sadie with a bucket of water, soaking both her and Nicholas. In an instant, Sadie was pulled out of her Pentwater dreams. Before Sadie could even react, Jayna shot Sadie with the hose, soaking her entire front. She threw the hose down with a squeal and ran the opposite way.

"Get her with your sudsy brush," Sadie yelled to Nicholas.

Just like that, Jayna was out of her funk. The siblings kept filling the bucket with soapy water and sudsing each other until at last they gave up and jumped in the pool, fully clothed. Nicholas was bobbing around his sisters with his swimmies around his arms in pure delight.

Kurt stopped trimming the bushes and did a cannon ball in the pool, sending waves over Nicholas's head. He was laughing deeply from his little belly, begging his dad to do it again.

Nicholas stood proudly at the edge of the pool and jumped in: doing every twist and turn he could to get his father's attention. "Watch, Dad! Look at me! Watch this!" They all cheered as he splashed his way to the ladder, climbed out, and raced toward the diving board.

For weeks, Sadie had been urging him to jump off the board and into her arms below, but he hadn't quite mustered up the courage. But with Dad present, well, of course, that was all it took. Before he could even think about it, Nicholas stepped up onto the diving board and kept on going. He never even paused to jump, just basically ran right off the edge.

Kurt, Sadie, and Jayna all swam towards Nicholas as he popped up and sputtered water out of his mouth. His eyes were as big as saucers, and Sadie thought for sure he had taken a gulp of water and was going to panic and cry, when instead, he started clapping. "WOOHOO, NICHOLAS!" he cheered for himself.

They practiced swimming in the shallow end without Nicholas's swimmies on. Sadie had been working with him, and he was doing really well. He just needed a bit of confidence. Tonight, in front of his dad, he swam the entire width of the pool underwater with no help. Sadie felt so proud, knowing she had taught her little brother how to swim.

That night, Nicholas and Jayna both ended up in Sadie's bed, which was tight, even if it was a queen. Nicholas was out the second he laid his head on the pillow. Jayna and Sadie were writing on each other's backs, as usual. Jayna confessed to stealing Sadie's green eye shadow and eating the last ice cream sandwich in the freezer, which Sadie had clearly marked “SADIE’S” with an orange Sharpie.

Sadie wrote out a long sentence to Jayna about asking their dad if he could take them on vacation to Pentwater. Jayna wrote back that they should write him a letter. Sadie responded with, “First thing in the morning.” Jayna wrote, “I love you.” “Me too,” Sadie wrote back.

CHAPTER 13

Sadie

Dylan took Sadie to a party at Libby Burton's house, and it really sucked. Libby had just graduated along with Dylan, and for the most part, everyone there had just graduated or was about to enter their second year of college. Normally the two-year gap didn't bother Sadie, but it did tonight. The talk was all about packing up and moving into dorm rooms.

Sadie felt like an outcast, like all the girls were whispering about her, telling secrets and giggling. They probably weren't. Sadie had hung with the girls in Dylan's class a lot, but she suddenly felt really young. She still had two years of high school left, was about to start her junior year, and they were all talking about the university adventures they were about to embark on. Most of them were sloppy drunk, and Sadie knew better than to feel insecure—it really wasn't her style—but tonight felt different.

Normally, Sadie always felt protected. Dylan always went out of his way to make her feel comfortable around all his friends, male or female, and Sadie had made some new friends herself. As the summer weeks had passed and the reality set in that Dylan would be leaving for college in the fall, it seemed like everything was slowly unraveling.

She told herself she was just afraid of change. With everything she had been through, she could definitely admit outright that she was afraid of losing Dylan. Didn't most girls in her situation feel the same? Or was she overly sensitive because of losing her mom?

Dylan was going to a university about thirty-five miles away. Sure, he would be leaving her, but he assured her they would see each other all the time. He was only a half an hour away, he reminded her. Dylan guaranteed Sadie they would see each other on both weeknights and weekends, aside from his lacrosse, rushing for a fraternity, her tennis, and both of them studying.

"Don't be such a pessimist," he had said when she mentioned that he'd be too busy for her. She had also said something about Dylan being surrounded by a bunch of floozies, day and night—trying to steal her guy. As soon as she said it, she regretted it. She *did* sound insecure, desperate, and pathetic! What was up with that?

She wished she had taken Myla and Kyla up on their offer to hang out at Myla's grandmother's house. Myla's grandmother lived in a huge beautiful Victorian house, all alone. Her grandpa died two years ago. Myla spent a lot of time with her grandma, helping her out with yard work and cleaning. Grandma Susie was always asking Myla to sleep over with "those two cute girlfriends."

Sadie could picture them now, sitting on the front porch in rockers, eating homemade cookies, and drinking real lemonade made with fresh squeezed lemons and sugar. Later they would be playing rummy or cribbage with Grandma Susie while sipping chocolate milkshakes that she made from her old time shake mixing machine.

Plenty of times they would lie in the grass next to the rose garden and stare up at the stars and talk until the wee hours of the night. Myla's grandma loved to tell old stories about growing up in a house with six other siblings, four sisters and two brothers. Sadie thought listening to an old woman reminisce about her life sounded way more exciting than the party or being with Dylan.

Maybe it was her, she thought. Maybe she was reading into nothing. Maybe she was just in a mood, a funk. She wanted her two best friends and their simple, uncomplicated friendship.

Sadie figured Dylan was probably off in the garage with the guys and would come up behind her any minute with a kiss, but he never did. She found him when it was time for her to be home, and he acted slightly annoyed that he had to leave the party.

Now as she lay in bed, she was questioning everything all over again. Was this how relationships unraveled? Was this how things fizzled out? Should she expect the call from him soon saying he wanted to take a break or he just wanted to be friends? He was going off to college. Why would he want to date a junior in high school?

She was startled when her cell rang. "Hey, babe, I felt like we didn't get to spend any time together tonight since you ran off with the girls. Can you sneak out and meet me at the end of the road. I'm here waiting, p-l-e-a-s-e."

Every bone in her body was telling her to say no, but of course, what came out was a pathetic, desperate, yes. If Dylan was slipping away, she was determined to do everything to make him want her, and only her, as his girlfriend.

"I'll be there in ten minutes."

"Sadie, wait."

"What?"

"Wear the black lace bra and panties I got you for Valentine's Day."

She hung up without saying anything because she felt a stab in her stomach. As if all the air had just been sucked out of her sails. But why? Plenty of times she had snuck out to be with Dylan. Why was this time any different? Was sex all he wanted her for now? Was she just being paranoid over nothing?

CHAPTER 14

Sadie

Sadie and Jayna had written a letter to their dad, explaining to him that they thought their mom would want them to stick with their traditional summer vacation in Pentwater. They were ready for their first family vacation without their mom, and they missed "their cottage" that they had rented year after year since they were babies.

Kurt wrote a letter back to his daughters, saying that he had planned on it as a surprise and booked it months ago. He was glad he didn't have to keep it secret any longer because he could really use their help planning and packing.

So Sadie had spent the better part of the last two days getting all the laundry caught up. She then packed all the clean clothes in laundry baskets, just as her mom always did. Instead of duffle bags or suitcases, Lydia used laundry baskets to haul their clothes, toiletries, beach gear, and pantry foods.

Ever since Sadie could remember, the days before they left for Pentwater were exciting. When she was younger, she would ask her mom every other minute how many hours until they left. Sadie would start a daily countdown on the chalkboard in the kitchen the month before, and then it would change to an hourly countdown around seventy-two hours prior.

She always had a hard time falling asleep the night before they left. Sadie remembered sneaking downstairs to see her mom in the kitchen, packing up the food. It would be dark outside, and she would have all the windows open in the house, letting the warm summer night breeze roll through. The echo of crickets and frogs would be ringing loudly as Sadie tiptoed through the house to spy on her dad next.

Kurt would be outside in the garage, packing up fishing gear, hobo pie makers, beach toys, and filling the bike tires with air. He would wash and scrub everything, which Sadie never understood since they were heading to the beach to live in a sea of sand for the next two weeks. Her dad would meticulously load all their belongings up in the small trailer he attached to the back of their old blue Suburban.

Before Sadie could read, Lydia would hand her a list of pictures cut out of magazines. There were three pages of neon orange construction paper with pictures of lifejackets, sunscreen, beach towels, sand toys, bug spray, flip-flops, and so on—all things for Sadie to collect around the house and put in a designated laundry basket. Once Sadie completed each sheet, Lydia would give her a Popsicle or a new container of bubbles.

When Jayna was old enough to help out, they would fight over who got to collect what, so Lydia made a second list on neon green construction paper for Jayna. Jayna and Sadie would race through the house to see who could collect their items first. It always ended up in a fight.

Obviously, their picture lists had phased out once they were old enough to read, but Sadie couldn't help but smile when she thought of them and how she looked forward to packing for Pentwater. That was the thing about Mom, thought Sadie; she took the time to do simple but special things like that for them.

Now, in the midst of checking off items on her hand written list, Nicholas had wrapped his arms around her leg. Sadie leaned over and kissed the top of his head and told him she loved him. He looked at her with the sweetest smile and asked for a pack of fruit snacks. The kid was turning into a fruit snack junkie. Lydia would have flipped if she knew Sadie let him have a package, sometimes two, every day.

A light bulb went off in her head. It was her mother's voice loud and clear. *Find the picture lists and let Nicholas help pack.*

Sadie picked Nicholas up and told him first he had a special job to do and, as soon as he finished his treasure hunt, he could have some fruit snacks. Knowing Lydia, Sadie was quite certain she wouldn't have gotten rid of the orange and green lists—it was only a matter of finding them.

She took Nicholas's hand, and they went down to the basement to scour through the plastic tubs. There were gazillions of tubs; purple for Easter decorations and mementos, orange tubs with black lids for Halloween and fall stuff, red and green tubs for Christmas decor, tubs labeled "Jayna's Souvenirs" and "Sadie's Souvenirs," and of course, the endless tubs of Lydia's diaries. They had so many tubs that her dad was always building extra shelving to store them on.

It was only a matter of finding the right tub, and Sadie knew she would uncover the lists she was looking for, because to Lydia, these were just as important as the letters her children wrote to Santa. *Ah-ha, that's where Mom would store them.* She began to search for a tub in which she had seen her mom throw homemade gifts, poems and cards they had given to her and dad over the years. She remembered it was labeled "Special Creations from the Kids."

Sure enough, as she dug through it, she found the ratty orange and green sheets tucked between some homemade Mother and Father's Day cards. They weren't quite as neon as they used to be, and the magazine pictures were a little frayed at the edges, but she knew Nicholas would have as much fun with them as she did, and who knows, maybe they could even make new ones if he wanted.

As soon as Sadie shoved the tub back on the shelf, she noticed the lids on several of her mom's diary tubs weren't secured tightly. It was obvious someone had recently opened them.

Sadie's blood boiled as she pictured Jayna in the basement, snooping through their mom's diaries. Jayna knew they were off limits. Or weren't they anymore? Sadie pushed down on the lids until she heard each one snap into place. She wasn't sure what to think.

Should she say something to Jayna or just let it go? Maybe it made her feel close to Mom. Sadie felt a little twinge of jealousy. What things had Jayna learned about their mom that she hadn't? Had Jayna been reading about their mom's childhood or teenage years, or maybe even her deepest thoughts in her last year of her life?

Sadie turned off the basement light, led Nicholas back upstairs, and decided not to bring up the diaries with Jayna yet. One thing was for certain though: Sadie was suddenly intrigued by the diaries more than she had ever been. Would they reveal the secret about what Marissa had done to her mom?

CHAPTER 15

Kurt

Kurt remembered Lydia always being a cheerful, bubbly woman from the moment he met her, but something in her had changed after she had Jayna, and she was never quite the same again.

At first, the doctor had said it was postpartum depression, or the "baby blues," and talked with her about simple ways to cope like exercise, getting more sleep, taking time for herself, and eating right. By the time Jayna was one, Lydia still hadn't shed the "baby blues" and was prescribed Xanax.

The medication seemed to be helping, and after a few months, Lydia seemed to be her old self again, someone with a zest for life. After a year, Lydia figured she didn't need the medication anymore and weaned herself off of it. In a matter of weeks, Lydia had fallen back in her slump but figured it would take her body a little time to adjust and come around.

Several months had gone by, and Lydia's anxiety and depression had only worsened. She went back to the doctor and once again was given a prescription. However, this time the medication wasn't helping as it had before, and Lydia found herself in and out of the doctor's, trying this and tweaking that. After months of trial and error, Lydia was improving and felt like herself.

Out of the blue, Lydia had begun feeling dizzy, suffering from insomnia, nausea, and even having chest pains and palpitations. Luckily, after a host of tests, no major health problems were revealed. Her doctor thought she was just feeling anxious. So it was back to tweaking the anti-depressants once again. Over time, Lydia's symptoms subsided, and she felt like she had her life back, despite the fact she felt like she couldn't cope without her daily dose of benzos.

During this time, Marissa and Marcus were on the brink of divorce, and Lydia poured herself into being there for her best friend. Helping her best friend through something so difficult gave Lydia a sense of purpose she desperately needed at the time

Kurt had mixed feelings about vacationing in Pentwater. He had planned it as a surprise well in advance, and after reading Sadie and Jayna's letter asking to spend their *usual* two weeks there, he couldn't back out. He was sure everything would be fine, but all the firsts without Lydia were trial and error for him and the kids (mostly error on his part).

It would be good for the kids. They missed out on Pentwater last summer when Lydia's death had been just that May, but now that it had been over a year, they were more than ready to go as a family of four.

They needed to get away from the house and be carefree, especially Sadie—she had so many responsibilities at home. Kurt was also looking forward to getting away from the daily grind and relaxing on the beach, fishing, and having a few beers with Benton. As a single father of three, he needed this vacation, and probably a vacation from the vacation.

CHAPTER 16

Sadie

Going around the last curve and seeing Pentwater Lake always put Sadie at ease. She was officially on vacation. Passing Snug Harbor Marina, the familiar restaurants, gift shops, and ice cream parlors made the memories of years gone by come flooding back. Within two minutes, they would be pulling up to their rented cottage, and she would be greeted by the familiar sights and sounds of Lake Michigan.

She had spent two weeks of her summer in Pentwater since she was an infant, and it never seemed to get old or lose its appeal. She secretly envisioned bringing her own family to Pentwater for vacation someday—watching sunsets with her husband on top of the dunes while her children chased after seagulls in the sand.

She briefly thought of Dylan, tried to envision him as a father, but her thoughts were soon replaced with thoughts of Travis and their little fling two summers ago. Sadie hoped it wouldn't be awkward between the two of them this year. She felt guilty being so excited to see him.

She rolled down the window to let the breeze blow in. Pentwater even had its own smell. The lake's fresh water, mixed with the town's scent of baking waffle cones and greasy food from the bar on a hot day, filled their SUV. Sadie inhaled the sweet fragrant smell and felt giddy. She had really, really missed this town.

Nicholas slowly opened his eyes after sleeping the entire one-hour-and-twenty-minute drive. Even Jayna turned off her phone and removed her ear plugs. They were going to be just fine on their first vacation without their mom; Sadie could feel it.

The door was always left unlocked to the cottage, which Sadie loved about the feel and safety of the small beach town. Kurt barely shifted their SUV into park before the doors flew open and they were all dashing inside the cottage.

Sadie took her laundry basket and backpack straight to the room she and Jayna shared. It was updated three years ago to an almost exact replica from a page in the Pottery Barn Teen Magazine.

There were two kids' bedrooms—one decorated for girls and one for boys. Both were decked out in a beachy, surf motif with surfboards as shelves and pictures of seashells and starfish on the walls. The comforters had huge Hawaiian-looking flowers on them, and even the furniture was a distressed beachy pale blue and sea green.

Within minutes, Sadie, Jayna, and Nicholas all had their bathing suits on and were running through the thick sand to the water. Sadie was chasing Nicholas with a bottle of spray-on sunscreen because she knew he wouldn't stay still long enough for her to apply the lotion.

They hit the water full throttle, and luckily didn't go into instant shock. The chalkboard inside the cottage had reported the water temperature to be a steamy seventy-five degrees, very warm for Lake Michigan. It still felt cool against the hot afternoon sun, but Sadie knew Nicholas was not going to let her chill out in her beach chair just yet.

Jumping waves for a half an hour tired Sadie out, and she coaxed Nicholas onto the shore with a promise to build sand castles and eat Cheeze Kurls. Jayna was lying on her back with her eyes closed, ear buds in, foot thumping to her music, and sucking on a piece of cherry licorice. Kurt had promised he'd be out to play with Nicholas as soon as he unloaded the cooler and put away the groceries. Sadie figured he was probably sneaking in a call to Marissa as well.

Sadie dried off and dumped the bag of sand toys out for Nicholas when she caught site of Travis playing catch with a football in front of the cottage next door. He was facing her and gave her a wave mid-throw. She suddenly felt silly for the way she was jumping and splashing in the water with Nicholas, making motor-boat noises and acting more like a twelve-year-old than a sixteen-year-old.

She waved back to Travis and quickly plopped down in her beach chair and grabbed her book. Her heart fluttered and she felt nervous to talk to Travis, which was stupid, really. She had known Travis her whole life, had built sand castles next to him for hours on end on this very beach.

She heard the familiar ding from her cell announcing she had a new text message, which she figured was probably from Dylan. She immediately felt guilty for the nervous excitement she felt towards Travis. Sadie knew she would be absolutely lost without Dylan, so who cared what Travis thought—why not just walk up and say hi, as she had every year of her life?

Kurt's voice caught her off guard. "Did you say hi to Travis yet? Looks like he brought a friend this year. You can still change your mind, Sadie. I don't care if you want Myla and Kyla to stay with us for a few nights."

Sadie ignored her father's first question. "Not this year, I just kinda feel like being alone. Maybe at the end, for a night or two, I'll ask Myla and Kyla to visit. I don't know . . ." Sadie trailed off and grabbed her sunscreen and sunglasses from her beach bag just as Nicholas yelled for their dad to dig with him.

Kurt collected a shovel and several buckets from the pile and began digging with Nicholas. "We're gonna build the biggest sand castle this beach has ever seen," he told his son, dropping to his knees.

Sadie noticed her dad had lost some weight. The small dad gut he was starting to accumulate over the years was gone. His facial features even stood out more; he looked more defined, a little older but actually better than he had in a long time. He was wearing the sunglasses and swim shorts Sadie and Jayna picked up for him at the mall last week.

Kurt had given the girls his credit card along with his measurements and asked them to pick up a few summer outfits for their vacation. Besides a few golf shirts, Kurt went from his daily work suits and ties to his old T-shirts and ratty cargo shorts from summers past. Even his swimming trunks were old and faded from the chlorine of their pool, so updating was a necessity, Sadie informed him.

Sadie and Jayna actually had a lot of fun shopping for their father and made sure he was going to be the hippest dad in this small town. As Sadie was watching her brother and dad play, she was stricken when she realized he wasn't wearing his wedding ring. *When did he stop wearing it*?

Sadie thought of Marissa. *Did she ask him to stop wearing it? Would she dare show up at the cottage over the next two weeks?*

Before Sadie knew what happened, she had been splattered with sand. She flew out of her chair with a scream and began to spit sand out of her mouth. It was caked onto her lips, since she had just applied lip protector, and glued to her body via her oily sunscreen.

"I'm so sorry. I didn't mean to skid out in the sand and douse you. Travis threw it long, and I thought I could catch it no problem. Are you okay?"

Thank God Sadie had her sunglasses on, saving her eyes from the sand. She gritted sand in her teeth and muttered, "I'm fine."

Travis came running up, handing a bottle of water to Sadie. "My fault—I threw it a little long."

As Sadie swished the water in her mouth and spit it out, she saw Travis's friend glare at him. Something told her that Travis threw the ball *long* on purpose.

"Well, Sadie, this is Cody. Cody, this is Sadie." Travis picked up the football and began to toss it in his hands nervously. “Hey, Mr. Booker.” He nodded towards the shore. “Hey, Nicholas. Hey, Jayna.”

Kurt and Nicholas said hi to Travis through their chuckles. Sadie was glad she could give everyone a laugh. Jayna gave the boys a half smile and laid her head back down on her towel.

“My parents said to say hi. They’ll be out shortly—they’re still unpacking,” Travis informed Kurt.

Travis turned back towards Sadie and nudged her arm. A gesture that sent Sadie’s heart racing. “Uh . . . how about a swim?”

Sadie gave Travis and Cody a friendly glare as she tried to wipe the sand off her arms. “Are you going to splash me or just go straight for the dunk?”

Instantly, Travis put Sadie at ease. That old familiar feeling swept over her—she was used to being sarcastic and a little sassy with him. The dorkiness of the kid she used to know might be gone, but underneath the svelte teenage version, he was just the same old Travis that she had buried in this very sand a million times. How many times had they slept next to each other in sleeping bags on the beach chairs under the Big Dipper?

Travis threw his arms up. “No splashing or dunking, I promise.”

They hit the waves and Sadie took a deep breath as the water hit her belly button. She noticed Travis’s eyes go straight to her abdomen and then her chest. His eyes didn’t linger, and he averted them soon enough, but nonetheless Sadie saw the glance just before she dove into a wave. When she came up for air, Travis was right next to her.

Cody tackled Travis for the football, propelling him into Sadie. He caught the football with one hand and Sadie’s waist with the other as they plunged backward.

When they both popped out of the water, he held the ball up in the air and tightened his hold on Sadie. “Double save.”

He looked to Sadie. “Threesome?” They all giggled, formed a triangle, and played catch in the water.

CHAPTER 17

Sadie

Sadie told Dylan she loved him and tossed her cell phone on the nightstand. Jayna rolled in the bunk bed above her as Sadie closed her eyes and listened to the sound of the waves through the open window.

She liked keeping the window open and seeing the sheer curtains blowing from the breeze off the water. The damp sheets stuck to her skin, so she kicked them off and thought of the Jason Derulo song, "Want to Want Me," where he sang, "It's too hard to sleep. I got the sheets on the floor, nothin' on me. And I can't take it no more. It's a hundred degrees."

She had just closed her eyes when she heard a small ping on the window screen. She knew instantly it was Travis and Cody and hopped out of bed.

Sure enough, standing below her were two huddled figures trying to look inconspicuous. "Two minutes," Sadie called down in a whisper. She felt in the dark for her shorts and tank in a pile on the floor and slipped them on.

The cottage was dark and silent as she exited through the sliding glass door, figuring it was the quietest. Not that Kurt would have really cared that she was going out. It seemed that, in Pentwater, there weren't any real rules. What kind of trouble was there to get into anyway? Besides, she wasn't with Dylan, and that always meant the rules were relaxed.

The three of them walked down the beach and over the sand dunes into the campground, hoping to see some other teenagers hanging out there. They walked up and down the rows of motor homes and trailers, smelling the smoke from the campfires and hearing the laughter from the lingering night owls sitting in circles around the glowing flames.

Cody took a big sniff. "I smell s'mores."

"I smell dough boys," said Travis, shaking his head.

"What the heck is a dough boy?" asked Cody.

Sadie and Travis both looked at each other and then at Cody in disbelief. "You've got to be kidding. You don't know what a dough boy is?" Sadie teased.

Cody shook his head. "Never heard of it."

"Dude, you've lived a sheltered life," said Travis. "A dough boy is the best flippin' homemade cinnamon roll you will ever have. You take the dough from a crescent roll and wrap it around a wooden dowel and cook it over the campfire until it's golden. Then you roll the dough in a stick of butter until it's dripping, and then roll it in cinnamon sugar. It's freaking awesome! We'll make some tomorrow night."

After hanging out on the beach all day and grilling burgers for dinner, the families had skipped a fire on the beach and had ridden their bikes into town for ice cream instead. By the time they had gotten back, it was late and everyone went their own ways, tired from the first day's excitement.

The campground was void of teenage life, so they decided to head down to the beach and walk the pier. That too was quiet, so they walked the channel and back roads into town.

As they were walking, Sadie kept getting a whiff of Travis's cologne. It smelled good, different from Dylan's. She was so used to the comforting smell of Dylan, his voice, laugh, his walk, and the way her hand felt in his. She wondered what Travis's hand felt like. She couldn't remember the last time she had hung around another guy besides Dylan and his friends. It felt good to have a real guy friend of her choosing.

Sadie wondered if Dylan would be mad if he knew she had snuck out with Travis and Cody. Of course he would, she thought. Just as she would be pissed if she knew he had snuck out with two girls. She told herself this was entirely different, completely harmless. Travis was like a brother, she had known him forever, and Dylan would never know anyway. He had nothing to worry about.

She kind of wished Myla and Kyla were with her after all. They would all have a lot of fun together. Cody was really sweet and funny. He and Myla would make a cute couple.

After walking the quiet streets of Pentwater for the better part of an hour, they decided to call it a night. Travis and Cody walked Sadie to her cottage and made sure she got in before they snuck back in next door.

Back in bed, Sadie was wide awake. She couldn't stop thinking about Travis. When they were walking, his arm brushed hers a couple of times, and she felt that same ripple of excitement flutter through her as it had when she and Dylan first started dating.

There was something about the way Travis looked at her too. He really looked, took her in. Sadie had caught him peeking at her several times throughout the day when he thought she wouldn't notice. She did, and it had gotten her thinking about him way more than she ought to be.

As if on cue, Travis sent her a text. A Bitmoji actually. Travis rode a leaping sheep under the stars with the words *Sleep Tight*.

Sadie sent her own Bitmoji back to Travis. She chose the one of herself sleeping on a half moon.

Dear Sadie,

The summer after Dad and I got married, we spent a week in a tent, camping in Pentwater. The record heat had us sweltering every night. Well, except for the night we had a terrible thunderstorm and the tent leaked like crazy.

Anyway, Dad and I carved our names into the wood on the lookout halfway up the Old Baldy foot trail.

I don't know why I never pointed it out to you. I guess I didn't want you to think it was okay to vandalize and carve your name into things. It's in the corner facing west, so next time you go, check it out.

The night we carved it, we sat up there and watched the sun set with a pitcher of margaritas that we hauled up all those steps. It is still one of the best memories I have with Dad. It's a simple memory—that's why it's so special. We were so in love and so content just watching the sun set and being with each other.

As my life comes to an end, it's those simple memories that fill my head, Sadie. It's not about fancy jewelry Dad bought me, or whether our house was bigger than the neighbors', or even if my kids were the smartest in their class, or the star players on their sports teams. It's about love and the margarita moments—private moments shared by you and your loved ones that no one knows about or can try and compete with.

So someday when you're married, make a pitcher of margaritas, carve your names (and encircle them in a corny heart the way we did) next to Dad's and mine on the Pentwater lookout, and watch the sunset.

I love you, Sadie,

Mom

CHAPTER 18

Sadie

Sadie's voice was still groggy as she answered her cell. She couldn't remember the last time she slept in this late. The clock on the nightstand read 10:08 a.m. Usually Nicholas had her up by 7:30. Even on weekends when their dad was home, Nicholas ran to Sadie's room first.

"Were you sleeping?" asked Dylan.

"Yeah, I can't believe Nicholas didn't wake me up." Sadie crawled out of bed and looked out the window facing the beach. Sure enough, Nicholas was splashing in the water, and Kurt was lounging in a beach chair with his coffee and the paper. Jayna was still zonked in the upper bunk, so Sadie snuck out of the room and down to the front porch.

"Were you up late or something?" Dylan asked, and Sadie's heart raced.

"Not really, I guess it's just the fresh air and everything."

"Fresh air?" Dylan chuckled. "You sound like my grandma. Sadie . . . I miss you."

"I miss you too."

"So when can I come see you? Remember, in a few short weeks, I'm moving on campus."

Sadie wanted Dylan to come visit, she really did, and the thought of him moving to the dorms made her stomach sick. So why was she dreading this question? She shifted in the Adirondack chair and crossed her legs. "Why don't you wait a couple of days for us to get settled in? I want you to really feel what it's like to miss me."

"Believe me. I miss you." Dylan's voice was seductive and made Sadie wonder if he just wanted to visit her so they could sneak off. "I love being at the beach with you—you're different when you're there, more carefree. It's like you let go and have fun."

She *was* more carefree at the beach. She felt a sense of peace whenever she was there. She pictured the two of them bobbing in the water, holding each other close, flirting, and even playing paddle ball together. She did miss Dylan—they did have fun together. "How about tomorrow?"

Sadie grabbed a bowl of Honey Nut Cheerios and went back out to the Adirondack chair on the porch and watched the boats enter and exit the channel. People began to claim their spots on the beach.

As the towels were stretched out and the umbrellas were pushed into the sand, Sadie felt an overwhelming sense of loneliness. She missed her mother so much at that moment.

Lydia used to walk the beach at the crack of dawn every morning with Andrea, Travis's mom. By the time they got back, their husbands would be having coffee on the porch, and the four of them would drink coffee and make the most amazing breakfasts.

Most mornings, after all the kids were up, they would gather on their porch for the works: egg casseroles, frittatas, bacon, sausage, croissants, donuts, fresh fruit, and fresh squeezed orange juice, compliments of Benton, Travis's dad.

Sitting here on this empty porch with a bowl of Cheerios sucks, thought Sadie. Everything was different without Mom around. She set the bowl down and looked next door to see Andrea wave at her over her novel. Sadie waved back and hoped Andrea couldn't tell she was on the verge of tears.

Still in her pajamas, Sadie walked down to the beach. As she passed her dad, she mumbled she was going for a walk. She decided to head north, away from the public beach and people. How many times had her mother walked this very stretch of beach, she wondered? Did it ever cross her mind that someday her life would be cut short because she was going to be diagnosed with a fatal disease? The last summer they vacationed here, did Lydia have any inclination that it was her last time here? That, three months later, she would learn her fate?

The sound of gentle waves crashing on the shore brought Sadie some peace, but there were times when sadness engulfed her. She said a prayer and asked God to please help ease her pain. She didn't know what else to ask for. She walked until the sun felt hot and intense and turned around.

Tired, she sat down in the thick sand that was already hot from the sun. She could feel her shoulders burning—all she had on was a thin sleeping tank and shorts. As she sat quietly, looking over the water, she felt a presence wash over her so powerfully it almost brought tears to her eyes again.

Whether it was God's presence or her mother's, she didn't care; she felt it. She felt strong. She felt her mother's love. She felt the love she had for her family and Dylan. She may not have had her mother, but she had a lot to be thankful for.

With each step towards the cottage, Sadie felt better. She couldn't help but wonder if her mother's spirit lingered here. She was certain her mother was in heaven, but she wasn't so sure about where else her mother was. Could she be present in the breeze that made the dune grass dance? Was it possible for her to be riding the crest of the waves? As the cottage came into view, she could see everyone out on the beach. When her foot hit the first step, she was greeted by the cooing sound of a mourning dove perched on the roof. The sound soothed her. She remembered her mom always loving the sound of the bird, and she felt like it was some sort of a sign that her mother was with them in Pentwater.

Sadie saw from the large clock hanging on the porch wall that it was nearly one o'clock. She had been gone for over two hours. Her dad was probably freaking out. Sadie went straight inside and changed into her suit and sunglasses. When she came out, she was surprised to see Andrea waiting on the porch for her.

Andrea wrapped her arms around Sadie and held her. Sadie hadn't felt this kind of motherly hug in so long. Even though it was comforting, it was also a bit awkward.

Andrea pulled back and held Sadie by her shoulders. "How about going for a walk with me tomorrow morning?"

Sadie nodded in agreement.

Sadie kept to herself most of the day and read magazines as she flipped from her stomach to her back, soaking up the scorching August sun. Nicholas was busy driving trucks through the sand with some other kids on the beach, while Jayna had reunited with Liz, a girl her age who visited her grandparents every summer a few cottages down.

Kurt and Benton were sitting under an umbrella, having a beer and talking politics while Andrea lay in the sun next to Sadie, reading a novel. Sadie was glad to have Andrea next to her physically, but she wasn't interested in much conversation.

Travis and Cody had been on their boogie boards most of the day, and even though they had made a little small talk, Sadie wasn't in the mood to hang out with them. It wasn't personal; she just wanted to chill and get over her mood.

She wondered if Andrea told him to back off, because normally he would be egging her on to try boogie boarding or throw a football around. Travis could always bring out Sadie's masculine and playful side.

When it came to playing sports at school, Sadie was all about tennis, a rather girly sport, Sadie realized. But here, with Travis, she was always throwing a football or Frisbee around. Travis had sent her another Bitmoji while she was on her walk. In this Bitmoji, he was riding a Popsicle like a surfboard, the words *STAY COOL* above him.

Sadie's Bitmoji reply was herself sporting the word *COOL* across her face, her eyes peering through the two O's.

As Sadie sprayed on another layer of sunscreen oil, her phone chirped with a text message from Paige, Marissa's daughter. Sadie had finally broke down at tennis camp this summer and mentioned to Paige what was going on with their parents. Paige was clueless, which really didn't surprise Sadie.

From time to time the girls would text; mainly Sadie would text Paige to see if Marissa was at home when Kurt had said he was meeting with clients for dinner.

Sadie couldn't figure out Paige's true feelings about their parents' relationship. She acted annoyed by it, but yet Sadie knew Paige wasn't nearly as miffed as Sadie was. She had to hold her tongue too. She wasn't about to bad-mouth Marissa to her own daughter, even if Marissa had done something evil to her mom.

Paige had confronted Marissa, and Marissa told Paige that they had casually dated a few times—that they were enjoying each other's company and weren't making a big fuss about it.

When Sadie read that text from Paige, she was ready to throw her phone—*she* was making a fuss!

Paige, by Sadie's request, even spied on their parents together once at a restaurant and once playing golf together. Luckily, Paige had never followed them to any sleazy motel rooms, thus far.

As Sadie read the text from Paige, she felt herself break into a sweat. Paige reported to Sadie that she snuck a look at Marissa's phone earlier and read several text messages between her and Kurt. It looked as if Kurt was either going to meet up with Marissa for an afternoon somewhere or Marissa was going to visit them at Pentwater for a day.

Sadie was fuming. How dare she! She hadn't even come over to their house since Sadie's birthday party last spring.

Why would she think intruding in on their vacation would be appropriate? Especially a place so sacred to Lydia!

Sadie looked over at the man sitting ten feet from her. She was disgusted with her father and wanted nothing more than to rub sand in his face. Here he was laughing without a care in the world and at the same time plotting some secret rendezvous or, worse yet, Marissa crashing their family vacation.

Kurt had said that Lydia forgave Marissa for whatever she had done to her, but Sadie was positive Kurt was exaggerating. Knowing her mom, she probably did tell Marissa she forgave her because she was dying and that was the kind of person she was. Sadie didn't buy the tale entirely.

If they became so close again at the end, then why didn't Marissa come around more often and why didn't Lydia mention it? Sadie didn't buy her dad's story that her mom wanted to keep it mum to focus on her family. He was doing some serious sugar coating. She was sure of it.

Andrea must have sensed Sadie's anger. She closed her book and turned to Sadie. "Anytime you need to talk about anything, Sadie, you can trust me. I'm a good listener, and I won't give you a bunch of nonsensical parental advice. You can get anything off your chest with me . . . okay?"

"Thanks, Andrea . . . maybe sometime . . . I don't feel much like talking today. I hope you don't think I've been being rude; it's just that . . ."

Andrea put her hand on Sadie's arm. "You don't need to apologize or make excuses, Sadie. I get it. I really do."

Sadie looked at her with questioning eyes.

"My mom died when I was nineteen. I was away at college, my freshman year. I went through it too. No, I wasn't as young as you, and I didn't have to take care of a younger sister and brother, but I understand what it's like to lose someone you love and need so much."

"I'm sorry. I never knew."

"It was twenty-four years ago. She's been gone more than half my life now—not a day goes by that I don't think about her."

Sadie looked down. That really wasn't what she wanted to hear. She wanted Andrea to tell her it was going to get easier, that she would move past it and pretty soon it wouldn't be a big deal. Sadie was hoping that, by the time she was in college, she would be old enough to handle it better.

"But in a good way, Sadie, not in a sobbing, missing way. Little things I do remind me of her and it's comforting to know she is a part of who I am. I have her bony wrists, I love to paint abstracts the way she used to, and I'm a diehard Tigers fan like her. My mom walked every morning and I do the same. She drank her coffee lukewarm and so do I. Her right toenail always split down the middle and so does mine, and our smiles were identical. I've been told by my grandmother that our laughs sound the same."

Andrea took a deep breath and continued. "I love looking at pictures of my mom and reminiscing about making cakes and pies together. She was this skinny little thing, who was constantly baking in the kitchen. She had her own little business, "Kate's Cakes," and she pumped out towering wedding cakes right from our own kitchen. She had me baking alongside her by the time I was eight. And she was a talker—the woman loved to talk to everyone. She had more friends than I could keep track of."

"Sometimes I think those things of my mom too, and I smile, but so often it just makes me miss her even more. And then there's Jayna and Nicholas. I try to be so strong for them, but I think it just makes it harder. I get so frustrated sometimes."

Andrea nodded. "You have a lot on your plate, Sadie. I won't argue. I was the youngest of three. My brothers were older than I was, and we were all spread across the U.S. at different colleges when my mom passed. But I didn't face my mom's death for a long time. I buried myself in books, boys, and booze." Sadie and Andrea both laughed. "It made it worse. I dealt with my mom's death in all the wrong ways throughout my college career. I was twenty-five when I saw my first counselor, and I did more healing in that first month with her than I had in the six years since I lost my mom."

"So what's the secret?" asked Sadie.

"I wish there were one, honey. The best advice I learned is to talk about her, keep her memory alive. Allow her to stay a part of your life. I also learned getting angry doesn't solve anything. It won't bring her back.

"My counselor told me on the first session that I couldn't control the circumstances, but I could control how I chose to react to them. She also told me that it took a lot of practice every day.

"I kept asking why my mother had to die. The counselor looked me in the eye and asked 'Why not?' I wanted to slap her, but she was right. I had to accept the fact that my mom was never coming back and I had to move on. She taught me to realize I still had a full life ahead of me and I was the only one standing in my way of living it."

Andrea paused and bit her lip. "You're young, Sadie, but I can honestly say you already have one up on me. I wasn't nearly as mature at nineteen as you are now at sixteen. If it's any consolation, with age comes understanding. I know that it might not help right here, right now, but getting things off your chest will." Andrea laughed and pushed her sunglasses up her nose. "We're women—what we do best is vent our frustrations."

Hadn't Sadie said she wasn't up for conversation? But wow, it was really easy with Andrea. She seemed so . . . on Sadie's level. Andrea was also a neutral ear. Sure, Sadie talked about her mom with her dad, but not like this, and not often enough.

Sadie and Jayna talked about their mom and tried to keep her memory alive around the house, but the outside world didn't seem to care so much about her mom dying anymore; they were past it. Except for family, Dylan, and occasionally Myla and Kyla, Sadie felt funny mentioning her mother around most people. And the last thing she wanted to be was morbid and whiney, needing sympathy from others.

Dear Sadie,

As you go through life, you are going to make mistakes. Don't be too hard on yourself. Ask for forgiveness, forgive yourself, and move on. I can't tell you how many nights I lay in bed, wide awake, beating myself up for not being the perfect mother, wife, sister, daughter, or friend. It's stupid really—a waste of time.

I'm not saying that you should go through life being selfish and living carelessly. Please work your hardest to be a kind, compassionate, loving, giving, and selfless person. BUT allow yourself to make mistakes. Just own up to them, promise yourself you'll try your hardest to do better, and be done with it.

I wasted so much time in my life feeling guilty over things I said and did. If I blew up at you kids, I would convince myself I was the worst mom on the planet. If I turned one of you kids away because I just really didn't feel like playing Barbies that day, I would lose sleep over it that night. Pretty soon I was so consumed with me and my "bad" behavior that I was literally caught in my own trap.

You're probably rolling your eyes about this right now, but it will make sense someday. You can't be everything to everyone, Sadie, so just know your best is good enough. Don't sweat the small stuff, honey, and the big stuff, well . . . you've got to rely on your faith.

I'm trying my hardest not to lecture, because I know you tune me out anyway. But someday you'll appreciate my words of wisdom. Remember on the days you feel like you have nothing to give, a smile or a hug might be all someone else needs!

I love you, Sadie,

Mom

CHAPTER 19

Sadie

Dinner was beachside over a roaring fire that no one could get too close to because it was already scorching hot in the evening sun. The fireball in the sky was lowering toward the lake, but the temperature was not.

Sadie buttered two pieces of bread and placed them in the hobo pie maker for Nicholas. "What do you want on your pizza?" She spread sauce over the bread and sprinkled a handful of mozzarella.

"Extra cheese and pepperoni," he said, grabbing a fistful of pepperoni and throwing it toward Sadie.

"Slow down, champ," she said, grabbing the bag of pepperoni before Nicholas dove into it again.

"Hey, why don't you let me cook his pizza while you make one for yourself," said Travis. He folded the hobo stick, clamped it, and carried it over to the fire before Sadie had a chance to protest. Not that she cared if he did it, she was just used to preparing Nicholas's food for him.

Sadie stood there for a second, dumbfounded that the thought would even cross Travis's mind. She watched Nicholas run behind Travis to the fire, and the two of them knelt down in search for the hottest coals. Nicholas was already clinging to Travis, desperate for a big brother to play with.

Andrea walked up behind Sadie, juggling a dish of coleslaw, a bowl of tortellini salad, and a bag of chips. She dropped them on the picnic table and looked toward the fire. "Looks like Travis finally found his long lost brother."

Sadie smirked. "Ha, I was thinking the same of Nicholas."

Andrea and Benton also had a daughter, Bella, but she was nineteen, three years older than Travis, and studying abroad this summer in Europe.

"Sometimes I wish Jayna was a brother to Nicholas instead of a sister." Sadie chuckled. "Maybe she would be a little more help and play with him, at the very least, a good role model."

Andrea smiled. "Jayna reminds me of myself. I was never much for kids growing up. I babysat twice and never again. I hated it! I couldn't stand crying babies, or playing dolls, or trying to calm them when their parents left."

"And you had two of your own?"

"Believe me it took a lot of coaxing from Benton to get me to agree to children. I went into it with my armor up. I told him I was still going to work full-time, be in my book club, my walking group, and we were not going to give up our Tuesday night golf league or our Saturday date nights.

"Then, there I was in the hospital with Bella in my arms, telling Benton there was no way I was going back to work in six weeks, or ever. Hitting a golf ball and chasing after it suddenly seemed petty, and I couldn't keep my eyes open long enough to read two pages in the best of books.

"Once they put her in my arms, I was a changed woman forever. Jayna may change someday too. Unfortunately, that doesn't help you much now with Nicholas."

Sadie laughed. "I'll probably be the one who doesn't have kids because I'll be so worn out from Jayna and Nicholas. Jayna will probably have a half dozen!"

"Where is Jayna, anyway?"

"She's having dinner with Liz and her grandparents. She said they're having real food—steaks and salmon on the grill." Sadie rolled her eyes and sighed. "She was the one who was so excited to be in Pentwater and cook hobo pie pizzas and cherry and apple pies over the fire. Now it's not good enough for her."

"Well, once we whip out the dough boys tonight, she'll come running."

"Oh, don't get me wrong—it's quite alright she isn't here. When Jayna is in a mood, it's best she isn't around. She is either sweet as pie or a royal pain in my rear! Speaking of dough boys, can you believe Cody has never had one in his life? Travis and I were teasing him last night."

"Sheltered." Andrea laughed. "By the way, why didn't you bring a friend? I put the bug in your dad's ear. I was kind of hoping you would, and the four of you could hang out, you know. I mean, not that you can't with just you three, but, well, you know," Andrea fumbled.

Sadie glanced sideways at Andrea and wondered if Travis ever talked about her or if Andrea noticed the way Travis looked at Sadie. She immediately felt bad. What did it matter anyway? She had a boyfriend.

"I mean . . . I know you have a boyfriend, Sadie, but I just thought then you wouldn't feel like a third wheel."

Sadie tried to hide her feelings. She didn't even understand them herself, but she wondered if Andrea knew something Sadie didn't or if she could read into Sadie or something.

"I don't mind all the attention. Besides, I wanted to get through this first week alone. Maybe next week I'll invite a friend up, maybe two, one for Travis and Cody." However, Sadie knew that Travis was off limits for Myla and Kyla.

Kurt and Benton arrived to the fire, carrying a cooler filled with drinks and some Tiki torches to light when the sun set. Kurt put his arm around Sadie's shoulders and gave her a squeeze. "Thanks for getting Nicholas going. He was starving. Why don't you make yourself something, honey? I'll get the rest of his plate. Does he eat coleslaw?"

"No, Dad, Nicholas hates coleslaw. Give him some tortellini." Sadie didn't mean to sound annoyed, but it kind of came out that way. Didn't he pay attention to anything?

Sadie decided she would make Travis a pizza at the same time she made her own. She knew all he liked was cheese. He had always been an extremely picky eater. Andrea would always scold him when they were kids, telling him he should try new things and eat more like Sadie. Funny, the things she remembered.

She slipped in next to Cody by the fire. He was on his third attempt to try and *not* scorch his pizza. He was clearly an amateur at this beach living stuff, but he was adamant about experiencing it all. Sadie was quickly learning that Cody brought out the fun side in people wherever he went. He was a bit of a prankster, but basically a big goofball that she couldn't help but like. He was cute too, with dark hair and deep blue eyes.

Cody looked at the two pizza pies in Sadie's hands, "Hungry?"

"I thought I'd make one for Travis, since he helped me out with Nicholas." She ignored Cody's sly grin. "But . . . if you burn yours again, you can have it."

"Third one's a charm," he said, unclamping the sticks and peering inside at his pizza. "Oh, damn!"

Sadie rolled her eyes. "Again?"

"Kidding—it's perfect!" Cody sauntered off to the picnic table like a proud little boy who just used the potty for the first time.

Sadie, Travis, and Cody were out for their nightly walk. No sneaking out this time. After watching the sunset and making doughboys over the fire, they told their parents they were going to walk the pier. It was nearly eleven o'clock and the beach was deserted.

The sky was clear and starry and the air was still warm. Nothing more than the slightest ripple came ashore as they walked barefoot along the water's edge.

"My gut hurts," Cody said, placing his hand on his stomach.

"That's because you ate an entire roll of dough, you idiot!" Travis gave Cody a friendly push, and he stumbled in the water, almost tripping.

Cody groaned and belched. "But they were sooo freaking good I couldn't stop."

"Don't be a pig, man. There's a lady here."

Sadie wondered when Travis had grown up. He seemed so much more mature than most of the guys she knew from school, aka Dylan's friends, and they were older, graduated! Not that Travis wasn't a typical sixteen-year-old, but he was different somehow, more caring. Was he like this to every girl or just her?

Travis was a lot like his dad. Benton was the kind of husband who catered to his wife. He was always affectionate and helpful and eager to please Andrea. Travis had a good role model.

Sadie didn't remember her dad being like that with her mom. They were more traditional. Lydia stayed home and cared for her family while Kurt worked hard and took care of the lawn and played "Mr. Fix It" around the house.

Sure, her mom and dad kissed each other when they came and went and said "I love you" to each other, but they didn't hold hands in public, or rub each other's shoulders, and they certainly never made each other's plates and ate off each other's forks the way Benton and Andrea did.

There was no doubt in Sadie's mind that her mom and dad loved each other, but Andrea and Benton had the kind of marriage that people were envious of. Sadie not only could see this with her own eyes, but she remembered overhearing her mom telling Andrea those exact words only two summers ago. She had forgotten about it until now.

As the three approached the pier, they could hear voices of other kids. Travis chuckled. "Wow, maybe there's teenage life around here after all."

They climbed on the cement pier, and Sadie couldn't believe how warm it felt under her feet. Up ahead they saw several silhouettes and a lantern sitting on the edge of the channel side. In the silence of the night, the splash of bodies jumping in the water echoed. A few squeals and screams followed.

"Holy crap, it's freezing!" a girl squealed.

Every hair on Sadie's body stood up as she registered the voice she heard—Jayna! Sadie took off in a sprint towards the ladder next to the glow of the lantern. As Jayna reached the top rung and placed her foot on the pier, Sadie grabbed her arm and gave her a yank, sending them both flying backwards.

"What the hell!" screamed Jayna, her face falling flat as she recognized her sister.

"That's what I should be asking! Have you lost your flippin' mind, Jayna? Do you want to drown? There could be an undertow, a riptide. You could hit your head . . . and that would be the end of you." Sadie's chest was heaving. "Not to mention you can't see a damn thing out here."

"Relax, Sadie. I'm fine," Jayna snarled. "Quit trying to act like you're my mother."

Before Sadie realized what she had done, it was too late. She hauled off and slapped Jayna across the face. "How dare you?" Sadie meant it in so many ways. "You have no respect, you selfish, brainless little brat."

Jayna lunged toward Sadie, ready to attack. "Jayna, back off!" Liz yelled as she grabbed her and pulled her away from her sister.

"What? Are you on her side, Liz?"

"I'm not on anyone's side, Jayna, but I am the one who talked you into coming out here. Seriously, Sadie, don't be pissed at Jayna. I was the one who coaxed her into jumping into the channel. She said no at first. I'm sorry."

Liz sounded sincere, but Sadie wasn't ready to cave. Dead silence met her as she stood in a crowd of at least ten kids. She was mad, no doubt, but she also felt humiliated. Leave it up to Jayna to pull something like this.

Sadie knew she didn't always make the best choices herself, but if there was ever one thing their mother and father were adamant about, it was no jumping or swimming off the pier. And here was Jayna in all her glory doing it in the pitch black of the night, all to impress a bunch of barely pubescent boys and girls.

"You so much as put your little toe in that water again, and I swear I'll drown you myself." Sadie pushed through the wide-eyed bodies surrounding her and stormed back towards the beach.

A few minutes later Travis and Cody caught up with her. "You okay?" asked Travis.

Sadie plopped down in the sand and the boys did too. "Yeah, I probably overreacted. I know I'm no angel, but I'm not stupid."

"Well, if it's any comfort, I don't think Jayna will be jumping in again. She grabbed her towel, and she and Liz took off down the pier leading into town."

"Wonderful, next I can bail her out of the bar. Actually, what I wouldn't give for a drink myself right about now." No sooner had the words left Sadie's mouth than the three of them looked at each other, knowing exactly where they could score some alcohol—their parents' cooler by the fire.

CHAPTER 20

Sadie

Kurt knocked on the bedroom door as he pushed it open. "Sadie, it's 9:30, and Andrea is on the porch, wondering if you want to go for a walk."

Sadie's head was pounding. Mixing beer and tequila from the cooler was not a bright idea. They hadn't necessarily drunk a lot. All it took was two beers for Sadie to feel drunk, but they each did a few shots on top of it, and Sadie was not used to downing straight tequila with nothing but beer as a chaser.

Who made the stupid choice now? Sadie's inner voice teased her.

"Tell her I'll be down in a second." Sadie tried her hardest to sound normal and wondered if her dad could still smell the alcohol on her. She doubted Travis and Cody felt like this, and they were probably still sleeping, anyway.

Kurt nodded and left her room without another word. Sadie ran to the bathroom, splashed water on her face, and scrubbed her teeth and tongue until her mouth felt raw. She threw on her favorite yoga capris, a tank top, baseball cap, and sunglasses.

It was Sadie that sent the *REGRETS* Bitmoji to Travis this morning. Her cute little comic self was sprawled out across a chair with a cool cloth on her forehead.

In the kitchen, she guzzled a glass of water and bypassed her usual cup of coffee. The thought of it made her want to puke. She passed through the living room of the cottage on the way to the porch to find Nicholas glued to Sponge Bob with a bowl of dry Fruit Loops resting in his lap.

"Are you supposed to be watching that, champ?"

"Dad don't care."

"Dad doesn't care or dad doesn't know?"

Nicholas didn't answer. He was too engrossed in the TV show to even hear Sadie, and Jayna's voice echoed in Sadie's head. *Stop trying to act like my mother.* She wasn't their mother, so she kissed Nicholas on the forehead and walked out on the porch.

Kurt and Andrea were laughing about something and stopped when Sadie came out.

"Sorry I slept so late."

"No worries. You ready?" asked Andrea.

Sadie tried to sound enthusiastic as she bounced down the steps to the sand. "Yep!" This was going to be painful.

Andrea had on a short white running skirt and a black and white Nike tank top. She was in very good shape. Andrea was athletic-looking with long muscular legs and toned arms. She was a natural blonde with a slight tint of red to her hair.

They were both barefoot since they were going to walk down the lakeshore through the sand. Andrea carried a bottle of water with her, and Sadie wished she had grabbed one as well. They quickly fell into pace on the quiet beach.

Andrea held out her palm. "Do you need these?" Two ibuprofen rested in her hand. She offered Sadie her water as well.

Sadie looked at Andrea's face, but she couldn't see her eyes through the tinted sunglasses Andrea was wearing. She did notice a smirk on Andrea's face though.

"Thanks." Sadie scooped them up and swallowed them down with the water.

"You can have the bottle," said Andrea. "Hangovers suck!"

"How'd you know?" Sadie felt a little stupid and also wondered if her dad knew too.

"I went to clean out the cooler this morning, and my tequila bottle was half empty, not to mention the beer was completely gone."

"Oh, sorry." Sadie winced. "We were just going to do one shot of tequila each. I guess we went a little overboard. Did you mention this to my dad?"

"No, I figured your body was punishing you enough as it was. And besides, Travis and Cody will be hearing from me. I should have woken those boys up and made them scrub floors or something."

"It was my idea. We found Jayna and Liz out on the pier, jumping in the channel with a bunch of other kids, and I blew up at her. For some reason, I thought hitting the cooler would help." Sadie couldn't believe how easy that just came out to Andrea, but wondered if she should have kept her mouth shut.

Sadie felt her eyes get hot and her throat well up. "I get so sick of having to protect and take care of everyone. I made such a scene and complete idiots out of both of us. I don't know why I even care. I do worse all the time—like raiding the cooler."

"You care because you love her and don't want your sister to get hurt, plain and simple, Sadie."

"She yelled in my face to stop acting like her mother, and I know she's right."

"You would protect your sister whether your mom was alive or not, Sadie. You were only doing what you thought was right, and it was. Don't be so hard on yourself."

Sadie needed to hear these words from Andrea, from an adult. It was hard explaining these things to Myla and Kyla. They compared Sadie's scenarios to fights they had with their siblings, which was fine, but it was different—they weren't responsible for their siblings.

Jayna and Nicholas were Sadie's responsibility; her mom had told her to take good care of them. Keeping them alive was a big part of that, especially since their dad was so oblivious to most of the crap Jayna pulled.

Sadie had never been one to run to their parents to tattle on Jayna, even when they were little, and she wasn't ready to start now. Besides, what would Kurt do? Ground her? That would only backfire in Sadie's face because she would be the one in charge of making sure Jayna obeyed the terms every day while he was at work.

Sadie was feeling better. The ibuprofen, water, fresh air, and Andrea were helping. They picked up their pace and chatted easily. Sadie pictured her mom and Andrea out there walking and talking about their lives and families. She wondered what her mom vented to Andrea about. Her kids? Her husband? Marissa?

Taking in the familiar view of sandy dunes and occasional homes and cottages put Sadie at ease. She was always at peace here. The sun beating down on her back, along with the lull of waves, made everything in life seem a little easier. Times like this she wished summer would stick around all year long and they never had to leave. Sadie dreamed of being a recluse, being homeschooled on the beach.

Sadie was considering talking to Andrea about Marissa, but she didn't know how to bring it up, and she didn't know if it was even worth it. The text from Paige was still eating away at her. Would Marissa seriously dare show up in Pentwater? It had been years since their families vacationed in Pentwater together.

What the heck? She couldn't hold her tongue any longer. "Do you remember Mom's friend, Marissa Jenkins? They used to rent the cottage with us?"

"Sure, I remember. We used to have some great times out here. We talked a bit at your mom's funeral."

"She and Marcus are divorced now. You knew Mom and Marissa had a huge falling out, right?" Sadie didn't wait for Andrea to respond. "Well, of course you did; that's why they stopped coming here with us. Did Mom ever mention to you what it was about?"

Andrea was silent for what seemed like several minutes. "Lydia did talk with me about it, but Sadie . . ." Andrea inhaled deeply. "Sadie, it's complicated and really not my place to comment on anything."

Sadie was now aware of one thing her mom and Andrea talked about on their walks. "You do know they reconciled when Mom was sick, don't you?"

"Yes, your mom told me that."

"So what's the big deal then?" Sadie heard that snotty tone in her voice and hoped Andrea didn't catch onto it. She didn't mean to be rude. "I mean . . . what could have happened that was so bad it had to be kept a secret from me? I'm her daughter and she's dead."

"Can I ask why it's so important for you to know?"

Sadie bit her lip. Maybe she should have kept her mouth shut after all. Was it worth telling Andrea and getting herself all worked up?

"Dad and Marissa are secretly dating—that's why I want to know."

Andrea stopped dead in her tracks. Sadie was a few feet ahead of her before she realized it and stopped to see her standing there, dumbfounded.
"What did you say?"

"Dad and Marissa have been talking and dating for the entire summer—ever since last spring, actually. They started getting cozy during tennis season. I don't know how often they see each other. He's never let on to the fact that he goes out with her, but I have my sources, and I know they date. I've also seen some of the text messages from her on his phone. In fact, I'm waiting for her to show up here."

Andrea looked at Sadie, stunned.

"Are you sure about this, Sadie, or are you just suspicious? Maybe they've met a few times to talk. Maybe it's strictly platonic. I mean your mom and Marissa were lifelong friends."

"I wish. Believe me. I wish. Paige, Marissa's daughter, and I have been keeping a close eye on them. They're spending more and more time together, and yes, they're affectionate."

They started walking again, slowly. Sadie's mind was racing, and from the look on Andrea's face, she was shocked. Was it just because Lydia and Marissa used to be best friends, or was the look of shock because of what happened between the two of them?

"I can't believe it," said Andrea.

Sadie got the feeling that Andrea hadn't meant to say that out loud. "Neither can I, so now are you going to tell me what happened?"

"Sadie, I really can't, not now at least. I can't disrespect your father like that. And Lydia, I . . ." Andrea was definitely lost for words. "Oh Sadie." She touched Sadie's arm.

"What, Andrea? What could be so bad?"

Andrea looked away from Sadie. "It's not my business, Sadie, you have to understand that. It's simply not my place to say anything."

"But I'm asking you to."

"I can't, Sadie. I just can't."

CHAPTER 21

Sadie

Jayna waltzed down the beach from Liz's cottage just in time for lunch. Sadie didn't even bother to look at Jayna as she stomped up the porch steps and sat as far away as she could get on the picnic table. Kurt smiled and kissed her head and offered to make her a roast beef sandwich. Jayna said she hated roast beef and dug her hand in the bag of Chex mix.

"How about turkey and provolone then," Kurt suggested, always kissing Jayna's butt and not wanting to get on her moody side.

"Whatever, I want lemonade too."

"Sure, sweetie."

Jayna glanced Sadie's way with daggers shooting out of her eyes. Sadie shot hers right back. For a minute, Sadie seriously considered apologizing to her for overreacting last night. Forget it. With the way Jayna acted, she didn't deserve an apology—she seriously had issues.

Kurt walked into the cottage to get Princess Jayna a glass of lemonade, and Sadie could tell Jayna was nervous sitting across from her at the picnic table. Nicholas was too busy sticking his carrot sticks in his sandwich to even notice anyone else was present.

"I wasn't planning on saying anything to Dad about last night, but if you're going to act like such a little snot, I have no problem slipping."

"You would, Sadie. Actually, I can't believe you didn't run home and tell him last night—anything to make you look like the good girl, always high and mighty and in charge."

"Yeah, because that's me. I'm always running to Dad and tattling on you. I usually do it in the spare time I have between doing your laundry, driving you to Chrissie's house, making your meals, and covering for you when Dad calls home from work to check on us and you've taken off on your bike for the day without bothering to tell anyone where you're going."

"You always have to bring that stuff up. What does jumping off the pier have to do with how much I help around the house? You complain about everything."

Okay, Jayna had a good point. It didn't exactly have anything to do with it, and every time they fought, Sadie did bring up what a slacker Jayna was.

"Ya know, Jayna, I'm sick of having to take care of you. When are you going to grow up? Jeez, Jayna, you can't even make your own sandwich!"

Kurt walked out with a pitcher of lemonade and seemed to feel the tension in the air between his daughters. So he did what he always did, ignored it, and tried to lighten the mood by offering to do something fun as a family. "Anybody want to go fishing after lunch?"

"I do. I do!" screamed Nicholas, jumping up and down, raising his hand.

"Sadie? Jayna?" asked Kurt.

Jayna shook her head no. "Liz and I are going to lie in the sun with some friends down by the pavilion, but thanks, maybe tomorrow."

Sadie couldn't believe her ears. Was Jayna being polite?

"I think I'll just hang out here today with Travis and Cody. I might try skim boarding. You two boys can bring us home some fish for dinner." Sadie squeezed Nicholas's shoulder.

"You hate fish, Sadie," said Nicholas, looking concerned.

"I like fish, just nothing that swims in Lake Michigan. Why don't you throw them back in and let them live with their fish families, okay, champ?"

Nicholas nodded and Sadie felt bad for bickering with Jayna in front of him. He didn't need to hear it. Who was she kidding? He heard everything and pretended he didn't. She probably warped the kid for life.

After Kurt and Nicholas left, Sadie went up to change into her swimsuit. She chose the baby blue and brown Roxy bikini, the one her dad said looked as if it was missing some thread. She hoped she wouldn't lose her suit while falling on her face skim boarding.

Jayna was already in the room, digging through her laundry basket of clothes, holding up different suits. Sadie was irritated that she couldn't just throw her clothes in the drawers or put the laundry basket in the closet so they wouldn't have to trip on it for two weeks. Sadie held her tongue, though, and said nothing as she stepped over Jayna's pile and changed.

Jayna dipped her head. "Hey, if you want to hang out at the pavilion with us, you can. I was thinking of buying a blue raspberry slushy. I mean . . . I know they're your favorite. If you want your own, I'll buy you one too."

Sadie was caught completely off guard. She wanted to tell Jayna off, but knew this was Jayna's way of apologizing, so she had to practice what she preached and act maturely. "I'm looking forward to skim boarding, but maybe after a while I'll walk down and you can buy me a slushy."

"Okay, see ya later." Jayna threw her sunscreen in her bag and left the room quickly.

Sadie sang Katy Perry's "Hot and Cold" under her breath as Jayna left. She had always thought the song was written for her sister.

As she dug through her drawer trying to find her Roxy swim cover up, she received another Bitmoji from Travis. She was instantly flattered. *Wanna Hang*, was above Travis in a hammock, holding a drink in a coconut with a cute umbrella in it.

After hitting send, Sadie wondered if her response was borderline desperate. Her Bitmoji was her cartoon self, running, and read, *On My Way*!

CHAPTER 22

Sadie

Sadie knew her way around the tennis court, but when it came to skim boarding, she was very much an amateur. It didn't help that she felt like Travis was totally checking her out. Here she was again, confused, because as much as she doubted herself, she very much liked the attention from him.

She had talked to Dylan earlier, and because of work, he couldn't come for a visit for two more days. Sadie was excited to see him and missed him, so how could she be so flattered by Travis?

Sadie ran, threw the skim board down, and hopped on, skimming across the shore with ease.

"Now that's my girl—that's how you do it!" yelled Travis, running up to Sadie to give her a high five.

Cody smirked. "She's better than you, dude." He threw his board down, ran, hopped on, and sailed by.

"I'm tired," said Sadie, handing the board back to Travis. "I'm going to sit in the beach chair for a while."

"I don't think so," he argued. "You're on fire. Keep practicing." Travis got close to Sadie's face and playfully shoved the board back in her hands.

Sadie swatted Travis on the butt with the board. "Get out of my way, then." She perfected another run, knowing all too well she was acting like a tease. When she stood up with the board, she had to take a second glance. Dylan was walking in the sand toward her. Holy shit, he obviously just saw the exchange between her and Travis because he did not look happy.

Sadie swallowed hard as she started jogging up the sand to meet Dylan. She wanted to keep him as far away from Travis as she could, even if it were only twenty feet. She still had the board in her hand and could feel both Travis's and Cody's eyes on her back. Three pairs of guy eyes, how nerve-wracking!

"Hey, what are you doing here?" asked Sadie, leaning in to give Dylan a kiss. His jaw was clenched, and although he kissed her back, his attention was not on her.

"Ends up I got the afternoon off of work, so I thought I would surprise you, but it looks like you're having too much fun with your new buddies to care."

Dylan's voice was cool to say the least, and Sadie didn't blame him. He looked over Sadie's shoulder to the shore and nodded to Travis and Cody, but hardly in a friendly way. It was the upward chin nod, the arrogant, bad-ass nod Sadie so hated from boys. They all did it to act tough and cool, and she thought it was so annoyingly rude.

"Travis and Cody are teaching me how to skim board. I'm getting pretty good—can't wait for you to watch me," she said flirtatiously, trying to make light of the situation. Sadie hugged him and whispered in his ear, "I've missed you," and planted another kiss on him. It was a tasteful kiss, nothing inappropriate. Not only did she feel uncomfortable in front of Travis and Cody, but Benton and Andrea were also on the beach in front of their cottage, pretending to read their books but obviously peering her way.

"I'll introduce you and then we can take a walk." Sadie headed towards Travis and Cody, and Dylan followed. The tension between Dylan and Travis was thick, but thank God for Cody. He instantly started talking football with Dylan. As soon as Cody gave Dylan a "Congrats" for winning the state championship last fall (his senior year), Dylan loosened up.

Travis even piped up, and soon, all three of them were talking high school teams and scores.

Thankfully, Travis and Cody lived in a district about forty minutes away, and the schools weren't in the same class, so they didn't play each other. The tension was still present, but had eased somewhat in the uncomfortable ten minutes the guys had been talking.

A few minutes into the conversation Sadie felt Dylan take her hand and pull her close to him. She felt warm and loved by his touch, but at the same time, she couldn't help but wonder if he was holding her hand out of pure love, or if it was to show some sort of ownership over her. She felt a tad embarrassed and awkward in front of Travis.

There was a pause in the conversation, so Sadie gave Dylan's hand a tug and suggested a walk. As they strolled away, she had the biggest urge to turn around and look over her shoulder to see if Travis was watching her. Why was she feeling like this? And what was it exactly? Guilt? Pity? It wasn't as if there was anything between her and Travis anyway. And Dylan was the one she loved.

Hand in hand they walked past the public beach and saw Jayna out in the water, playing Frisbee with Liz and several other kids her age. It was obviously the same group of kids from the pier that Sadie made a scene in front of and didn't really want to confront.

It felt like all of a sudden she had a lot she didn't want to confront—the strange feelings about Travis, her dad and Marissa, even the secret as to why her mother and Marissa had their falling out—all this on top of dealing with Jayna. Why couldn't she escape from all these issues bogging her down? It always seemed like there was something. She was a teenager—wasn't her life supposed to be carefree?

Dylan brought Sadie's hand up to his mouth and kissed it. "Why are you so quiet? Are you pissed that I showed up here?"

Dylan didn't sound cocky, which surprised Sadie. He seemed more scared, almost the way she had heard girls her age talk to their boyfriends. Girls were always so jealous and afraid of getting dumped for another girl. Sadie felt bad; she didn't want to make Dylan feel like that. She realized his tough guy act was just that—an act!

She brought his hand to her lips and kissed it. "This was the best surprise ever. I thought you were working at the golf course today, so I was a little shocked is all."

"My dad gave me the afternoon off. Of course, I'm sure I'll be working overtime the next couple of days to make up for it. You still seem kinda off though . . ."

"I got a text from Paige, saying Marissa was planning to visit here. It's really bugging me, my dad hasn't said a word, and I don't think this is the place for her to come and expose their relationship to everyone. This place was sacred to my mom, my family. Not to mention our families vacationed here before Marissa cut my mom off."

They stepped onto the pier and felt a light breeze off the water. The air was incredibly humid and thick. "If I'd known, Marissa and I could have carpooled." Dylan tried to make light of the situation, and Sadie just glared at him. "I'm kidding. Why don't you confront your dad, Sadie? Tell him you're not comfortable with her coming here."

"It's not that easy, Dylan. First, I know I would start to cry if I brought it up, and second, I know I would start yelling—we'd just end up in a huge fight. It's not like we haven't fought about it already."

Sadie told Dylan about the conversation she had with Andrea. She explained Andrea's stunned reaction to the two of them dating and about how Andrea wouldn't spill a word about the fight between her mom and Marissa.

Dylan was a good listener while Sadie vented, and she was feeling better just getting her troubles off her back. They sat down at the end of the pier and watched the waves splash over the rocks, the boats come and go, and people fish.

Dylan offered to talk to her dad for her, acting as if Sadie didn't know what he was up to. Sadie turned his offer down, but was touched by his concern. How many boyfriends would put up with hearing all these family sagas all the time? Suddenly, she was feeling closer to Dylan than she had in weeks. All her worries about him going off to college and falling out of love with her melted away. He obviously really loved her.

"Don't you think it's odd that no one will breathe a word about their falling out, though? I mean . . . it's not like I'm four. Why can't I know what happened? What could really be so bad?"

"Does anyone else know, besides your dad and Andrea?"

"My Aunt Josie and Aunt Nevie both know, but I think I have a better chance of finding out from my mother than I do either of them."

Dylan smirked. "So pretty impossible to get your aunts to talk?"

"Yeah, you could say that."

Stepping off the pier, Sadie could see Jayna and her friends were out of the water and lying on their beach towels in the sand. A couple of kids were playing paddle ball, and a girl was standing in the middle of the towels, dancing. They were too far to hear the music, but Sadie laughed to herself because she now had a clear picture of what she and her friends all looked like at the beach, playing around, dancing, and being carefree.

It shocked her that Jayna, at fourteen, looked more like seventeen. She was turning into a stunning young woman. She looked so much like their mother. Sadie wondered if Jayna realized that when she looked in the mirror.

As they made their way up the beach, through the scalding sand to Jayna, Sadie gave Dylan a brief version of what happened on the pier with her last night. She told him Jayna's attempt at an apology was to buy her a slushy.

The dancing girl stopped and looked embarrassed when Sadie and Dylan stopped to talk to Jayna. Liz turned down the radio, and everyone grew a little silent. Sadie felt like an idiot. Here she was standing in front of a group of kids within two years of her own age, and she felt like she was a forty-five-year-old wicked mother whom all the kids hated.

"Oh, hey, Dylan," said Jayna, breaking the silence. "What ya guys doin'?"

Sadie smiled. "We went for a walk, and I thought we'd say hi and take you up on that slushy."

For once, Jayna didn't hesitate. She popped right up from her towel and grabbed her cut-off shorts. Sadie could see a few dollar bills hanging out of the front pocket. She laughed to herself. It would be like Jayna to lose her money before they even got to the counter.

Since Jayna only had enough money for two slushies, she insisted she didn't want one and gave hers to Dylan. Sadie rarely saw this side of Jayna. Dylan was teasing Jayna as they walked back to the group of kids, asking her which of the boys she liked. Much to Sadie's surprise, Jayna pointed out a shaggy blond kid sitting on a towel next to Jayna's vacant one.

"Does he like you? I mean are you a couple?" Sadie couldn't imagine Jayna with a boy, especially a boy that would put up with her attitude.

Jayna rolled her eyes. "I just met him three days ago." The blond looked towards the pavilion, and as soon as he spotted the three of them staring at him, he quickly looked away.

Dylan smirked. "He's definitely into you, Jayna." "What's his name?"

"Brody," said Jayna, staring his way.

Dylan and Sadie looked at each other and smiled behind Jayna's back. They thanked Jayna for the slushies and headed towards the dunes as Jayna ran back to her friends.

"She's not so bad, Sadie. She's just immature. She'll grow out of her attitude. Don't be so hard on her. Not everyone is a perfectionist," he teased and poked at her ribs.

"I'm not a perfectionist, Dylan, and she's as moody and flighty as they come."

Dylan squeezed Sadie's waist as they walked. "Lighten up, babe. You're too uptight!"

CHAPTER 23

Sadie

Sadie couldn't believe how welcoming her dad had been when she and Dylan came back from their walk. He shook Dylan's hand and gave him a warm pat on the back. Dylan, Travis, and Cody threw the football around while dinner was cooking. Sadie was relieved that everyone was getting along.

She took a sip of her lemonade and locked eyes with Travis. He stared two seconds too long before looking away, and she quickly looked down at her plate. What was that about, she wondered, feeling awkward. She felt a pull at her heart, but why? She was in love with Dylan. Right?

Liz's giggling brought Sadie out of her trance. She and Cody were acting quite flirtatious next to each other at the picnic table. Liz was approaching fifteen, so she wasn't much younger than Cody, but Sadie still had to roll her eyes at her giddiness. Even funnier was that Cody seemed to be completely enjoying the attention.

Dylan stayed well after dinner. They watched the sunset, and then everyone pitched in and helped build a bonfire on the beach. Sadie noticed Travis had grown quiet, and again it bugged her, and it bugged her that it bugged her.

The stars filled the clear Pentwater sky, and Sadie quickly pointed out the Big Dipper to Dylan—the same Big Dipper, she reminded herself *again,* that she and Travis slept under as kids on this beach. They roasted marshmallows and let off some leftover fireworks from the fourth of July that Benton had brought.

Shortly after midnight, Dylan said he should get going. All the parents had gone to bed an hour earlier, leaving Sadie, Dylan, Jayna, Liz, Travis, and Cody hanging out by the fire. Everyone seemed to be getting along, especially Cody and Liz, but Sadie couldn't decipher whether the slight tension she felt between Dylan and Travis was real or was just her worried mind.

Sadie walked Dylan to his car behind the cottage and kissed him good-bye. Just as he was about to get into his car, he told her to stay put, that he had forgotten his baseball cap on the beach.

After several minutes of standing in the dark, waiting for Dylan to return, Sadie got antsy and started walking around the side of the cottage toward the beach. She quickly stopped when she heard his low but threatening tone of voice.

"I'm not trying to sound like a dick or anything," Dylan said. "It's just that I know you've got it for her, and I want to make sure you understand she's mine. You better not be hitting on her or making any moves. I'm serious, Travis. Hands off!"

"No worries, dude—Sadie's like a sister," said Travis.

"Okay. We're cool then. See ya around."

"Yeah, see ya."

Sadie ran back to Dylan's car before he rounded the corner. She was instantly fuming with Dylan, playing back in her head what she had overheard. How dare he talk to Travis like that! She wasn't going to let her annoyance show to Dylan, but there was no denying that his words definitely got under her skin.

Dylan wrapped his arms around her and kissed her again. When he pulled away, he looked her in the eyes. "Be good."

She stood in the dark and watched his taillights fade in the distance. *Be good? What the hell was that supposed to mean?*

Walking back to the fire, she found only Cody and Liz.

"Where'd everybody go?"

"To bed," said Liz cuddled up close to Cody.

"Alright, goodnight," Sadie called over her shoulder as she turned and walked back toward the cottage.

"Hey, don't lock up. I'm staying over."

Sadie gave Liz that motherly look, and as soon as she did, she wished she hadn't.

"I'll be inside in a bit, I promise."

"I promise too, Sadie," said Cody with a smirk.

Good thing it was Cody, because she trusted him. "No biggie—stay out as long as you feel like."

Sadie crawled in the bottom bunk and wondered if Jayna was still awake. She didn't talk about too many intimate things that happened with her and Dylan to her younger sister, but she felt like it right now. Sadie desperately wanted to vent about what she overheard. She wished Travis had still been at the fire. She could have smoothed things over.

Instead, she grabbed her phone and decided to text Myla; she was the level-headed one and the best listener. After waiting several minutes with no reply, Sadie figured Myla was asleep and gave up, tossing her phone on the nightstand with a sigh.

"What's wrong?" asked Jayna.

Sadie thought for a moment before answering. "Even though I love Dylan like crazy, he can be so irritating sometimes."

"Like how?"

"Like how he's jealous of Travis. I overheard him telling Travis to stay away from me." Sadie looked out through the gauzy curtains and stared at the Big Dipper and wondered if she should apologize to Travis on Dylan's behalf.

"I'm not trying to defend Dylan or anything, Sadie, but it's quite obvious you and Travis have a thing for each other. You're always flirting and hanging out. It's no wonder he's pissed."

"Whaaat? Travis and I do *not* flirt."

"Uh . . . yeah you do, big time."

Sadie thought of their flirtatious Bitmoji texting, but no one knew about that.

"Well, it's only in a friendly way, and it's certainly not intentional. I mean . . . it's Travis. How could we be anything more than friends?"

"How couldn't you be?"

"Jayna, you're not helping."

"Maybe I am."

"Whatever. I'm tired and you don't know what you're talking about," said Sadie, declaring the conversation over. So much for thinking it would do any good to talk to Jayna; she'd never even had a real boyfriend.

Liz slipped in the bedroom and found the sleeping bag on the floor. She smelled like Cody's cologne, something Sadie noticed him wearing for the first time tonight. "He is such a good kisser!" beamed Liz.

"What about Ryan, Liz?" asked Jayna. "Don't you feel the least bit guilty?"

"Ryan will never know. He's two hours away. Besides, I'm staying with my grandparents a whole month. I need some excitement."

Liz and Jayna began chatting away about Cody and other boys Liz thought were cute that Jayna should like. She was definitely way ahead of Jayna when it came to boys, thank God, and not the best influence.

Sadie buried her head under the pillow. Jayna's words were ringing in her ears. She had to admit she wasn't sure what bothered her more: was it Dylan's threat to Travis, or Travis's comment about her being nothing more than a sister?

She knew she wouldn't be receiving any goodnight Bitmojis from Travis and desperately wanted to send him one, but she was too afraid he might not respond.

CHAPTER 24

Sadie

The second Sadie opened her eyes she was already thinking about how embarrassed she was for what Dylan had said to Travis. She hated that kind of attitude in boys, and she was definitely miffed at Dylan. The question was whether she should say something to Travis about it or just let it be. He had no idea she had overheard, and she didn't want an awkward wall between the two of them.

She stepped over Liz on the floor, grabbed some clothes, and went in the bathroom to change. When she came out into the bright airy kitchen, she smelled coffee. She saw an electric fry pan, a box of pancake mix, and syrup sitting out on the counter ready to go. Her dad must be planning breakfast.

Sadie grabbed her favorite mug from the glass cupboard—the ceramic one with bright colored flip-flops painted on it that had been at the cottage since she was little—and poured herself a cup of coffee. With a banana in hand, she headed for the porch.

Sure enough, Sadie found her dad staring out at the water with a cup of coffee in his hands and an unread paper folded on his lap. Even though she was far from quiet as she padded onto the porch, he hadn't heard her coming or noticed that she had plopped down in the Adirondack chair next to him.

"Morning, Dad."

"Oh, hey, sweetie. You're up early. How'd you sleep?"

"Fine."

"Are you and Andrea going for a walk?"

"Yeah, in a bit."

Kurt smiled at Sadie. "Just as she and your mom used to do." Kurt leaned his head back on the chair as if it helped him remember Lydia better. "They used to come back and make a huge breakfast, the works. I always loved the smell of bacon wafting out onto the porch from the kitchen. I thought I would make bacon and pancakes this morning once everyone was up and around."

It made Sadie feel good that he cherished the same memories she did. She wondered what his favorite memories of Pentwater were. "One summer, you, Paige, and Travis decided to take a walk into the dunes after dinner. Your mom, Marissa, and Andrea had gone inside to do dishes and left us dads to watch over the kids. We failed!

All of a sudden you kids were just gone! You couldn't have been more than four at the time, so it was utter panic around here. We all feared the worst, that the three of you waded into the water after each other and drowned. We were running around, frantically yelling your names.

Finally, about fifteen minutes later, we found all three of you together over at the public beach, hanging with the teenagers at the volleyball courts. I will never forget the feeling when we came over that last dune to see you running around so carefree. Your mother, Marissa, and Andrea were all in tears, hugging and kissing you kids, and Benton, Marcus, and I all felt like the biggest losers. Of course, we all got chewed out."

Sadie wasn't so sure where this story was going, or where it had even come from, but she was pretty sure her dad had been sitting out here thinking about her mother and the past. She wondered if he felt as close to her here as she did.

Sadie took a sip of her coffee. "I bet Mom is glad we're here. It might sound weird, but I feel like this place was sacred to her."

Kurt's face paled, and he lowered his eyes for an instant. "Sadie, look. I need to talk to you about something. I'll be honest with you, sweetie. I understand if you're upset or confused, but—"

Instantly, Sadie felt an elephant step on her chest and anger rise up in her like she couldn't believe. "I already know about Marissa, Dad, and it makes me sick. Have you loved her all along? Did you two have an affair? Is that why she and Mom had the falling out? Did Marissa beg Mom on her death bed to forgive her?"

Sadie stood up from her chair and slammed the coffee mug down on the railing, sending the hot liquid splashing all over her hand and arm. She welcomed the burn—it only added fuel to her fiery rage.

Kurt sat, looking stunned in his chair, staring up at Sadie. "No, Sadie, Marissa and I did not have an affair, I promise you that."

"So you just waited until Mom died to start sleeping with her?" As soon as the words left Sadie's mouth, she regretted them, and from the look on her dad's face, she knew she had crossed the line.

"Don't you ever talk to me that way, Sadie. Do you understand? Have some respect." Kurt's voice was deep and firm, a voice Sadie rarely heard. "Not that it's any of your business, but I am not sleeping with Marissa." He clenched the arms of his chair in anger.

Sadie's voice was rising, and against her will, tears began spilling out. "What happened then? Why is it such a big secret? And why, out of all the women in the world, do you have to be with Marissa? How could you do that to Mom and our family? You're betraying your dead wife and embarrassing us!"

Kurt leaned forward, rested his elbows on his knees, and buried his head in his hands. "It's complicated, Sadie, but I assure you . . ." Kurt hesitated, seeming to choose his words carefully. "What has developed between Marissa and me was not there before Mom died. We have only been casually seeing each other over the last couple of months."

"So that's supposed to make it alright? Your girlfriend is your dead wife's ex-best friend, *Dad*. How does that sound to you?"

"What it sounds like to me is that two people who have known each other for a long time suddenly found themselves pulled together by unthinkable circumstances, and they realized they really care for each other. And frankly, Sadie, I don't even need to explain this to you. I'm an adult and I will make my own choices.

"If you must know, I have been agonizing over this for weeks, all because I love you kids with all I have in me, and I will always love your mother. She wasn't just your mother who died, Sadie; she was my wife, my best friend, the mother of my children, and the woman I held and adored for over twenty-two years of my life."

Kurt stood up and wrapped his arms around Sadie, and she buried her head in his chest. He kissed the top of her head. "I don't know how it happened, Sadie, but it did. I care for Marissa, and I need you to accept it."

"How can I when no one will tell me what Marissa did to Mom?"

Sadie could feel Kurt's grip on her tighten. "Sadie, let it go. It was between your mom and Marissa, and they forgave each other."

Sadie pulled back from Kurt and looked him in the eyes. "I was eleven when it happened, Dad. It wasn't just between Mom and Marissa. I remember hearing you and Mom arguing, and when I asked Andrea about it the other day, she freaked out." Sadie turned and headed down the porch steps to the beach to find Andrea for their walk. She couldn't look at her father for one more second.

Kurt yelled after her. "Marissa is visiting us today, Sadie. Please, at least be courteous."

Not a chance, thought Sadie.

CHAPTER 25

Marissa

Marissa was a ball of nerves and anxiety. She loved Sadie like her own child. So why did she fear her? She was a sixteen-year-old child for crying out loud!

Sadie had been through enough, and Marissa didn't want to put her through any more stress or sadness. So here she was at 5:11 a.m. pulling out her third batch of peanut butter chocolate chip cookies from the oven, wondering if she was the cruelest woman in the world for seeing Kurt Booker, the husband of her deceased best friend.

Ugh, was she wrong for dating Kurt? Was she crazy for having feelings for him? Was she completely out of her mind to think they even had a chance at making this work? What was she thinking imposing on their family vacation? Their first vacation since Lydia died.

She swallowed her last cold gulp of coffee and realized she had downed four mugs. Not good. Marissa usually drank two mugs each morning; any more and she was cranky and irritable. She indulged herself with a hot gooey cookie and decided she needed eggs—eggs and a green smoothie.

The countertops were piled high with bags of licorice, chips, homemade puppy chow, and homemade trail mix. She remembered how much Sadie loved puppy chow and Jayna the trail mix with peanut M&Ms.

The cooler was stashed prematurely with fixings for chicken kabobs, summer beer, chocolate milk boxes, sodas, fresh cut melon, the sweetest berries, veggies, homemade ranch and dill dips, an assortment of cheeses, summer sausage, and beef sticks. She would have to stop and replace the ice on the way, she knew, but this was what Marissa did when she was in a tizzy. She went overboard. She tried to please everyone. She was sucking up!

What would Kurt think of all the fuss she had gone to? Already loaded in her car were a bag chock-full of sand toys, glow sticks, water balloons, Frisbees, a paddle ball game, a new dart gun for Nicholas, and a couple of extra boogie boards.

It was a day trip to the beach, and she had enough food, drinks, and gear for a week. Then there was Paige. What did Paige really think of all this? What would this do to Paige and Sadie? Was Marissa putting Paige in danger of getting hurt too?

Last night Paige seemed excited to be going to Pentwater, but when Marissa had brought it up, she also noticed Paige trying to act somewhat cool about it. As the blender roared to life, swirling her spinach, banana, avocado, celery, and almond milk to a beautiful bright green, she scolded herself for all her irrational behavior. “Get a grip,” she told herself out loud.

“No doubt!” Paige scowled with a yawn. “What the heck are you doing?” she asked her mother, looking around the disarrayed kitchen.

“Oh sorry, did I wake you?”

“You could say that.” Paige moaned, while filling a glass with water. “Timers beeping, the mixer whirling, the blender screaming . . . who could sleep?”

Paige grabbed a cookie and started to head back up the stairs.

“Where are you going?” asked Marissa. “I thought you would help me start loading all this food in the car.”

“Jeez, it’s not even 6:00 a.m., Mom!”

Marissa let out a sigh as she stuck a straw in her smoothie and told herself to calm down.

CHAPTER 26

Sadie

Andrea was just walking out the sliding door onto the porch as Sadie came up the stairs. The two cottages were identical structures but painted and decorated differently. The Bookers always stayed in the red cottage with the blue door, and the Sutherlands always stayed in the blue cottage with the red door.

Andrea's eyes immediately went from Sadie's red, puffy face to Kurt, who was diligently sweeping sand off the porch next door.

"Are you ready?" asked Sadie as she turned back down the steps, her eyes fixated on the shoreline.

Andrea could barely keep up with Sadie as they walked in silence for a few minutes. "Do you want to talk about it?"

"Marissa is coming here today. I hate it. I hate it that he has to like her, and I hate it that she's coming here. Of all places, why here?" Sadie flung her arms in the air. "Dad says that he and Marissa didn't have anything going on before Mom died, but I think it's a lie. I think they had an affair. What else could it have been?"

Andrea pressed her lips together. "Sadie, your dad and Marissa did not have an affair. I wouldn't lie to you."

"Then tell me what did happen."

Andrea shook her head. "No, Sadie."

They walked in silence again for several minutes. "Sadie, you know your mother was so proud of you. She used to talk about what a good tennis player you were and how she was sure you were going to go pro one day.

"Your mom and I would meet at a café halfway between our houses in the winters for lunch so we could catch up. For dessert, your mom always ordered the triple fudge brownie, smothered in hot caramel sauce, served with peanut butter cup ice cream. Of course, this was after her spinach and kale salad loaded with beets, broccoli, and tomatoes." Andrea laughed. "She loved her dessert, and it somehow never clung to her. I bet you never knew your mom was a soap-opera addict. She secretly taped 'Days of our Lives' and watched it either when you kids were napping or later when you were in school full-time and your dad was at work. She never wanted anyone to know.

"Oh, and when you kids were little, we used to set the clocks ahead to get you to bed early so we could have some peace and quiet around the fire at night. And your mom told me more than once that she had always dreamed of taking guitar lessons. Which reminds me what a pretty voice she had—she used to sing you to sleep and it was beautiful."

Andrea went on and told story after story about Lydia, helping Sadie forget about her dad and Marissa for the time being. Before Sadie knew it, she was actually smiling and laughing, remembering her mother.

"She was such a beautiful woman, Sadie."

When Sadie got back from her walk with Andrea, her family, including Liz, was just sitting down at the picnic table for breakfast. The bacon and hot syrup smelled amazing, but the last thing she wanted to do was eat breakfast near her father.

Nicholas begged Sadie to sit next to him. She noticed her dad's coffee mug next to the empty plate on the other side of Nicholas. At least she wouldn't have to look at him, she thought. Sadie helped Nicholas cut up his pancake as her dad walked out on the porch with a bowl of pineapple and strawberries. Pancakes, bacon, and fruit—this was huge for him, and to Sadie's surprise, it all looked edible.

Jayna and Liz were gossiping about some girl from the beach, giggling that she had no boobs to fill out her bikini top. Kurt overheard the girls and cleared his throat, giving Jayna the "shut-up and do not talk like that especially in front of Nicholas" look. They snickered and changed the subject to what color wire Liz was going to get at her next orthodontist visit.

Sadie was mid-bite in her pancake when she noticed Travis and Cody walk out on their porch with bowls of cereal in hand. They plopped down on their red Adirondack chairs, looking half asleep.

Cody took a sideward glance towards their cottage, most likely looking for Liz. But what really caught her attention was that Travis didn't even bother to peek at their porch. She knew he could certainly hear them, and a cold shoulder wasn't normally his style. She felt a pang of guilt in her stomach and wondered what was going through his head?

Was he going to ignore her for the next week and a half? Sadie hoped not.

After breakfast, she took a long shower, shaved her legs and underarms, and then slathered lotion from head to toe. From the bathroom, she could hear her phone on the dresser blowing up with text messages.

There was even a text from Paige, warning Sadie that she and her mother were on their way to Pentwater.

Sadie wasn't so sure what Paige thought about their parents dating. At first she seemed equally annoyed; she eagerly volunteered to spy on them and report back to Sadie. But lately she acted like it was no big deal. Maybe it was easier for Paige since her dad had moved on to another woman long ago. Maybe she thought the fight was Lydia's fault?

Whatever the case, Sadie had a mission, and that was to make sure Paige put up just as much of a stink as she did. She liked Paige well enough—they were inseparable as kids—but their parents becoming a real couple, nah-uh, not going to happen.

Sadie didn't feel much like going down to the beach quite yet and decided to ride her bike into town and shop instead—nothing like a little retail therapy, she reasoned.

She quickly sent Travis a Bitmoji before she could talk herself out of it. It was generic; she was holding a spray can with the word *SUP?* above it.

Several suspenseful minutes later he texted back, and Sadie was disappointed with the *YO* he was sitting on. What did she expect? Something with hearts? No, but something more.

The cottage was empty when she came out of her room. She left a note and hopped on her bike. She took her time and rode through the campground and down by the pavilion and by the channel on her way, stopping at a coffee shop for a frozen mango smoothie. It felt kind of good to be alone—at home, she always had Nicholas clinging to her side.

She walked in and out of the surf shops, trying on bathing suits, summer skirts, sunglasses, and countless tanks and shorts before deciding on a purple cotton strapless dress studded with tiny rhinestones across the top. When she was checking out, she found some earrings and a toe ring.

Sadie walked out of the store at noon. The town whistle blew loudly as little kids covered their ears. Sadie loved it that they still blew the noon whistle every day.

The air was thick and sticky. The digital readout on the bank sign read eighty-four degrees. The temperature was expected to reach ninety today, which meant the water would feel refreshing.

As she tied her bag around the handle bars and lifted the kick stand up, the whistle died down and she heard two familiar voices from around the corner. "I can't believe you got away with that, Jayna. You are the master. I was freaking out the whole time! What a rush that was!"

Sadie held still. What were Jayna and Liz up to now?

"It's so easy, Liz. Why don't you just try it? The secret is to do it right in front of the clerk so they won't suspect it. It's not like they count the rings on your fingers when you walk in the store."

"But what about cameras—doesn't that freak you out?"

Was Sadie hearing what she thought she was? Was Jayna stealing?

"They don't have someone sitting in the back staring at cameras all day, Liz. Those are for nighttime robberies. Besides, I doubt these little stores have cameras. It's only a couple of bucks anyway, big deal."

"I'm still too chicken," said Liz. "Besides, my grandma would hand me a twenty everyday if I asked."

Sadie wheeled her bike around the corner to find Jayna and Liz sitting at a café table, sipping frozen Cokes. Jayna's back was to Sadie, but Liz's eyes grew wide at the sight of Sadie peering down on her little sister.

"Or maybe Liz is just honest, Jayna. Did you rip off the drinks too?"

Jayna whipped around and glared at her sister. "What are you talking about, Sadie?"

"Don't play stupid with me." Sadie grabbed Jayna's hand and looked at the silver ring with pink stones in the shape of a peace sign. "What would possess you to steal this? And what else have you stolen?"

Liz took a nervous drink from her straw and looked down at the table. Jayna pushed her chair back, grabbing her purse and drink. "Nothing, this was the first time, and I'll never do it again, so just keep your mouth shut, Sadie. I don't need another lecture from you."

Jayna began walking down the sidewalk, and Liz quickly got up to follow. "The ring is all she took, I swear. Give her a break, Sadie. Lay off a little." Liz picked up her pace to catch up with Jayna, and Sadie just stood and watched them go.

Riding all the shady back roads to the cottage, Sadie decided to forget the stolen ring. She figured, if Jayna wanted to be stupid enough to steal, she could risk getting caught. She was done dealing with Jayna.

However, Sadie couldn't help but wonder what went through her sister's head. One minute she was happy, the next pissed off at the world. One day she did something stupid and swore she'd never act like that again, and sure enough, within a couple of days, she was back at square one. Did she think anything through? Did she have a conscience?

Back at the cottage, Sadie slipped on her suit, grabbed her phone and ear buds and went out to the beach. She had no idea where her dad and Nicholas were, but if it meant no Marissa, she didn't care. Sadie laid her head back on her beach chair, closed her eyes, and sang along with Adele, One Direction, The Weekend, and Taylor Swift.

Just as she started to drift off, Cody came up from behind her and held an ice cold Gatorade on her cheek, which sent Sadie flying out of her chair.

"Nice, couldn't you see I was relaxing," Sadie said.

"Sorry, where's your sister and Liz?"

Sadie bit her tongue, even though she wanted to make a sarcastic remark about Liz being into more boys than just Cody. She really liked Cody and didn't want to see him get hurt, but maybe he was just having a fun little fling too. "Isn't she too young for you?"

"She's only a year and two months younger. Isn't Dylan, like, two years older than you?"

"That's different. I'm sixteen and she's only fourteen."

Cody rolled his eyes. "She'll be fifteen in three weeks."

"So the calendar says. Are you sure you want to get involved with her? I mean I just don't see you two as a couple. You're, like, way sweet and she's kinda trouble."

Cody smirked. "I know what this is about, Sadie. You want me. I didn't see it before, but it all makes sense now. How could I have been so blind?"

Sadie laughed. "Shut up, Cody."

Cody grabbed Sadie by the shoulders and gently shook her. "What is it? My physique? My charm? My athletic ability? Tell me, Sadie, what is it about me that turns you on? Why do I set you on fire?" Cody started pushing her towards the water.

"It's not your brain, that's for sure, cuz I'm not so sure it's all there!"

"That does it!" Cody scooped Sadie up and began running towards the water with her kicking and screaming. She chucked her iPhone on her towel as he carried her away. They had barely made it five steps in the water when Cody tripped over the surf, and they both tumbled face first into the lake.

They were barely knee deep, but Sadie was laughing so hard she couldn't get up and felt sand rushing in to her bikini bottom. She grabbed a fistful of sand from the lake bottom and threw it at Cody's head. He reciprocated, and before long, they were covered in thick, wet sand.

Sadie had sand in her ears, hair, mouth, just about every crevice of her body. She ran and dove out into deeper water to wash off and Cody followed. "Game over," she said when she came up for air. "You can find out for yourself what you're getting into."

"Thank you," said Cody. "How do you know I'm not just a player anyway?"

Sadie only frowned at Cody. She knew he wasn't, and she also knew she was butting in his business, so she kept quiet.

When Sadie and Cody reached the shore, she froze at the sight before her. Marissa and Paige had arrived and were making their presence known. It looked as if they were getting reacquainted with the Sutherlands. Benton and

Andrea were greeting Marissa with hugs, and Travis even gave Paige a hug. What was up with that? They hadn't seen each other in six years. Why would he give her a hug?

"Who's that?" asked Cody.

"My worst nightmare," Sadie said coldly. "My dead mother's enemy—now my dad's girlfriend."

"Oh, ouch," said Cody. "Let's play catch." Cody threw the football at Sadie, hitting her in the stomach. She picked it up and chucked it back at him. He knew just what she needed to get her aggression out.

Sadie was doing a good job of ignoring their guests for about three minutes until Paige ran up to say hi. Sadie was a little irritated that she and Travis hugged, and she wasn't so sure they were on the same team when it came to their parents.

Paige was sweet, but kind of a floater, always hanging out with different crowds, like she wasn't sure where she belonged. Besides tennis, she was kind of a book worm. Paige would end up being valedictorian; that was for sure.

Sadie introduced Paige and Cody and asked her if she wanted to play catch with them—surprisingly, she did. A few minutes later, Travis joined them, and Sadie attempted to make eye contact with him, but it was impossible. He wouldn't give her the time of day. Marissa's laughter suddenly echoed out, making Sadie glance towards the cottage. Her dad, Marissa, Andrea, and Benton were all laughing about something, and it made Sadie's stomach churn. She wished Andrea would send Marissa on her merry way, at the very least talk some sense into her dad.

A few minutes later, Kurt and Marissa came walking closer to the shore with Nicholas running ahead of them. After he begged to play catch, Sadie told him he could be on her team.

Marissa stopped at the beach chairs and set her bag down in the sand and waved to Sadie. "Hey, Sadie, how are you?"

Sadie managed a not-so-polite "fine" and half smile. A twinge of resentment swept over her when she noticed the way Paige eyed her. She had to remember that Marissa was Paige's mother, and she would of course defend her to the end.

Kurt and Marissa took seats next to each other and began chatting. The sight was irritating to say the least. Sadie tried hard to put her mom's face on Marissa, but for the life of her, she couldn't get a mental picture of her mom in her head, which made Sadie want to cry or, better, scratch that woman's eyes out!

Travis spread his towel down on the other side of Paige, and anger seared through Sadie. Paige was usually quiet and reserved, but Sadie swore she was flirting with Travis and he was flirting back.

So here she sat, wanting to reach over Paige and pull Travis next to her and ask him what he was doing. Paige and her mother were quickly becoming double trouble.

Was Travis acting like this because of Dylan's threat, trying to prove he didn't care about Sadie at all? Or was he really attracted to Paige? She could understand if he was; Paige was beautiful and one of the nicest girls Sadie knew. That bothered Sadie even more and made her feel selfish and cruel. Who was she to stand in the way if they liked each other? Travis certainly wasn't hers.

Before Sadie knew what she was doing, she had grabbed her sunscreen, walked around to Travis's towel, and started squirting lotion on his back, telling him she was worried that he was getting burnt. Halfway through, she realized what an idiot she looked like. He had propped up on his elbows, turned his head, and gave her the strangest look.

She was so embarrassed, mortified, so she made the excuse that she had to rinse her hands off in the water and practically sprinted to the shore. You idiot, Sadie, what were you thinking?

It was obvious Sadie was jealous, and she hated herself for it. She never swam out to the swim buoys by herself, even though she was an excellent swimmer, but for some reason she was drawn to them. Usually the thought of not being able to touch the bottom while swimming in Lake Michigan bothered her, but this time she felt like she could swim clear across to Wisconsin to escape her family, Dylan, Travis, and most of all, herself.

Once at the buoy, Sadie swam parallel to the shore from one buoy to the next. The water was calm with barely a ripple, and Sadie quickly fell into a rhythm, alternating between the breast stroke and freestyle. Even though she had never joined the swim team, her mother insisted on swim lessons every winter so they were strong swimmers at home in their own pool. It paid off; she was quick yet graceful.

When Sadie felt like she had reached near exhaustion, she swam to the shore. The mass of beach towels was deserted when she got back. She scanned the beach and caught sight of Travis, Paige, Cody, and Liz all playing volleyball against Jayna and her new friends, and she felt like she didn't have a place anymore.

Up until yesterday, she had Travis and Cody all to herself, and she liked the bond they shared, but today she felt like she didn't fit in. Sure, she could go join in on the game, but she truly didn't feel like it, so she lay down on her stomach and closed her eyes. Soaking up the warm sun on her back helped her relax and drift off.

CHAPTER 27

Kurt

When Kurt came out of the bathroom from his shower, he noticed Marissa had changed into a white sundress. She looked beautiful with her hair swept up, showing off her bare, delicate shoulders.

She handed him a glass of lemonade mixed with beer and vodka. One sip and Kurt had remembered Lydia and Marissa making their "summer beer" drink almost every night they were in Pentwater.

Kurt remembered himself and Marcus teasing their wives about their froufrou drinks until they decided to try them one night. After a few too many, they both ended up puking next to the fire. Thank goodness the kids were young then and actually went to bed *before* their parents.

"You're remembering that Lydia and I used to drink this stuff while we were here, aren't you?"

Kurt nodded. "I can't believe how crazy we got sometimes as young parents."

"Why don't you take the pitcher next door and give some to Andrea and Benton so I don't make a fool of myself tonight. Let her know I'm five minutes from putting the kabobs on the grill."

Kurt stood staring at Marissa for a few seconds, and she looked up from her chopping. He tilted her chin up with his finger and gave her a soft kiss on the lips before walking out the door with the pitcher in hand.

Marissa

Sadie came into the cottage, after watching Kurt leave with a pitcher in his hand. Even though Marissa's back was to her, she could tell by Sadie's footsteps that she stopped dead in her tracks when she spotted Marissa alone in the kitchen. Marissa quickly turned and offered Sadie a glass of regular lemonade, but she declined with a polite, "No, thank you," taking Marissa by surprise.

Sadie was halfway to her bedroom when Marissa decided to take the opportunity to talk to her alone. "Sadie, I know you aren't exactly excited that your dad and I are dating, but I wish you would give me a chance. I really care about you. I have since the day you were born—actually since the day your mom told me she was pregnant with you."

Marissa followed Sadie to her room and leaned up against the door frame.

Sadie ignored Marissa and dug through her clothes, lifting up different outfits, inspecting them like it was the first time she had ever seen the clothes.

"Sadie, I was like your second mom for the first ten years of your life. Can you cut me some slack?"

Sadie dropped the mini skirt in her hands to the floor and glared at Marissa. "I don't need anyone, especially you, barging into our family and replacing my mom. We're doing just fine without your help. I'm quite sure you are the last person on this earth that my mom would want dating my dad. So if you're looking for a warm welcome, you're certainly not going to get it from me, ever!"

Marissa's jaw dropped, but then she stood up straight and continued. She had no idea of the level of hatred Sadie had towards her.

"Lydia and I had a really rough time for several years, you know that. But, Sadie, we worked through all of it before she died. We weren't enemies, if that's what you think. And me and your dad—it just happened. It wasn't planned or premeditated. Believe me. Not in a million years did I ever expect anything like this to come about."

"Whatever happened between you and Mom, or whatever you did, you made her suffer for years. I could even hear her and Dad fight about it sometimes. Then she got cancer and died and here you are. Why can't you just make it easier on all of us and go away?"

Marissa inhaled deeply and tilted her head. "What happened between me and your mom is in the past. You've got to let it go, just as we did. I assure you your mom and I had completely worked through our problems. All was forgiven—we were once again as close as sisters.

"I know you're only trying to protect your mom, and I respect that, but, Sadie, you're not being fair to me or your dad."

"Fair? You want to talk about fair? It's not fair that my mom is dead and you're here. That's not fair!"

With that, Sadie crumpled on the bottom bunk and turned her back to Marissa and sobbed. Marissa felt like she had been punched in the gut. The last thing she wanted was to leave Sadie crying like this. She knew she ached for her mother, and Marissa felt for her and wanted so badly to wrap her arms around Sadie and comfort her, but she also knew that would be a mistake at this point.

Instead, she closed Sadie's door and went back into the kitchen where she found Kurt standing, looking out the slider, watching Nicholas play trucks on the porch steps. She could see his muscled back through the ice blue fitted T-shirt he was wearing. He turned, and when their eyes met, she knew he had heard everything.

"I'm sorry. I should have kept my mouth shut. I just wanted a chance to make it right."

Kurt took Marissa in his arms. "You said all the right things, much better than anything I could have said."

"Maybe I should go. This has been enough for her today."

"No, I want you to stay. We need to show her that we're adults and she isn't in control."

Marissa backed away from Kurt. "She's hurting, Kurt, and I don't want to ruin everyone's night and your vacation. We can try again when you get back home."

"You're not going anywhere, and leaving isn't going to make the situation any better in the long run. I really want you to stay." Kurt looked at the beach and saw Paige hanging out with the other kids, Travis in particular. "And Paige is having a great time. Maybe there's still hope Paige could help smooth things over."

Jayna

Jayna pushed open the bedroom door to find Sadie lying on the bottom bunk, facing the wall. The room was quiet except for the light sound of the fan swiveling in the corner and then a sniff from Sadie.

She dropped her wet sandy towel on the floor and peered over her sister's shoulder. "Are you crying?" Jayna saw the redness of Sadie's face and eyes and felt guilty. "If you're that upset about me stealing some stupid ring, I'll take it back! Jeez!"

Sadie rolled on her back and looked up at Jayna, whose long, thick sandy blond hair was piled on top of her head and all strays secured away from her face with a bright yellow stretchy headband that matched her suit. Her large almond eyes popped against her tan, and not only did she resemble their mother to a T, she actually looked concerned.

Wiping her eyes, Sadie laughed out loud. "You always think everything is all about you."

Jayna sat on the edge of the bed, and Sadie scooted over for her. "Yeah, well, what's your deal, then?"

"The bitch in the kitchen, ya know, the one trying to replace our mother."

"What? You think they're into each other like that?"

"Jayna, open your eyes. We've even talked about it a few times. They're dating and who knows what else."

Jayna felt a mixture of emotions. She wasn't sure how she felt about her dad dating. The fact that it was Marissa, someone she knew, was probably better than a total stranger, right? Paige was nice enough, actually a lot more fun to be around than Sadie most of the time. But she had to agree that she kind of liked the way things were, just them and her dad. "So tell dad he can't date her," Jayna said very matter-of-factly.

Sadie rolled her eyes. "It's things like that, Jayna, that show how immature you are. They've been seeing each other for months. Dad isn't going to break it off just because we tell him to."

"Okay then, we'll be so mean to her that she'll leave him."

Sadie hadn't thought of that exactly, but wasn't that possibly her underlying motive? If they made it difficult enough, maybe her dad and Marissa would both see that it wasn't worth it.

Jayna's eyes widened. "Liz and I can put laxatives in her drink at dinner, or better yet poison. Can't you cut the lines to the brakes in her car?"

Sadie shook her head and let out a sigh and a laugh. "Get real, Jayna."

"Hey, you're the one with the big issue. I was only trying to help."

"Maybe we can figure out what Mom and Marissa had the big blowout fight about in the first place. The thing is, Jayna . . . whatever Marissa did to Mom . . . it took Mom until her death bed to forgive her."

Jayna seemed slightly confused. "Dad won't talk?"

"No, and neither will Andrea. She is the only other person who knows."

Jayna thought for a minute. "What about mom's diaries? I see Dad reading them sometimes at night. He sits outside and reads them next to a lantern. I've gone down to the kitchen for a drink and seen him out there. I think I've even seen him crying."

Sadie's face lit up. "Sometimes you can be brilliant, Jayna."

"So does this mean you're not mad at me anymore for stealing?"

"Seriously, Jayna, how can you be so smart and so stupid at the same time?"

Jayna shrugged and grabbed a swimsuit cover-up before heading back outside.

~*~

Sadie

Sadie kept to herself during dinner. Thank God the two picnic tables between the cottages were pushed together and long enough so that Sadie could stay clear of Marissa. Being around her was unbearable.

Andrea seemed to sense the tension in the air, and she was being extra sweet to Sadie. She didn't expect Andrea to give Marissa the silent treatment; however, they seemed to be catching up like old pals. What was up with that? For a split second, Sadie questioned whether she was acting immaturely, but then she quickly reminded herself that she was simply being true and loyal to her mother.

Travis and Paige were definitely flirting, and to say that it was getting under Sadie's skin was an understatement. Seriously, why couldn't these two women just go away?

Sadie knew Paige was clueless, but it still didn't make it easier.

She wished Dylan were there, even though she was still pissed at him for threatening Travis. He was working for his dad, helping with the maintenance of the landscaping at the golf course his father ran. When Dylan texted earlier, he asked if she was hanging out with "Travy boy," which irritated Sadie, but she replied back that he and Paige suddenly seemed to be in a sizzling summer fling.

Sadie pushed around the contents of her chicken kabob on her plate and dipped a piece of summer squash and zucchini in barbeque sauce, something her mom used to do to get her to eat vegetables. If it was covered in sauce it usually made it past Sadie's lips.

Dumping her paper plate in the fire pit, Sadie announced to no one in particular that she was going for a bike ride. Andrea heard and offered to go with her, but Sadie politely turned her down and agreed to meeting up for a walk in the morning.

She wasn't more than two minutes down the road when she heard Jayna yelling for her to wait. Jayna rode up next to Sadie, huffing and puffing.

"Don't you want to hang out with Liz and your friends?" Sadie asked.

"Nah, Liz, Cody, Travis, and Paige were going to get ice cream and watch the sunset from the pier. I didn't really feel like being a fifth wheel. It sounded kind of boring."

Sadie just nodded at her sister, and they rode through the streets of Pentwater in mostly silence, going up and down the roads they knew so well from their many bike rides with their mom as kids. Sadie noticed which bed and breakfast inns had been repainted, and which ones that time and the weather had taken their toll on over the years. Some had new additions and beautiful flowers and a quaint feel, and others were sparse and tired, desperately in need of TLC.

They rode past Pentwater Lake, Snug Harbor Marina, Cenzos, House of Flavors, and Cosmic Candy. "I'm thinking a peanut butter cup flurry sounds good. Do you want something?"

"I don't have any money on me," said Jayna.

"No, really?"

"Sadie, shut up . . . like I knew."

Sadie did shut up. She was only teasing, but she knew when she genuinely hurt her sister's feelings, and now was one of those times. "I'm kidding. C'mon, I'll buy you whatever you want."

They ate their flurries on a bench overlooking the channel that led from Lake Michigan to Pentwater Lake. Halfway through, Jayna asked if Sadie would be willing to switch her peanut butter cup flurry with Jayna's Oreo cookie flurry.

Jayna was notorious for doing this, and not only when they got ice cream, but when they went out for dinner too. She expected her family to trade meals with her halfway through and couldn't understand why everyone thought it was rude. Sadie just handed her sister her ice cream and accepted the Oreo cookie flurry without a word.

The sun was about to set when Jayna spoke up. "So, if we stay away long enough, maybe Marissa will be gone by the time we get back."

"She better take her daughter with her," mumbled Sadie.

"What's wrong with Paige? I thought you two were friends?"

"We are, but I don't want her up here."

Sadie felt Jayna's eyes studying her. "Yeah, she kind of left you in the dust. I mean she saw Travis and just kind of ditched you for him."

Sadie shrugged. "Somethin' like that."

Sadie and Jayna hung out most of the evening, riding their bikes to the beach and sitting in the dark, gazing at the stars on the end of the pier, climbing Old Baldy, and running down in the dark, and making lap after lap through the rows of the state campground, listening to the campfire stories and songs.

Sadie came out to watch the thunderstorm with her dad and pretended she hadn't seen him reading her mother's diary. It was dark out, almost midnight, but she would recognize the diaries anywhere. Even though she was still pissed at her dad for inviting Marissa and Paige out, she couldn't help but soften a little at the sight. Maybe he would realize he was making a mistake.

Another thing that occurred to her was that he had brought the diary to Pentwater with him. That meant he still thought of her—enough to pack it ahead of time and bring it here. Sadie was curious what was in this diary that was so special to him. She longed to read it too, but felt like it would betray her mother's privacy and trust.

A huge crack of thunder broke, and Sadie jumped as lightning highlighted the building waves. She wrapped her arms around her knees and pulled them close.

"This is going to be a good one," Kurt said, staring out to the water.

"Uh huh—they always are over the lake," Sadie muttered. A cool breeze blew through, and Sadie shivered for what seemed like the first time this steamy summer. Lightning was flickering every few seconds, moving closer and closer. It was beautiful.

"How about some hot chocolate?" asked Kurt.

"I didn't pack any. I figured it was way too hot."

"I did. There's always at least one good storm in Pentwater every time we're here."

Sadie shrugged. "Sure."

While her dad went to make hot chocolate, Sadie retrieved Dylan's hooded sweatshirt from her bedroom.

Jayna was out like a rock. They were so different. Jayna would sleep through every storm and never know it even rained, whereas Sadie was up faster than lightning at the first clap of thunder.

She peeked in on Nicholas, turned his fan from low to medium to drown out the storm, and, once back out on the porch, slipped the sweatshirt over her head. The sweatshirt smelled like Dylan. He had given her this sweatshirt to bring to Pentwater. It was orange with black lettering, their school colors, and had Dylan's last name, McCabe, written across the back, along with his football number.

They had done this throughout their entire relationship. Every couple of weeks Sadie would trade Dylan for a new sweatshirt, which he would spray with his cologne. She would wear these sweatshirts around the house or to bed to keep him close.

Sadie put the sleeve up to her nose and smelled Dylan as she looked next door at Travis's cottage. It was dark, but she wondered if he was listening to the storm, or if he slept right through it like Jayna. She thought about him and Paige and wondered if they were a real thing already. She wished she didn't care.

Maybe she just needed to get away from Travis or at least get her mind focused back on Dylan. She was still very in love with him, so how could any of these crazy feelings for Travis even mean anything? Kurt came back out with a mug of hot chocolate topped with a swirl of Reddi-Wip. They sat in silence for the next hour, watching the storm until it died down to just a heavy rain.

CHAPTER 28

Sadie

Even though the rain had stopped, the sky hung low with a thick haze. The air was just as thick with humidity, and the sand on the beach was wet and sticky as Sadie made her way over to get Andrea for their morning walk.

As the words came out of Sadie's mouth, she regretted them. "Looks like Travis and Paige really hit it off yesterday."

Andrea looked at Sadie a second too long, and she prayed her face showed nothing but indifference as she stared straight ahead at the shoreline. When would she learn to think before she opened her mouth?

"Probably no more than catching up with an old friend."

Sadie wondered if Andrea was just saying this because she knew that's what she wanted to hear or if she truly believed that's all it was. "Yeah, with Cody and Liz flaring up, Travis probably felt like he needed a girl by his side too." *Ugh what was she saying?* She really needed to shut up, already.

"Ah, I remember a few of those little summer romances too. They died down as quickly as they flared up. So is Dylan visiting again? You must miss him."

Sadie sensed Andrea knew her struggle and wanted to see where Dylan really stood. "He might drive out today."

"I bet you can't wait! You two have been together a long time. Hasn't it been over a year and a half?"

"Yeah," was all Sadie could say. She did want to see him, but knew how awkward it would be between Dylan and Travis. As much as she wanted Dylan around, she wasn't so sure she wanted to be without Travis all day, and knowing Travis, he would most likely avoid both of them. As much as she loved Pentwater, she never thought it would get this complicated.

Pentwater had always meant simplicity and carefree days, but maybe she was just confusing that with the days when her mother was still alive. Really, when she stopped to think about it, most of her problems wouldn't even be an issue if her mother were alive. She wouldn't have to worry about Marissa and Paige moving in on her dad and Travis. Jayna would still be a pain in the butt, but it wouldn't be her responsibility.

Sadie changed the subject to Marissa, not necessarily an easier subject, but one that was bound to come up anyway. "Do you think I'm acting immaturely and irrationally about Marissa?" Sadie asked, point blank.

A couple of seagulls swooped down in front of them to eat some leftover popcorn on the beach. They walked around them in silence, and Sadie could tell Andrea was choosing her words carefully. "I know it has to be hard to see your dad dating, and the fact that it's Marissa, well, I can't blame you for being confused and even upset."

"But . . .?"

Andrea laughed. "But they're adults and will make their own decisions, and I don't think you acting out towards them will make them change their feelings for each other."

Sadie thought about her dad's reaction to Dylan when they went out on their first real date. It wasn't that he didn't like Dylan; it was more that he didn't like that his daughter had grown up and was dating anyone, period. Sadie knew she would date Dylan no matter if her dad approved or not. He had only softened in the beginning because of her mother, anyway.

"So I am being immature?"

"You're acting out of love for both of your parents and also respect for your mother, which is wonderful, Sadie. Don't forget to take a step back and try to understand what other people are going through and feeling. The older you get, the easier that is to do."

Marissa

Marissa grunted as she slammed the ball with all her might into the wall at the far end of the tennis courts. Sweat ran down into her eyes, and she wiped it away with the bottom hem of her tank, exposing her stomach. She quickly laid it back down when she realized two older gentlemen watched her with wandering eyes from the courts. *Dirty old pigs*, she thought, not feeling the least bit flattered.

When she needed to think, she played a solo tennis match with the wall. Maybe it wasn't so much thinking that she had to do today, rather work through a wide range of feelings.

She looked at her watch and saw that it was nearly ten and figured she'd get home as Paige was probably just rolling out of bed. She slung her tennis bag over her shoulder and guzzled a lukewarm bottle of water as she walked to her car. Inside, it was scorching, so she cranked the air, rolled down the windows, and slid back the moon roof, hoping the breeze would dry her sweat. She felt like she was sitting in a pool of it! Marissa was just about to pull down her road when she decided to drive past it. There was someone she needed to go check on. As she drove, she spotted a rickety wooden stand with home grown vegetables and fresh cut flowers in the yard of an old farm house that was recently restored. She pulled in and bought the prettiest bouquet of gladiolas, dahlias, daisies, and coreopsis.

Pulling into the cemetery, she shuddered at the sight of a burial in progress in the far back corner. She said a quick prayer that the deceased had lived to the ripe old age of one hundred.

Lydia's stone was beautifully kept. The pots of flowers were well shaded by an oak tree, and the begonias and sweet potato vines were thick and lush.

Marissa sat down and gave the flowers to Lydia. She talked to her like she was sitting next to her. Marissa explained her complicated feelings for Kurt, and she explained the torn emotions, the anger from Sadie, the delight of Nicholas, and Jayna's nonchalance. She swore to Lydia she had never fantasized about Kurt or in her wildest dreams thought some day she would be in the position she was in, but she knew Lydia already knew and understood.

Marissa heard the cooing of a mourning dove and shuddered at the timing of the bird. She looked up but couldn't see it in the trees. On cue, it cooed again, and she looked over her shoulder and spotted the bird perched on a fence behind her.

"There you are, friend." She laughed at herself. "Really, Lydia, I feel like this is one of those moments we'd be lounging poolside at your house, laughing hysterically at the thought of me talking out loud to you at your grave and you talking back (or mocking me) through a mourning dove.

"Thank God no one else is in earshot. They would think I've completely lost it, but it feels so real, sitting here, talking out loud to you."

"*Whoo-ahh-whoo-whoo-whoo,*" the bird cooed again.

"Seriously, Lydia, I'm taking this as your acceptance, your approval to stick it out. Life would be so much easier if you were still here. Damn you, cancer, why did you have to take her? By now you would have talked me into dating one of the New Yorkers that your sisters had already had their way with. Nothing would be complicated. No hurt feelings."

Marissa sighed and thought of how ugly their relationship had gotten a few years ago. It robbed them of a perfect friendship. What a nightmare their lives would be if Sadie uncovered the truth.

"I'll do my best, Lydia. I promise I will love them the best I can."

Marissa stood and turned to face the bird, but it was gone. She blew her best friend a kiss as she left.

As expected, Paige thumped down the stairs as Marissa was opening the fridge gathering the contents for a smoothie. She was ravenous.

"Did you, like, just get back from running a marathon or something?" asked Paige. "Your face is all red and blotchy, and the back of your tank top is soaked in sweat."

"I was hitting balls at the wall."

"Hmm," mumbled Paige. "Alone?"

"No, Ly— Yes, Paige, alone."

"Weird."

"What's so weird about it, Paige?"

"No, not that. Jayna texted me and asked if we were going to PTW again today. I didn't even know she had a phone."

"Ha! PTW, that's what we always called Pentwater. Anyway, are you sure it's Jayna?"

"It's a number I don't recognize, but it says, 'Hi this is Jayna.' So can we go?"

Paige leaned against the counter, her hair piled in a bun on top of her head, her shorts barely covering her rear, and the strap of her tank top was hanging down to her elbow. Marissa couldn't wrap her head around how Paige had grown up so quickly. She wished she had been able to give her siblings. She bought some time by flicking on the Vitamix.

Marissa poured a tall glass for herself and a smaller one for Paige. As expected, Paige crinkled her face, and Marissa quickly went into her spiel that it tasted better than a McDonald's strawberry shake.

Paige eyed the purple smoothie while still texting and asked if there was spinach in it.

"Only a handful, it's mostly blueberries, strawberries, and bananas. Could you please put one healthy thing in your body today?"

"So can we go or what?"

"I had too much sun yesterday, so why don't you take my car and go."

"Reeeally?"

"Really. And try to hide your enthusiasm that you get to go without me."

Paige laughed, grabbed her smoothie, and ran off to her room to get ready. Marissa figured the smoothie would either be dumped down the bathtub drain or left sitting on her dresser, attracting fruit flies.

Sadie

When Sadie returned from her walk with Andrea, she had a text message from Dylan, saying he would be up around noon, and a text from Myla and Kyla wondering when they were going to get invited. Sadie suddenly missed her girlfriends more than she realized.

She was sure she was way out of the gossip loop at this point and felt the need for an escape from her reality. Only Myla and Kyla would understand what she was going through with her crazy feelings for Travis, her guilt over Dylan, how irrational her father was being, and what a burden Paige had become.

Sadie was brushing her hair when Nicholas came barging in her room and invited her to go play mini golf. He told her all the kids were going, rattling off Jayna and Liz, Travis and Cody. Nicholas was excited beyond belief getting to hang out with the "big kids" as he stated it.

Figuring this was the perfect time to be close to Travis with no Dylan or Paige, Sadie agreed. Besides, she and Travis had always battled it out on the mini golf course several times each summer during their stay. This was one area where the competition was real and fierce.

In fact, they both kept score throughout the game to keep each other honest, and the standing bet had always remained the same: the loser buys ice cream, and not just a wimpy soft serve, whatever the winner chose, which usually turned out to be a large flurry or sundae overflowing with toppings.

Remembering all the score cards from years past tucked in an old Sketchers shoe box at home, Sadie knew this wasn't something she would ever pass on. On the bike ride into town, Travis kept his distance. He said nothing more than "hey" when they got on their bikes. He wasn't being rude, but the air was thick between the two of them. Sadie couldn't help but be a tad bitter. A few days ago they were having so much fun together, just as they had every summer growing up. Then, *bam*, Dylan had to get in Travis's face, and then Paige showed up, flirting with him, instantly throwing a wrench in the works between the two of them, an unspoken one, but one nonetheless.

Sadie was determined to get things back to normal. Travis was *her* summer friend—he had been since they were in diapers, and no one was going to change that.

"Looks like I'm getting a free Oreo cookie sundae." Sadie tallied up her score at the ninth hole to discover she was in the lead by three points, twenty-three to Travis's twenty-six.

"Since when did we agree that the loser buys ice cream?"

Sadie got a sarcastic smirk on her face. “Ah, since every year we’ve been in Pentwater, which happens to be since we were crawling.”

Travis looked up before putting and rested his club on his foot. He had a sleeveless shirt on with a rope necklace around his neck that he and Cody had each bought at Bones’ Surf Shop. His skin was already about three shades darker than it had been the first day, and it made the white around his brown eyes glow. Sadie was sure he looked hotter than he ever had, but that was the case with Travis—he got better looking every year.

“I figured you were past that, Sadie.” His voice was cool, but she could tell he was fishing for something.

“Why would I ever pass up free ice cream?”

“Oh, so you weren’t going to bring it up if you lost?”

Sadie thought a minute. “I had every intention of bringing it up, just as I have every intention of kicking your ass, Travis Sutherland.” Sadie wasn’t holding back—she decided to go full throttle and lay it on thick with Travis. She took her putter and gently smacked his butt with it. Travis studied her for a second. She could tell he was flattered, but hesitant to play along as usual.

“Don’t lick the whipped cream yet,” Travis said before taking his shot. He got a hole in one and only smirked at Sadie. She rolled her eyes.

On the seventeenth hole, Sadie screwed up. It was a par three that took her seven shots and gave Travis the lead by two points, his forty-five to her forty-seven. Sadie was sweating, and the fact that everyone was rooting for Travis didn’t help.

Of course, Jayna would want anyone but her overbearing sister to win, and Nicholas had taken to Travis like he was his long lost brother. Cody said he wasn’t taking sides, but Sadie thought he may have silently been rooting for her because no one else was. Liz was too oblivious to anyone else but Cody to care.

Realizing she would probably have to get a hole in one on the eighteenth hole to win, Sadie was taking her time analyzing her shot from every angle. She didn't care that she was backing up the entire mini golf course. There wasn't a speck of shade whatsoever, and it was fast approaching ninety degrees, so people were getting impatient.

"Today, Sadie," groaned Travis.

"You so can't wait to beat me and rub it in my face, can you?"

"I'd just like to get my free ice cream before they run out!" he pleaded, sweat trickling down the side of his hairline.

Sadie made her shot and it bounced off the wooden oar, went straight along the green towards the spinning ship's wheel, and missed it by a half inch. She swore under her breath and quickly putted the ball in. There was no way it was going to take Travis five shots to get the ball to the ship's wheel. Sadie was defeated with a final score of forty-nine.

It took Cody three shots, Nicholas at least nine, Jayna four, and Liz five. Sadie figured it would take Travis two or three. He stepped up, acting like a hot shot and aimed at the wooden oar in the exact spot Sadie had. Sadie made a comment about him having to use her tactics to win, which he ignored.

Luckily, he had hit it too softly, and it barely bounced off the oar, so he had to squeeze his putter between the ball and oar, and it ended up being a messy shot. He wasn't in line with the ship's wheel in the slightest, so his next shot had to consist of just getting out of the trap of the wooden oars.

After two shots, he had the ball lined up perfectly. Travis eased the ball toward the spinning wheel, and it plunked right in. Travis had won by one point . . . so she thought. As the ball slowly spun around on the ledge of the wheel, it rolled off right at the top, a true miracle. Had the ball followed the wheel around, it would have immediately dropped down the hole and been swept away.

"WHAT? I got robbed!"

"Sadie probably stuck her club in the wheel. Were you watching her?" Jayna retorted.

Travis just smirked as Sadie glared at her sister.

"Dude, you are totally screwed!" Cody shook his head and laughed.

Sadie couldn't help it either and laughed. "Seriously, Travis, I don't think that has ever happened before . . . to anyone!"

"Well, the game isn't over yet," Travis said, eyeing the ship's wheel again. "If I make it in one shot, we tie."

"There's no way you're going to make it in one shot unless you can put the ball straight and somehow make it miraculously turn at a ninety-degree angle. You'll be lucky to make it in two, and I'm betting on three." Sadie cocked her hip and leaned on her club, feeling confident she had just won.

"You have a bad habit of speaking too soon, Sadie."

Cody sighed. "This is gonna get ugly."

Sure enough, somehow Travis pulled it off. He whacked the ball hard enough for it to first hit the decorative lighthouse in the corner, bounce off a rock placed off to the side of the green, and go tumbling back into the ship's wheel, which this time carried it all the way around. Travis said a silent "yes" and pumped his fist, Tiger Woods' style.

"Pure luck! You had no clue it was going to do all that, so don't go trying to act like a hot shot!"

"It just kills you not to win, doesn't it, Sadie?"

"Excuse me, hot shot? You did not win. We tied!"

"Yes, we did, Sadie, and it kills you just the same. You've always got to be one up on everyone, don't you?" Travis shoved his score card in his pocket and walked toward the club return.

Sadie ran after him. "What's that supposed to mean?"

"Just what I said. You always have to be one up on everyone. You can't stand to be second in anyone's eyes."

Sadie's heart sank. What exactly was Travis referring to? Did he recognize that she was a bit jealous of the way he and Paige were hitting it off? Thankfully, with all the commotion of everyone returning their clubs, no one overheard what Travis had said . . . except, of course, Jayna.

Jayna grabbed Nicholas's hand and started walking to the ice cream window. "He's got a point, Sadie," she said as she passed.

What the heck? Was everyone out to torment her today? It wasn't like she was seriously pissed—she was truly joking.

As everyone ordered their ice cream, Sadie realized she had lost her appetite. Travis's comment stung. She envisioned making amends on this mini golf trip, not building even more tension. This entire vacation was slowly letting her down, and here she thought Pentwater was just what she needed.

On the bike ride back to the cottage, Sadie had to hold back tears. She felt like such a failure. She felt like she was on everyone's bad side, and no doubt it was her fault. Possibly she would volunteer to dig a hole in the sand with Nicholas and climb in.

As soon as she parked her bike, she got a text from Dylan saying two things: first, he was getting gas and he was only twenty minutes away, and second, he had a surprise for her.

She had gotten so wrapped up in golf and everything else she had completely forgotten he was coming. Maybe this was exactly what she needed, a quiet day alone with Dylan. They could find a secluded spot on the beach and just chill together all day. He was her boyfriend after all, and obviously there was nothing between her and Travis, so she assured herself that spending the day with Dylan would make her forget about her worries.

Sadie was on the porch, touching up her toenail polish as she waited for Dylan. She had already changed into her suit and packed a small cooler with drinks. Her dad had taken Nicholas fishing, and Jayna and Liz were hanging out with Travis and Cody next door.

Sadie was enjoying the peace, but couldn't help glancing over to the porch every so often. It looked like they were playing cards. Whatever they were doing, they were crowded around the table, laughing and having a good time. A pang of jealousy ripped through Sadie, but she quickly shook it off. She could easily go over there and join them, but she convinced herself she would rather wait for Dylan.

Travis looked up two seconds too early and caught Sadie staring. Their eyes met for a minute, and Sadie quickly looked away. This was a little awkward, her sitting here alone while they all hung out, just feet away.

Thankfully, she heard the crunch of tires on gravel, telling her Dylan had arrived. She walked to the corner of the porch and saw Myla and Kyla running up ahead of Dylan. The girls embraced and started chatting instantly, until Dylan interrupted, "Ah, h-e-l-l-o, I'm here too."

Sadie broke away from her girlfriends and gave Dylan a kiss. "This was a good surprise, thanks."

"They cornered me. I really had no choice," Dylan teased.

Kyla gave Dylan a playful swat on the arm. "Puh-lease, you thought you were hot shit with the two of us in your car."

"What I was really thinking about was walking down the beach with all three of you in bikinis."

Now Sadie was the one to swat Dylan, along with a glare. The four of them made their way toward the water in front of the cottage, Dylan calling a name out and haphazardly throwing a Frisbee.

Sadie noticed Dylan nod towards Travis and Cody and the two of them give the same gesture back. She wondered what Travis and Cody said about the whole ordeal. She told herself not to think about it.

A half hour later, Travis, Cody, Jayna, and Liz all came down to the beach and plopped their towels amongst Sadie's little group. Everyone was introduced, and in no time, they were all hanging like one big group. The tension between Dylan and Travis was slight, but nothing too intense.

Travis was acting rather cool about the ordeal, like he could care less, which Sadie admired. He was being mature about it. Dylan, well, he probably felt like he had the upper hand, so he was extra chummy. Things were going smoothly, so Sadie figured that was all that mattered.

Myla and Kyla were filling Sadie in on what had been happening at home. Lauren Holley had made a complete idiot out of herself. After staggering over to her ex-boyfriend and his new girlfriend, she made a huge scene when she begged him to take her back in front of over fifty people.

"It was frightening," Myla explained. Can you believe that? I mean, really, I felt bad for her."

Sadie was feeling better already, not that she thrived on other people's misfortunes, but that she was hanging with her friends and having fun, not worrying about her own issues for a change. Dylan was even making an effort to chat with Travis and Cody. They were, of course, talking sports again, this time college football. Sadie felt content until Kyla sat up on her beach towel, shaded her eyes, and asked if that was Paige walking toward them.

Travis heard Kyla and jumped up from his towel to meet Paige. Sadie's heart sank as she cranked her head around, and sure enough, Paige was strutting toward them. She felt her good mood dissipate in an instant and her stomach lurch. She was glad she had her sunglasses on; otherwise, she was sure the daggers shooting from her eyes would have pierced Paige's skin. What she didn't notice was that Dylan, lying next to her, was watching her from the side and, despite her sunglasses, could see she was pissed with Paige's presence.

"Are they some sort of item?" whispered Kyla.

"Paige is definitely workin' it," Sadie said in a catty tone that Dylan picked up on. Myla and Kyla both knew from Sadie's texts that Marissa and Paige had paid a visit and that Sadie was none too happy about it.

They all watched as Paige and Travis said hi to each other. Whatever Travis said must have been hysterical because Paige burst into laughter, throwing her head back for emphasis. She flung her hair over her shoulder and adjusted the strap of her beach bag while looking straight up into his eyes.

"Really?" sneered Sadie.

Travis quickly took Paige's bag and walked her towards the group. Sadie couldn't help but think that Dylan didn't perform such gestures as carrying Sadie's bag or opening her car door as often as he did when they first started going out. It was all very nauseating!

"Hey, everybody," Paige said in her chipper voice.

Everyone said "hey" or "hi" back to Paige, except Sadie. All she could manage was a muted grunt. Did Travis call her and invite her when Dylan showed up? Just to get back at her or throw it in her face? It had been just over an hour since Dylan arrived, just about the same amount of time it took to drive from home to Pentwater. Was Paige waiting by the phone for his call, or did they already have this planned? Either way, Paige's presence did not settle well. Sadie knew she wasn't being fair, but she couldn't help it.

It was hard not to stare at Travis and Paige. Everyone was talking as a group and having a great time, but Sadie knew her attention was focused on the two of them, and Dylan noticed too. As they all headed for the water, Dylan grabbed Sadie and gave her a playful shove that almost sent her tumbling back in the waves. But at the last second, he grabbed her and she fell into his arms. He nuzzled her nose with his and kissed her.

They were crouched in the water up to their shoulders, and Dylan's hands were moving up and down Sadie's stomach. Sadie flinched, pushed Dylan's hand, and pulled away, looking over his shoulder at Travis and Paige playfully splashing each other.

Dylan grabbed Sadie's chin and turned her head towards him. "What's your deal, Sadie? Why are you so pre-occupied with Travis and Paige? Ever since she got here, you've been acting pissy. Are you jealous?"

Sadie couldn't swallow the lump in her throat; it was too big. "Jealous of what? I just . . . I guess I'm holding a bit of a grudge, you know. I don't really want her or her mother around." Sadie thought this would surely get her out of the corner; it was even partly true.

Dylan looked at Sadie with a steely stare, and she had to look away. He was definitely studying her and not buying it. "I think there's more to it than that, Sadie."

"Like what?" she asked, playing dumb.

"Like you've got a thing for him."

"Please, I've known Travis all my life. He's like a brother to me."

"So you two have never messed around?"

Sadie thought back two summers ago to their tiny fling. It was so long ago, not to mention she was fourteen and clueless. It really hadn't meant that much. When Dylan came along the following fall, Travis wasn't even a thought, but she knew her answer would still piss Dylan off.

Sadie shrugged. "We kissed a few summers ago, but it was more experimental than anything, not a big deal."

Dylan looked angry and it annoyed Sadie. He really had no right.

"Whatever," he said.

Sadie knew this was where she should try and comfort Dylan by kissing him and reassuring him that she had absolutely no feelings for Travis, that Dylan was the only one she could ever love, but she couldn't, and she wouldn't.

"You're not trying to line him up for when I take off to school?"

"Puh-lease Dylan, don't be ridiculous."

Sadie couldn't have been more thankful when the group swarmed around them, interrupting what was definitely the start of a fight. Dylan broke free from Sadie and dove into a wave, swimming out towards the swim buoys. She let him go, acting as if nothing happened, and decided to enjoy some time with Myla and Kyla.

Dylan acted coldly toward Sadie the rest of the afternoon. He hid it well from everyone else, but it was obvious to Sadie that he felt threatened. He made no effort to hold her hand, touch or kiss her, all the things he would normally be doing. Oddly, he was extra chummy with Travis and Cody. What? Was he going to hang out with them all day?

Myla sensed something was askew and whispered to Sadie. Sadie filled Myla in on Dylan's accusations about Travis and how immature Dylan was being. "He needs to get over it. He's being an ass!"

Myla continued to question Sadie, putting her on the spot. She was never one to let her get away with anything, at least not without a complete drilling.

Sadie confessed to Myla that she was bothered by Paige coming to visit Travis, but she sloughed it off as a territorial thing, that she was just being protective of Travis. He *had* been *her* friend since they were in diapers, and she was just looking out for him, plain and simple.

CHAPTER 29

Sadie

Pentwater was supposed to bring her peace, not angst. The trip that had started out so wonderfully had taken a serious nose dive, and Sadie was feeling helpless. Everything was out of her control!

She was nervous about losing Dylan. In their almost two-year relationship, which she realized was almost unheard of at her age, they rarely fought. Lately it seemed like they were always on edge, happy one minute and irritated with each other the next.

She stared at Dylan across the fire, yes, across, not next to her. He had been floating around all night, barely speaking to her, and as much as she wanted him here, just as much of her wanted him to leave. She was so indecisive!

He was standing there with the light from the flames flickering across his face and a chip on his shoulder, looking hot as ever because he was, but also looking ugly as could be because jealousy was ugly. But could Sadie blame him? Wouldn't she be jealous? Was she jealous?

Was it obvious to everyone, well, except Paige, that she felt something for Travis? Oh shit, jealousy is ugly, guilty, and admitting feelings for Travis was someplace she'd rather not go. But the more she sat there and watched Paige and Travis flirt, the more she couldn't stand it.

Who could blame Paige? Travis was the total package—good-looking, outgoing, easygoing, athletic, funny—the kind of guy that could be friends with anyone. He had that natural confidence without being cocky, something that, until recently, Sadie had always overlooked in Dylan.

Dylan, though, had been by Sadie's side through her mom's illness, death, and thereafter. Besides Myla and Kyla, he had been her social life for the first two years of high school. Two years, exactly how long Sadie still had left of high school, while Dylan was off at college, doing who knows what!

Sadie wished she could ask her mom's advice on this one; she wondered if her mom had written her any letters about choosing boyfriends. She looked at Travis and Paige sitting next to each other, both digging their bare feet in the cool silky sand. She probably didn't even have a choice when it came to Travis. From the looks of it, they had both made their choices. Sadie wondered if they had kissed yet.

"Earth to Sadie." Kyla nudged Sadie with her elbow. "What's the deal? Are you and Dylan totally at each other's throats?"

Luckily, between the roar of the fire, the music, and everyone talking, no one heard Kyla. She wasn't the subtlest person.

"I mean I've never seen you two like this," she went on.

"It's so complicated, Kyla."

"Or rather, you are!" She grinned.

Sadie gave Kyla a friendly glare. "Okay, you know me well enough to get away with that, and I half agree with you, but that's just the way I am. As hard as this is to say, I'm wondering if our relationship has run its course. At the same time, I can't imagine losing him. Quite frankly, the whole college thing terrifies me. It always felt so distant, and now it's almost here, and I'm freaking out."

"Are you worried he's gonna break up or cheat?"

"Kinda both."

"That's it?"

"It's the long-distance thing in general and the fact that I'm only going to be a junior. For the first time, I suddenly feel so much younger than Dylan."

"Hmm, that all?"

Sadie looked at Kyla. "What are you getting at?"

"Travis."

All Sadie could do was shrug. She wasn't about to lie to her best friend. What good would it do anyway?

A couple of hours later, Dylan announced to Myla and Kyla that he was ready to go. Sadie felt relieved. All she wanted to do was go for a walk on the beach in the dark, alone, just her and the Pentwater stars.

Their good-bye was awkward, a cold kiss that normally would have left her in tears, but she wasn't feeling in the mood to be kissing Dylan or his ass, and she knew that was what he was expecting.

The second they pulled away, the text messages from Myla and Kyla came pouring in. Dylan was clearly pissed, driving like a maniac and cussing about Sadie, asking Myla and Kyla what was going on. *How were they getting away with texting her while riding in his car? He must be livid if he wasn't even noticing.*

Sadie couldn't help the surge of joy she felt. If they ever fought, it always seemed like it was Sadie worried about Dylan breaking up with her. She found it comical that her friends were watching, listening, and reporting firsthand to her how Dylan was reacting when the tables were turned.

While her phone was still in her hand, she decided to be daring and send Travis a Bitmoji. Why not? They were friends and friends texted each other. She decided to play it safe with *YO DAWG* above her cute smiling face.

Whenever she had a pause from a text message, Sadie enjoyed the stars overhead, especially *her* Big Dipper. It was a calm night, and the waves came to shore gently over her feet as she walked. She said a small prayer for everything to just work itself out—her mother's advice was *trust God to handle whatever is heavy on your heart*—and felt a wave of peace wash over her, probably more from her surroundings than anything.

On her way back to the cottage, a text came through from Kyla that they had made it back to her house safely, despite Dylan's reckless driving. She responded back, and when she looked up, she was temporarily blinded from the bright glow of her cell phone screen and didn't see the two figures right before her. One more step and she would have run into them.

Sadie's eyes registered a gut-wrenching sight. Standing before her were Travis and Paige, arm in arm, embraced in a kiss. Sadie felt as if she had just been punched in the stomach, and she wanted to puke.

Both Travis and Paige jumped. They clearly hadn't heard Sadie walking up. Sadie didn't stop. She kept walking and muttered an "Oops, sorry." When she got far enough away, she couldn't help it. The dam broke, and the tears came flooding over. She picked up her pace and started running along the beach, kicking up sand and water on the backside of her legs.

She ran past the cottage, past the public beach, and ran down the cement pier full throttle until she reached the lighthouse at the end. Her tears came even harder as she stood alone, gasping for breath and staring out at the black mass of water.

Sadie cried over Dylan and Travis, she cried over her mom, and she cried over the fact that her dad was dating Marissa and he didn't care that it was killing her. She even cried over Jayna and Nicholas. She felt overwhelmed by the duty to care for them. Heck, she couldn't even take care of herself. What was happening? Sixteen wasn't sweet at all! It was sour and it sucked!

What if Travis showed Paige her Bitmoji and they were laughing at her? How hideous!

Fifteen minutes later, Jayna startled Sadie when she sat down next to her. “What’s up?” she asked.

Sadie sniffed and was glad it was dark. Maybe Jayna wouldn’t notice she had been crying. “How did you know I was here?”

“I was still sitting by the fire when you went streaking by. I wasn’t sure if you were on another health kick, out for a late night run, or if something was wrong, so I followed you.” Jayna giggled. “I wasn’t worried enough to sprint to catch up.”

Sadie couldn’t help but crack a smile. She probably did look a little ridiculous running down the beach at midnight. “I thought I heard something in the dunes, and it freaked me out, so I took off running to the pier.”

“You’re a horrible liar, Sadie. You saw Travis and Paige walking on the beach, didn’t you? It’s obvious you like him, Sadie. Just admit it.”

“But I still love Dylan too. And they were doing more than just walking—I saw them kissing. I can’t believe he likes her. Why can’t she and her mother just get away from us?”

“I’m not trying to defend Paige, but she has every right to have her fling with Travis, and you do have a boyfriend. You can’t be mad at her. She has no idea.”

“I know. I need to get over him. I’m sure I will once we’re home. Myla and Kyla think I’m in panic mode since Dylan is leaving for college. I’m sure they’re right.”

“Let it be, Sadie. Dylan loves you. He texted me and told me to talk some sense into you.”

Sadie was half flattered, half annoyed. Dylan had texted Jayna, *really*? “Ugh, I can’t deal with it anymore.”

“Okay then,” said Jayna. “I’ve been thinking about snooping in Mom’s diaries to find out what really happened between her and Marissa. Before you go and give me a lecture, just hear me out. Mom poured her heart out in her diaries.”

"I'm not going to give you a lecture, Jayna. You make it sound like I'm always such a bitch."

"Not always!" Jayna snickered.

"I'm going to feel guilty as heck reading Mom's diaries, but I think this is a good reason to break the rules."

"So are you done crying now? Can we go back?"

CHAPTER 30

Sadie

Sadie and Jayna were sitting on the bedroom floor, playing cards. Peanuts had been their favorite card game since they were little. Their mom had taught them how to play by the time they were five. Sometimes their games would last hours or would even continue on for days if they set the score high enough.

It always irritated Sadie that Jayna was faster at throwing her cards out. She was sloppy, but quick. Sadie liked the piles in the center to be neatly stacked, and Jayna always had the cards flying. Lydia would let the girls stay up late in the summer, and they would play cards outside in the screened porch while listening to the sounds of the summer night. They would play until Lydia couldn't stand the bickering between Sadie and Jayna any longer.

They listened to the crickets through the window and sat in front of the fan swiveling back and forth on the floor. The old fan wasn't very powerful, so the cards didn't even rustle.

"I have no clue what's in the diary Dad brought here, or when it's even from, but do you think we could sneak it out of his room?" Jayna suggested to Sadie as she laid out an eight, nine, and ten of clubs.

"Yeah, probably in the morning if he takes Nicholas fishing or something."

"I meant tonight, right now, Sadie!"

Sadie threw out a two of diamonds from her peanuts pile and scanned the playing field before she flipped over three cards from her hand. "How are you going to manage that? Dad's in there asleep."

"I'll walk in, grab it, and walk out. Dad sleeps through anything."

"Do you know where he's been keeping it?" Sadie asked, while looking at Jayna closely. Maybe she had been reading it all along.

"No, but chances are it's either on the nightstand or lying in his basket of clothes. He's not going to hide it under lock and key," Jayna said sarcastically.

Sadie raised her eyebrows in concern. "And if he wakes up and catches you?"

"Ugh, seriously, Sadie, do you ponder, question, and analyze every move you make?"

"Pretty much, yes."

Jayna rolled her eyes at her sister. "Just let me handle it, okay?"

"Go for it. I forgot you're good at stealing."

"You can be such a bitch, you know? Are you ever gonna let it go?"

Sadie laughed. "Sorry, couldn't resist." She slapped the last card from her peanuts pile on top of the four of spades and yelled, "Peeeanuuuts!" while doing some goofy jive.

"Big deal, no doubt I still racked up more points than you. Going out first doesn't mean squat in this game."

"Who's the bitch?" asked Sadie.

"Whatever. You comin' or are you scared? For once, can you live on the edge? Be spontaneous, even a little daring?"

"It's probably not wise for both of us to be clunking around in there."

Jayna popped up and headed out of the bedroom faster than Sadie could even get to her feet. She did a tiptoe run through the cottage, trying to catch up to Jayna, who was being anything but quiet. Sadie knew she was probably doing it just to aggravate her.

When she got to the living room, Sadie stopped and waited while Jayna pushed open the door and waltzed in like it was the middle of the day and the room was empty. Luckily, the cottage had been gutted a few years ago, and it was new enough so the doors and floors weren't squeaky, because Jayna was the furthest from graceful.

Not seven seconds later, Jayna emerged with the diary in hand and bopped right by Sadie in mockery.

It only took one glance to know this diary was the diary from the year of the blowout between Lydia and Marissa. It had 2009 stamped across the front. "I can't believe we're actually doing this. I'm having serious second thoughts. I mean, Mom made it very clear that no one was to touch her diaries," said Sadie, rubbing her fingers along the purple cover.

"That was when she was alive," argued Jayna. "She never said anything about after she died."

"Off limits means off limits, Jayna."

"Seriously, Sadie, I went to all this trouble, and besides, there is no other way to find out what Marissa did to our mother. You're the one that needs to know *sooo* bad!"

Sadie took a deep breath and opened the diary to a page that was sticking out. Tucked in loosely was a very battered piece of Lydia's personal stationery, the one stamped with a big *L* encircled in pink and green spirals. Sadie read it out loud.

Dear Marissa,

I've never had to write a letter like this in my life, especially to my best friend, my confidant. To say I'm sorry will never be enough, but I'll say it anyway. I'm so sorry, Marissa. What I've done is incomprehensible, even to me.

I can't imagine the pain I'm putting you through and the turmoil I have created. From the bottom of my heart, I want you to know that it was not intentional. I'm not making excuses for my behavior or placing blame somewhere else, but I was not even aware of my actions. In fact, to this day, I still don't even know how it happened or remember anything more than bits and pieces.

I know you, Marissa, and I know you must be seething at every word of this letter. I don't blame you one bit, but I had to write you anyway. I know you aren't ready to talk to me in person, and to be honest, I don't think I could even face you. I only hope that one day you can forgive me and find peace in your heart.

It kills me to think I have destroyed our friendship. I can't imagine a life without you in it. I understand it would be nothing short of a miracle for you to accept me as a friend again, but I can only pray that someday you will.

Forever I will cherish the decades of our friendship, everything we have been through together, the good, the bad, and now, because of me, the ugly. One more time, Marissa, I'm sorry.

With love & deep regret,

Lydia

Sadie and Jayna sat in silence. The whirl of the fan seemed to take on a roar in the room. "What the heck?" said Sadie, completely stunned.

"So it was Mom that did something to Marissa?"

The way Jayna said "Mom" made Sadie recoil. "We don't know what happened, Jayna. I doubt Mom was completely at fault."

"Sure sounds like it, Sadie."

Sadie glared at her sister.

"What? I'm not saying it in a bad way, Sadie. I'm just saying I thought all along that Marissa was to blame. I never considered Mom could, you know, do something as bad as this letter makes it sound."

"It probably wasn't. Mom could be pretty emotional sometimes. I'm sure she just offended Marissa and felt really bad."

"Well, we'll know soon enough. Let's start reading the entries right before this letter."

Sadie folded the letter to Marissa and stuck it in the back of the diary, wondering if it was a copy or if she chickened out and never gave it to Marissa. She took a deep breath as she stared down at her mother's slanted script.

August 15, 2009

I have single-handedly ruined our Pentwater vacation. I mentioned to Kurt that I told Andrea the real reason Marissa and Marcus aren't vacationing with us this year. He was upset, as I figured he would be, because we had decided together to keep this mess quiet.

Kurt looked right at me and said it was bad enough what I did, but now to have other people know, just makes it that much worse and embarrassing. I told him that was not my intention. My intention was to be open and honest. I felt keeping quiet from Andrea was no different from lying to her. And I'm in no position to jeopardize another friendship. Both Andrea and Benton had asked several times about Marissa and Marcus and whether they were still separated. I confessed that Marissa was more than willing to grant him a divorce.

I know I'm being selfish, but I'm glad Marissa and Andrea never developed a close relationship. They had both remained "friends through a friend," and only saw each other in Pentwater or when we had get-togethers at our house. I could never replace Marissa; she will always hold the title of best friend in my heart, but I'm hoping Andrea will be there for me. God knows I'm going to need her.

Sadie flipped the page quickly and began reading aloud again even though Jayna was sitting next to her on the floor following along.

August 16, 2009

I puked twice on our morning walk. Andrea rubbed my back and assured me we could go back if I wanted, but I refused. I never threw up with Sadie and Jayna. It was always lingering in the back of my throat, but it never came out. It's probably the extra anguish I'm going through!

I pray this baby is at least healthy. Who knows what kind of toll all the stress I'm under puts on a fetus. At least I'm getting exercise and trying my hardest to eat healthy. All I crave is salt, mostly chips, and that has been extremely inviting while vegging on the beach all week. I'm forcing the fruits and vegetables down my throat when all I really want is to binge on junk!

August 17, 2009

I confessed to Andrea that I considered not keeping the baby. I have to get this crap off my chest; otherwise, I'm going to go crazy! Not that it's guaranteed to save me.

She said she was relieved I decided not to, and agreed with Kurt that in the long run it would only make matters worse. I'm still not so sure I agree with either of them! I only hope I can love this baby whole-heartedly. I only wish, hope, and pray Kurt will.

"What the heck?" said Jayna. "Go back further, like into May."

Sadie flipped back the pages frantically with a bad feeling that what they were about to uncover was *not* going to be good!

May 20, 2009

Thank God Kurt got the girls off to school! My head feels like it's going to explode, and the room is still spinning. It's taking my all to sip coffee and write. I feel like I'm still rocking from the boat. No, that can't be. We were tied up to the dock. There wasn't even a wake.

Anyway, I met Marcus last night, as Marissa asked me to, on their boat in Grand Haven. He welcomed me warmly, despite knowing I was there as Marissa's best friend and advocate. She had given me an agenda.

Number one—find out if there is another woman, which he swore there wasn't, but I'm certain there is.

Number two—see if there is any hope in trying to save their marriage or if divorce is going to be her reality.

Number three—get him to remember their happier times, and convince him they could have that again (if only he gave the effort and showed up to their weekly marriage counseling sessions).

The first thing I noticed as we sat on the back deck of the fifty-foot Sea Ray (with a bottle of wine) was that Marcus seemed happy living aboard the boat—the happiest I have seen him in well over a year or two. I will definitely keep that to myself.

I know Marissa wants me to tell her that he looks miserable and misses her like crazy. She wants to hear that he is willing to make things work. That is not the case, and it makes me so sad for her. Marcus wants out, just as he has told her a thousand times, but poor Marissa, she can't accept it.

The few times Kurt and I were out with Marissa and Marcus this past year were tense and extremely awkward. I admit I even started to hold a grudge against Marcus. How couldn't I? He is being a total shit to Marissa! But I went because I would do anything for my best friend.

Marcus says the marriage has been over for at least two years. That they have just been going through the motions, living together more as distant roommates than husband and wife. Their interests are different, they have grown apart physically and emotionally, and the air had gotten so thick around the house that he escaped to the boat just to breathe.

He explained how she's hounded him for a boat for years, and he has worked his ass off to give it to her. From the second he surprised her with the boat, she has ridiculed it, and then she was pissed that he spent so much money on it. Marissa's version is entirely different. She wanted the boat for them to reconnect, they agreed on a price range, and he spent double. I understand both sides.

I heard it all. He feels like their sex life is a chore on her to-do list. That instead of saying "thank you" when he folds the laundry, she bitches because he folds it sloppily. If he wants to go out, she insists they stay in. She complains that he works too much, so he cuts back his hours, and then she complains that he just sits around and watches sports all the time. Typical problems in any marriage, I thought, but when not dealt with, they become destructive.

Another constant fight between the two of them is how much Marcus drinks. After he popped the cork off of the *third bottle of wine (or whine, should I say?), I don't think I could even comprehend a word Marcus was saying. In fact, I don't remember anything after Marcus topped off my glass that last time. Bad, bad idea to drink more than one glass while taking Xanax.*

I zonked out and Marcus had to drive me home! What I do know is that somehow I have to tell Marissa her marriage is over. At this point, I can only be the best friend I can be and let her cry on my shoulder while her husband serves her divorce papers. Jackass!

So, despite nursing one fierce hangover, I have to meet up with Marissa at the club to play tennis and be the bearer of bad news—this sucks!

"I don't get it. Why would Mom go and talk to Marcus about Marissa?" asked Jayna. "Why did she have to go see him on his boat, anyway?"

"Because that's how Mom and Marissa were—they were like sisters. They would have done anything for each other. Marissa must have asked her to go and try and talk to him about saving their marriage."

"Not all sisters!" retorted Jayna.

Sadie snorted. "Whatever."

May 20, 2009

It started raining this morning, so Marissa and I canceled our tennis match and met up for a late breakfast. After all the wine from last night, I was in no shape to play, anyway. I needed some serious grease, and let me tell you, that was the best western omelet I've ever had! On top of it, I ate four sausage links, dripping in grease, and a bagel thick with peanut butter. If I ever have a hangover again, which I pray I never do, I know the exact cure!

Anyhow, as soon as we sat down and ordered coffee, Marissa begged me to fill her in on the good news from Marcus. She knew from the look on my face the news was grim, and I only got five words into it before she started crying. My heart broke for her, and soon we were both in tears. Not only was my best friend losing her husband and it killed me to see her so distraught, but Kurt and I were losing the relationship with Marissa and Marcus that we had cherished for over fifteen years. It really did suck! And poor Paige!

I repeated what Marcus had said over and over to Marissa. Yes, it's really over and he has already found a divorce lawyer. No, there's not another woman. And yes, they shared many amazing years, but the last few have been anything but, and he is ready to let it go.

Those words really stung Marissa. "Let it go," she kept repeating. "How can he just let the last fifteen years go? Not to mention walk out on your wife and daughter!" After spending three hours rehashing the same things we have been rehashing for months, I left her, feeling helpless. I wish I could fast forward her life two years from now. I would have her sitting pretty under the arm of a sugar daddy, ready to sweep her off her feet.

I didn't mention to Marissa that I got super drunk and Marcus had to bring me home. Not that I feel the need to hide it, but I don't want Marissa to think I'm in agreement with him, like we had this fabulous time laughing and hanging out together. She wants me to hate him, and even though I'm disappointed and angry with him, I don't hate him, but for my best friend, I will.

After talking at length to Kurt about this tonight, he suggested we work hard at keeping our sex life top on our *want-to-do-list. Easy answer for any guy, I guess—just have sex and everything will work out just fine! Well, it did make for some passionate love making, so I guess I can't argue. Now if I can only make him understand how sexy he looks cooking dinner for me and doing the dishes!*

Jayna cringed. "Ew, gross! Please skip ahead if Mom starts talking about her and Dad having sex."

A thump followed by a creak of the door startled the girls, and Sadie slammed the diary shut. Thank goodness it was only Nicholas stumbling in rubbing his eyes still half asleep.

"What's up, champ?" Sadie scooped him up in her arms as Jayna quickly closed the door.

"I have to go potty. Dad always leaves the light on in the bathroom." Nicholas looked around. "How'd I get in your room?"

CHAPTER 31

Sadie

After tucking Nicholas back in bed, Sadie and Jayna eagerly flipped through the pages to find where they left off.

June 14, 2009

Marcus left me the strangest voicemail today. He was apologizing up and down for the way he acted when I visited him on his boat. Um, I was the one that blacked out! But, he obviously regrets some of the harsh things he said about Marissa and is paranoid I will tell her. I wonder if he has been agonizing over it for the past three weeks! Odd of him to wait so long. I don't know what he's worried about, it's not like I would say anything that would hurt her any more than he already has.

I'm not calling him back, that's for sure. It's not that I hate him for what he is doing to Marissa and Paige, but I need to stay clear of the "he said, she said" mess. I talked to him once for Marissa as she asked, and I consider that enough. I will be there for her during this mess, but somehow I need to respect Marcus and his decision too, even though I have to admit I think he has turned a little selfish and arrogant over the past couple of years.

Anyhow, I need to get some sleep. Kurt and I are invited to an engagement party tomorrow night for one of Kurt's business clients. I think this is his third marriage and the woman is twelve years younger than he is. The guy is loaded. He owns dozens of high-end retail buildings in the Chicago area. The party should be quite the show!

June 16, 2009

If I don't puke on this ride home from Chicago, it will be a miracle! The party last night was amazing, I think. Honestly, I can't remember half of it. I do remember champagne in my hand the second we walked through the doors and everything from martinis to Long Island iced teas after that. We were at least sixty floors up, in an elegant ballroom with a view of both Lake Michigan and the city.

There had to be over three hundred people in attendance, and they served the best filet of sole I've ever had. They had a sushi bar and served lobster, crab, prime rib, mussels, and oysters. The dessert table was exquisite, complete with a chocolate fountain. And this was only the engagement party—I can't wait to see what the wedding and reception will be like.

After dinner is where the night gets quite fuzzy. I remember dancing and doing shots. Shots! What the hell was I thinking? I don't remember so much after that. I recall laughing at Kurt when he kicked open the door to our hotel room because he was carrying me and had no free hands.

We went straight for the bed and began to tear each other's clothes off! Poor Kurt, he really wanted me to tell him what an animal he was last night, and unfortunately, I have no recollection. None. I can't remember a single thing after going through the door.

At this point, all I'm concerned about is trying to find a greasy cheeseburger to settle my stomach. I pray that my five-hundred-dollar dress isn't ruined from a wine stain that mysteriously appeared at some point during the night. Not to mention the tear along the zipper. It was definitely a wild night!

June 18, 2009

I cannot shake this hangover sickness thing, and it's been three days!!! I will never mix my meds with alcohol again. I've learned my lesson—twice!

Seriously though, this blacking out crap and not remembering anything really sucks. It's one thing when I'm in the comfortable presence of my own husband, but something I can NOT do around other people. At least when I blacked out the first time on Marcus's boat, I was with a longtime friend, someone I know more like a brother and who was kind enough to drive me home safely. How embarrassing it would have been had I been with someone else.

I called my doctor, and she said it was definitely a bad idea to consume a lot of alcohol while taking benzos, but that I shouldn't still be this sick. Well, I am!

I've thought about easing off some of my meds to avoid some of these side effects, but I'm too scared. I would never admit this to anyone else, but I feel like my life depends on and is controlled by the medication. I know I feel better and don't have the radical mood swings, but knowing that I have to be drugged up to act like a "normal" person is incredibly irritating at the same time.

Taking a low dose anxiety and depression medication sounded so harmless in the beginning. I can't imagine *functioning without my benzos. There has to be another way to escape this way of living.*

June 20, 2009

Ugh, not only do I still feel like crap, I have been tossing and turning the last few nights and feel like a zombie. Not to mention I have been having the strangest dreams ever. I had a dream Kurt left me for a twenty-year-old bartender, another dream that Jayna was kidnapped, and also a nightmare that I had sex with Marcus, ew! Where in the world do dreams come from?

I'm thinking I need to go to the doctor and either get on antibiotics for a stomach bug or see if my meds need to be tweaked because I'm miserable.

Here it is summer vacation and the girls are bugging me to take them to the beach, and I have been nothing more than a slug, wanting to hibernate in the air conditioning and sleep, so unlike me. The second the heat hits my face, a bout of nausea washes over me. I can't even bear to be sick in a lounge chair by the pool!

"Did you know mom took depression meds?" asked Jayna.

Sadie shook her head no. What Sadie did remember was her mom taking her multi-vitamin, a B-12, and a D-3. She knew this because she also set the same vitamins out for Sadie.

Jayna wouldn't swallow anything, so she still took the gummy bear vitamins—but they tasted so good that the entire family ended up eating the gummies every day.

Sadie closed her eyes and thought hard. Were there any other pills that she saw her mom swallow? Were there any strange bottles in the cabinet?

"SADIE," Jayna whisper shouted, "READ!"

June 22, 2009

My period is twelve days late. It's NEVER late. I doubled up on my anti-depressants today to try and lessen the panic settling in my gut and the anxiety-induced heart palpitations. Kurt knows something is up with me. I can feel his eyes looking me over, studying me.

Not only has my "hangover" from the engagement party lasted an entire week, I got up to use the bathroom twice last night. I never get up to go to the bathroom in the night, well, except when I'm pregnant. That's usually my telltale sign I know I'm pregnant even before I take a test. Some women don't get up until late in their pregnancy. My weak bladder starts right off the bat. This morning I was gagging while brushing my teeth, and when I popped a mint in my mouth while driving, I had to spit it out the window! I can NOT do mint when I'm pregnant!

I'm also craving salt like a crack addict needs her next high. I downed almost an entire bag of chili cheese Fritos this afternoon, and I'm eating soup every day for lunch when it's eighty-five degrees outside. The nausea builds as the day goes on, and by night, I feel like I'm on the verge of puking everything, including my organs, out of my body. Unfortunately, my body never surrenders.

These are all identical symptoms from my pregnancies with Sadie and Jayna!

I'm scared to death to take a pregnancy test!

Did I mention how tired I am? I took three naps this week!

June 23, 2009

I bought the pregnancy test today, but didn't take it. Ugh, I was so nervous I was going to run into someone I knew at the grocery store and they were going to see it in my cart or on the check-out counter. I hid the test between Sadie's chocolate chip waffles and Jayna's Fruit Loops.

What am I doing buying them this garbage? I never let them eat that sugary processed crap. I just don't feel like arguing. I just want them happy and out of my hair because I'm too sick and exhausted to deal with anything.

Seriously though, I can't handle another baby. What would happen if I got post-partum depression after another baby on top of being whacked out already? How could this happen, anyway? Kurt had his vasectomy years ago.

Funny how I can sit here and stress myself out with worry, and I haven't even taken the stupid test yet, but I can't! I hid the box behind the towels in the bathroom cabinet the second I got home. I'll take it in the morning. Isn't that when it's most reliable, anyway? I know stalling won't change anything. Do grown, married women give their babies up for adoption? Wait. I would never consider that. Or would I?

June 24, 2009

My worst nightmare has come true. I'm pregnant!!! This poor, poor child. What kind of life is it going to have with a mother like me? Sure, I've been able to keep it together well enough for Sadie and Jayna, but will this be my breaking point?

How the hell did this happen? I will sue the doctor who performed Kurt's vasectomy for every penny he is worth, that son of a bitch! Even as I write this, I can see what a nut case I am. What kind of person reacts to a pregnancy like this? Especially when I'm married and already have *two children? Sadie and Jayna would be ecstatic to have a baby brother or sister. What a crazy, selfish bitch I am!*

Sadie and Jayna looked at each other, wide-eyed. "I'm having second thoughts about reading this, Sadie. I don't think I could live with knowing that Mom didn't want Nicholas and considered an abortion."

"Don't jump to conclusions, Jayna. We both know how much Mom loved Nicholas. She was probably just in shock, not to mention she was on medication, confused, and hormonal!"

June 26, 2009

I have to tell Kurt that I'm pregnant before he comes right out and asks. Why am I so scared? Why do I feel so overwhelmingly distraught? It's not like Kurt was dead set against any more kids after Jayna. He was the one that left the decision up to me.

I can't even call Marissa. She has her own problems to deal with. Besides, she always wanted an entire brood of kids, and Marcus was dead set against more than one. It's not right for me to go to her and throw a fit about being pregnant with a third child.

If I decide to keep this baby, I'll have to get it together at some point and fake happiness. If I decide not to keep this baby, this may be the first secret I ever keep from my best friend. Maybe Marissa could adopt this child. She would certainly be a better mother than I could be.

I'm paranoid that something isn't right though. Why? Why and how have I gotten like this? I'm worried about something I can't even write in my own diary. I've never in my lifetime not been brutally honest in my diary, but this, I just can't bear to put it in writing.

June 28, 2009

Kurt woke me up last night because I was crying in my sleep. I had to change my pajamas because they were soaked with sweat. Kurt wrapped his arms around me and told me he was concerned about me. I have made it so that he's so uncomfortable talking about my depression and mental status that it's as if it barely exists. It's becoming the big white elephant in the room, in our relationship.

I made up a story that in my dream we were in a horrible car accident. He knew not to push any further, and soon I heard his breathing become steady as he drifted back to sleep. I stared at the clock the rest of the night, scared to death about the recurring dream I've been having. It's beginning to haunt me.

June 29,2009

Kurt left early this morning for Chicago and won't be home until tomorrow. What a relief. I'm so exhausted, both physically and mentally. I couldn't bear to keep up a charade in front of him this evening.

Sadie and Jayna were both invited to friends' houses this afternoon, so I am thanking God for that since I slept the entire afternoon away. The sky was a beautiful bright blue and a comfortable eighty degrees, so I slept in the screened porch. I rationalized my nap with the fact that I wasn't in a dark bedroom on such an amazing day. I am not the kind of person to be inside on a summer day, so this feeling alone gets me down.

I picked the girls up from their friends at dinner time and took them out for Mexican, even though I was on the verge of throwing up across the booth. They wanted to go for a bike ride when we got home, but I couldn't muster up the energy. They both looked at me very accusatory. I never turn down a bike ride, and usually I'm the one always begging them. See. I can't even be a decent mother to the two children I already have!

June 30, 2009

Since I feel at my best in the morning, I thought I had better not cancel on Marissa and our doubles match. Julia and Gretty are our biggest rivals; I had no choice but to suck it up and play my hardest. I should play under pressure and sickness more often—we blew them away.

Unfortunately, my day did not stay on a high note. I overdid it and didn't drink enough water or eat soon enough. Kurt got home from Chicago early and decided he wasn't going back into work the rest of the day, so we planned on an outside lunch at the bistro in town, followed by a lazy afternoon, swimming in the pool with the girls.

Walking to our table on the terrace, I felt it coming. The wave of nausea swept over me quickly, along with the clouded, blotchy vision, and muffled conversations around me. I knew I was going down, and there wasn't a thing I could do to prevent it. Luckily, we had reached our table, and I was able to clutch on to the side of it, thinking I could go down easy. Not the case!

My passing out was anything but graceful! I bumped my head on the chair so hard it knocked me out cold. Kurt was on his cell dialing 911 immediately, and next thing I knew I was being loaded up in an ambulance. At this point, I should have just blurted out that I was fine, only pregnant, and overdid it playing tennis in the heat, but with the girls and Kurt all staring over me, telling me *they were following me to the hospital, I just closed my eyes and wished it were all a dream.*

So I told Kurt the news at the hospital, and he was relieved. I think he thought there was something seriously wrong with me. We decided to keep it quiet from the girls and everyone else until we know how far along I am and that everything is healthy.

After I assured Kurt I wasn't having any steamy affairs, he has been gloating all night that our crazy evening in Chicago at the engagement party released some ferocious sperm that were bound and determined to reach my eggs despite his vasectomy! I pray to God he is right.

Sadie hadn't realized she was holding her breath and exhaled in relief. "I knew Mom wasn't capable of having an affair!"

"I hope Mom is done talking about her and Dad, sex and sperm, and vasectomies." Jayna giggled.

July 4, 2009

I somehow made it through our annual 4th of July pool party. Entertaining thirty people was the last thing I wanted to do, but I made it through. The fireworks were spectacular! Of course, Kurt had enough fireworks of his own that it wouldn't have mattered if we couldn't see the town fireworks from our backyard.

I actually felt pretty good today, probably because I didn't have a second to think about it. I feel like Marissa knows something is up. I hope she doesn't ask if something is wrong because I'm afraid I'll break down and cry and spill my guts. I'm just not ready. It was odd having her here without Marcus, not that I missed him, but she and Marcus are the only ones to have split in our circle of friends. She did well, probably because she was able to drink margaritas all day while I had to sneak inside and fill my glass with the non-alcoholic pitcher I hid in the back of the fridge.

Two more days until my appointment with Dr. Carter. I know I'm going through withdrawal from quitting my benzos cold turkey. Hopefully, I can get some meds that are safe to take during pregnancy. Maybe I'll be able to see all this clearer, possibly even accept it, and somehow be at peace. I'm scared.

July 5, 2009

Kurt is insistent on making an appointment to have the doctor check his vasectomy so if he needs to get it fixed he can do it well before the baby is born so we aren't both laid up at the same time.

I feel ill when he talks about it. But I feel ill all the time for that matter!

July 6, 2009

I've never been so happy to see Dr. Carter and walk out of her office with a scrip in my hand. Usually, it makes me feel defeated, but today I felt liberated. I just wish I could have talked to her more about my concerns. I clammed up! Maybe at next week's appointment, after I have been on these meds, I will be relaxed enough to open up.

My dreams are getting out of control. I can't yet write about them. There has never been anything in my life so terrible that I haven't been able to write about it in my diary.

July 12, 2009

I'm sitting here at 6:00 a.m. with a cup of tea by the pool, watching the sun rise. I still can't stomach coffee this early in my pregnancy. This should be a blissful summer day. Instead, I think it may be the beginning of the worst day of my life. Kurt is going to the doctor to get his vasectomy checked. I'm such a coward. Why haven't I confronted my worst fear?

The dreams are always the same. They are so vivid it's frightening! If the dreams are actual memories, I don't know what I'm going to do!

With every passing day, Kurt gets more excited about this baby, asking when we can tell the girls they're going to have a sister or brother.

July 12, 2009

My life is a freaking mess of a nightmare! Kurt's vasectomy checked out perfectly. No swimmers. Here I am at 11:30 p.m. sitting out by the pool, alone, wondering where Kurt took off to. He's been gone for hours, not that I blame him.

All his excitement vanished, gone! What if he leaves me? And here I can't even explain how it happened. And that is the truth!!!!

The girls heard us fighting, even though we had locked ourselves in the bedroom. So now they're upset too. Sadie came downstairs at 10:30, asking if Daddy was home yet and why he was mad. Ha! I don't even know the answer to that!

I told Kurt about my dreams. I explained, pleaded, that I don't remember any of it actually taking place in real life, but it would explain . . . How pathetic am I? This isn't even real life! This is crap that happens on fake reality shows!

July 13, 2009

My head is pounding from crying all night long. If I got two hours of sleep, that's a stretch. When Jayna crawled in bed and put her arm around me this morning, I was in such a fog I thought for a split second it was Kurt, and when I realized he may never lie in this bed next to me again, I couldn't help but break down in tears.

When I saw the headlights come down the driveway around 3:00 a.m., I met Kurt outside. By the look on his face, I knew instantly where he had been—to visit Marcus at the marina on the boat I'd like to sink.

Apologetic, Marcus confessed everything, saying we had several bottles of wine and it just happened. Kurt couldn't go into detail. It was too painful, and honestly, I don't need to know much more, except one thing: who initiated? Unless I ask Marcus, I may never know that answer, and even then, I may not get the truth.

It might not make one bit of difference, but I am glad I blacked out after our night in Chicago and don't remember anything about that night either. I brought it up to Kurt, and he shot me a look that, even in the dark, I saw in his eyes he didn't want to hear my excuses.

Kurt said he was tired and had to get a couple of hours of sleep so he could function at work. He turned away from me, and when I went inside an hour later, I found him sleeping on the couch. In our fourteen years of marriage, neither one of us has ever slept on the couch.

Sadie stopped reading and put her hand to her mouth. She looked Jayna square in the eyes. "I can't flippin' believe it!"

"Mom and Marcus," whispered Jayna in disbelief. "So, Nicholas . . ."

A gazillion things were running through Sadie's head. Her mom slept with Marcus! It was Mom! Marissa did nothing. *My own mother slept with her best friend's husband. She cheated on dad! Mom cheated! Mom cheated! She slept with Marcus!!!*

CHAPTER 32

Sadie

"Nicholas is the spitting image of Marcus. He looks nothing like Dad. How could we have been so blind?" said Jayna.

"Because most people don't go around looking to see if their siblings look like other dads, that's why."

"Keep reading. I want to hear every word, cover to cover."

July 14, 2009

Okay, I'm not playing this off as a victim because I truly don't remember a goddamn thing, but between my meds and the wine, I was clearly out of it! How could I even, you know, be an active partner? Did Marcus take full advantage of me? Or was I so out of it that I came on to him and then blacked out after the fact and have no memory?

I've been considering calling Marcus, but that might just make this all worse. I guess that explains the tone in his voice when he left the voicemail two days afterward, asking if I was okay. I thought he sounded odd. I just figured he was mocking me a bit for being so drunk.

He also had made a comment about wanting to be the one to bring me home instead of calling Kurt to pick me up because he didn't want Kurt to visit the crime scene.

Again, I thought he was just making a wise crack at my drunkenness.

After telling Marissa that Marcus was going to be filing for divorce and seeing her so distraught, I had no intention of speaking to him again, so I ignored both his phone calls. I should have called him back. Maybe I could have found out sooner and . . . Ugh, I can't even write it. What the hell. This is my place to vent it all. I could have ended the pregnancy immediately! Now I will probably lose my husband, my best friend, and who knows, maybe even my girls.

I want to tell Kurt it's not my fault, but I don't even know if that's the truth. I want to beg him for forgiveness, but I don't even know if he will come home after work.

What will it be like if he does walk through that door? Do we fake that everything is fine for the girls' sake? Do we sit down and eat dinner as a family and try to make conversation? Ha, that's assuming Kurt doesn't come home, pack a bag, turn right around, and walk back out. Could he do that? Would I if I were in his shoes? Probably.

Sadie covered her mouth with her hand and mumbled, "Holy . . ."

"Shit," Jayna finished.

July 14, 2009

The kids are busy swimming, and I'm sitting here in a lounge chair, crying behind my sunglasses. I think they sense something is up because they haven't even asked me to get into the pool and play with them—that never happens!

Marissa called and asked if she and Paige could hang out this afternoon. I told her I was doubled over with period cramps and was super cranky, so I wouldn't be good company. Of course, she offered to come hang by the pool and watch the girls while I took a nap or went for a massage or something. I turned her down.

Maybe it's my paranoia, but I felt like she could sense something. Probably because I never turn her down. We see each other at our worst all the time and help each other out. She even argued with me a bit and teased, "Where is Lydia, and what have you done with her?" If she only knew . . . and when will she?

Is Marcus going to tell her? Kurt would never go that route. Will I have to be the one? How long can I avoid it? We are supposed to play tennis in the morning. Do I cancel? Do I play and act like nothing has happened? She and Paige always come over to swim after tennis . . .

I know this is crazy, or maybe not, but maybe Kurt would agree to uprooting his family and moving us thousands of miles away. Maybe we ought to just leave the country and start over. Here I go again, assuming I still have a husband and a family.

Sadie kept the book in her hand and jumped up to lock the door. She suddenly realized her dad could walk in at any minute, even if it was almost two in the morning. There was no way she was going to give this diary up until she read the entire thing. Her dad would have to break the door down if he wanted it.

She already made the decision that she wasn't going to keep quiet about any of this. First thing in the morning she was going to confront her dad.

July 14, 2009

Well, there was no need to worry about awkwardness between Kurt and me in front of the kids because he sent me an email that said he was working late and wouldn't be home for dinner. I needed a distraction, so I took the girls to get Italian takeout, and we had a picnic in town by the dam and got ice cream. Not that all this garbage left my mind for the entire evening, but from time to time, I think I may have gone a good two minutes without condemning myself.

So here I am again, sitting outside by the pool, this time looking up at the stars and writing by the glow of the lantern. What a beautiful, blessed, peaceful life I had until I screwed it all up. My marriage wasn't perfect, no one's is, but it was darn good, with a lot of love, respect, and trust. Will I ever even get a chance to earn Kurt's trust back?

When I tucked Sadie and Jayna in bed, I couldn't help but wonder if I have ruined their future too. Have I single-handedly destroyed everything we've worked so hard to create? Our goal has been simple: to bring them up in a loving, secure home where they will develop good morals and values. It would be nice if their mother could model that! What do I say to them? "I swear it was a mistake! I never would have done what I did in a right, conscious state of mind. I was foolish. I'm not used to drinking large quantities, and I didn't realize the effect that mixing alcohol and Xanax would have on me."

Marissa texted me a couple of times this afternoon to check in and see if I was feeling better. Every text I get from her makes this whole mess worse. I wonder how long it will be until the texts from Marissa stop, well, at least the friendly ones. She begged me to not back out of our doubles match in the morning. How am I going to be able to look her in the eye?

July 15, 2009

It's only 11:38 a.m., and all I can think about is getting this day over with and going to bed. Kurt came home just before midnight last night and never even came into the bedroom. I heard him out in the kitchen, and I couldn't force myself to go out there. I couldn't face him! And I figured he didn't want to face his pregnant wife, either.

The more I think about it, the more I want to know about Marcus and Kurt's meeting. Did Kurt scream at him? Did he take a few swings? Or did they talk openly and honestly? Was Marcus apologetic? Or was he arrogant about it? I can't and won't call Marcus. It only makes me look and feel guilty. I pray this baby looks nothing like the bastard. I never want to hear his voice or see his face again.

I felt like I had the word "guilty" written all over my face at tennis. I was trying too hard to act normal, and I came across acting a phony, fake happy. I felt like I was going to get sick the entire time, and I played like crap. I'm usually the one that hates to lose and Marissa blows it off, but I was acting all giddy, saying stupid things like we needed a loss because we were getting too threatening and our heads were getting too big. She finally looked at me and asked if I was okay because I was super chatty, almost nervous chatty.

As we were walking to our cars, Marissa made a comment about being sick of waiting for Marcus to file for divorce. It's not a new comment. She has been saying it for weeks. She knows it's coming. They have talked about it, and he told her that he wanted out, but she refuses to be the one to file. So basically, every day she waits in agony.

I completely ignored her, acted like I didn't hear her, and I could see her glance awkwardly at me out of the corner of my eye. She probably figures I'm sick of hearing about it because she didn't say another word. I have a feeling the papers will be arriving sooner than she thinks.

July 15, 2009

I need to vent again today. I'm as close to hyperventilating as I ever have been. What an afternoon! First Marissa and Paige stopped by after their shopping spree at the Rockford sidewalk sales. Again, I felt like I was trying too hard to act normal, and I felt like Marissa was eyeing me suspiciously. I overdid the oohs and aahs when she showed me her new handbag and shoes.

When Paige and the girls started swimming in the pool, I insisted on going in and blending us a margarita even though she said "No" twice since she had to leave to pick her mother up from the airport in thirty minutes. So I hurried inside anyway and blended a quick virgin for myself and added the tequila to hers. Why did I have to be so adamant and try to act not pregnant when she has no idea I am? It's draining! So I sucked mine down super-fast and made some stupid comment about needing that to relax after getting creamed this morning in tennis. Again, overdoing it . . .

Now, I'm nervously sitting here waiting for Kurt to get home. He called me a couple of hours ago and asked me to go drop the girls off at his sister's house. He called her earlier and asked her if the girls could have a sleepover so we could have a night out. Stacy was thrilled when I dropped Sadie and Jayna off. Her boys are both in high school, and she's always saying she wished she'd tried one more time for a daughter.

She questioned me about where we were going for dinner, and I told her Kurt was surprising me. Stacy then commented on how sweet and romantic her brother was and teased me that I was lucky to have him. Under normal circumstances, I would have laughed it off, and of course agreed, but instead I felt like I had just gotten stabbed: knife inserted, twisted, and slowly pulled out!

So, here I sit and wait for Kurt to pull into the driveway and wonder if this is the day he tells me he wants a divorce. Maybe I'll get my papers before Marissa gets hers. The longer I sit, the more my mind races. Would he seek custody of the girls? Will I be living alone with this baby? Will my own daughters disown me?

Sadie paused and wiped a tear from her cheek before turning the page. "This is too much. How could all of this have happened and we were so blind?"

Jayna sniffed. "Maybe some secrets *are* better kept a secret!" but they both knew there was no turning back now.

July 16, 2009

I am so drained. My head is pounding from lack of sleep and all the crying I did last night. Kurt went into work late this morning. He made sure I ate breakfast, attempting to make me a toasted egg sandwich. It was a flop, but I ate it anyway, with more love, admiration, and respect than I have ever had for him.

Luckily, Stacy asked if she could bring the girls home after dinner tonight, saying she had a special day planned for them. Of course, I took her up on it, dreaming of taking a nap followed by floating on a raft all afternoon.

Last night was horrible and wonderful all rolled into one. Kurt walked in the door with a bag of Chinese takeout, which sat on the kitchen counter, untouched for hours. He went and changed, got himself a beer, and suggested we go out to the porch. After a deep sigh, he gave me a hug, and at that moment, I knew I hadn't lost him, at least not physically.

When I began to speak, basically pleaded through tears, he put a hand over my mouth and said he gets to be the one to talk first. He told me about showing up on Marcus's boat after sitting at the bar, ready to tear his head off. He was glad he didn't because he never would have gotten the truth or the apology. Not that it will ever change the outcome or his hatred for Marcus, but it probably saved our marriage.

Kurt admitted he blew up. He went on a rampage and overturned a small table Marcus had set up on the boat deck holding a makeshift bar with wine and liquor bottles. Marcus stood calmly as the bottles exploded around him. When Kurt went after Marcus with his fist, he stopped short and took a long look in Marcus's eyes. He said he felt something come over him; he knew it wasn't worth it. He had to hear it for himself. Why? Why, after all these years of being friends . . .? Even though it was a friendship created through their wives, how could he do this? They had hung out for decades, gotten to know each other well through barbeques, golf outings, dinners, births, and vacations.

Sitting at the bar, Kurt had thought hard about two things in particular. One, Marcus was a cheater. He had known Marcus was fooling around on Marissa from time to time for the last several years. It wasn't his business, so he'd stayed out of it. He knew if he told me I would tell Marissa, which is correct, and Kurt figured it was only a matter of time before they were divorced anyway, since Marissa was always crying to me. Our "couples" dates and vacations were already getting a bit strained because of their fighting. I guess guys are just wired differently, what can I say?

The other thing Kurt told me he had thought about at the bar, which is making me cry all over again, is that he knows me, and he knows I love him and would never cheat on him . . . voluntarily. And as I had prayed he would, he did compare the situation with my Chicago blackout and how, to this day, I still don't remember anything about returning to the hotel, our amazing romp, and blacking out.

So, to this he asked me to tell him what I do remember. I told him I remembered driving there, and I emphasized it was per Marissa's request, which Kurt knew anyway. Kurt had even told me that evening that I should just stay out of it. But I went anyway, for Marissa, because she is my best friend, and that's what we do for each other. She begged me to talk to her husband, begged me to go to the boat, so I did.

I went on to tell him that Marcus and I basically talked about their marriage being over. Marcus was sick of the marriage counseling and basically didn't love her anymore, and he didn't even want to try and work it out. I had told Kurt all this the very next day, because I was dreading facing Marissa with the truth she didn't want to hear.

Anyway, I told Kurt I remember Marcus opening bottle after bottle of wine and me telling him that I couldn't have anymore because I had a long drive home. He said not to worry, that we'd eat something, and one more glass wouldn't hurt. It did. It will hurt many people for the rest of their lives!

I told Kurt I remember Marcus bringing up crackers and dip and that he kept topping off my wine, saying I've always been so uptight, that I needed to relax and enjoy the moment from time to time. I remember thinking he was right. It was a beautiful night and what was the big deal? I also remember thinking if I loosened up, so would he, and the more dirt I'd get out of him to relay back to Marissa.

At one point, Marcus even said we should call Kurt and tell him to come out. I couldn't look at Kurt as I told him this. Of course, he was at home with the girls that night and couldn't leave them.

I vaguely remember Marcus and Kurt helping me inside, but I don't remember getting into Marcus's car, him driving me home, or how I got into bed.

Kurt had asked Marcus how he could do something like this. His reply was quite simple. He said he had gotten caught up in the moment and he kissed me. He was so upset with Marissa that it could have been partly to get back at her. Marcus admitted to Kurt that he made a mistake, but he swore it had nothing to do with Kurt. He was regretful and knew he was in the wrong.

When Kurt told Marcus I was pregnant, he didn't even argue that it wasn't his. Marcus knew that Kurt had gotten a vasectomy years ago. It was a joke between the two of them for a long time because Marcus was adamant about not "capping his bubbles," as he called it.

Other words were spoken, but the bottom line was Kurt threatened that, if Marcus didn't keep his mouth shut and move far away, he would make his life a living hell. Even though they didn't work out of the same office, Marcus was in the same line of commercial real estate for a sister company. Kurt had gotten him the job about five years ago, and he could easily help him lose it.

He told him he had better find a way to keep Marissa's mouth shut too, because he knew how women could be, wanting to spread gossip all over town, trying to get women to take sides (basically hate me). Kurt reminded Marcus how expensive child support is and how hard it would be to pay Marissa if he lost his job, so if she were to go blabbing the truth, she would suffer in more ways than one.

I was slightly confused, wondering if this meant we were going to tell Marissa or just try and keep it from her. I suggested we lie and tell her that Kurt's vasectomy was no good. I think I even had Kurt convinced for a few minutes that it could possibly work. He quickly pointed out that he and Marcus look nothing alike. Marcus is Italian with dark skin, hair, and eyes, unlike Kurt's green eyes and sandy hair. If Marissa ever questioned it and did the math, this baby's due date would be dead on.

Kurt looked me in the eye and told me telling Marissa was the right thing to do. It made me feel like a cheater all over again, like complete scum. I know I'm only trying to justify it to myself, but wouldn't telling her only hurt her more than she is already hurting? I can't help but wonder if he wants me to tell her as part of a punishment. I will do whatever it takes to keep him from leaving me.

So, I'm relieved that my marriage isn't over. Yes, it's going to be a long rocky road, especially through this pregnancy, and I have no idea what the delivery room will entail, let alone the years to come in this child's life. I guess time will tell and we'll take it one day at a time.

My agony over Marissa is mounting by the minute. I can't keep this a secret for much longer. It won't be long before I start to show, and I know she'll get served with divorce papers soon. I can't sit around and listen to all of that while I'm carrying Marcus's child.

I've heard of women being in scandals, having affairs, catching their husbands cheating, and I've known one or two that have strayed. Even though I don't consider myself as having had an affair, I still carry the responsibility of creating a huge mess. To think I'm capable of hurting Kurt and Marissa to the degree I have kills me. Not that I'm solely to blame, because it takes two, and Marissa and Marcus were on the brink of divorce anyway, but I can't help but feel like a home-wrecker, and the fact that it's my best friend is unbearable.

Now the big question is how am I going to tell her? Kurt told Marcus that I was going to be the one to tell her so he couldn't lie or twist the truth. So, do I do it face to face? Ask her over? Go to her house? Meet her for lunch or at a park? Will she believe me that I blacked out because of my medication? How would she react if I told her I believe Marcus took advantage of me? Would she call me a liar and defend him?

Ha! As I'm writing this, she is calling me on my cell. I let it go to voicemail. She asks if I want to hit the beach tomorrow with the kids.

CHAPTER 33

Sadie

Sadie couldn't flip the pages in her mother's diary fast enough. It was so much to digest. "This is all so bizarre!"

"Tell me about it! Did you ever, in a million years, suspect any of this?" asked Jayna.

"Never!"

"What are we gonna do? I mean do we keep it a secret that we know, or do we tell Dad that we read Mom's diary? And what about Nicholas? Shouldn't he know that Marcus is his dad?"

Sadie interrupted Jayna. "Slow down. First, we need to get through as much of this diary as possible tonight. Second, you bet I'm confronting Dad. Third, don't you dare open your mouth to Nicholas. He's too young and there's no point in it anyway. The big question is what about Marissa?"

Jayna waited for Sadie to explain, but she just sat, deep in thought. "You mean should we be nice to her and accept her and Dad?"

"I mean that and more. Honestly, I can't imagine why she would want anything to do with Dad, with any of us, especially Nicholas! How can she even look at the kid knowing it's her ex-husband's son? How can she not hate all of us?"

"She is sweet to him too, playing with him on the beach, and even showing affection," Jayna pointed out. "This also means we share our brother with Paige. He's her half-brother too!"

Sadie glared at Jayna. “Paige is the least of my cares right now, Jayna.”

“You’re just saying that because of Travis, Sadie. Either get over him or dump Dylan and go after him.”

“Let’s not go there right now, okay, Jayna!”

Jayna held a hand up. “Fine, I was just saying—”

Sadie didn’t want to hear it, so she cut in. “Maybe Marissa wants Paige to have a relationship with Nicholas? Maybe Paige knows everything?”

“No, I doubt it. Paige couldn’t ever keep something like this to herself, and she doesn’t pay Nicholas any extra attention as she would if she knew he was her brother.”

Sadie agreed with Jayna, but she still couldn’t see why her dad and Marissa would want to date. “I guess this explains why Marcus moved to California—Dad forced him to.”

“Yeah, what a slime. I knew he had some young, blond girlfriend out there, but what a jerk to be cheating on Marissa and then, you know, do that to Mom.”

Sadie didn’t want to say it out loud because she didn’t want to plant anything in Jayna’s head, but wasn’t that kind of like rape? He totally took advantage of their mom! “Too bad Dad didn’t get one good punch in!” admitted Sadie.

July 17, 2009

I had a breakdown in the middle of the night last night. I woke up soaked with sweat and crying, more like convulsing.

I have no idea if it was only a dream or if it was an actual memory. I was feeling very loopy and closed my eyes and slumped over on the plush pillows lining the sofa on the deck. Marcus was then kissing my neck. I pulled myself up instantly, saying, “I have to leave,” but Marcus insisted that I couldn’t drive and that I should go below and sleep it off for a bit.

He carried me below and plopped me down on the bed. My sundress blew up, and I reached to smooth it down, but when I did, Marcus was already crawling on top of me. He started kissing me, hard. At first, I was confused. I kissed back, thinking that it was Kurt.

Within seconds, I realized it wasn't him and began to push Marcus off. He was telling me to go with it—no one would ever know—that he had always wanted me. I pulled the back of his hair, trying to peel him off. His hands were all over me, and I was so tired and weak. My eyes closed.

I woke up shaking, crying, and couldn't catch my breath. Kurt asked me about the dream, and for some reason, I couldn't tell him. I felt like he would think I was making it up to try and look like the scared, innocent victim. I felt so dirty. I feel so dirty.

In the shower, I cried. When I got back in bed, Kurt wrapped his arms around me. It felt phony. I don't deserve it. Was that a real memory? Was it only a dream? Did I play an active part? Or was I taken advantage of? Does it matter? Will it change anything?

July 17, 2009

So here I am again, writing for the second time today and it's only 9:12 a.m. I'm being foolish, selfish, and cowardish (if that's even a word). The girls and I are going to the beach with Marissa and Paige today. I can't tell her yet—I just can't do it! How am I supposed to tell my best friend that I'm pregnant with her husband's child? She's going to hate me. I'm going to lose my best friend!

I need this day with her. Maybe she 'll see how much I care about her and that I wouldn't ever do anything (knowingly) to jeopardize our friendship.

I'll do it tonight. Maybe after the beach I'll see if she'll meet up with me for a late-night walk. I can offer to go in her neighborhood so she can have the neighbor girl sit with Paige. If we're walking, I don't have to look her in the eye. Ugh, I'm a first rate coward!!!

Sadie and Jayna were too engrossed in the diary to hear the knock the first time, but the second *rap, rap, rap*, sent them both in a panic.

"Yeah," Sadie yelled nervously through the locked door as she scrambled to her feet and threw the diary under the crumpled comforter on her bed.

Jayna hopped to her feet as well. She swallowed hard, looking at Sadie wide-eyed and panicked.

"Can you open the door, please?" asked Kurt, his voice smooth, unruffled.

Sadie glanced at Jayna, mouthed "oh shit," and slowly pulled the door open. Sadie and Jayna stood dumbfounded, staring at their dad as he stepped in the room and ran his hands through his hair and over his face, looking tired and defeated.

"I guess this means we need to talk," he said.

Sadie could feel herself shaking, and a trickle of sweat ran down her back. She wasn't sure if she was going to cry, scream, or, weird as it was, laugh. Instead, both she and her sister stood there in silence, waiting for their dad to make the next move, fearing to admit anything.

"Look, girls. I know you've been in here reading Mom's diary. Jayna, you're lucky you didn't get clocked or tackled—it's a bad idea to sneak in my room when I'm sleeping. For the record, you suck at creeping around."

Jayna shrugged.

"Why didn't you try and stop us?" asked Sadie.

"I don't know, to be honest. I guess, well, you're old enough, and all these secrets . . . It sucks. It's hard. I don't want to keep living a lie. By letting you read it for yourselves, I was taking the easy way out. Let's get one thing straight right here, right now—it stays in this family. We don't tell our friends, boyfriends, no one. Not a soul."

Sadie and Jayna nodded, and Kurt told them to follow him to the beach. As they stepped off the porch into the cool sand, Sadie glanced up and found the Big Dipper, right where it always was, at two o'clock in the Pentwater sky. She pictured her mother sitting in it, dangling her feet over the scoop, ankles crossed, looking down on them. Sadie couldn't quite figure out what she felt toward her mom after what she had discovered.

"How far did you get?" Kurt asked as they sat down a few feet away from the shore.

Jayna piped up, "August 17th, in the morning, Andrea knows about the baby."

It was quiet for at least a full minute before Kurt spoke again. He had finally gotten through the diary and was thankful he had. Not only did he need the confirmation that Lydia truly was not aware of her actions on that night, he was glad he knew exactly what his daughters had read.

"Marcus took advantage of your mom. She honestly had no intention of doing what happened."

"You mean having sex with Marcus?" Jayna blurted.

Sadie closed her eyes. Leave it up to Jayna to be so insensitive. Would she ever get a clue?

"Yes, Jayna, that's correct. She went to see Marcus on his boat because Marissa asked her to go talk to him. They were separated and on the brink of divorce. Anyway, Mom had been taking some medication for anxiety, and when mixed with too much alcohol, it made her black out."

"It was depression medication, right? Why was Mom so depressed?"

"Seriously, Jayna, cool it already!" snapped Sadie.

Jayna sneered. "What?"

"Girls, both of you cool it. Mom wasn't depressed about any one thing. She just . . . She was an intense person and sometimes felt overwhelmed, or sad, anxious, or even really happy. She described it as being on a roller coaster. Her doctor suggested that she take an anti-depressant and anti-anxiety medication to help regulate her emotions a bit. You know . . . feel calmer."

He sighed in frustration. "Mom loved all of us, and it's not that she was unhappy . . ."

"So Marcus was at fault? Not Mom?" interrupted Jayna.

Even though the question was quite shallow and pure Jayna, Sadie wanted to hear her dad agree that it was all Marcus, that their mother was nothing more than a victim. She wanted badly to blame it all on Marcus. The thought of a tainted picture of her mom wasn't what Sadie wanted to remember.

"Mom wasn't herself that night. She had way too much to drink, and along with her medications, she, well . . . Marcus took advantage of her."

"So Nicholas, he isn't even your son? He's Marcus's kid?" Sadie knew the answer to this question, but she needed to hear it point blank from her dad.

"He is my son, maybe not biologically, but I was the one in the delivery room, who held him as he took his first breaths. He is Mom's flesh and blood too, and so he is just as much a part of our family as we are to each other."

"And Marcus, he doesn't want anything to do with him?"

"Marcus wasn't really given the choice, but no, he didn't ever put up a fight about wanting custody or even visitation rights. Nicholas's birth certificate has no mention of Marcus. I'm listed as his biological father."

"Isn't that illegal? Like kidnapping or something?" asked Jayna.

Kurt gave Jayna a look that told her to never raise that question again. "Someday Nicholas will know the truth. If he wants a relationship with Marcus, well, that will be for the two of them to figure out. I had hoped to wait and tell all of you when Nicholas was an adult, but part of me wanted to talk to you two sooner. I feared you would find out the wrong way somehow."

"Is that why you've been reading Mom's diaries, to see if she wrote about it?" asked Jayna. "I've seen you at night, for a long time."

"I can't pinpoint any one reason why I decided to read through some of Mom's diaries. In part for more understanding, and partly because I can hear her voice, and I feel close to her when I'm holding her words. I miss her too, girls."

This brought tears to both Sadie's and Jayna's eyes, and they all sat in silence under the Pentwater stars with the dark Lake Michigan water at their feet. The girls had so many more questions that needed answering, but instead, they relished the moment, sitting in peace and feeling Lydia watching over them.

CHAPTER 34

Marissa

Marissa woke in a sweat and a fury. Her emotions were definitely getting the best of her. In her dream, she was seething, yelling at Lydia, even clawing and shoving her.

She was crying in her dream and began to cry in her sleep, which woke her up. As she walked to the kitchen for a glass of water, she could feel herself still shaking. The feelings of being so upset at Lydia all came rushing back: the stomach aches, crying fits, and sleepless nights. She hadn't had a dream like that in years.

Fresh air was what she needed, so she made her way to the front porch and cozied herself on the comfy new cushions she bought for her rocking chairs.

The night was warm, and she wasn't chilled the least bit, wearing only a silky shorts and tank pajama set. She leaned her head back as she rocked and gazed at the stars, finding the Big Dipper. Beautiful. Simple. Peaceful.

She remembered how finding the Big Dipper with the girls when they were little was such a big deal when they were in Pentwater. A smile spread across her face as Marissa remembered she and Lydia taking Paige, Sadie, and Jayna up in the dunes to stargaze one summer. They had brought their dried-out beach towels, still smelling of coconuts from that day's sunscreen.

The girls had flashlights to navigate the trails through the dunes, and as they lay on their backs staring up at the stars, they used the flashlights as pointers, making up constellations because their sorry mothers didn't know any.

Marissa closed her eyes, and she could still hear the girls giggling, the rustling of the dune grass in the breeze, and the faint sound of the waves rolling to shore below them. The kids always smelled of summer: sunscreen, the lake, ice cream, popsicles, and camp fires.

Those were the best years of her life, thought Marissa. They were young, she and Marcus were still in love, and everyone was healthy.

Please give me a second chance, prayed Marissa, and then she even went as far as singing, "Star light, star bright, first star I see tonight, I wish I may, I wish I might, have this wish I wish tonight," just as she and Lydia had with the girls that night.

That night she had wished so badly for another child. At that point, there was still a chance.

CHAPTER 35

Sadie

The next morning came sooner than later. The conversation with their dad had lasted only a few more minutes. Kurt had suggested they all get some sleep and talk again over breakfast, followed by some morning fishing.

By the time Sadie and Jayna stopped talking, it was after three in the morning, so when she heard Nicholas scream, "Nooo . . . Pop Tart!" and saw that it was already 9:42, she figured she might as well get up. She snuck out, letting Jayna sleep, and heard her dad bargaining with Nicholas that he could have another Pop Tart after he finished his bowl of blueberries.

"I hate blueberries," she heard Nicholas say as she rounded into the kitchen.

"You loved them yesterday," her dad said in response. "And please don't use the word hate, little buddy."

Nicholas huffed. "I'm NOT little."

Sadie surprised Nicholas from behind and nuzzled his head with her nose. He turned around and had an instant smile on his face at the sight of his sister. Sadie loved Nicholas like crazy, no matter if Marcus was his father—nothing was going to change that.

She felt a sudden protectiveness come over her. She would do anything so that Nicholas would never have to know that Kurt wasn't his real dad, and at the same moment, she realized something herself. She realized why her dad was so adamant about her not knowing the real reason behind her mom and Marissa's falling out. It was a protective thing, a love so great that he would do everything in his power to protect. It wasn't just Nicholas he was protecting either; it was his entire family, his wife, her friends, and so many others.

Sadie scooped a handful of blueberries from Nicholas's dish. "I'll help you out, little buddy. I love 'em. They're brain food, good for your memory, and they'll make you smart."

At the sight of his sister, Nicholas grabbed a handful of blueberries and gobbled them down too. "I'm already smart, Sadie. Dad is the one who should eat them, so he'll remember what I don't like to eat."

Sadie snickered and saw her dad behind Nicholas raise his arms and shake his head in defeat. She knew nothing, or no one, could break the bond that held their family together.

Sadie's head was pounding from lack of sleep and the fact that there was so much on her mind.

One of the biggest burdens was Marissa. Realizing it was her own mother who caused their fall out, and not Marissa, changed everything. It didn't make it any easier to figure out why her dad and Marissa had a thing going on. If anything, it seemed even more twisted. And Paige . . . well, they shared a brother. Did this mean she would find out too? And what about Travis and Paige?

Just as Travis popped into Sadie's head, she saw him out the kitchen window, heading towards their cottage. Sadie panicked a bit as he knocked on the door. She hadn't even brushed her teeth yet, she was still in her pj's, and she knew she looked like crap. It had been a long night.

At the sight of Sadie, Travis pushed open the screen door, letting himself in. "Hey, morning."

"Good morning," Sadie said, taking two steps back, hoping she didn't have the worst morning breath ever. She scrambled over to the cupboard to grab a glass and quickly got herself some water. "Want something, water, juice?"

"Nah, thanks, I just came to grab Nicholas. Cody and I are taking him mini golfing. Your dad asked if he could hang with us for a while so you could go out to breakfast."

Nicholas scrambled from the table faster than he could scream *Pop Tart*. "I'll get my flip-flops, Trav!"

Travis and Sadie watched Nicholas run to the porch and then looked at each other. Sadie felt the unspoken tension and she hated it, so before she knew it, she was rambling nervously.

"So . . . meet up with you on the beach this afternoon? The waves are supposed to be big. It will be a good day for boogie boarding. That's waaay easier than skim boarding, if you ask me." She laughed nervously.

"Actually, we were thinking about heading over to Silver Lake. My dad brought his Jeep up so we can take it on the dunes. Do you want to go with us? We have an extra spot. Liz was going to go, but she has to do something with her grandma now."

"That's okay. You don't have to wait for me. I think my dad wants to do some fishing after breakfast anyway. You two go ahead."

Sadie saw Travis shift uncomfortably, and she instantly knew why. One spot in the Jeep was reserved for Paige. The extra was now available since Liz couldn't go.

Travis couldn't seem to look Sadie in the eyes. He took his baseball cap off and spun it around, placing it backwards on his head. Why did he have to do that? He looked so incredibly hot with his hat on backwards. "Paige is driving up around one-thirty, so we have to wait for her anyway. It's no big deal, we can leave whenever, and it'll be fun if you come with us."

Sadie hated the fact that the dunes had been planned as a double date. No way was she going to hang out with Travis and Paige all day, even if Cody was there as a buffer. She didn't need to see Paige hang all over Travis.

What came out of Sadie's mouth wasn't true or what she wanted, but she said it anyway. "Dylan had mentioned driving up, so I better stick around here." She knew she sounded both competitive and pathetic at the same time, but she had no choice.

"Okay, we'll catch up with you later then. But really, Sadie, you should reconsider. I mean, if you reconsider, shoot me a text or something and we'll wait for you."

Travis winked at Sadie, and just like that he was gone, and Sadie was left standing in the kitchen, mad at herself. Mad at what exactly, she was unsure. That there was this weirdness between her and Travis? Or wasn't there? He winked at her, was that a peace offering? Did it mean something more? Did he want her to go to the dunes because he wanted to spend time with her? Get her away from Dylan? Or rub Paige in her face?

She now felt like she had to invite Dylan over, and she wasn't sure she wanted to. She wished she had the courage to look Travis in the eye and ask him if he had feelings for her. Were the Bitmojis a way of flirting or simply for fun? She also wished she knew if she wanted to love or leave Dylan.

Kurt

An hour later, Kurt was sitting with his daughters, having omelets and French toast on a deck with the mid-morning sun hot on his back. The charter boats had pulled back into the marina, and the captains were busy skinning the fresh caught salmon in front of many spectators.

It was already too hot to be drinking coffee, but after last night, Kurt needed it. Both Sadie and Jayna were sipping on their icy, blended, flavored-syrup laced, whipped-cream-topped coffee drinks—something Kurt knew Lydia would not go for. He could almost hear her freaking out about how much sugar was in the drinks, not to mention they shouldn't be having that much caffeine at their age. Sometimes it was easier to cave. *You've got to pick your battles, and this certainly wasn't going to be a battle,* Kurt reasoned.

Jayna was first to speak, asking her dad if they could finish reading their mother's diary. After they talked on the beach, he had taken it from them. He hesitated and said he would have to think about it.

Jayna argued that they had already read the major stuff, so everything that followed would just help them to understand what their mother had gone through.

Kurt knew arguing with this would be tough; Jayna had a good point. Kurt also knew that it wasn't always the bold print that did the most damage; more often it was the words in small print, the details. Lydia poured out her feelings, and they weren't always pretty. He knew there were upcoming pages that would be hard for the girls to digest.

"Will you at least tell us what happened when Mom told Marissa?" asked Sadie.

"Honestly, that was the day all hell broke loose."

"I don't get why Marcus didn't confess to Marissa right after you went to his boat."

"I told him he couldn't. I wasn't going to let the bastard put his twist on the story. If he was the one to tell Marissa, it would have been your mom's fault. The entire thing would have been worse had Marcus been the one to talk to Marissa first. I didn't need Marissa driving over in a fit of rage, screaming at Mom in front of you girls."

Kurt went on to explain that, after the day at the beach, Lydia did take Marissa on a walk and told her something went wrong the night she went to visit Marcus and that she was pregnant. He flat out told the girls that it was bad, very ugly for weeks. The months that Lydia was pregnant were not easy on anyone, and the divorce between Marcus and Marissa was an all-out battle, to say the least.

Kurt clenched his napkin in his hand as he explained that he even got harsh with Marissa, letting her know what he threatened Marcus with, if either of them spoke anything about the mess to anyone. What happened was horrible, but he had to be certain that it wouldn't spread like wildfire through the neighborhood, their school, the tennis club, and the small town they lived in.

"I was not going to let you girls grow up and be whispered about. Most of all, I didn't want you to find out what happened through trash talk. Marissa understood quickly enough that, if word spread, Marcus would be losing his job and she could kiss her child support and alimony good-bye.

"Anyway, our main focus should be on protecting Nicholas. He's far too young to be told any of this. I love that little guy. You girls know that."

Sadie

It was nothing new that Sadie felt nauseated at the mention of Marissa's name, but for an entirely different reason now. Knowing it was her mother and not Marissa that was responsible for the end to their friendship added a new awkwardness. Sadie's defensive wall was still up towards Marissa. It had just shifted from defending her mom's honor as Marissa's victim, to defending her mom's honor as Marcus's. She wondered what Marissa really thought and if dating Kurt was part to get back at Lydia in a really weird passive-aggressive way.

She half felt like an idiot, wondering why Marissa hadn't just come right out and told Sadie she wasn't the one at fault, even when Marissa was well aware that Sadie thought she was the one to blame. Sadie felt embarrassed about the way she had been acting, but she had no intention of apologizing. Facing Marissa was going to be harder now than ever!

Sadie couldn't help the anxiety rising from the pit of her stomach. "So how in the heck did you and Marissa end up dating? It sounds like you were pretty pissed with each other too."

"I was never angry with Marissa, honey. I was certainly standing up for and protecting my family, and if that meant putting Marissa in her place, that's all it meant—it wasn't personal. Believe me. Marissa and I were both in a lot of pain. We had all been friends for a long time. I felt awful for what she was going through, but my job was to protect my wife and kids, not her."

"Had you"—Sadie paused and spoke slowly, knowing she was on the brink of tears— "ever had feelings for her back then?"

Kurt looked both his daughters in the eye. "No, never!"

"So how . . . why now? Why her?"

Kurt seemed to choose his words carefully. He explained that, in Lydia's final months, Marissa and Lydia had spent a lot of time talking and working through three years' worth of issues and emotions. Marissa had been the one to reach out to Lydia and forgive her.

In the months following Lydia's funeral, Marissa had called every so often to see how Kurt was, but mostly she was concerned about her best friend's daughters and even Nicholas. Kurt affirmed to Sadie and Jayna how much Marissa cared about them. It made Sadie uncomfortable. He went on to explain that Marissa would check in from time to time, letting him know that, if he needed help with looking after them, she was there.

It wasn't until they started seeing each other at Sadie's tennis matches that they began to talk more and eventually started meeting up from time to time for a cup of coffee or lunch. Kurt assured his daughters that their relationship had nothing to do with their mother and what happened in the past. He had never, in all their years of friendship, thought of Marissa as anything other than their mother's friend.

"So how long have you been sneaking around seeing her?" As soon as she said it, Sadie knew her tone was snotty and she deserved the look her dad gave her, but luckily, that was all he did, and she almost felt guilty for getting away with it.

"It's been a few months, mostly since late spring."

Sadie had a flashback to her sixteenth birthday party, wondering if that's when their relationship started.

"We are taking things slowly. It's been nice having someone to talk to."

Both Sadie and Jayna shifted in their seats and sipped their frozen coffees. What could she say to that? The rest of the breakfast went mostly question and answer, and for the most part, Sadie was surprised with how much they were able to get out of their dad. At times like this, she actually appreciated Jayna's bluntness. She asked all the questions that Sadie wanted to ask but didn't dare.

CHAPTER 36

Sadie

After breakfast, Sadie, Kurt, and Jayna went fishing off the pier. They didn't catch much more than a bunch of gobies, but it was peaceful, without a whole lot of conversation. When they got back to the cottage, Sadie changed into her suit and found Nicholas and Benton digging holes in the sand (sand pools Nicholas called them) while Andrea filled the holes with buckets of water.

Sadie appreciated the fact that Andrea didn't baby her with hugs and a bunch of consoling words. Kurt had told Andrea why he was taking off with just his girls. Andrea handed Sadie a bucket and told her to start filling the holes with water.

Nicholas was on a mission to have several pools for his Spiderman, Batman, and Iron Man figures to swim in. Sadie was drained both emotionally and physically, and this monotonous, mindless work felt soothing.

She was glad Travis, Cody, and Paige had already left for the dunes. Sadie purposefully acted interested in fishing longer than she really felt like it. The last thing she needed was to see Paige hanging on Travis. She felt relieved that the Jeep was long gone when they got back.

Dylan was working at the golf course today and had texted her several times, asking her what she was up to. His tone in his texts seemed bitter, so Sadie kept her responses clipped. She didn't feel like dealing with his jealous, pissy attitude.

She hadn't called Dylan to tell him what she and Jayna discovered in her mom's diary. Normally, she would have called him immediately with something like this. She knew her dad didn't want her to talk to anyone about it, but under different circumstances—mainly if she wasn't annoyed with him—she would have told him.

Sadie could feel things unraveling between them, and it scared her, but then again, maybe it was for the best. He would soon be a college boy joining a fraternity and beer-bonging with the sorority girls in a matter of weeks. The thought of being boyfriend-less scared Sadie. He had been her crutch through plenty.

Sadie excused herself from dumping water in the sand holes, grabbed her phone, and fell to her beach towel. It was Myla and Kyla she needed right now. She thought about calling, but honestly, she was so sick of talking, so instead, she just sent them a two-page email explaining what happened.

She knew her dad said no one, not a soul was to know, but she could trust her two best friends not to breathe a word to anyone. She needed them, needed their support and their advice, especially on how to handle Marissa.

Sadie's cell rang and she saw that it was Kyla.

"Can you flippin' believe it?" was Sadie's greeting to Kyla.

Sadie poured her heart out to Kyla for a solid thirty minutes before taking a deep breath. Wow, it felt good to vent! She could tell her friend was sincerely concerned, but she could also tell Kyla was distracted and had something else on her mind.

"I'm sorry. I'm going on and on about my family saga. Something's up. What's bugging you? Dish your problems on me for a change."

Kyla took a deep breath and let out a groan. Sadie knew it was big. "I wish that were the case, Sadie. I heard something today."

Kyla's voice sounded grim, and Sadie got that prickly feeling she got before she heard bad news. "Lay it on me, girl. How terrible can it be?"

"Well, not so hot. I ran into Madison Cruz at the mall today, and she asked if you and Dylan were still going out. I told her yes, that I had just spent the day with you two in Pentwater, and that he drove me and Myla out there to see you."

Sadie's heart was pounding hard. "Talk faster, Kyla."

"Madison was at Allison Cooper's party last night and so was Dylan. She said he got there late, but was still there when she left."

Sadie could feel her blood begin to boil. Allison Cooper was Dylan's ex-girlfriend, the one he dumped for Sadie. Allison hated Sadie and talked nasty about her any chance she got.

"He must have gone there after he dropped Myla and me off. On the way home from Pentwater, he got a call from Jake, and I heard him say, 'Yeah, I'll stop by,' but I figured he meant at Jake's house, so I didn't think twice about it."

Sadie was fuming. "What an ass. I can't believe he had the nerve to go to her house. He says how much he can't stand her, so he shows up on her doorstep? He's doing this to make me jealous because he thinks I have a thing for Travis."

Kyla went on to describe that Madison saw Allison hanging all over Dylan. Allison was really drunk and talking trash to Dylan, something about how she knew he'd eventually come begging her to take him back. Madison didn't say much more, only that when she left at 2:00ish Dylan was still there along with about ten people, none of which were his close friends.

Sadie's head pounded. Could this day get any worse? She had reached her limit, was on information overload, and needed some time to process everything.

Dylan hadn't mentioned anything today in his texts about stopping at Allison's. At first, Sadie thought he was trying to make her jealous, but wouldn't he have mentioned it then? Was he trying to hide it? Did he kiss Allison? Or more?

Sadie wanted to pick up the phone and chew him out. She checked the time. He was just finishing work at the golf course. She needed an escape, but she knew Travis, Paige, and Cody would be getting back from the dunes anytime, and she certainly didn't feel like dealing with that either.

So there she was, kicking back on the couch, seething, and trying her hardest to read the latest celebrity trash in the tattered *People* magazine Andrea gave her. From the couch, Sadie had a clear view out the screen door to the picnic table on the front porch where Jayna was playing a game of *Memory* with Nicholas.

Ever since they got back from fishing earlier, Jayna had been by Nicholas's side, playing in the sand with him, swimming, getting him snacks and drinks, and now playing games. Sadie was usually the one doing this while Jayna was off being Jayna. She wondered what was going on. Was Jayna afraid of losing Nicholas? Or was she analyzing him to see if he was anything like Marcus? Whatever it was, it was out of character, but Sadie enjoyed the break and hoped Jayna's behavior stuck.

Sadie couldn't help but get annoyed by the fact that Nicholas was her half-brother instead of her full brother. Mostly because that meant she shared him 50-50 with Paige. Petty, yes, but Paige barely knew him. Sadie had more than earned the right to full sisterhood, practically motherhood. She felt defensive, hoping Paige wouldn't try to win him over once she knew the truth.

Sadie had a clear view of her dad pacing back and forth, up and down the beach in front of the cottage, and talking on his phone, surely to Marissa. He wouldn't be talking business for that long at dinner time. She wondered when Marissa would tell Paige and what her reaction would be, and felt the knife twisting in her stomach again.

She heard footsteps coming up the porch steps and knew it was Andrea when Nicholas began to brag to Miss Andi that he had three more matches than Jayna! From the sound of it, Andrea had brought over something yummy, because next Sadie heard both Jayna and Nicholas cheer and yell, "Yummo!"

Andrea had brought over lemonade slushies and her homemade Heath bars, which she made with saltine crackers, brown sugar sauce, and melted chocolate chips. She kept them cool in the fridge, but they always stayed good and gooey.

"Figured I'd find you in here," she said as she came in the screen door, bearing treats for Sadie.

Instantly, Sadie knew Andrea was here for a talk. She must have seen her dad on the beach, Jayna and Nicholas on the porch, and figured all she needed to keep them put, and talk with Sadie alone, was a cup and plate full of sugar.

For some reason, Sadie felt nervous, and she started making excuses why she was sitting alone inside, saying she was tired (which she was), and had cramps (which she didn't and wasn't sure why she said it), and finally saying that once she picked up a *People* she couldn't put it down.

Andrea handed Sadie her cup of lemonade slushy and didn't waste any time making small talk. She started talking about what a wonderful person Lydia was—that she would never do "that sort of thing" intentionally. Andrea also apologized for the additional hurt that this news was bringing.

"If I could take all the pain away from you girls, I would."

Sadie scoffed. "Ha! I'm immune to it now. My skin is so thick a razor couldn't slice it."

Andrea gave Sadie her motherly look. She wasn't buying it, and neither was Sadie, really. She patted Sadie on the leg and stood up. "Let's go for a walk. I'm sure your dad and

Benton can handle getting dinner together while we're gone. Besides, Travis isn't back from the dunes yet."

Sadie hesitated. She really wasn't up for it, but Andrea was already holding the screen door open for her before she could protest. Once Sadie's feet hit the wet sand and the waves spilled over her ankles, she knew this was exactly what she needed. She felt like hugging Andrea, pretending for a moment that she was her mother. She hadn't had that kind of motherly hug in almost a year and a half.

Andrea opened right up, explaining that Lydia's actions were not intentional and that her family and friends were everything to her. Several times, Andrea gave reference to what a good woman Lydia was and that Marcus did a horrible thing, taking advantage of her when she was completely out of it.

Sadie didn't talk much. She just listened to Andrea speak highly of her mother—probably painting a much better picture than was true. But Sadie didn't mind; she hung on every word.

"Marissa and I had a long talk the other day when she was visiting. Bottom line, Sadie, is Marissa forgave your mom a long time ago. She knew your mother better than pretty much anyone. She knows the truth. It just really hurt, and it was easier for Marissa to keep her distance with your mom. Seeing your mom pregnant and then with a young Nicholas in her arms wasn't easy.

"Also, between us, I asked her about the relationship between her and your dad. I can assure you it started well after your mom passed, and it has nothing to do with your mother. They are simply two people who know each other well and enjoy each other's company. Sure, they spent a lot of time together in their younger years, but the feelings they have for each other have developed slowly over the last few months."

"Those were almost my dad's identical words."

"It's the truth, Sadie."

This eased some of Sadie's anguish, but it certainly didn't take it away. Andrea knew what Sadie needed to hear and it was definitely helping, but she still didn't want to accept Marissa and her dad. She didn't want to accept that her mom slept with Marcus, and she didn't want to accept that she might have to share Nicholas with Marissa and Paige.

"I'm not ready for someone else to fill my mom's shoes."

Andrea said nothing; instead, she grabbed Sadie's hand and squeezed it. Sadie was grateful for Andrea. She already knew how immature and selfish she sounded when she said these things, but it didn't change how she felt.

They walked back to the cottage without a word. Sadie loved spending this time with Andrea, but it almost made her miss her mom even more. It made her think about what she was missing. Just before they rounded the bend that would put their cottages into view, Sadie had one last thing to say.

"Thanks for being so loyal to my mom."

Marissa

Marissa hung up with Kurt and poured herself a glass of Riesling, took three big gulps, topped off her wine glass, and found her way to the front porch and her beloved rocker. She took another drink as she took off her earrings, bracelet, and necklace and placed them on the table holding several magazines she swore she was going to take some time to look through.

With another sip, she kicked off her high-heeled sandals and finally rested her head back and closed her eyes. She had been so busy with work that she had skipped lunch. Her stomach growled, but she didn't have the energy to make herself something just yet. Instead, she was going to dull her senses and enjoy a slight buzz.

She was in shock that Sadie and Jayna had read Lydia's diary and knew the truth. She ached for them. She ached for Kurt, Nicholas, Paige, and herself too, everyone except Marcus—that pig!

Oh Lydia, I wish this didn't have to be. These girls are far too young to have to deal with such heavy issues. Marissa couldn't help but think she was partly to blame for the anguish she was causing them.

The big question now was how to tell Paige. What should she say to Sadie and Jayna? *"Whoo-ahh-whoo-whoo-whoo."* Marissa laughed out loud. *Seriously Lydia, I'm beginning to really think you've come back to us in the form of a mourning dove.* The bird cooed again, so Marissa got to her feet to see where it was.

As Marissa looked to her roof, the bird cooed a third time. There it sat on the peak of the dormer. *Now you're showing off, Lydia.*

Feeling extremely light-headed, Marissa finished her glass of wine and brought it inside to refill. She decided it was a finger food kind of night, so she sliced orange and red peppers, zucchini and summer squash, washed some raspberries and blueberries, grabbed the pretzels and crackers, piled them all high on a paper plate, and added a mound of guacamole in the center. She refilled her wine, found a can of honey roasted peanuts and tucked it under her arm, as her hands were already full, and went back out to the porch.

The dove was gone. Marissa was fine with that. The last thing she needed to do was have her neighbor witness her talking to a bird while downing a bottle of wine. She still had no idea how to approach Paige with the news that Nicholas was her half-brother, but thought she had better text her to come home so they could talk tonight. Kurt had assured her that both Sadie and Jayna swore they weren't going to say anything to Paige until Marissa had a chance to tell her the truth.

Marissa wasn't so sure she wanted to be the one. Paige adored her father, and even though it ate away at Marissa, she would never want that to change. She thought it was healthy for Paige to have a somewhat normal relationship with Marcus. Paige's relationship with her father was just that, *her relationship*, and Marissa would always try hard not to influence it, good or bad.

CHAPTER 37

Sadie

The smell of barbecued chicken hit Sadie's nose far before they reached the grill. Her walk with Andrea had given her a sense of understanding and relief. She had even considered ways she could somehow work on coming to terms with accepting Marissa. But as soon as she saw Paige and then heard her squeal as she got bombarded with water balloons, her relief quickly turned to irritation.

The entire gang was in an all-out water balloon war! Even her dad and Benton, standing by the grill, were throwing cheap shots, splattering Nicholas, as Cody (three times his size) tried to hide behind the little guy. Sadie saw Jayna loft one at Paige's back, and it made a loud splat as it soaked her strappy little beach cover-up, sending her into another fit of squeals.

Paige was chasing Travis around in circles, throwing balloons that bounced off of him instead of breaking. *Seriously, put a little muscle in it.*

"Oh boy, looks like we're about to get bombarded," said Andrea, ducking from a balloon her own husband chucked at her.

"Have fun," said Sadie as she turned toward the campground and started to jog. She knew Andrea would think it odd that she was taking off, especially since their walk ended on such a good note, but she couldn't handle the sight of Travis and Paige once again, and she knew what that meant. She liked him, possibly loved him, and he didn't feel the same way.

Sadie could feel that lump in her throat, but refused to let a tear slide down her cheek. She took the steps two at a time up Old Baldy foot trail and wished she had her watch on, because after all the times they had timed themselves as kids, this certainly was bound to be her record speed breaker.

When she reached the lookout deck, she contemplated stopping, but knew, even though it was empty now, it was only a matter of minutes before a group would step up, heaving and out of breath. She needed to be alone, so she kept going, following the trail through the woods until her feet hit the thick dune sand and she was at the highest peak overlooking the campground, Lake Michigan, the pier, boats, and the sinking sun.

Thankfully, she couldn't see their cottage—the trees obscured that view. Sadie found a spot over by the massive roots of a tree that were showing because of sand erosion. It was out of the way just enough so that no one would bother her, or see her face, and she could still see the incredible view.

As she sat silently, she could hear the gentle sounds of people below her. She could hear babies crying, kids playing, the screech of the swing set in need of oiling, and the roar of a speed boat barreling by in the distance. There were puffs of smoke from grills and campfires rising—all signs of life, people living.

Sadie knew she was feeling sorry for herself, and she hated it—that wasn't the kind of person she was. She was in a major rut. Everybody and everything seemed to disappoint her lately, even herself. Though she kept telling herself to suck it up and get over it, she wasn't succeeding.

She thought of all the people below her. Everyone had issues. Sure, she heard laughter, and the sight before her made it look like everyone was living in bliss, but the truth was that, before her eyes, there was loneliness, anger, frustration, resentment, and bitterness. There were couples fighting, kids being mean to each other, and people mistreating others, most likely the ones they loved the most.

Sadie dug her feet in the sand until she felt the cool stuff underneath that didn't get scorched by the afternoon sun. She pulled her knees close to her chest, wrapped her arms around them, and rested her chin on those same bony knees.

She gave herself a much-needed pep talk. Things could be worse. Her family wasn't perfect or complete anymore, but she loved her dad, sister, and brother like crazy. She had great friends and she had Dylan. He loved her. She just had to get back on track.

She jumped at the familiar voice that said, "Hey," from behind her. Shit!

Travis sat down next to Sadie and her heart raced. What the heck was he doing up here? How embarrassing! Sadie could only imagine what she must have looked like running away from the cottage instead of joining in on the water balloon fight and fun.

"What's up, Sadie?"

Okay, this question was a little too general. Was he asking, "What's up?" as in "How you doin'?" or as in "What's your problem?" or "What are you feeling?" Or was it simply an ice breaker—the first thing that came to his mind? She wished she could just send him a Bitmoji.

Sadie shrugged and slid her feet back and forth, digging them down deeper in the sand. "Who can resist Old Baldy this time of day? Why'd you come up?" she asked, turning the tables.

Sadie could feel Travis looking at her profile, but she couldn't bear to turn towards him, so she stared out over the dune, pretending to be engrossed with the view.

"I came up here to see what was wrong with you, Sadie. I feel like you're pissed off at me. It's been really awkward between us. Did I do something?"

Sadie almost laughed. If he only knew the truth, which he never would! "Jayna and I discovered something in my mom's diary last night, and I guess it's just been a tough day."

There was a long pause before Travis spoke. "Is that it? I mean . . . that's the only thing bugging you?"

Travis had an awkward look on his face, and he spoke with a touch of a nervous laugh that Sadie couldn't figure out.

"That about sums it up," Sadie said way too quickly.

"Hmm . . ." Travis got a bit squirrely and grabbed a twig and started drawing circles in the sand. "That's not what your sister said."

Sadie's head snapped towards Travis. His face was bright red. "What are you talking about? What did Jayna say?"

"Ah, well, man, this is awkward. She said that you've got a thing for me." Travis took off his Detroit Tigers baseball cap and put it back on backwards.

She noticed he did this when he was nervous. It was more than okay with Sadie because he looked so, so, so incredibly hot like that.

"She said that's why you took off the way you did."

OMG, Jayna is going to get a piece of my mind. "I wanted to be alone."

"That doesn't answer my question. And for what it's worth, I was hoping it was true."

Sadie's heart was about to jump out of her chest. She could barely look at Travis, but yet she couldn't turn away either. *Double OMG! Was this for real!!!* She saw a trickle of sweat run down the side of his tanned cheek and could feel her own trickle of sweat run down her back.

"I, um, what exactly are you saying?" asked Sadie. She wanted him to do the talking.

"I guess I'm saying I've got a thing for you."

"A thing?"

"Seriously, Sadie, do I have to spell it out?"

Sadie laughed. "What about Paige? You two definitely have a thing going on."

"I like Paige. I really do, but not as more than a friend. I've tried, but the feelings just aren't there. When you saw us kissing on the beach, I swear that was the first time, and I knew right then she wasn't girlfriend material."

"So why are you still hanging around her?"

Travis shrugged. "To get my mind off of you, get this vacation over with, go home, and break it off with her over the phone."

For some reason, this made Sadie smile. Typical Travis, he was one of those "nice boys," the ones your mother wants you to date, but instead you go for the ones that break your heart.

"Okay, and maybe try and make you jealous too."

Now Sadie laughed out loud. She leaned over and bumped the side of his arm with her elbow.

"You still haven't answered my question?" he said in an even tone.

Sadie was just about to speak when she changed her mind and grabbed Travis's hand and kissed the back of it. Then she took his chin lightly in her fingers and kissed his lips. "Does that answer your question?"

She then took out her phone and texted him the Bitmoji she had wanted to text him all along; it read *SWOON* and Sadie was falling backward with her hand on her forehead.

Travis's Bitmoji said *CRUSHIN'* and he had hearts circling his head.

CHAPTER 38

Sadie

"This is really weird," said Sadie as she and Travis looked out over the water from the dune. "I mean now what? Now that we have this established?"

Travis had his hand resting on Sadie's knee. It felt so awkward and yet so comfortable at the same time. She remembered the two of them kissing two summers ago. It seemed like forever ago, and here they were now.

"We could just sit here until nightfall—go back after everyone has gone to bed."

Sadie laughed. "Yeah, that would never happen. I'm giving it ten more minutes before the entire search party reaches the top of this dune."

"Maybe you should go down ahead of me," suggested Travis. "Everyone will ask if you saw me, and you can act like you didn't. I'll wait fifteen minutes or so and act surprised that you made it back."

"So then I can watch you and Paige hang on each other all night? Sounds fun, but no thanks."

"We don't hang on each other."

Sadie cocked her head to the side and gave Travis the "whatever" look.

"Okay, Paige can be a bit touchy-feely, but she's harmless. It's not like she's groping me. Besides, you're the one with a real boyfriend. What about him?"

Sure, Travis had a point, but Dylan was at home, so he wasn't an immediate threat. Paige was basically at the bottom of the dune. Everything was suddenly hitting Sadie at once. She had just kissed Travis, confessed she liked him, and cheated on Dylan.

"I overheard Dylan threaten you the other night. I'm sorry."

"Ah, don't be sorry. I don't blame him. Does this mean I get to be the one threatening other guys now?"

"If that's what it takes."

"No, seriously, Sadie, is it going to be over between you two? Something tells me he's not going to let you go quietly. I'm not so sure you want to break it off with Dylan, either."

"It's over between us. I think he knows it too. I think he would have dumped me in a couple of weeks anyway, once he's an all-out college boy."

"So I'm just your fallback? Your backup plan?" Travis said this jokingly, but Sadie knew there was more seriousness behind the question than he was letting on.

Sadie decided to go the same route, joking and seriousness all rolled into one. "Does it matter? Do you really care how you got me? As long as you have me, what's the difference?" For reassurance, she put her arm around his back and squeezed his shoulder.

Travis pulled his phone out of his pocket and handed it to Sadie. "How about you call Dylan right now and tell him it's over, before he shows up here."

"Right, Travis, I'm going to call and break up with my boyfriend of almost two years using your cell phone. Talk about pouring salt in the wound!"

Travis shrugged and said it would definitely get the point across in a big way. Sadie agreed, but didn't find it necessary to be cruel. This was definitely a phone call she was dreading. There was no way she could keep Dylan away from Pentwater for the next week and break up with him face-to-face when she got back home.

Even though a phone breakup was tacky, Sadie knew that was her only choice. She couldn't bear to look at Dylan in the face and break up with him. He would try and talk her out of it, and she would feel so guilty she would probably end up giving him the false hope that there was still a chance for the two of them. They had been through a lot together.

"I'll make you a deal. You go down and get rid of Paige and I'll call Dylan."

Travis stood up. "Let's go!" He started full force down the hill, and Sadie had to run to catch up. Her mind was racing. *What was he going to say to Paige?* She suddenly felt terrible that she basically stole Travis outright from her. But, it wasn't as if Travis had feelings for her anyway, so technically, she didn't steal him from her because he was never *hers* to begin with.

At the bottom of the hill, they were both red-faced and out of breath. Sand stuck to their feet and calves. They looked at each other and laughed, neither really knowing exactly what about. Travis leaned in and gave Sadie a long and lingering, but gentle kiss. Every square inch of her body tingled.

Sadie frowned. "Look. I feel kinda shitty about Paige. Don't say anything tonight. Just play along. Call her tomorrow."

"So I get to kiss two girls tonight?"

Sadie swatted Travis in the butt. "Ha-ha! You could fake being sick."

Travis snickered. "Deal, but it's not my fault if she lunges at me with those lips."

Travis grabbed Sadie's hand, and they took the long way back by walking up and down every row of the campground and then to the beach where they walked along the shore towards their cottages. Sadie dropped Travis's hand when the cottages came into view.

By this time, dinner was finished, and everyone had congregated back behind the cottages in the driveway, getting on their bikes to head to town for ice cream. Sadie and Travis approached cautiously, probably trying too hard to act like nothing was going on.

Sadie was searching for Paige and didn't see her, but she didn't want to say anything. She figured she was probably inside using the bathroom, so she went straight to her bike.

Even though it was chaotic as usual when the entire group went anywhere together, there was an obvious vibe going on that was hard to ignore. Everyone was acting extra giddy and mentioned nothing at their return, just "grab your bikes—it's ice cream time."

No one asked Sadie where she had been or Travis where he found her. Nothing was mentioned that they missed dinner or where the leftovers were. Something was definitely up!

Finally, as they all started riding away, Travis asked to no one in particular where Paige was. Cody was the one who said she took off for home. Paige had a babysitting job she forgot about. Travis hadn't noticed until then that her car was gone, and neither had Sadie, obviously too nervous.

On the ride into town, Sadie stayed next to the Doodlebug that pulled Nicholas behind her dad's bike. At the ice cream shop, she did the same, kept her distance, mostly talking with Andrea and wiping Nicholas's face every three seconds. Sadie kept catching Travis glancing at her, and she couldn't help but smile and quickly look away so no one would notice. She was nervous he was going to make it obvious.

It was band night in the center of town at the gazebo, so they went and joined the several hundred people gathered on the grass. Kids were running around, dancing, there were men making animals out of balloons for the kids, the police officers were handing out stickers, and every kid under ten was getting their face painted. It brought back so many memories of her mother dancing with her and Jayna, twirling them around and acting silly to the classical jams.

Sadie was in her own world, playing the drums on Nicholas's back when Jayna sat down next to her.

"Everybody knows, Sadie, so you two can stop ignoring each other."

"What are you talking about?"

"Oh, don't play dumb. It's obvious what happened between you and Travis when he went looking for you."

With the look Jayna had on her face, Sadie knew something was up. "What did you say to him?"

"Nothing really, I just looked at him and told him now was his chance. We both knew there was only one place you would be."

At first, Sadie wanted to tell Jayna to mind her own business from now on, but she knew she didn't mean it. She was glad Jayna gave Travis the push to come look for her. Jayna never knew when to keep her mouth shut, but this was one of those times Sadie was glad she didn't.

"Only one downfall," Jayna said, biting her lip. "I'm pretty sure Paige knew what was going on. The second Travis left, she grabbed her stuff and made up some excuse about babysitting."

Sadie instantly felt a knot in her stomach. Even though she was jealous of Paige and Travis, and the way Paige had been acting was super annoying, she didn't dislike Paige, and she truly didn't want to hurt her. But yet, she couldn't say she would change the way things happened either. *What if Paige called Dylan? Would she?*

"Did she seem really upset?"

"Actually, she seemed embarrassed, like she couldn't leave fast enough. I felt bad for her, Sadie."

It was really starting to hit Sadie what she was going to have to deal with between Dylan and Paige. She had witnessed breakups with a lot of fighting, tears, and drama more than enough around school, and even a little bit when Dylan dumped Allison for her, but nothing like this.

"This part really sucks."

"I hope you're serious about Travis. You're not going to go running back to Dylan as soon as we get home and screw Travis over?"

Sadie knew her relationship with Dylan was over and she wasn't going to ditch Travis, but she also knew she still had feelings for Dylan and it wasn't going to be easy. He was her first boyfriend, her first everything, and he would always be the boyfriend that was there for her when her mom died. She was scared he was going to hate her—she didn't want that. The situation truly saddened her.

"I'm not going to screw Travis over, Jayna."

Jayna looked at Sadie, studied her sister. "You better not, cuz I like Travis, and I went out on a limb for you."

"Don't push it, matchmaker," snapped Sadie. She grabbed her sister's hand and pulled her up, telling her to go dance with Nicholas. To Sadie's surprise, she actually did! Sadie decided not to play a charade and went and sat down next to Travis.

Andrea was thumping her foot in the grass to the beat of the music when Sadie caught her looking and grinning towards her and Travis. Sadie smiled back and had that urge to hug her again. Instead, she grabbed Travis's hand, completely catching him and Cody off guard.

Cody smirked. "About time."

CHAPTER 39

Kurt

Shortly after 1:00 a.m., Sadie pushed open the screen door and joined Kurt sitting by the fire. The soft glow of the hot coals in the fire pit blazed before him.

"If you're trying to sneak Mom's diary, I hid it really well," he joked.

"Only Jayna would try that again." Sadie didn't dare ask, but wondered if that meant it was going to be off limits.

Kurt smirked. "Aw, give your sister a break—she means well."

Sadie knew she did, and that she needed to cut her sister some slack, but it seemed every time she did, Jayna pulled another stunt.

"So, what's going on with you and Travis?" he asked bluntly.

Kurt seemed surprised when Sadie opened up. She spilled about hanging onto Dylan because that was all she ever knew, about being nervous that he was going off to college, and losing yet another important person, and that she knew she wasn't as in love with him as she thought she was because she had strong feelings for Travis.

She asked for Kurt's advice on how to break it off with Dylan. She had chickened out tonight when she talked to him and knew she had to tell him in the morning.

She'd talked to Dylan after he got out of work, and he acted like he didn't have time to talk to her. He'd said he was in a rush to get to Brady's house because they were headed to a party near campus. She almost blurted out that she was dumping him, but she didn't have the energy to fight. Sadie knew he was trying to make her jealous.

Kurt took the direct route and told Sadie it was best to be honest. "Sometimes the truth hurts, but not as bad as when the lies catch up to you."

Sadie wondered if her dad was talking about more than just Dylan, but wasn't in the mood to go further with it. She was emotionally exhausted and really just wanted to go to bed. Sadie kissed Kurt on the cheek as she got up from the steps.

Kurt grimaced. "I noticed Paige and Travis were hanging around each other quite a bit. Is she upset about the two of you?"

Sadie stood on the steps, looking down at her dad's back and thought for a second about how to answer the question. She suddenly felt like she was on the defense. "Do you think I'm only after Travis to beat out Paige? Because of Marissa? To stir the pot?"

"That's not what I meant, Sadie—that's not what I asked. I was just curious to know if Paige was really hurt about Travis or not."

"Travis and I have nothing to do with Paige. He didn't even like her, and it's not like they were even a couple, so I don't know what to tell you."

Kurt turned toward his daughter. He could tell she was getting upset; he could hear the quiver in her voice. He stood up to face her, and since he was a couple of steps below her, they were eye to eye, until she dropped her head.

"Look, Sadie. I just want us all to be able to get through this as easily as possible. Marissa hasn't told Paige about Nicholas yet. She was here all day with Travis, and last I talked to Marissa, she hadn't come home yet."

"Did you tell Marissa about Travis and me?"

Kurt shook his head. "No. I'm staying out of that."

"Travis texted Paige and asked her to call him, but she didn't. I feel bad about it, Dad. I really do. It's not like I planned all of this, and it's not like I dislike Paige or anything."

Kurt reached out and hugged Sadie. "I'm sorry if I sounded like I was accusing you of trying to start something with Paige through Travis. That's not what I meant."

"It seems like ever since Mom died there is so much drama. I hate it! Everything was so simple before."

Marissa

When Paige finally returned Marissa's call, Marissa caught her in a lie but decided not to hold her accountable. Marissa asked who it was that she left Pentwater to babysit for, and Paige said she actually had the days confused and shortly after getting on the highway she realized it, but by then didn't feel like going back.

Marissa already knew from talking to Andrea that Sadie and Travis were becoming a couple. Andrea was worried about Paige when she left, so she had called Marissa to fill her in.

It sat uneasy with Marissa because Paige didn't date often and she seemed really excited about Travis. No mother wanted to see her daughter crushed and heartbroken. She only hoped Sadie's feelings for Travis had nothing to do with Paige.

One thing was for certain. Marissa was not going to be one of those mothers who got in the middle of her teenage daughter's relationships. She was a firm believer that kids needed to figure out their problems on their own. Of course, she would always be there for Paige if she asked for advice or even as a sounding board, but this was a life lesson for Paige to work through.

She was also not going to let this get between her and Kurt. What went on between their daughters, friends, and boyfriends was between them. She was not going to let it interfere with her relationship.

Marissa told Paige to stop and grab a movie for them on her way home, but Paige begged and pleaded to stay out. She said she had just hung up with Megan and she was going straight to her house for a sleepover.

Rather than argue with Paige, Marissa caved. She really wanted to tell Paige tonight that Nicholas was her half-brother, but quite honestly, after three glasses of wine, she wanted nothing more than a shower and her bed. Tomorrow they would talk.

CHAPTER 40

Sadie

Sadie woke feeling both giddy and full of anxiety. She felt that new-love giddy feeling for Travis. She couldn't wait to be with him all day, no pretending, and no feeling confused or jealous. No wondering what he was thinking or trying to read into his actions.

The anxiety, well, that had settled in her stomach for the call she had to make to Dylan. She knew he didn't have to work today, so he would probably be calling, asking to drive out. She thought she probably had a couple of hours before he rolled out of bed—no doubt he was probably out until the wee hours of the night at his college party.

Dylan had sent her a text around three in the morning that said he couldn't wait to tell her who he ran into. She didn't see the text until she woke up this morning. She felt like texting back "Allison?" but decided it wasn't worth it.

To Sadie's surprise, the cottage was quiet. Nicholas usually had the TV tuned into cartoons as he played with his trucks and Legos on the floor while Kurt sat on the porch with his coffee, paper, and talk radio jabbering away.

The chalkboard by the door where they left messages for each other read "Gone fishing" with a picture of a fish drawn next to it by Nicholas. The chair was still pushed up to the wall under the chalkboard, and the chalk was sitting on the seat along with several dusty little fingerprints.

Sadie grabbed a banana off the counter and pushed open the screen door. It was supposed to reach ninety degrees today, and the temperature was climbing fast. The air was so thick with humidity she felt like she was stepping into a steam room.

"Don't eat that!" she heard as she plopped into the Adirondack and began to peel her banana.

Travis came jogging through the sand toward her. "Don't eat that," he said again as he approached her.

Sadie eyed her banana, wondering if it carried some sort of disease. "Uh, okay, why?"

"I thought we would go into town for breakfast."

Sadie sighed. "Here I thought there was an emergency recall on bananas for salmonella poisoning or something."

"Sorry, I just had a craving for cinnamon French toast."

"Are you asking me on a first date, Travis Sutherland?"

Travis smiled. "I guess."

Sadie went back to peeling her banana. "Breakfast sounds good, but I'm starving, so can I eat my banana too?"

Travis and Sadie took their time walking into town, hand in hand. She thought for sure that Cody would be tagging along with them, which would have been fine with Sadie, but instead, he went for a run with Benton.

Travis confessed that Paige called him in the middle of the night and left him a message and he hadn't returned her call yet this morning. He said she sounded like she had been drinking and it was loud in the background. *Sounds like both Dylan and Paige were leaving drunken messages in the middle of the night.*

The smile on Sadie's face as they shared a gigantic cinnamon roll was contagious. Travis couldn't help but beam. He hadn't seen Sadie like this their entire vacation. She was actually acting like the Sadie he had known all his life. Carefree. Happy. She even looked prettier.

There was never a dull moment between them. They had so much to talk about since they went to different schools and didn't know each other's friends. They gossiped a bit about their friends, they remembered stories from when they were little, and they tried to count how many times they had eaten breakfast at this restaurant over the past sixteen years.

Travis brought up the time they were racing down Old Baldy and Sadie was in the lead, but only by an arm's length. Travis had stuck his arm out just far enough to give her a little shove. Sadie had tumbled forward, landing face first in the sand, getting a mouthful. Sand was in her eyes, ears, pretty much every crevice of her body. Travis kept running, whizzing by, and grateful to be in the lead.

The memory was still fresh in Sadie's mind, especially since they were eleven when it happened! Sadie remembered bursting into tears, and being embarrassed that she did, but being thankful it was one of those times when all the parents were at the bottom of the hill, taking pictures and videotaping, so there were plenty of witnesses. Benton had not gone easy on Travis!

"You were kind of snotty to me the rest of that vacation," recalled Travis with a smirk.

"Snotty? You're lucky I ever spoke to you again! I mean you pushed me from behind. I should try and dig that video out."

Travis got a funny look on his face. "If you can't find it, we can watch mine." He paused for a moment. "After your mom's funeral, my mom dug out all of our vacation videos and we watched them. We all laughed and cried together. Your mom was really cool and made the best brownies ever!"

Sadie felt no sadness at the reminiscing—it made her so happy. "That's awesome, thanks." They kept talking, until they realized the restaurant was starting to seat people for lunch—it was nearly eleven thirty.

On their way back to the cottage, they took the long way, walking up and down the streets of town, down the channel, out to the pier, and along the beach. Sadie opened up and told Travis everything about her mother's diary. It was so easy talking to him, and the more she talked, the more she felt okay with it. She knew her secret was safe with Travis.

They held hands, and with every step they took together, Sadie felt surer about Travis than she ever felt about Dylan. That was until their steps brought them back to the cottage, where Dylan and Paige were waiting for them. Panic seared through Sadie as she dropped Travis's hand. Crap. Busted.

Of course, it wasn't just Dylan and Paige before them—it was everyone. It appeared to be a normal afternoon on the beach, but Sadie knew this was *so* not going to be normal.

Sadie mumbled quietly to Travis, "Either this is going to be a huge spectacle in front of everyone, or our families are going to be the best buffer ever."

As Sadie and Travis got closer, all eyes were on them. Jayna's eyes looked like they were going to fall out of her head as she stared back and forth between Sadie and Travis and Dylan and Paige. Everyone else suddenly tried to busy themselves in the sand or head for the water.

Dylan was next to Nicholas; he looked up with a glare and then back at the sand. He was digging vigorously with his shovel, his biceps flexing and his veins popping. Yep, he was really pissed!

Paige was sitting near Dylan, grabbing handfuls of sand and letting it slowly sift out of her fist like an hourglass timer.

"There might still be time to turn around and run," joked Sadie nervously.

"Yeah, this is definitely awkward," Travis whispered.

When they were about thirty feet from their crowd, Dylan stood up, chucked the shovel, and walked toward them. Both Sadie and Travis slowed to a crawl so the confrontation would be semi-private. Dylan's eyes were shifting back and forth between her and Travis.

"What the hell, Sadie? Was I going to be the last to know? Or were you going to cheat on me your entire vacation and then come home like nothing happened?"

Dylan's voice was ice cold, but at least he wasn't yelling or putting his fist in Travis's face . . . yet. Sadie could barely look at Dylan. Half of her wanted to wrap her arms around him and tell him she was sorry, not that she wanted to be with him, but because she didn't want it to be like this. She really didn't want to hurt him or have him completely hate her.

"It's not what you think, Dylan; nothing's happened." Well, except for a couple of kisses, but what Sadie really meant was that this just happened last night. "We haven't been sneaking around all vacation, Dylan, I promise. It just sort of happened last night. I was going to call you first thing."

Sadie started to fumble, and her eyes filled up with tears. She actually wished Dylan would try a cheap shot at Travis. It would make it easier for her to get mad, scream at him, and tell him to get lost.

"A phone call? Wow, Sadie, how big of you. And you," said Dylan, looking at Travis. Dylan took a step forward and poked a finger at Travis's chest, obviously trying to intimidate him. "I thought we had an understanding. Sadie's already taken; that means *not* up for grabs, asshole!"

Travis held his ground and didn't step back. He wasn't as much of a hothead as Dylan, but he could definitely hold his own if he had to. "Dude, I had no intention of anything happening."

Sadie interrupted Travis and stepped between the two of them. "I hate to break it to you, Dylan, but it's really not up to you who I go out with. I'm perfectly capable of making that decision myself. To be quite honest, you can blame me. I'm the one who went after Travis. And don't act like everything was all perfect between the two of us. We both know it wasn't."

Sadie folded her arms in front of her. "We both know we weren't going to last once you took off to school."

Dylan grinned and eyed Travis. "Nice, dude, she just admitted that you're just her fallback guy."

Sadie spoke up again. "First, keep Travis out of it. This is between us, Dylan. Second, call him whatever you want. It won't change the fact that I have feelings for him and it's over between the two of us. Third, why don't you leave before we both say and do things we'll regret. Making a spectacle in front of everyone is so not cool."

"The only thing I regret, Sadie, is hooking up with you in the first place. You use people, and when you don't need them anymore, you get rid of them." Dylan snickered towards Travis. "Don't think you'll be an exception."

Travis looked like he wanted to put his fist in Dylan's face, but knew better, especially since there were so many people around. "Thanks for the warning. I'll gladly take my chances."

Dylan and Travis looked as if they were ready to pounce on each other, so Sadie put her arm between them and rested her hand on Dylan's arm, turning him away. "Why don't the two of us go talk."

"Screw you, Sadie." Dylan flung her hand away. "There's nothing to talk about. You were right. I would have dumped you for someone else once I got to school, anyway."

"How mature of you, Dylan," she said to his back, as he started through the sand towards the cottage where his car was parked.

As she watched him walk, she did feel bad for him—how humiliating, but then again, he was the one who drove here. Wait. Paige wasn't budging. Shouldn't this also be her cue to leave? For some reason, she was almost dreading confronting Paige more than Dylan.

No sooner than Dylan turned his back, Travis nodded toward their parents. "Oh man, look who else is here."

Sadie's jaw dropped as she saw Marissa approaching. If she could've dug a hole and climbed in, she would have. "This day is really starting to suck."

Marissa had a smile on her face as she waved to Kurt, and he jumped up from his beach chair to greet her with a hug and a small peck on the lips. She had on big round sunglasses, a large brimmed straw hat, and a sheer white beach cover-up. Marissa was beautiful. It was no wonder her dad was attracted to her.

Marissa plopped down her beach bag. She was definitely here to stay. Translation: Paige was too!

Sadie cocked her head to the side and frowned. "You know I'm starting to wonder how Marissa can't hate me. I mean I'm the one who's been assuming and accusing her that she did something horrible to my mother for all these years, and now I've done this to Paige. Ugh, I've kinda been a real bitch."

Travis put his arm on Sadie. "Don't be so hard on yourself. It's only natural to defend your own parent. Besides, you've been through a lot. Marissa knows that. Why do you think she's been so understanding and kind?"

"In other words, while I've been so mean?" Sadie thought of Taylor Swift's song titled "Mean." She sang the words in her head, the part about being pathetic and then, "Why ya gotta be so mean?"

"That's not what I meant," said Travis.

Sadie shrugged. "It's true."

Dylan rounded the corner of the cottage and was out of sight, but not out of earshot as he peeled out of the gravel driveway, no doubt, throwing up rocks behind him, most likely spraying her dad's Denali. Kurt glanced over to Sadie with an annoyed expression, and Sadie looked the other way.

Paige still sat in the sand. She had filled in for Dylan and was playing with Nicholas.

"Let's get this over with," Sadie said, kicking her way through the sand.

CHAPTER 41

Sadie

To Sadie's surprise, Paige ignored her and Travis as they approached. She kept playing with Nicholas, head down toward the sand, acting completely engrossed in perfecting the shape of the mermaid she just made with the purple mold.

Jayna, on the other hand, grabbed Liz and the paddle ball set, and quickly started a game five feet away from where Paige was so she could eavesdrop.

Sadie felt so awkward, but she could only imagine how Paige felt at the moment, probably pretty ridiculous, humiliated. Sadie was waiting for Marissa to come up and reprimand her, but honestly, she couldn't see it really happening. It wasn't Marissa's style.

As Sadie was frantically searching for the right words to say to Paige, she was caught off guard when Paige popped up from the sand and started walking down the beach, blowing by Travis and asking Sadie to follow her, as she took hold of her arm.

Reluctantly, Sadie followed, looking over her shoulder at Travis with worry as Paige pulled her along. She noticed Jayna throw down her paddle and walk into the water, obviously disappointed there wouldn't be a show.

Catching up with Paige, Sadie figured she had better start with the apologies. "Look, Paige. I'm sorry about all of this."

Paige held up her hand and interrupted Sadie. "Save it, Sadie. Let me talk."

Paige did just that. She talked and talked and talked some more, but Sadie was relieved. Paige actually apologized to Sadie and explained how, when she left last night to "babysit," she and another friend, Megan, ended up texting Dylan to see if he could get them into the college party.

They drove to the party with one intention: to get back at Sadie. Paige explained that she and Megan hung out with Dylan all night. She eventually told Dylan that Sadie was cheating on him with Travis—that she saw it with her own eyes. Paige confessed she stretched the truth and added a few extra details that weren't true, but she'd let her emotions get the best of her.

"When Travis took off after you yesterday, I knew. I knew he was in love with you. I made up an excuse that I had to babysit and I left. I called Dylan on my way home. I'm sorry. I was so mad or crushed or embarrassed. I don't even know," explained Paige.

Sadie didn't blame Paige. She could see herself doing something like that had she been in Paige's shoes. She was just glad Paige wasn't screaming at her, calling her what she deserved to be called.

Paige wasn't done, though; she had more to confess. After filling Dylan in, she decided she would get back at Sadie in a bigger way, so she kissed him. She admitted that at first Dylan pulled away, until Paige reminded him that his girlfriend was most likely doing the same thing at the same time with Travis. Paige said they kissed a few times, and it really meant nothing—she actually regretted doing it.

Sadie understood. She knew she had it coming, and honestly, it didn't really bother her. What surprised Sadie the most was what else Paige spilled. She went on to confess that she had been in love with Blake Howard for, well, forever, and he had been going out with Abigail Fleming for, well, forever.

Paige thought that, if she tried to make something work with Travis, she might eventually really like him and maybe even forget about Blake. She admitted she really never had anything more than "friend feelings" for Travis, and deep down, she knew Travis didn't for her either.

"I was more embarrassed than anything when Travis took off after you, Sadie. It's so obvious that you mean everything to him. It just felt like such a stab. I can't have Blake and Travis doesn't want me." Paige's voice quivered. "This probably sounds corny, but I just want a boyfriend."

This was supposed to be one of those times where she should have all the right words to say, but instead Sadie was scrambling. She couldn't remember what it was like to *not* have a boyfriend.

"Sometimes having a boyfriend is highly overrated." Sadie giggled. "Seriously though, it will happen. You can't think about it too much. Let love find you. You never know; maybe Travis has some other friends he could introduce you to."

What a lame thing to say, thought Sadie. She felt bad for Paige. Never would she have guessed that Paige felt like this. True, Sadie couldn't ever remember her having a boyfriend, but she was outgoing, always cheery, and she was cute too.

If anything, Sadie bet most guys were intimidated by Paige. She was a major overachiever, super book smart, and had that goody-goody aura about her.

"I'm sick of the flings. It seems like right when I think a relationship is going to take off the guy takes off instead."

Thinking of how forward Paige was with Travis made Sadie wonder if Paige just seemed needy and came on too strong. "Maybe you should try playing a little hard to get. Flirt, but don't overdo it. Don't act like you want a boyfriend. Guys need a challenge."

Sadie truly had no idea what she was talking about, but it sure sounded good coming out. They kept the conversation loose as they approached the end of the pier and rounded the lighthouse, turning back towards the cottage.

It was weird talking to Paige this much. They had been as close as sisters when they were little, constantly together because of their mothers. Then they grew apart in junior high and high school because of their mothers. Sure, they were on the same tennis team at school, had the occasional class together, and were always friendly, but they hadn't hung out in almost six years.

Paige touched Sadie's arm thoughtfully. "Hey, I know it really bothers you about my mom and your dad. I understand how it would be hard to watch your dad date another woman. I know we've talked about it before, and I've done some spying, but honestly, it has never really bothered me as much as I let you believe. I guess seeing my dad with someone else for so long and seeing my mom alone for equally as long made it easier for me to accept."

Paige hesitated and then went on. "My situation is different from yours. I haven't seen my mom this happy in years. Quite frankly, I'm glad it's your dad. I'm not saying it isn't a little weird, but at least this way it's not some whacko. I feel like it's comfortable. I already have so many childhood memories with him, you, and Jayna in them."

Sadie could definitely see Paige's point and maybe even agreed with her on some level. She felt that horrible sense of dread for what Paige would think after she knew what happened between her dad and Sadie's mom.

"I know our moms drifted apart for a few years. My mom pretty much went into hiding after the divorce. She outright ditched her friends. It might be kind of cool to reconnect after all these years."

Sadie swallowed hard. Was that what Paige thought? That *her* mom went into hiding after the divorce and cut *my* mom out of her life because she was devastated over her husband? If so, Sadie couldn't believe that Marissa basically took the blame. She never let on to Paige that the friendship shattered because of Lydia!?

So it was quite obvious Paige was okay with their parents dating. Sadie knew this was the time she was supposed to open up and say something about being okay with it too, but she just couldn't yet. Sure, she felt bad for the way she had treated Marissa, but Sadie wasn't ready to invite Marissa and Paige into their lives with open arms just yet—she had way too much to process. Besides, would Paige feel the same after she knew the truth?

Anyway, Sadie could still envision Lydia and Kurt sitting in their lounge chairs next to each other by the pool. She could see her parents receding down the driveway together as they went for their nightly walks. She could see her dad come into the kitchen after work and give her mom a kiss as she made dinner. Sadie wasn't ready for those mental images to be replaced.

There was a new normal around their house, and Sadie was mostly responsible for creating it. Paige didn't get that. Her dad had been out of the house for six years, and she had seen him move on. Not to mention she could pick up the phone and talk to him whenever she wanted. Sadie's mom wasn't a phone call or even an airplane ride away.

"No hard feelings?" Travis asked Paige as she pretended to be engrossed in a book sprawled out on her beach towel.

Paige's face flushed, and she had a hard time looking Travis in the eye. "Nah, let's forget about it."

The waves had kicked up to four feet over the afternoon, and they were having fun boogie boarding as Kurt, Marissa, and the Sutherlands relaxed in their beach chairs. Sadie was trying extra hard to be polite to Marissa. Even if it was excruciating and she'd rather avoid her most of the time, Sadie felt like she owed it to Paige and maybe her dad too.

When Kurt and Marissa went for a walk down the beach, hand in hand, Sadie looked away. She couldn't watch their receding figures. As she glanced away, she caught the eyes of Andrea on her. Andrea gave her a warm smile, showing she understood. How weird was it that Sadie was this close to her boyfriend's mom? *Boyfriend*, she thought as she watched Travis and Cody toss the football back and forth, *even weirder*.

CHAPTER 42

Kurt

Kurt and Marissa had decided that since all the kids were present, it was as good a time as any to tell Paige that Nicholas was her half-brother.

Kurt had asked Andrea to take Nicholas to her cottage to help her prepare dinner while Kurt and Marissa held a meeting with Paige, Sadie, and Jayna.

The girls all sat on the wraparound couch while Kurt took a seat in the chair. Marissa stood, looking fragile and uneasy, even though her arms were crossed and her face was set.

"What's going on?" Paige chuckled, looking around at everyone's straight faces.

"Well, Paige, there's something that you need to be told. Nicholas, well, honey, Nicholas, he's . . . he's your half-brother."

The room was silent for what seemed like thirty seconds, but was probably only five.

"What? Huh?"

"Your father"—Marissa cleared her throat and spoke louder— "Marcus is actually Nicholas's biological father." The room fell silent. Page's face went from confusion to astonishment to anger as she processed what she was told.

"You've got to be kidding me! Lydia had an affair with Dad? She slept with Dad?" Paige leaped off the couch in a fury. "Your mother slept with my dad? What a whore!"

Whoa, that did it. In an instant, everyone was shouting, throwing accusations left and right. Sadie screamed in Paige's face that her dad had raped her mom. Paige blamed Lydia for breaking up her parents' marriage. Jayna started sobbing and pushed Paige across the living room, and she flew back into the chair Kurt was sitting in.

Marissa and Kurt were refereeing accusations and obscenities that were flying left and right, trying to calm everyone down for a civil conversation.

"You're a lying bitch, Mother! How could you keep this from me? Nicholas is four, and I'm just learning he's my brother? Was that why you kicked Dad out and forced him to flee across the country?" Paige glared at Sadie. "Your mother slept with my father." Then Paige turned back to Marissa. "And your best friend slept with your husband."

Kurt piped in and defended Marissa. "Paige, calm down. You're being disrespectful to everyone."

Paige was seething, and now Kurt was under attack as well. "Your relationship with my mother is pathetic and disgusting."

"Okay, Paige, that's enough." Kurt's voice was firm as he looked into her eyes. "We need to discuss this in a mature manner. What's done is done. Accusations aren't going to change the outcome of what happened over five years ago."

Marissa spoke up, "Bottom line, we have a little boy to protect here. Your brother! Let's not forget that. We were waiting until all of you were older to discuss this, but Sadie and Jayna read Lydia's diary and uncovered the truth."

Paige wasn't ready to listen. She was still fuming, yelling at her mom for being a liar all these years, howling through her tears that Lydia was a home-wrecker and a slut, screaming at Marissa, calling her twisted, and telling her she was out of her mind for being in the same room with the family that destroyed her own. She also added that she *was* actually still pissed at Sadie for stealing Travis from her.

"Like mother like daughter!

Marissa tried explaining to Paige that she and Marcus had already been going through a divorce and that it wasn't a consensual relationship, but Paige wasn't ready to listen. She only screamed over her mother's voice.

"Lydia was a slut! I knew it. I knew all along she did something terrible to you, Mom. Not in my worst nightmare would I have thought she was capable of seducing Dad."

They were caught completely off guard when Nicholas came bounding through the door in search of his favorite bandana, which he called his chef's hat, and had to wear while he helped Andrea prepare dinner. Andrea was running two seconds behind him, apologizing profusely that Nicholas ran out before she even realized what he was up to.

When the little guy stepped into a room full of yelling and saw his sisters crying, his little lip trembled. The room fell silent, and Paige stared at her half-brother with astonishment, curiosity, resentment, and longing. It was as if it was the first time she had ever laid eyes on him.

Kurt quickly swept Nicholas up and took him outside to comfort him. Luckily, Andrea's beach bag was lying on the porch and her stash of licorice was hanging out. Andrea easily redirected Nicholas's attention with the licorice and walked him back to her cottage to cook with her.

Paige stormed out of the cottage behind them and shut herself in the car.

"That bombed completely," said Marissa, exasperated. "I think it's best that we leave. At least we have a long car ride home. Hopefully, I can get Paige to settle down and hear the truth. It was probably for the best that Nicholas barged in. Things were only going to get uglier."

Kurt agreed, saying that everyone needed to cool off and Nicholas didn't need to see any more outbursts. Nicholas was a smart little cookie. He didn't need to overhear the wrong thing and start asking questions. Back in the cottage, Kurt tried talking to his daughters about how they could help smooth things over with Paige. Sadie and Jayna weren't so willing. They were deeply offended when Paige called their mother a whore and a slut, putting full blame on Lydia, acting like Marcus was the innocent one.

Kurt sighed. “Paige’s reaction wasn’t surprising, under the circumstances. Most likely, she just needs time to chill out, to process it all. You should reach out to Paige.”

Jayna scoffed. “What! How can you be on her side?

Sadie folded her arms over her chest. “You should be defending Mom and this family.”

CHAPTER 43

Sadie

Sadie was still struggling, trying to comprehend what happened between her mom and Marcus, and now, the things Paige said about her mom . . . She had been tempted to call or text Paige and tell her what a slime her father was for taking advantage of her mother.

Luckily, Travis was the distraction Sadie needed. She could be herself and spend every waking minute with him without hiding her feelings.

They were inseparable, holding hands, hanging on the beach, kissing, and laughing. She couldn't remember the last time she was this happy.

She had told him she loved him when they went back to the top of Old Baldy to watch the sunset. They sat in the exact spot they had when Travis came looking for Sadie a few days earlier. It was now and forever their spot.

Sadie had no worries about Paige showing up. Marissa had called her dad to let him know that Paige was going to California to stay with Marcus for a couple of weeks. Thank God!

In a twenty-four-hour period, Paige had gone from being mad at Sadie when Travis took off looking for her at Old Baldy, to forgiving her the next day on the beach, to later that evening hating her and her family, and once again accusing Sadie of stealing Travis from her. Sadie wondered where they would stand once Paige flew back to Michigan.

Sadie was relieved when her dad told her Marissa wouldn't be visiting them in Pentwater again. Sadie's feelings towards her were complicated. For now, she was going to forget everything and spend every waking second absorbed with Travis.

Myla and Kyla advised Sadie to steer clear of social media. Dylan had been making a few snarky remarks about their breakup that would only get Sadie riled up. It wasn't anything super bad, but nothing Sadie needed to read or, worse yet, respond to, and she would be tempted. Sadie had seen enough on Instagram of his wild nights of partying. *Really, how many selfies hanging on girls must he post?*

Dylan hadn't called, but he had texted that he left a box of her things on the front porch of her house. Sadie figured it was probably gifts she had given him, pictures of the two of them, and a sweatshirt he had of hers. She supposed she would clean out her room of his belongings when she got home.

Sometimes, when Sadie looked at Nicholas, she caught a glimpse of Marcus and Paige. It was strange, and she tried to push it aside, knowing Nicholas's heart belonged to her, Jayna, and their dad, and it would forever.

Chilling on the beach one afternoon, Travis told Sadie how beautiful she was when she smiled and that she needed to more often. It wasn't until then that she realized how little she had until recently. Ever since the night on Old Baldy, she had every reason to. Even Jayna had made a comment about Sadie being nicer now that she and Travis were together.

Only five days remained to spend in Pentwater with Travis. Sadie tried not to dwell on it. She liked spending every minute of the day with him. Once they went home, they would be thirty-some miles away from each other. Sure, it was only a half hour drive to see each other, but it wouldn't be the same as being right next door.

Luckily, Cody and Liz were keeping up their little fling as well, so Cody didn't feel like the third wheel. Jayna complained of being the fifth wheel, but actually she didn't mind much at all. They had one rainy day where they all drove to Ludington and caught a movie and then spent the rest of the night playing board games.

Sadie and Andrea kept up their morning walks where Andrea told Sadie amazing stories about her mother. She loved hearing about the quirky things her mother did, all the way down to the thoughtful gestures she was known for.

Travis and Sadie managed to sneak off for nightly walks under the stars. There was something about the Pentwater stars. They always seemed brighter, and there were thousands more over the water than at home. They walked the beach, pier, town, and campground, talking, laughing, and sometimes without a word at all.

One bright night, the moon was full and illuminated the heart that Travis drew in the sand with their names in it. The gesture gave Sadie goose bumps. He kissed her, told her he loved her, and confessed it wasn't the first time he'd written her name in the sand.

On their last day, they both woke up early to go out to breakfast, alone. They walked hand in hand into town as they had nearly a week ago. Sadie sighed. "I wish we could stay just one more week."

"Yeah, too bad more renters are coming this afternoon; otherwise, I know I could talk my mom into it," agreed Travis.

"I doubt my dad would go for it. He's probably eager to get back to work and to Marissa." Sadie thought of going back to her life at home and school starting in another two weeks, and it depressed her.

"I have football practice anyway," said Travis. "Two-a-day, ugh, rough!"

"Can I watch?"

Travis was grinning so big she could hear it in his voice. "Talk about pressure, not to mention everyone will be wondering who the hot chick is hanging on the fence!"

Sadie gave Travis a kiss on his hand as she held it. "Well, you can tell them the hottie is your girlfriend."

"Yeah, right, you'll probably start ignoring me in a couple of weeks and start dating another guy, an older guy, the way you did after our first kiss two years ago."

"Whaaat! I wasn't the one that dissed you! You dissed me. Then, on the rebound I might add, I started going out with Dylan."

"Not the way I saw it," teased Travis.

"Whatever!"

"Yeah, whatever," he agreed. "We were, like, fourteen, just about to be freshman. It never would have lasted."

Sadie had a weird thought go through her head that she didn't dare mention out loud. Travis was turning seventeen in two months. It wasn't unheard of for people to start dating as teenagers and date through college and get married. Would they be one of those couples? Would they rent these cottages with their family and friends some day?

Sadie knew she didn't want to get married young. She wanted to go to a big university, hopefully not close to home, and then work and travel for a couple of years before getting married and starting a family. However, the thought of being all grown up with Travis and a family made her giddy.

They had breakfast outside on the deck of the restaurant, surrounded by mostly senior citizens since it was barely after eight and most of the vacationing families were still snoozing. One family had young toddlers, who were screaming and throwing fits, and it made Sadie chuckle to herself. She definitely didn't want to rush the marriage and kid thing, especially since she knew what it was like to be the mother around the house. Nope, she definitely wanted some freedom.

No, right now she was enjoying being sixteen, about to start her junior year in high school, totally in love. Her feelings for Travis were so different from those she had for Dylan. With Dylan, she felt like she needed him and depended on him for security, maybe to fit in, maybe to get her through a really bad time in her life. With Travis, it just seemed real and really comfortable.

There wasn't that awkward feeling of getting to know someone and feeling pressure to always be at her best. She was one-hundred percent herself with Travis. She was who he always knew her to be, and how great that was—even though he knew a lot of embarrassing things from her childhood.

After breakfast, they got iced caramel lattes and shopped the surf shops. Sadie bought Travis a new T-shirt, and he bought her a new pair of flip-flops.

The rest of the day was spent hanging out at the beach, playing volleyball with Cody, Liz, Jayna, and some other friends (mostly Jayna and Liz's gang from the pier). Sadie felt like that was a lifetime ago and simply let it go. But if Jayna ever did something as stupid again, which Sadie knew was probably right around the corner, she would be there knocking some sense into her sister all over again.

CHAPTER 44

Sadie

"Well, I guess this is it, the end of summer vacation." Sadie and Travis sat on the steps of her cottage and stared out toward Lake Michigan. She had packed up everything and set it in a pile by her dad's Denali for him to load. Andrea and Benton had left an hour ago. Luckily, Travis and Cody drove separately from his parents, so Travis hung back to spend every last second with Sadie.

"So, will you come to my practice this week?"

"I promise to be cheering from the sidelines. Can I watch every day, or will I look like a stalker?"

"Are you kidding? All the guys will be so jealous! Hey, the pressure might be good for me. So I was thinking . . . next Saturday I could pick you up for a real date?"

Sadie inhaled the fresh scent of the water and exhaled slowly. "I'm counting down the days."

Travis kissed her. "I miss you already." He took out his phone and made her pose as he took a profile picture of her. She then sent him a text saying, "I love you," and they laughed as her picture popped up on the screen of his cell. She was actually surprised at how good the picture of her was—she was tan, her hair was "beachy," blowing in the breeze, and her smile was just right, not too toothy and cheesy. A good pic for Travis to have with him at all times.

She then snapped one of Travis for her screensaver. While she was adding him to her favorite people, he snapped a picture of his flexed bicep and sent it to her as a text. "This is for those guys that try to get with my girl. Tell them you're taken and show them this."

He kissed her as they laughed together. "Travis, my He-man."

"You know you're the only one that calls me that. Everyone calls me Trav, not Travis."

He was right; she never called him Trav. "Is that okay?"

"More than okay. I just like hearing your voice; doesn't matter what you call me."

Kurt stepped out on the porch and told Sadie everything was loaded and ready to go. The cleaning crew was waiting in the driveway for them to leave. He shook Travis's hand and said good-bye and left them alone.

Travis wrapped his arms around Sadie and told her this was the best vacation ever. She teased him, agreeing that it was rather eventful, with the best ending. She was sad that it was ending; she was happy in Pentwater with Travis, really, simply happy. The happiest she'd been since the day she found out her mother's fate.

They lingered on the porch for another minute before Travis walked Sadie to the passenger door. He opened it up for her and then stuck his head in the window of the backseat where Nicholas was already strapped in and gave him knuckles. "See ya, little buddy."

Jayna got in, grumbling that it was too hot, and snipped at Kurt to crank the air conditioner. Sadie rolled her eyes at Travis and held her hand up for knuckles. "Don't leave me out."

They pulled out, and Sadie watched Travis get in the Jeep, wishing she was next to him. She gave him one final wave and silently said good-bye to the cottage and to the entire town of Pentwater as they drove by the ice-cream shops, surf shops, and the restaurant deck that she and Travis ate breakfast on only a few hours ago. The smell of hot grease and waffle cones filled the air, and Sadie inhaled the scent and closed her eyes.

The ride home was typical. Nicholas fell asleep, and Jayna was zoned out with her ear buds snuggled in place, music cranked in her ears. Sadie was heavily into texting both Myla and Kyla. They had so much to catch up on. Both girls were already on their way to Sadie's house, informing her they would be hanging out by the pool until she got home.

Myla and Kyla had looked after the pool and kept it clean the last couple of weeks. They both knew the code to the keypad for the garage door to Sadie's house. They also took turns watering the plants and getting the mail. Kurt promised the girls one of his famous bacon cheeseburgers for dinner as a thank you.

Dylan was still a huge topic in their texting. The rumors about their breakup were running wild. Of course, Dylan's story was quite different from the actual truth—mostly that the breakup was his doing and that Sadie had some rebound guy because she couldn't stand to be alone. "Needy" was the exact word he used.

Kyla heard that he had already hooked up with his ex-girlfriend, Allison, which probably was true. This definitely struck a nerve with Sadie. Allison always tormented Sadie any chance she got, whether it was with a nasty look, a sly remark, or a ridiculing giggle. Sadie hated to admit it, but she had always felt threatened by her. She knew Dylan was only doing this to get back at her, and even though she wanted nothing to do with Dylan, it still stung.

When Sadie wasn't texting, she was waiting for her dad to bring up Marissa or Paige, but he never did. She knew it had to be on his mind. How couldn't it be? It was on everyone's mind. Sadie thought of her mother, thought of the strain her pregnancy and the birth of Nicholas must have been on their marriage. She wondered if her dad resented Lydia, if deep down Kurt ever wanted to divorce her.

For the life of her, Sadie still couldn't wrap her brain around why her dad would want to get involved with

Marissa. She also wondered if Marissa was somehow getting back at Lydia and Marcus by dating her dad. Sadie stared at the passing trees along the highway. It was almost too bizarre to understand.

Even though Paige was clear across the country in California, Sadie felt like Paige had been a greater distance from her when Sadie was in Pentwater. Going home meant back to reality, the reality that Paige would be flying back before school started and she would have to face her every day. Tennis practice would be a real treat too!

Sadie could practically hear the buzz in her ears from all the gossip swirling around from her and Dylan's breakup, to the fight between her and Paige over Travis, to the fact that their parents were dating. Thank God no one knew the truth about Nicholas. Sadie would seriously switch schools if that ever got out.

CHAPTER 45

Kurt

Eager to get back to work was an understatement. Not that Kurt didn't love and cherish the time in Pentwater with his kids—he wouldn't trade it for anything—but being a single parent was hard, and parenting around-the-clock even harder.

He always knew the responsibility of taking care of Nicholas was tough on Sadie, but he did pay her, and in his eyes, it kept her out of trouble too. Two days off each week to hang at the beach or pool with her friends was plenty, in his eyes. Kurt remembered having a summer job bagging groceries nearly thirty hours each week when he was Sadie's age.

The fact that he was meeting Marissa for lunch also helped him pop out of bed an hour before his alarm went off that Monday. He hadn't seen her since she and Paige left the cottage six days ago.

As he swallowed his last gulp of lukewarm coffee, about to walk out the door, he heard the padding of little feet on the wood floor, coming down the hallway from behind him. Nicholas had fallen asleep in his clothes on the couch in the screened porch last night, so Kurt had simply carried him up to bed.

"Hey, champ, you're up early."

Nicholas only nodded and rubbed his eyes with a yawn. "Chocolate milk," he said.

Nicholas was famous for his simple but direct choice of words. It was never, "I want this," or, "Can you get me that," just a simple one or two-word statement. Kurt was trying to get him to at least incorporate a please or thank you, here or there.

Kurt got him his chocolate milk and a granola bar from the pantry and tucked him in on the couch with cartoons. He gave him a hug and kisses and told him to wake up Sadie or Jayna if he needed anything.

"Why do you have to go back to work?" asked Nicholas, without looking away from the TV.

Kurt felt that pang of guilt sear through him. He told Nicholas that's just what dads have to do; otherwise, they wouldn't have a house to live in or food to eat. Nicholas was either content with this answer or was already too wrapped up in *Paw Patrol* to be listening anymore. Kurt figured the latter and decided it was a good note to leave on.

He kissed his forehead and had a flash of Marcus pop into his head. The thought that someday Nicholas would learn that Kurt wasn't his biological father killed him. He did what he always did when the thought entered his mind—forced it out just as quickly.

The guilt of leaving the little guy alone on the couch followed Kurt out to the yard, where he adjusted a few sprinkler heads and pulled out of the driveway, wishing there was a mother in a soft robe cuddling on the couch with Nicholas.

He pictured Lydia, coffee mug in one hand, spatula in the other, flipping pancakes laced with bananas, chocolate chips, or blueberries. She had fed her children French toast and pancakes as often as possible when they were little because they loved them, but more so because Lydia loved the way her kids smelled after they ate syrup at breakfast.

Lydia had kissed her children like crazy and even more so when they were laced with the sweet smell of Aunt Jemima. Kurt wished he had hung back ten more minutes to at least give Nicholas a toaster waffle drenched in syrup. *Tomorrow*, he thought, *tomorrow I'll get him his breakfast gooey with syrup, and a side of fresh blueberries arranged in a smiley face just as his mother would have.*

Shortly after twelve-thirty, Marissa came bounding to the table on the patio of Blue Lake Grill overlooking the small, turquoise man-made lake. She had a cream pant suit on with heels that gave her a good three-inch boost. She kissed Kurt and sat down, taking off her suit jacket, revealing a silk camisole and toned, tanned, bare arms.

"Sorry I'm late. Mondays are always a nightmare at the office." She took a sip of the iced tea Kurt had ordered for her and a glimpse at the sparkling lake. "It's no Lake Michigan, but it's pretty, isn't it?"

"I'd like to take you there."

Marissa cocked her head to the side. "Hmm, where?"

"Lake Michigan, just the two of us. Maybe we could rent a cottage someplace for a weekend. I was thinking Saugatuck or Frankfort."

Marissa put her glass down and looked Kurt in the eyes. "I'd like that."

Their casual dating, though sporadic, had been going on nearly five months. Kurt was ready to take the plunge. A getaway was the perfect, and only, way they would be able to have any quality time together.

The waiter came and took their order of two chicken Cobb salads and a side order of fries for Kurt. He joked that it was the manly thing to do when you ordered a salad for an entrée.

"So, what's the next step with the girls?" asked Marissa.

Kurt squeezed lemon in his iced tea and set the rind down on his bread plate. "Leave it alone, stay out of it, and let them figure it out," he said, bluntly.

"You're giving up?" Marissa looked at Kurt with doubt, as if it were that easy. "Did you forget we're dealing with two teenage girls with emotions cranked on high?"

Kurt chuckled. "I knew you'd get it. That's exactly why we stay out of it. You see, if it weren't for the two of us dating, we wouldn't even know about the quarrel over Travis. You can't tell me that Paige would have run home and told you all the details about this girl named Sadie (pretending you didn't know the other girl) who dumped her boyfriend and moved in on the guy she just started seeing . . . even though supposedly they didn't really have feelings for each other anyway . . . blah, blah, blah . . ."

Marissa

Marissa considered this. She was very close with Paige and they talked about a lot. Okay, it took a bit of prying from Marissa, and she probably didn't always get the full story, but she felt like she was pretty informed when it came to Paige's social life.

"I disagree. I definitely would've heard about it. She would've been upset, I would have pried, and she would've caved, eventually told me what was upsetting her, and then asked me to buy her something she has been wanting. Out of guilt for any amount of anguish I've ever caused her, I would have taken her shopping and then regretted it because, before we would have gotten back home, she would have been snotty or disrespectful about something." Marissa chuckled and rolled her eyes.

Kurt frowned. "Then we may have an issue."

Marissa countered. "Not necessarily. I think you're right. I think I'm going to leave it alone. I won't even bring it up. So far, when I've talked to Paige, our conversations have basically been about all the fancy restaurants, hip beaches, and designer boutiques her dad and Felicia have taken her to. We've barely even talked about Nicholas being her half-brother. Paige was embarrassed over Travis, but she didn't really like him. She just wanted more to be upset about. She's angry and wants to blame Lydia and Sadie, even me.

"To be honest, I think Paige is in a state of denial. She has Marcus up on this pedestal, always has; he can do no harm. I'm always the bad person. If anything, she is more upset at me for keeping it a secret all these years. Or should I say, 'making her father keep it a secret,' as she puts it. Go figure, huh? I'm the innocent party, only trying to protect my daughter, but yet I take all the blame."

"Have you talked with Marcus about how to handle it?"

They paused as the server brought their lunch and asked if there was anything else he could get them. *All the answers*, thought Marissa, as Kurt asked for ketchup.

"Typical Marcus—he says he will handle it, which is the scary part because that means he will give her the sugar-coated Marcus wonderful-father version, not the truth."

"But I thought you and Paige pulled a near all-nighter talking about it before she left for California?"

"We did, but as I said, she has always placed her father on a pedestal."

Kurt seemed to think about this for a moment. "So she's going to hate me for being the reason her dad divorced you and fled to California."

Marissa looked out to the water. She would never mention to Kurt the crazy accusations that Paige came up with, along with the name calling. Paige had laid the full blame for her parents' divorce, and the fact that her dad took off to the other side of the country, on Lydia for sleeping with Marcus. Paige also had this crazy idea in her head that Kurt threatened to kill Marcus if he tried to take Nicholas.

"Paige has no idea that you gave Marcus an ultimatum, and she never will. Paige has several different versions twisted up in her head. She has accused Lydia of seducing him. She's accused me of divorcing him even though it wasn't his fault. She accuses you of stealing his fatherhood and forcing him to flee to California because he couldn't bear to watch his son grow up not knowing his real dad. Our conversation wasn't pretty. I know Paige, though, and I know that she just needs to spew it out of her system and then she'll move on."

CHAPTER 46

Sadie

Sadie woke up, thinking about Travis. She wished she were back in Pentwater with him. It was almost ten, which meant he was already at football practice. Myla and Kyla were both still sleeping: Myla in the bed next to Sadie, and Kyla curled up on the window seat/bed.

Lydia had made a super thick pillow bed, covered in a peace sign fabric for the large window seat, since it seemed Myla and Kyla always slept over in a pair. At one time, the three of them fit into Sadie's bed. Once they got older and started fighting over who had to sleep on the floor, Sadie bagged up the mound of stuffed animals displayed on the window seat and converted the space to a bed.

She grabbed her phone and snuck out of the room. Chances were Myla and Kyla would be sleeping awhile since they didn't turn out the lights until nearly three in the morning. They had spent way too much time on Snapchat and Instagram and way too much wasted time reading Dylan's ridiculous posts.

On her way downstairs, she texted Travis three simple words, "I miss you," for him to see after his first practice.

Nicholas was playing on the kitchen floor, smashing two monster trucks together and eating his second package of Pop Tarts. The open box, wrappers, and crumbs lay next to him as evidence. Last night Nicholas had gone to the grocery store with Kurt, and they had come home with a boatload of junk food—the telltale sign that their dad was feeling really guilty about stuff.

Sadie scanned the countertops, and sure enough, there they were. Donuts! An entire box of glazed, chocolate sprinkled, powdered sugar, and even a couple of bear claws. *Mom has got to be rolling in her grave.* All this, especially after the loads of junk they consumed while in Pentwater. Nicholas was always begging for donuts at the store, and from the looks of it, he hit the mother lode.

It wasn't long before Sadie found herself back in Mommy mode: collecting piles of laundry, sweeping up Nicholas's mess, and helping him get dressed and brush his teeth. Would it ever end? He was already begging her to go swimming or ride bikes or bring his trucks out to the swing set.

She felt herself getting frustrated, especially since Jayna was still sleeping, or pretending to be, and here she was doing it all, as usual. She had had freedom in Pentwater, a taste of what it was like to be a normal teenager, without so much responsibility. But then she caught a glimpse of Nicholas out of the corner of her eye. He was staring at himself in the bathroom mirror and flexing his muscles, blowing at his "guns" and grunting.

Sadie couldn't help herself—she melted, watching the little guy. He was so incredibly cute and sweet, and the last thing she was about to do was snub him and let him feel lonely. *The poor kid doesn't have a mom to love and cuddle him, but he has me.* She refused to let him down. He didn't even have a sibling close to his age to play with as she always had.

So a few minutes later, Sadie found herself drawing a race course on the driveway with cement chalk for her and Nicholas to ride their bikes on. It wasn't long before Myla, Kyla, and even Jayna were outside, donuts in hand, playing race-car drivers with them. It was fun being a kid now and then when she got her mind off herself, and she knew her mom would be proud.

Dear Sadie,

Since I'm not there to keep you on the straight and narrow, and be a nag, (Hehe!) I'm going to give you some advice. You need to choose your thoughts, and you need to choose them carefully. You also need to make good choices. Doing what is right instead of doing what you feel like doing will always pay off in the long run.

Every day, in every situation, stop and take a breath and think before you speak, before you act. Replace the wrong thought with the right thought and follow through by doing the right thing. Love always believes the best of every person. That's all I'll preach about today.

I love you,

Mom

CHAPTER 47

Sadie

In the days that followed, Sadie hung out with Myla and Kyla by day and Travis at night. She drove to his football practice, once, with her friends in tow.

The girls enjoyed scoping out new boys, and it seemed the entire football team was overly flattered as well. From the sounds of it, many of them got reamed by the coaches for being distracted by the threesome and were threatened with extra practice time at sun-up the next morning if they didn't focus.

After practice, the girls went back to Travis's house with a couple of his friends, Cody included, and hung out for a Mexican dinner prepared by Andrea. Liz had not returned any of Cody's phone calls or texts since Pentwater, and he was still in the dumps over it. Sadie felt obligated to give him a pep talk and include the lowdown about Liz—that it was her typical behavior and not him. Jayna had talked to Liz and gotten the scoop—she had simply moved on. Poor Cody.

Sadie wondered if Myla or Kyla might be a good fit for him. How fun would it be if one of her best friends dated her boyfriend's best friend?

Without Dylan in her life and Travis living in another town, Sadie was thankful that Myla and Kyla were willing to give up days at the beach with the school crowd and spend days babysitting Nicholas with her by the pool. She had missed her friends while dating Dylan. It felt good to catch up.

When the weekend came, Kurt agreed to let Sadie have a small pool party with Travis, Cody, and two other friends, Bo and Caleb, along with Myla and Kyla. Kurt asked if he could invite Benton and Andrea along with Marissa, and Sadie reluctantly agreed.

She half expected Marissa to show up at their house since coming home from Pentwater, but in the week they had been home, Kurt never even mentioned her name. Weird, thought Sadie, but she wasn't complaining. She wasn't stupid—she was smart enough to figure out that her dad had spent some time with Marissa.

Sadie had been with Travis one evening, Jayna was at a sleepover, and the next morning, Nicholas had mentioned that he and Dad picked up Marissa at her house and went out for dinner and then to the park. Sadie probed Nicholas and got a few details out of him.

Nicholas really liked Marissa. She gave him a lot of attention. Also, with Marissa around, so was Kurt, and they were doing fun things: first Pentwater, now dinner out, and the park. Sadie was baffled that Marissa would even want to be around Nicholas. Sadie couldn't figure out why Marissa didn't harbor resentment towards the kid.

Sadie thought about Paige, and it made her skin crawl. What if Paige came back from California, mad as ever at Sadie? What if Marcus decided he wanted custody of his biological son, Nicholas? What if Paige blabbed all over town that Sadie's mom slept with her dad? Sadie was dreading Paige's return.

The small pool party was super fun. Travis had cool friends, highly approved of by Myla and Kyla. The day turned out better than Sadie imagined it would. The way her friends and Travis's friends hit it off was perfect. Sadie was nervous that it would be an awkward day, but it was one of the best pool groups she'd ever had.

Her dad, Marissa, Andrea, and Benton pretty much kept to themselves, so Sadie never had to directly deal with

Marissa. She did find herself acting extra sweet in general. She felt like she needed to prove to Marissa that she wasn't a horrible person and boyfriend stealer.

That night Sadie had an unexpected visitor. Her cell chimed as his text message came through at 2:15 a.m. It simply said to meet him outside. Sadie changed from her bedtime tank into a short-sleeved shirt, brushed her teeth, and snuck out the sliding glass door.

Dylan was out on the swing set, gently swinging side to side. Sadie could tell immediately that he had been drinking. "Hey," said Sadie as she sat in the swing next to him.

Dylan ignored her and dug his foot in the pea stone and then kicked a wad of stones, spraying the slide. "How was your pool party?"

Sadie swallowed hard. She was certain she had heard a car's engine rev in front of her house this afternoon and the car peel away. She thought it was Dylan, but then she thought she was just being paranoid.

"Good. It was really only a few people."

"You mean your boyfriend and his friends."

Sadie cringed. She knew her ties with Dylan wouldn't be broken easily. She feared that they would end up fighting and hating each other. She knew being great friends was out of the question, but she really was hoping somehow, in time, they could be cordial. Dylan would always be linked to the hardest time in her life. He would always hold a special spot in her heart for being there for her. He was her high-school boyfriend who had been there for her when her mother died.

"Is that what you came over to hear? Do you want me to tell you he's my boyfriend?"

Dylan shrugged. "Well, is he?"

Even in the darkness, Sadie could make out Dylan's face well enough in the moonlight to see it looked like he had been crying. His eyes were swollen and his face blotchy. She wasn't going to lie, but she didn't want to hurt him either, even though he had already said some pretty nasty things about her on social media and to their other friends.

"Yes, we're seeing each other."

"So just like that, we're over? What the hell, Sadie? I was there for you. Travis is a little punk. You're screwing up!" Dylan turned to look at Sadie for the first time. His face was filled with anger.

"Have you slept with him?" Dylan snarled.

Sadie hadn't, and hadn't planned to, and wished she hadn't with Dylan, but his question pissed her off. "It's none of your business, Dylan—we're no longer a couple, remember?"

"So you have?"

"No . . . I, Dylan, what's the point?"

Dylan jumped up from the swing and got in Sadie's face. "The point is that I don't think it's over between us, and you don't either. You're making a huge mistake. I'm giving you this chance to change your mind."

"Dylan, we both know we needed a break. You're going off to school. I have two years left here."

"So you're dumping me because I'm going off to college a half hour away, but your new boyfriend lives a half hour away and that's okay?"

"I've changed, Dylan. I'm not the girl I was my freshman year. You've changed too. We're different people and that's okay. I will always have feelings for you, but I need to move on, and so do you."

Dylan stared directly in Sadie's eyes, and she had to look away. She folded her arms in front of her and got a chill. Never did she expect any of this from Dylan. Maybe she had always underestimated his feelings for her. Or was it that he just couldn't stand the fact that he was dumped?

"That's a bunch of bullshit, Sadie, and you know it. You got caught up in some fantasy of having a summer fling in a beach town. I'm here to give you a second chance, but this is it. Don't think you're going to come crawling back to me in another month after you figure out what a boring loser Travis is."

Okay, that struck a nerve with Sadie. "Really, Dylan, who's the loser? Who is the one showing up at my house in the middle of the night? In secrecy, no less, and let me guess: if word got out that you showed up here, you would deny it!"

"You really are an immature bitch, Sadie. You deserve everything that happened to you."

The tears came instantly, and it only seemed to fuel Dylan's fire. He grabbed her by the jaw and held her face two inches from his. She could definitely smell the beer on his breath.

"Ya know I got a phone call from Paige the other day, and I defended you. She accused you of being a selfish bitch. Now I see she's right. She also spilled her guts about what kind of person your mom really was, a home wrecker. You're just like her. You don't care who you hurt as long as you're happy. Have a nice life, Sadie. Hope Travis can handle all your crying fits over dead Mommy dearest."

Dylan jerked his hand away from Sadie's face, and she howled. *What? Paige had told Dylan the truth about Nicholas?* He turned and started walking away, but Sadie couldn't let him go, not like this, not without him promising to keep silent. She ran after him and grabbed his arm. "Please, Dylan, don't tell anyone. You'll only hurt Nicholas if you do."

He flung Sadie's hand off his arm. "Why should I do you anymore favors?"

"I never meant to hurt you, Dylan. I still have feelings for you, okay? Are you happy I said it? It's just not that simple though. Just because we're no longer a couple doesn't mean that I don't still care about you, but it's not enough anymore. Besides, getting back at me is one thing; screwing with Nicholas and my entire family is another."

His face softened and Sadie waited, waited for him to promise to keep their family secret quiet. Instead, he shook his head and cut across the lawn. Sadie could picture where his car was parked two streets over, where it always was when he snuck over to get her. Half of her wanted to run after him, but she held back. She knew she missed the familiarity of him, but there was so much more that she needed to let go.

When he was almost out of sight, he stopped and turned around. He stood for a second and they stared at each other's silhouettes. "You're right about one thing, Sadie. You aren't the same girl you used to be. Once upon a time, I really loved that girl."

Sadie fell to the ground and cried.

CHAPTER 48

Marissa

"I can't believe we actually went through with it!" exclaimed Marissa.

"Meaning you're glad we did or you wish we hadn't?"

Marissa gave Kurt a light swat on the leg as they pulled into the driveway of their weekend getaway in Frankfort. It was perfect, with its wraparound porch and plushy, cushioned Adirondack chairs.

They were greeted by Cecile, the bubbly owner of the bed and breakfast, and showed to their room. The house was painted a cheery yellow, and the colors inside made them feel like they were already sitting on the tranquil beach. They relaxed for a moment on the second floor patio outside their room with a glass of wine.

"Could it get any better than this?" asked Marissa as she tilted her head back toward the sun.

A smile crept across Kurt's face. "A lot better." He winked.

She teased him by rubbing her bare foot up his calf. Marissa emptied her glass. "Let's hit the beach and climb the dune Cecile told us about."

They walked the mile stretch hand in hand along the water's edge until they reached the massive dune. Kurt's jaw dropped. "You've got to be kidding me! That is one fierce-looking dune, and the incline is straight up! It looks like a heart attack waiting to happen!"

Marissa rolled her eyes at Kurt even though the sheer angle of the dune frightened her. "Suck it up, old man! Last one up is a rotten egg," she said as she dropped her sundress and began to climb the hill in only her bikini. This acting like a tease stuff was quite fun.

Kurt and Marissa were struggling to keep their footing. The sand would switch between a slippery clay base, back to the hot silky sand, which made it extremely difficult to keep from sliding and tumbling back. The dune was so steep they were forced to climb it on their hands and feet. It felt as if they would tip over backward if they stood straight up.

About three quarters of the way, they stopped for a break, both panting, with sweat dripping down their faces. "Remind me why we're doing this?" asked Kurt.

"The views will be worth it, but really it's all about the climb," said Marissa as they both peered over their shoulders. The view was already amazing, but too scary to turn around and risk falling to your death.

"Hey, I've heard that, 'All about the climb.' Isn't that some song the kids listen to?"

Marissa chuckled. "It's Miley Cyrus, and it's a good song. It's okay if you like it—I won't tell anyone." Marissa looked deeper in Kurt's eyes. "No matter how steep, it's the challenge of the climb that will make getting to the top worth it."

Kurt wiped a drop of sweat from Marissa's forehead with his sand-covered finger and showed off his bright whites. "This deeper side of you is quite attractive, but I'm still a firm believer in getting to the top as quickly as possible."

He took off looking like a bear scaling a mountain. It took only a second for Marissa to catch up. Thank God for her tennis; it kept her fit and her legs strong.

Once they reached the top, they were silent except for a "wow" and "beautiful." As they stood there, they realized the dune they had just climbed was more of a cliff than anything.

The late afternoon sun dazzled the aqua water in front of them. The surf had picked up, but they were so high up that they could no longer hear the waves. Sailboats and cruisers bobbed up and down between the swells, and an occasional roar from a speedboat slapped by, completing the picture.

Frankfort's pier was much longer and thinner than Pentwater's pier, and it doglegged, creating a bigger splash when the waves crashed over it. A few brave souls speckled the pier, mostly seasoned fishermen.

Marissa felt Kurt take her hand, and they sat in the sand and admired the view for at least twenty minutes. He squeezed her fingers. "We should get ourselves one of those someday."

Kurt using the word "we" made Marissa blush. "One of what?"

"A big ol' boat. We could dock at a different port every night or, better yet, throw an anchor out and let the waves rock us to sleep."

Marissa wasn't sure which excited her more, the reference of a definite future together or the thrill of being aboard a yacht with Kurt. All of it rolled into one, she supposed. "That sounds fantastic." Marissa owned her house free and clear, so if she and Kurt were to ever get married, it was definitely doable, to sell her house and replace it with a boat.

"Frankfort one day, Holland to Saugatuck the next, Chicago after that," said Kurt.

She was engrossed in her daydream when Kurt pulled her to her feet. "Let's find the deck and bar Cecile told us about." They climbed even higher to a mini cliff on the dune and found a wooden deck with a built-in bar and stools. On the back side of the dune sat a couple of houses; obviously the owner of one was responsible for building the lookout bar.

"Incredible! To think these people can come out here every day and enjoy this. Sometimes it makes you wonder why you settled for where you settled," said Marissa, easing onto a bar stool.

"No more settling!" declared Kurt. They clinked their pretend beer bottles and hollered "cheers" as a late-sixty-something man walked up from behind them.

"Well, isn't it your lucky day, folks," he greeted, setting a small cooler on top of the bar. "I just happen to be the builder and bartender of this fine establishment." He handed Marissa and Kurt each a cold bottle of Corona from the cooler and cracked one open for himself.

He fished out a sealed bag with slices of lime and offered them each one. "I'm James. Welcome to my slice of heaven." James took the stool next to Marissa and stared out at Lake Michigan as he took a long gulp. "She's somethin', ain't she? I've been around the block in my days, and I tell ya, the Caribbean has nothing on this very spot."

"You're a lucky man," said Kurt as they introduced themselves.

"I am. Not only do I get to escape up here every day at five o'clock, but I get to meet some interesting people too. So, let's cut to the chase. What's your story? Where are you from and what's your business?"

James was a funny man, and Kurt and Marissa enjoyed talking with him for more than an hour. He was tall, muscular, and tan with thick white hair and striking blue eyes. They learned that he was a retired builder, an avid sailor, was father to five kids, had twelve grandkids, and the missus only let him hang out up here with his morning coffee and after five o'clock. She knew he'd become a lazy drunk if she allowed him anymore time to sit and stare at the water.

After an interesting hour with James, they heard a cowbell ring from the backside of the dune. James took his last swallow of his third Corona (as if he had the time it took for three beers down to a science) and said, "Six o'clock dinner bell. Don't want to keep the missus waiting. You two enjoy your evening. Coffee is served from seven to nine tomorrow morning if you're up for a hike." James grabbed his cooler and disappeared to his home on the backside of the dune.

"Race?" asked Kurt with a smirk.

"Ha! Are you kidding? Bring it on!"

Marissa took off, leaving Kurt in the dust, shouting, "Cheater, cheater!"

Marissa couldn't help but squeal as she tore down the dune with Kurt at her heels. She was waiting to go face first in the sand and flip and roll to the bottom. Instead, her legs took over, fast and furious. Her body felt like she was flying, her strides large and confident. She peered over her shoulder and saw Kurt's muscular chest and arms pumping behind her. He was so sexy. For all these years, she had never really noticed how good-looking he was. Or maybe she did, but she was always quick to remove the thought from her head.

At the bottom, she kept running straight into the water until she tripped on a wave and crashed face first. She came up for air and saw Kurt dive in next to her. The waves were huge, crashing over their shoulders and tossing them around like bobbers. Feeling young and free from a combination of an empty stomach, a glass of wine, and two bottles of beer, Marissa took hold of the back of Kurt's head and kissed him.

After their lingering kisses, Marissa pressed her forehead and nose to Kurt's and closed her eyes. She relished the peace of the moment.

"Marissa?"

"Hmm?" She answered.

"I've fallen in love with you."

Marissa's eyes shot open. Kurt had a smirk on his face that quickly turned into a big boyish grin.

"Ditto." Marissa giggled, their faces only an inch apart.

"Ditto? as in the movie, *Ghost*?"

Marissa threw her head back with laughter. "I love you, Kurt, now and forever."

"That's more like it," he teased, nuzzling back into her, "I love you, Marissa, now and forever."

They stayed in the water, playing in the waves as the late August sun started dipping in the sky and shimmering on the water. Then they strolled hand in hand back down the beach and to the bed and breakfast where Cecile was arranging fresh cut flowers in a vase. She greeted Marissa with a bouquet of her own to take to their room.

Later that evening, Kurt and Marissa walked through the streets of Frankfort and found themselves laughing over martinis on the deck of a bistro. Kurt admired Marissa in her red strapless dress. She teased him, telling him he didn't need to flatter her anymore, that he had already won her over. This time they clinked real glasses and said cheers, "To us, and to the times we have ahead of us," said Kurt.

"This is absolutely crazy. Back in May we had dinner on the beach and everything felt so surreal, so unsure and rocky. Now it seems like we have finally taken a leap and a bound forward. It still seems surreal, but in a good way."

Marissa couldn't help but think how wild it was that they were here together, no sneaking. Kurt had left Sadie, Jayna, and Nicholas home alone with the neighbor checking in frequently. Of course, he was also keeping tabs on them with frequent text messages, but he felt comfortable—Sadie was more than responsible. Kurt could tell from Sadie's mannerisms that she was excited to be home alone for the weekend. He told her no boys allowed and even informed Benton and Andrea that he would be gone.

Sadie had texted him and asked if Jayna could babysit tonight so she could go out with Travis. Kurt was fine with that, but nevertheless worried that Travis would "walk" Sadie inside when he dropped her off. He definitely trusted Travis more than Dylan, but he was still a sixteen-year-old kid!

Kurt's attention focused back to Marissa. "It's been an interesting summer."

"I don't want to dampen the mood, but Paige flies home in five days. I don't know what to expect." Marissa sighed. "I know we said we were going to stay out of the girls' relationship, but there's only so much we can stay out of. Somehow, at some point, we need to get a few kinks worked out."

"We need to be there to talk with them about what happened between Marcus and Lydia. Maybe Paige will want to get to know Nicholas better?"

Marissa sipped her martini. "What a mess we have on our hands."

"Depends on how you look at it. What we have between the two of us looks pretty good to me. Everyone else will have to come around on their own."

~*~

Kurt

After enjoying a breakfast of quiche, fresh fruit, and buttery croissants on the front porch, they decided they would visit James for a cup of coffee. Nothing like a little mountain scaling to wake you up!

James seemed happy to see his new friends. He greeted them with paper cups and a thermos of coffee. After some morning chitchat, he insisted that he take them sailing. He gave them specific instructions to meet him and his wife at the marina at 12:30, telling them to bring nothing but their sea legs. His wife, Kate, loved to cook, and she would provide lunch.

Kurt and Marissa began to protest, feeling as if they were imposing, but James wouldn't take no for an answer. He looked at his watch—it was five minutes past nine—and said he had to scoot. With a wave, he disappeared down the back side of the dune once again.

Kate was as sweet as they came. It was obvious that she had raised five children and was a hands-on grandma. She told stories about each of her grandchildren as she pointed to their pictures displayed in a collage on the wall aboard the *Knot So Tipsy*.

The Lake Michigan waters were calm and quiet as they ate cranberry-pecan chicken wraps with quinoa vegetable salad, and homemade sweet potato chips. James was right; Kate was an excellent cook and the two of them were both hospitable and kind.

For a minute, Kurt felt like he was far away, almost like being on a honeymoon. He looked at Marissa with her aviator sunglasses, straw hat, and sheer black cover-up over her black swimsuit and knew right then that someday it might just happen. She was beautiful, inside and out. He had known it for years, but yet he was discovering it for the first time.

James caught Kurt staring at Marissa deep in thought. "I haven't the slightest clue about either of your backgrounds, but if it's any comfort, she's a keeper. You're far too old to be first loves."

Kurt chuckled. "Ha! Far from it, but she's been in my life most of it."

"Well, life is short. Don't waste too many days dwelling on it," advised James.

Kurt knew all too well about wasting days. Losing Lydia taught him to cherish the moments and live life, but he also knew that actually living by that motto took work, and he needed constant reminders.

"It's complicated, James, but thanks for the advice."

"Agh, that's what you think, but it's really not complicated. Love is one of the simplest things in life. Follow your heart and everything will fall into place." James patted his heart as he stared out at the horizon, his thick white hair blowing gently in the breeze. "The only thing complicating things up is this," he said, pointing to his head.

"I'll be seventy-four next week, Son. Believe me it goes fast; don't drag your feet too long."

Kurt laughed. "I won't, and wow, I had you pegged at sixty-five."

"That, my boy, is what love does for the soul. I married that beautiful woman fifty-three years ago, and it just keeps getting better." James pretended to tip his invisible hat at Kurt and then looked at Kate. She and Marissa were sitting closely in the shade, chatting like they had known each other their entire lives. Kurt wondered who sent these people to him.

The rest of their getaway was exceptional, filled with plenty of romance, relaxing beach days with breathtaking sunset nights, and scrumptious food. They extended it one more day, even when the guilt about getting home set in. Kurt knew it was the perfect ending to the perfect beginning.

CHAPTER 49

Sadie

With a nudge from Travis, Sadie had texted Paige. As the days had rolled by, Sadie got more and more worked up and nervous for Paige's return. So Travis had talked her into just getting it over with, being the bigger person and texting her.

After nearly an hour of deciding what to say, she stuck with, "Hey Paige, I hope you are having fun in California. I really hate what happened between us. Can we talk?"

Yep, those three sentences took a lot of thought, and as soon as she sent it, she wished she had written something different. For hours, she checked her phone every couple of minutes, thinking for sure she had missed the chime when Paige texted back. She hadn't missed a thing. Paige had ignored her text for two days now, and Sadie was going crazy.

Sadie had confided in Travis about Dylan's nighttime visit and was worried that Dylan and Paige were talking, ready to divulge the family secret. It was tearing Sadie up inside. She even contemplated telling her dad, thinking maybe he would go threaten Dylan. She found herself obsessed with checking Instagram to see what both of them were posting. So far—nothing.

Sadie had been staring at the same page in her magazine for the last half hour. Jayna was over at Chrissie's, and Nicholas was playing with Play-Doh on the porch. She got up to pick a nail color out for her toes when her dad flew through the door.

"Hey sweetie, how are you? Who's here?" he asked, looking frazzled and sweaty.

"Uh . . . just me and Nicholas. What's up?"

"Oh, well, the battery in my cell is dead, and I left my charger in the mudroom here today, so I couldn't call." Her dad was flustered, spitting his words out fast and talking with his hands, which he never did.

Sadie started to panic. What had happened? Was it Grandma or Grandpa, could it be Jayna? Wait, no, he didn't even know Jayna wasn't home. "What's going on, Dad?"

"It's not a big deal. I just wanted to talk to you first." The doorbell rang, and Sadie could see Marissa through the glass panels running alongside the front door. She stood, her arms full with a foil-covered pan, a large salad bowl balanced on top, and a loaf of bread draped across that. "I wanted to let you know that Marissa was on her way over. She made us dinner."

Just like that, Kurt scooted around Sadie and rushed to the door. Sadie stood in the living room with her jaw on the floor as Marissa stepped in the foyer and kissed her dad, saying something like, "Hey, good-looking."

Barf, thought Sadie.

"Hey, Sadie, how are you?" asked Marissa in an extremely chipper voice.

Sadie barely had time to mutter that she was fine, before her dad shoved a loaf of Asiago cheese bread in her hand. He grabbed the rest of the dishes from Marissa and nervously headed towards the kitchen. *What the heck is going on*, thought Sadie.

Marissa propped her sunglasses on top of her head and followed Kurt into the kitchen, leaving Sadie standing in the living room with a loaf of bread in her hand and a dumbfounded look on her face.

"Oh wait. I almost forgot," said Marissa, turning back around. "I made dessert too." She stepped outside to her car, and Sadie ran to the kitchen.

"Daaad, what the what?"

Kurt held up his hand and interrupted Sadie. "Honey, Marissa spent all afternoon making us baked ziti. Could you please just, I don't know, could you just . . ." Kurt scrambled for words as he looked over Sadie's shoulder, worried Marissa would walk back in.

Sadie saw the pleading in her father's eyes, and something deep within her crumbled, and she let her guard down. Her defensive wall collapsed. "I'll go get Nicholas. He's playing on the back porch." She walked out, knowing that, from this moment on, her life was going to go through another big change. This was no longer her mother's home.

Fighting back anger and fear, Sadie sat down next to Nicholas and grabbed a fistful of Play-Doh. She squeezed it so hard it crept out between her fingers. "Are you hungry for dinner?"

"Did you make pizza rolls?" Nicholas asked, excited.

Sadie snickered. "No, champ, I didn't, but Marissa is here, and she brought you noodles, your other favorite."

With a "Yippee," Nicholas was gone, tearing through the porch and into the house to find his newfound love. Sadie sat alone for another minute and gave herself a pep talk. She loved her dad, and she was doing this for him. He deserved to be happy too, right? It was just really confusing knowing how to feel about Marissa now that the truth was out. When she wasn't around, Sadie felt like she could be okay with the two of them dating, and then, *Bam!* Marissa was here, and all these strange emotions invaded Sadie. She had no choice but to suck it up, so she made her way back inside.

Marissa moved around the kitchen like she owned the place. She gathered plates, salad bowls, and silverware and stacked them on the counter. "We should eat *al fresco*. It's such a gorgeous night."

"Sounds fantastic," said Kurt as he disappeared outside with the dishes.

Al fresco? Fantastic? Double barf! Was this a dream?

Marissa pulled out Lydia's salad tongs and mixed the salad with dressing. Sadie acted distracted by Nicholas, helping him get his milk, but all she could think about was the fact that Marissa still remembered where everything was in their kitchen. Sadie wondered how many hundred times Marissa had moved around this kitchen with Lydia. If it wasn't a weekend barbeque in the summer, it was homemade pizza night in the winter, or baking birthday cakes together, or holiday cookies and bake sales for school.

"Taste this, Sadie, and tell me if it has enough dressing." Marissa was holding up a fork full of salad for Sadie to test.

Reluctantly, Sadie took the fork and tried to act normal, even though she was screaming inside. This was far from normal; it was weird, awkward, and extremely uncomfortable, even though Marissa was acting as if she came over every night and did this.

That's it, thought Sadie, as she took the fork from Marissa. *Halfway through dinner she's going to let me have it. She's going to reprimand me and tell me what a horrible person I am for the way I treated her and her daughter.*

Sadie ate the salad and nodded. "It's fine."

Marissa was smiling at her and it made Sadie edgy. *How can she be so nice to me? I've been anything but pleasant to her.*

"It's really good," she added and turned away to fill their glasses with water.

Thankfully, her dad came back in to help carry the food out. Rescue me, thought Sadie, but Marissa was intent on having a conversation with Sadie, or at least small talk.

"Can you slice the bread, please, Sadie? I'm going to mix some fresh parmesan, garlic, and olive oil together for a dipping sauce. Doesn't that sound good?"

"Uh, yeah, sure."

As Sadie headed for the cutting board, she caught a glimpse of her father's eye as he was walking out with the ziti in his hands. He was obviously tense. He wasn't acting all cool and nonchalant like Marissa. Sadie was glad. She wanted to make him sweat a bit, even though she had promised herself to be on good behavior.

The conversation, or babbling as Sadie thought of it, never stopped. Sadie had to admit the ziti was awesome, but yet she couldn't bring herself to compliment Marissa. When Sadie took her third helping, Marissa made a comment about Paige loving the ziti too. Sadie felt her cheeks heat, but nothing else was said.

Nicholas loved having Marissa around. He wanted to sit next to her, and he even asked if she would spread "that oily stuff" on his bread and sprinkle parmesan on his ziti. Nicholas was going through a phase where he had to do everything for himself, so the fact that he was asking Marissa to do things for him told Sadie his attraction to Marissa was the real deal. Could she blame the little guy? It was his chance for a real mommy.

Sadie asked if he wanted more ziti, and he said yes, but wanted Marissa to scoop it on his plate for him. Slap!

Dessert was margarita bars. Margarita bars reminded Sadie of her childhood summers. Either her mom or Marissa made them for every pool party they ever had. Most children would not like them, as they were a cross between key lime pie and a lemon bar, with an amazingly thick graham cracker crust, but since she grew up on them, she acquired the grown-up taste.

Just as Sadie was about to excuse herself, Marissa asked Sadie to play tennis with her in the morning. She explained that she and Paige were on a mother/daughter doubles team and she had to cancel their matches since Paige had been in California. She was hoping tomorrow Sadie could play in place of Paige.

Sadie quickly started fumbling for words or, better, excuses, when Kurt interrupted, saying how fun that would be and that Jayna would be fine watching Nicholas for a few hours while Sadie played.

"Great! I'll pick you up at 9:00," offered Marissa.

Sadie panicked. *In a car alone with Marissa! I think not!* "Nah, that's okay. I'll meet you there. I need to stop at Target after, anyway."

Kurt started to say something and Marissa interrupted him. "That's fine. We'll meet at 9:15 at the country club. I have to show a house afterward, anyway."

Sadie finished her dessert and volunteered to do the dishes. She and Travis kept up with their obsession for Bitmojis, usually ones laced with hearts, kisses, and I miss you quotes, but not tonight, not with Marissa intruding. Sadie was sending him everything from *WTH, SMH, AWKWARD*, and *THE STRUGGLE IS REAL.*

From the kitchen window, she had a straight shot of the entire backyard and pool. She watched Marissa pushing Nicholas on the swing, even doing underdogs. He loved it, yelling out deep belly laughs. Kurt was watching both of them, his smile so wide his eyes crinkled in the corner.

She studied her dad, noticing how he looked at Marissa. It was different from the way he had looked at her mom, at least from what she remembered. Sadie was nervous she would forget the two of them together. And if she forgot what it was like seeing her parents together, would she soon forget the images of their family together?

In bed, Sadie and Jayna wrote on each other's backs and Sadie told Jayna about the night with Marissa and how bizarre it was. Jayna was easily softening towards Marissa and it scared Sadie. As defiant and reckless as Jayna was, Sadie knew she was lost without a mother. Sadie was lost too, but in a different way, especially since the mothering fell on her shoulders.

Jayna had helped herself to two plates of leftover ziti when she got home from Chrissie's and wrote on Sadie's back, "At least she makes good ziti."

CHAPTER 50

Sadie

Sadie drove with all the windows rolled down and the morning breeze blowing through her hair. She was sweating, not because she was necessarily hot, but because her stomach was a ball of anxiety. As she turned into the country club, she swiped some more deodorant on and threw it in the back seat.

She adjusted her skirt and slung her tennis bag over her shoulder. It had been a few weeks since she'd played, and to be honest, she was itching to get back on the court, just not with Marissa as a partner.

Luckily, they only had a few minutes to warm up. There was no time for idle chitchat. Sadie waved to a couple of girls and their mothers that she knew from school and her team and felt her adrenalin kick in.

Marissa was a good tennis player, a really good tennis player, actually. She was petite and quick on her feet and not much got by her. It didn't take long for Sadie to also find her groove, and before she knew it, they had won their first three matches.

"We make a great team, Sadie," Marissa said, as they drank from their water bottles. Sadie noticed Marissa had slices of lemon and lime in her water, just as her mom used to do.

They did make a great team, but Sadie hated open-ended statements like this. She felt like she had to elaborate on them and suggest they play together more or something. "Yeah, I haven't played in a while. I was nervous I was going to be a bit rusty."

"You're doing awesome."

"Thanks, you too." Sadie wiped the sweat from her forehead and stretched her serving shoulder. They went undefeated until their very last match. Sadie crumbled. She hit a wall and made a couple of mistakes that cost them the game.

If it bothered Marissa, she didn't let it show. She gave Sadie a big congratulatory hug and praised her for her hard work. She was sure their score had bumped them up a few rungs on the league ladder, despite their loss.

Marissa pulled an extra protein shake out of her cooler and gave it to Sadie. "I'm so used to making a double batch for me and Paige that I didn't realize what I was doing until I was done, so I brought you one. It's kinda thick because of the protein powder, but the flavor is good—pineapple and mango. There's also spinach and avocado in it, but I swear you can't taste them. Paige even likes it."

Just like that, Marissa was gone. She said she had to get home and shower because she had to show a house in an hour. Again, Sadie wondered how and why Marissa was being so sweet. Not that she was ever mean, but Sadie was well aware there were definitely a few things that could make Marissa not care for her much.

Sadie wondered if Paige had mentioned to her mother that Sadie had texted her. She wondered how much they'd talked since Paige had been in California, and how much Paige opened up to her mom. Sadie felt that pang, that pang of wanting the option of having a mom to talk to about friends and boyfriends. Of course, who knows how much she would actually tell her mom if she were still alive, but not having the option made her feel like she would want to tell her everything.

CHAPTER 51

Sadie

It was the night before the first day of school. Sadie had spent the day with Travis. They had gone to the mall so she could help him pick out some new clothes, and then they had spent an hour at Target, getting composition books, pencils, and a calculator.

Andrea had cooked them dinner and sent Sadie home with all the leftovers and a batch of peanut-butter-chocolate-chip cookies. She looked at the cookies sitting on her passenger seat, but what she really craved was the protein shake Marissa had made her the other day.

Now Sadie sat in her bedroom, staring at her cell as Travis modeled his new outfits over a Facetime call. Pitbull sang "I Know You Want Me" in the background, and Travis sang along as he danced for her. He could always make her laugh. They had fun together, and he was as much her friend as he was her boyfriend.

Jayna came barreling in Sadie's room after hearing her hysterics. A larger audience only made Travis put on more of a show, especially when Jayna repeatedly told him what a dork he was and that he had no rhythm.

Sadie hadn't heard her dad knock on her bedroom door. "Sadie, Sadie!" he yelled over the commotion.

When Sadie looked up, her room fell silent except for the thumping from the beat of the music coming through her phone. Standing next to her dad was Paige.

"Paige is here," he said and started to walk out of the room. "I'll leave you alone."

Travis was still dancing, and Sadie saw the corners of Paige's mouth creep up into a smirk. Sadie was fumbling, caught completely off guard. "Travis, I gotta go," she panicked into the screen, and she shut him off.

Paige looked really pretty. She was tan and her hair looked as if she had just had it professionally blown out. She only had a pair of cutoffs on, but she wore this cream lacy tank top and a stack of gold bangles that matched her sandals and made her look like she was pairing vintage with new, to come up with summer chic straight from a magazine.

Sadie told Jayna to get out, so in Jayna language that meant plop down on the window-seat cushions and get comfortable. Paige sat on the edge of Sadie's bed across from Sadie at her desk. "Looks like things are going well with Travis?"

Paige didn't look mad, which was a relief, but she didn't look overly happy either. So Sadie decided to follow suit. "Um, yeah, he was just, ya know . . ." Sadie flipped her hands around apprehensively. "He was showing off some of his new school clothes."

"Look, Sadie. I was pretty mad when I left Pentwater. It just hurts, you know, to be rejected, even if you know inside that it wasn't meant to be."

Paige was playing with the corner of a blue fuzzy peace-sign throw pillow lying on Sadie's bed. She kept her eyes down, like she was trying to find a tick deep in the plush pillow.

"There's been a lot to process. I've been trying to figure things out from all angles. I'm not just talking about Travis. I'm over that. It's more the other stuff . . ."

Sadie felt her body relax, realizing how tense she had been since Paige walked into her bedroom. She wasn't going to hate her because of Travis.

Paige continued. "I still feel betrayed. I feel like my parents are both liars. Up until a few weeks ago, I thought I was an only child. I'd always been alone, my dad left, and I had no siblings and never a boyfriend. The boyfriends never worked out, and the fact that I have a brother was kept a secret. I've hated being an only child."

Sadie and Jayna exchanged glances. They were both waiting to hear Paige bad-mouth their mother, blame everything on her. Sadie had not thought of Paige feeling the way she described. Despite losing her mother, Sadie knew she was fortunate to have so many people in her life that she was close to.

The bedroom felt really thick, so Sadie cracked a joke. "Let me know when you want to babysit our brother. Pick your day and I'm outta here."

Paige welled up. "He can't even know I'm his big sister."

Dumb, thought Sadie, dumb, dumb, and dumb! *Why did I say that?* Sadie watched as a tear trickled down Paige's cheek. She hadn't a clue how to respond. When Jayna started to speak, Sadie cringed, fearing what would come out of her mouth, no doubt even worse than what Sadie said.

"That doesn't mean you can't have a relationship with him. All it takes is ten minutes playing trains in the dirt and a pack of fruit snacks and he's your best friend."

The girls all giggled. "I always wished I had sisters." Paige sighed.

"It's not forever," said Jayna. "I mean, when Nicholas is older, we'll tell him the truth."

"I know." Paige looked down and Sadie felt bad for her. "I also know that what happened with your mom and my dad wasn't all her fault. I really wanted to blame it on her because it would be easier. I wanted to blame my parents' divorce on her and keep my dad perfect in my mind. I know he's not and we talked a lot in California." Paige wiped a few more tears away. "I could never figure out why my dad would want to live so far away from me. I figured he didn't love me enough."

Sadie felt a pang in her throat. Her dad was responsible for sending Marcus so far away. *No wonder she throws herself at guys' feet. She'll do anything to get the attention and love from a guy because she feels abandoned by her dad.*

Paige tugged at her gold surfboard necklace and sighed. "My dad said it was too difficult to be so close to the mess he created and it was best for everyone if he moved away. I screamed at him that it was best for everyone but me. I guess the more we talked about it, the more I understood his point, but it still hurts, ya know?"

Paige looked up and saw that both Sadie's and Jayna's eyes had filled. They all sat for a second and connected their own dots, their own perceptions of what took place six years ago.

"This is why kids are so screwed up nowadays. It's our parents' fault!" Jayna joked, and all three girls laughed.

This is one of those moments where I'm supposed to go hug her, thought Sadie, but she just sat there, still feeling uncomfortable. A chirp from Sadie's phone broke the spell. They all knew it was Travis.

Paige stood up. "It's late and we're starting our junior year tomorrow. I better get my beauty sleep. You never know. Maybe Blake will dump Abigail when he sees me."

Paige made the first move and gave both girls a hug. "I'm really sorry I said those things about your mom. I honestly have the best memories of her. Truce?"

"Truce," Sadie and Jayna agreed.

"She's kind of a sorry case," said Jayna after Paige left.

"Aren't we all?" Sadie snickered.

Jayna laughed. "Speak for yourself! I consider myself to be pretty well adjusted."

CHAPTER 52

Sadie

The first few weeks of school flew by. Sadie liked being a junior, an upperclassman. Or was it upperclasswoman? At first, it seemed weird not meeting Dylan by his locker between classes. When she passed it, she still glanced at it, remembering how her pictures had hung on the inside. A senior girl had it this year, a girl she didn't really know. Sadie thought she may have had an art class with her last year.

Dylan had not texted, called, or emailed her directly, but he had made a few more sly remarks about Sadie that traveled the gossip channels back to her. He posted some raunchy pictures on Instagram, always partying and smiling. Sadie ignored them. Paige admitted to Sadie that Dylan had called her and wanted to spread the family secret, but Paige begged him not to, explaining that he would be hurting far too many people, more than just Sadie. So far, he hadn't broken his promise.

She noticed that, since going off to college, Dylan had acquired one hundred seventy-eight new followers on Instagram. Sadie had heard that he was rushing a fraternity and enjoying the partying and girls that came along with it. It did bug her a bit, how couldn't it, but she was also relieved that she had moved on and wasn't sitting in a high-school classroom worried about her boyfriend cheating on her.

Every Friday night, Sadie went to Travis's football games. The first game she went alone and sat with Andrea and Benton. Myla and Kyla tagged along once when their own football team had an away game. Lately, Paige had asked to tag along with Sadie. At first, Sadie was reluctant, but it actually turned out to be kind of fun. Ever since their talk the night before school had started, Sadie and Paige were slowly on the mend, trying to put their family history and future into perspective.

After the games, they usually hung out with Travis and his crowd. Sadie and Paige had met a lot of new girl and guy friends through Travis and were surprised at how easygoing they were to the newbie girls.

Sadie noticed how different Paige was around his gang—more laid back and fun. The way Paige and Cody had been eyeing each other was obvious, but to Sadie's surprise, Paige hadn't mentioned a word about him.

This wasn't normal Paige behavior. By now she was usually throwing herself at whatever guy showed interest in her, obsessing over him. She was playing it cool, being a bit of a flirt, but not acting overly interested. Travis even asked about Paige on Cody's behalf, and Sadie was honest when she said she wasn't sure what Paige thought about him.

Tomorrow night Sadie, Paige, Myla, and Kyla were all making the trip to the game. Travis's friend was having a few people over to his house after the game. Kurt and Marissa were actually meeting up with Andrea and Benton for the game too.

Since Sadie and Paige had tennis practice together, they had started carpooling. On a few occasions, Paige had come home with Sadie after practice, and Marissa had also come over for dinner. Sadie wasn't thrilled with the situation, but she was slowly getting used to it. Spending more time with Paige helped ease the anguish.

The six of them either squeezed around the table to a dinner Marissa had prepared and brought over, or sometimes she had made dinner alongside Kurt in their kitchen. Marissa was slowly teaching Kurt how to cook. The apron her dad wore annoyed Sadie, but her dad loved Googling recipes and trying them out with Marissa at his side. There was something kind of cool about it, but Sadie kept that to herself.

On the nights Marissa ate at their house, she insisted on cleaning the kitchen herself; that was, after everyone had helped clear the table. Sadie would go to her room and do her homework, just as she had done when her mother was alive. She still took it upon herself to help Nicholas with his bath and read him books, but sometimes he would ask if Marissa could read to him instead.

Since Sadie's homecoming dance was on a different night than Travis's, they decided they would go to both school dances. She was excited to shop for two dresses. "Technically, I could wear the same dress to both, but that would be cheesy," she said to her dad when he furrowed his brow at the mention of purchasing double the dresses, two pair of matching shoes, and two sets of accessories.

Sadie had shopped with Myla and Kyla on a couple of different occasions, but had no luck. She had begun to scour the Internet, trying to find something she could order, but she was nervous about ordering the wrong size and then having to spend more money shipping it back.

The next morning Sadie awoke to the sound of Nicholas sword fighting the pillows on the couch, so she snuck down to the kitchen to make eggs, bacon, and bagels. She returned to her bedroom with breakfast on a tray for Myla, Kyla, and Paige. Cranking the windows open to a crisp, cool fall morning caused many groans and moans.

"It's the weekend, Sadie," moaned Kyla.

"Seriously," Paige said, "it's against my weekend conduct code to wake up before noon." She pulled the covers over her head.

“The fresh autumn air smells amazing,” Myla said, sticking her nose up to the screen.

After eating their breakfast picnic style on Sadie’s bedroom floor, the girls were all laughing and giggling, replaying the events of last night. They reminisced about the two floozy girls who ended up in the hot tub in their bras and underwear, the boy who thought he was the karate kid and tied a scarf around his head and karate chopped beer cans on the kitchen table, and the two girls with boy haircuts, obviously new to lesbianism.

All the girls decided it was fun to be in a town where there wasn’t any history or knowledge of cliques. There were no barriers—they could talk to whomever they wanted or be whomever they wanted without it flying through the Internet waves hours later or the hallways come Monday morning.

“Oh. My. Gosh,” said Paige. “I’m going to homecoming with Cody! I totally forgot he asked me last night. I mean, right, Sadie? He did ask me? Yes, he did, he asked me just before you threw me in the car. Ugh, I’m so embarrassed. I probably made such a fool out of myself, and he probably doesn’t want to go anymore.”

Paige wouldn’t stop rambling. “I’m so nervous I mean I barely know him, and the dance is in two weeks! Can we double with you and Travis? Where am I going to find a dress? What if it’s too late to get an appointment to get my hair done?”

Later that afternoon, Sadie was working on an English Lit paper when Paige called. “Pack your bags. We’re going to Chicago.”

“What? What are you talking about?”

“Me, you, and my mom. We just spent a wasted two hours at the mall. Talk about junk!”

“Tell me about it.”

Through the phone, Sadie could hear Paige rushing about, probably throwing clothes in her duffle bag. "So anyway, I looked at my mom and told her I wished we had time to go to Chicago and she said, 'Let's go!'

"Seriously, if we jump in the car and don't hit any traffic, we'll be there by five. We can shop until the stores close tonight and all Sunday afternoon."

Sadie grabbed a chunk of her hair and twisted it into a knot. This would be way too weird. Things were going okay with Paige, but driving to Chicago and staying in a hotel room with her and Marissa, no way. "I have an English Lit paper due on Monday that I totally procrastinated about. Besides, I'm going out with Travis tonight."

"Saaaadie, come on. Bring your laptop. We will have it written by the time we get there. I have that class two periods before you and I did my paper Thursday night in less than three hours."

"I promised Travis."

"Tell him you'll meet up Sunday night. We'll have you home by six. Pleeease, it'll be fun."

Sadie knew she wasn't getting out of it. Her dad would push her; Travis would push her. So twenty minutes later she was tossing her bag in the trunk of Marissa's sporty little BMW.

Kurt was elated, gave her his credit card, and for the first time set no limit. "Have fun, honey." Sadie kissed, hugged, and thanked him. "Thank *you*," he said, and she knew what he meant but didn't comment on it.

Nicholas cried as they pulled out of the driveway. He had begun calling Marissa "Rissy" and he was upset that he couldn't go with her. He had started in the developmental kindergarten class for five-year-olds not quite ready for full-on kindergarten. Socially, he was a bit behind, mostly separation issues.

Most of the pictures he brought home had Marissa drawn on them. He even had plenty of pictures he drew specifically for Marissa. He would pile them up in the pantry until he saw her next. Sadie caught herself one morning at breakfast, telling him to be sure to draw a picture for *her* that day. It never occurred to Sadie that she would be competing with Marissa for his attention.

The drive to Chicago was over in the blink of an eye. As promised, Paige helped Sadie with her paper, and Sadie knew that with Paige's help it was a definite A. Sadie also knew she would have spent double the time on it without Paige's help and gotten a B.

They checked into their hotel just for the sake of dropping their bags and sending the car off to an unknown parking garage. They were definitely on a mission, hauling armloads of dresses to the changing rooms at Saks Fifth Avenue, Niemen Marcus, BCBG, Bloomingdales, and some smaller boutique stores.

Thank God for the capability of cell phones to snap pictures and text them in an instant. Sadie had really liked at least a half dozen dresses so far that she texted pictures of to both Myla and Kyla for their honest opinions. Paige's and Marissa's opinions counted too, but the more the merrier.

Surprisingly, Marissa was fun to shop with. She had good taste and would tell them if a style made them look frumpy, smutty, or in some cases, like a bridesmaid. When they hit a shopping slump, she disappeared and came back to the dressing room with Starbucks Vanilla Frappuccinos.

After closing the stores, with several dresses being held at multiple shops, the trio plopped in a booth at The Cheesecake Factory. They shared gigantic plates of avocado eggrolls, fried macaroni and cheese, Factory nachos, four cheese pasta, and a California cheesesteak sandwich.

Sadie opted for the Reese's Peanut Butter Chocolate Cake Cheesecake, Paige the Oreo Dream Extreme Cheesecake, and Marissa indulged in the 30th Anniversary Chocolate Cake Cheesecake. Sharing was the best part. With each bite, Sadie felt a little more at ease with the two of them. They ate until they felt sick, but it was worth every bite.

"We won't be able to zip the dresses tomorrow," said Sadie, sipping her water.

Marissa chuckled. "Ha! You two have the metabolism of horses, thanks to tennis and your age. Just wait until you hit forty. It's like a switch, and, bam, gravity is your best friend, and every bite you eat clings to you like the plague."

"I didn't know horses had super-fast metabolisms," said Paige, squishing the last bit of cheesecake left on her plate with her fork.

"It was a mere figure of speech, dear, a cheetah, lion, or ape, whatever." Marissa flung her hand.

"It seems an ape would have a slow metabolism. Don't they just sit around? I mean, at the zoo, they're always just sitting there scratching themselves and eating bugs out of their hair."

"Do you always have to critique me, Paige?"

Sadie cracked a smile, remembering when she and Lydia would do this very same nonsense bickering. Now she did it with Jayna.

"Grab your bags, girls. I need a hot shower, a robe, and a pillow to prop my feet up."

Both Sadie and Paige had managed to purchase a new pair of skinny jeans and a few other loose ends they couldn't resist. Marissa slipped out of the booth with a moan, and Sadie and Paige followed suit.

They walked the streets of Chicago in the cold fall air amid the hustle and bustle of city life: cabs honking, sirens blaring every so often from a fire truck, night clubs pumping below the streets, silver and gold spray painted musicians trying to make a few bucks on the street, and the clacking of stilettos as the women dressed to the hilt exited the upscale restaurants.

Back in their room at the Omni Suites, they found *Sixteen Candles* on HBO. Marissa said it was her favorite movie in high school—she had watched it so many times she could recite most of the lines. "In fact, I used to make your mother watch it in college. It was the only VHS tape I owned. Lydia had the biggest crush on Jake Ryan the first time she saw it—actually, we both did."

Marissa held Sadie's gaze with a smile. Sadie wondered if Marissa knew how much she liked to hear people talk about her mother, just to hear her name spoken. Marissa, out of all people, knew so much and had so many stories about her mom.

Sadie wanted to hear more, but she couldn't just say the words, "Talk about her." It seemed strange, so instead she joked, "Now I know why she married my dad. They look like they could be twins. I mean when my dad was younger."

Maybe not twins, but Kurt did resemble Jake Ryan with the incredible eyes and dark hair.

"Ha! When your mom first met your dad, she teased that she was going to call him Jake!

"Do you girls remember the time we drove to Michigan Adventure for the day and got a flat tire?"

Sadie and Paige immediately started laughing and nodding. "Yeah, and the old man that stopped to help us . . ." Sadie could barely get the words out, she was laughing so hard. "He was changing the tire, and Jayna screamed, 'Ew, Mommy, that man's bum crack stinks so bad the flies are landing on it!'"

There had been a dead deer about ten feet away from where they had pulled over on the side of the road, and a few of the flies buzzed over.

"I had never been so embarrassed," said Marissa, covering up her mouth. "Lydia and I were apologizing profusely to that poor guy, and all he said was, 'That little girl is gonna keep ya on yer toes, Missus. You all have a good day now.' He yanked up his pants as he walked away."

They kept telling stories and laughing until almost two in the morning. Sadie went to sleep with a smile on her face and had the most amazing dream of her mother.

Sadie ended up with two completely different dresses. One was a deep purple, almost black, floor-length gown that hugged her tight. It was straight over her chest with beading and one crossover strap that ran from under her right arm to her left shoulder and around her back in a crisscross.

The other was a fitted, short, and strapless pale pink that showed off some killer strappy shoes. Paige and Marissa both agreed that she had picked two red carpet dresses.

Paige's style was bolder than Sadie's, and she found the brightest of bright yellow. It was Paige—it made a statement, and it was beautiful. Held up by two spaghetti straps, the sheer fabric fell elegantly over her skin, still lightly tanned from summer.

They both found shoes and jewelry, not the kind they admired from the window at Tiffany's, but perfect for their dresses and their budget. Sadie knew she would be raiding her mom's jewelry box for her tennis bracelet for the pink dress.

Since Paige and Cody were also going to both school dances and Sadie saw the way Paige had eyed her pink dress when she brought it in the dressing room, Sadie suggested they purchase it together and share it. One of them would wear it to the first dance and the other to the second. Even though Paige had two inches on Sadie, it still fit her great.

Sunday night, when Marissa pulled in Sadie's driveway, Sadie made a bold move. "Hey, why don't you two come in and we'll order pizza for dinner. I'm sure my dad won't mind," she said with a wink. Looking at Paige, she said, "Travis is coming over. I'll tell him to snag Cody on his way."

When Sadie crawled in bed Sunday night, she counted her blessings. She didn't have her mom, but she still had a lot of people to love; the houseful tonight proved it.

Marissa

Paige thanked her mother all the way home. "Chicago was so much fun," she had said over and over. Marissa was more than relieved the trip had gone as well as it had. They shopped, ate, and laughed until their stomachs hurt. It didn't get any better than that.

Marissa felt they had turned a huge corner. The three of them had spent good quality time together, and they were all at ease, even Sadie. Marissa had finally seen Sadie's genuine smile, something that rarely showed when Marissa was present.

The icing on the cake was that Marissa knew Paige wanted the relationship between her and Kurt to progress. Paige had begun to show affection to Nicholas, and he warmed right up to her. She had even picked out a new Iron Man figurine for him at The Disney Store and brought him home a bag of Garrett's Popcorn.

Marissa had watched Sadie's reaction closely, and she seemed completely okay with it, remarking that Nicholas would love the gifts. Nicholas gave Paige a huge hug, and Marissa saw Paige's eyes fill up.

Later, when Paige was on her way to bed, she remarked how quiet it was at their house. She mentioned that, at the Booker's, everyone bed-swapped. Sometimes Jayna slept in Sadie's bed, Nicholas slept in Jayna's, and sometimes all three siblings slept in the same room. "How cool is that?"

Marissa wrapped up in a sweater and called Kurt from her rocker on the front porch. The autumn air was refreshing, but she already missed the thick and humid summer nights. The night was dark, and only a few stars twinkled amongst a sliver of a moon.

"So tell me what she said, Kurt? I really had a great time. I think we may have cleared the hurdle this weekend."

"It's more of what Sadie didn't say. She didn't tell me I was a disgrace to the family. She didn't call you 'her.' She didn't refer to you as 'my girlfriend.' She didn't give me the cold shoulder and silent treatment. She didn't act as if I disgusted her."

Marissa could tell by Kurt's voice that he was smiling. "Sadie told me about watching *Sixteen Candles* and the reference with Jake Ryan. She talked of all the dresses you hauled in the dressing room and how she thought you would tip over if one more dress was in your arms. She bragged about dinner and the cheesecake. Thanks to you, Marissa, she had an amazing time."

She was silent for a moment, and Kurt asked if she was still on the line. "I'm here. This is all so bizarre, you know." She choked back tears. "I'm happy for us, of course, but you know what I'm most happy for? I'm happy that I could be there with Sadie as she picked out her dress because I know Lydia would want that."

CHAPTER 53

Sadie

Sadie hadn't thought much about her mother's diary since school started. She had been so busy it hadn't really crossed her mind, until now. She was home alone doing homework and eating noodles topped with Prego and parmesan cheese. Jayna was somewhere with Chrissie, and her dad and Nicholas were at the movies with Marissa seeing *How to Train Your Dragon 2*.

She went down in the basement and dug through the 2009 tub, but the diary from that summer that she and Jayna had read in Pentwater had not been put back. Did her dad hide it? He had made it clear that he thought they shouldn't read anymore of the diary, but would he go as far as hiding it from them?

Sadie was just about to go upstairs and look for it when she picked up another one labeled Fall 2009.

October 22, 2009

What a day. I'm beat. I spent the entire afternoon putting the final touches on the girls' Halloween costumes. Why don't I just buy costumes? Sadie wanted to be Britney Spears (from her younger days), and she wanted to look exactly as Britney does in the video of "Baby One More Time" where she wears the school girl outfit. So after watching the music video a hundred times, I made the pleated skirt and ran all over town to find the over-the-knee gray socks, the perfect gray sweater, and white collared shirt. Sadie does not have Britney's blond hair, so we bought a wig and styled it in braided pigtails.

Jayna's costume was a lot more fun to make than Sadie's. She is going as a butterfly this year. We picked out pretty purple, pink, yellow, and turquoise sheer fabrics for a dress design with a butterfly body sewn in. She has these gigantic wings that flutter ever so gracefully when she walks.

I just pray no one mistakes her for an angel. My dear Jayna will scream at them if they do!

I've never been so ahead of myself. I'm usually frantically finishing costumes in the eleventh hour. I guess this is what happens when my social life is pulled out from beneath me. No more tennis, no lunches with Marissa, no going for walks together, talking for endless hours on the phone, or going on shopping excursions after we drop the kids at school.

I hope Marissa and I don't run into each other at the school Halloween party. Paige's classroom is right next door to Sadie's. Maybe I should dress up in full disguise. I could wear a mask or be a ghost and drape a sheet over myself.

Now that my belly is showing, people are always making comments about how cute I look or asking when the baby is due and if we know the sex. I don't want all this attention, but I've become accustomed to putting on a good show when I need to. I fear someone will be gushing over my pregnancy and Marissa will walk around the corner.

Sadie flipped forward through a few pages and sat down on the cold cement in the storage room. She knew that once she opened the diary it would be difficult to put it down—

especially since, when she was reading it, she could hear her mom's voice crystal clear.

November 8, 2009

I had quite the scare today. I woke up and I was spotting. By the time I got home from taking the girls to school, it was heavy and I was cramping.

On the way to the doctor's office, I was trembling and crying. So many things were going through my head. I was frightened of losing the baby. I was frightened that something was wrong with the baby and I was going to have a premature delivery. I was frightened because the thought of losing the baby also made me wonder if it would be the best thing. I was most frightened because I realized how much I already loved this baby and I did NOT want to lose it! By the time I arrived in the parking lot, I was crying so hard I was nearly hyperventilating.

The ultrasound confirmed that the baby was fine. By the end of my visit, the spotting had decreased significantly. The doctor had questioned me about what I had done in the previous days, and I hadn't thought much about all the heavy lifting I had done: getting out all the tubs of Thanksgiving decorations and throwing out the rotting pumpkins on the front porch.

She concluded that I had just overdone it and that my body was reacting by spotting. She advised me to take it easy and ask for help when doing strenuous work. *Yeah, right,* I thought. I have been trying to be a super woman throughout this pregnancy, attempting to do it all, not complain or ask for help from Kurt. I feel like if I do, he will only think bad thoughts of how I deserve to feel lousy or I don't deserve help.

I tried to be strong all evening, but then after I put the girls to bed, I was so exhausted and so relieved and so angry for my thoughts that I broke down in his arms. I wasn't going to tell him about the spotting or the doctor's visit, but I needed him. I needed him so badly to hold me and tell me everything was going to be okay.

I sobbed in his arms as I told him my thoughts—that part of me had maybe hoped for a miscarriage, that the other part of me would be devastated, and that I was so, so sorry for what I had done.

He didn't say much more than "It's okay, it's okay" as he rubbed the back of my head and let me cry. When I went to go get a tissue, he called my name. When I turned around, he looked straight in my eyes and told me, "Everything will work out." I wonder if he realizes that is all I think about.

December 11, 2009

Kurt and I did our annual Christmas shopping day and dinner out tonight. I knew it was inevitable that I would run into her sooner or later. We saw Marissa, twice: once in the mall and again having dinner at Blue Water Grill. The first encounter was for sure coincidental. The second, I have a hard time believing the same, since Marissa out of all people knows that every year after Kurt and I finish Christmas shopping for the girls we go to Blue Water Grill.

I swear she was at the mall alone. I had held up a bright orange sweater that looked so much like Sadie, and next thing I knew, I was staring in the eyes of Marissa. She was holding the same sweater up in yellow.

I fumbled and started to speak to her, saying something about Christmas shopping for the girls, but she looked at me as if I were the biggest piece of scum she had ever seen and walked out of the store.

Kurt had seen it all unfold from across the store. He saw us standing next to each other, oblivious to one another, but he knew it was best if he stayed back at a distance. In other words, he was panicking, nervous as hell that we were going to get into a brawl!

I would be lying if I said it didn't bother me, but it didn't completely ruin my day either. For Kurt's sake, I didn't allow it to. When I was pregnant with Sadie and Jayna, I walked around a proud mother. Sometimes acknowledging this baby makes me feel ashamed. I wonder if Kurt is ashamed, disgusted, or repulsed by my growing belly.

Anyway, I really wasn't surprised when I saw Marissa sitting at the bar at Blue Water Grill with a man I didn't recognize. She had probably been there before Kurt and I even arrived, possibly watching us the entire hour we had been dining. I didn't notice her until I was walking back to our table from the bathroom. Thankfully, her back was to me.

Once I sat down, I realized she had a straight view of our table. Kurt handed me my spoon, waiting for me to dig into my favorite chocolate cheesecake, and I couldn't swallow one bite.

I couldn't help but look in her direction. She was laughing with this guy, throwing her head back like he had told the funniest joke she had ever heard. When she took a sip of her wine, our eyes met and locked. Once again, her eyes were full of hate and disgust.

Kurt followed my gaze and muttered something when he saw her, so we boxed the dessert and left. The fact that she just looks at me and doesn't say a word hurts worse than if she were to scream in my face. I'm not even worthy of that!

December 20, 2009

I'm feeling really weepy and I can't shake it. The girls are out of school for Christmas vacation. We've been wrapping presents, baking cookies, going sledding, and are set to go downtown and ride in the horse carriage and look at the twinkling lights around town tonight after Kurt gets home.

The girls are so excited about this baby, and when they talk about it, I get excited too. They kiss and hug my belly and talk to the baby. I even forget the circumstances for a moment and everything seems wonderful. It's when Kurt comes home that my attitude changes. The girls always want to talk baby names, and I hate to even bring it up around him.

I feel like our relationship is on a rollercoaster, climbing one minute, plummeting the next. I can't tell if it's from his attitude or my fear. As the pregnancy progresses, I get more afraid of Kurt rejecting this baby. Would he dislike a boy more than a girl because a boy would be more like Marcus? Will he hug and kiss this baby? Will he be helpful with feeding and changing diapers? Or will this baby be my responsibility alone?

Would it be worse if Kurt rejected the baby or me? I never know whether I should try and initiate sex. I fear he will shove me away. When we do have sex, I can't help but wonder if he is just going through the motions of marriage. I resent myself. How can't he?

Sadie wiped a tear from her eye. She couldn't imagine what her mother went through. She couldn't imagine how her dad dealt with it and Marissa too. It wasn't until now that she really, really thought about the deep feelings of each of them from their own perspective. Each one of their stories had their own twist of sadness.

December 25, 2009

It appeared to be a perfect Christmas inside the Booker household. The girls were up at 6:30 a.m., squealing and excited that Rudolph had led Santa Claus to our house once again. We opened presents with Christmas carols playing in the background, the fire crackling, and a fresh coat of sparkling white snow out the window.

The homemade cinnamon rolls reserved for Christmas and birthdays were heaven, the omelets cooked to perfection, and the aroma of freshly ground and brewed coffee filled the kitchen.

My parents, along with Nevie, Josie, and some guy she picked up at a conference two months ago named Rick, all came over for dinner, along with Kurt's sister Stacy and her family. Stacy knows something is up between Kurt and me. That is something I don't even have the energy to write about tonight. I will never willingly confide in my sis-in-law Stacy. NEVER!

I baked prime rib and steamed crab legs and made the Swiss cheese and onion poppy seed bread that I do every year. Mom made the au gratin potatoes and salad, Nevie made her seven-layer dip appetizer, Josie brought enough wine, beer, and vodka to last until next Christmas, and Stacy made enough desserts to last us until Easter.

It was the same as every year past. The only thing that changed was who Josie brought to the table. Nevie never brought a date. She said if she ever brought someone it would be because she married him in a drunken stupor in Vegas. My sisters will forever live the New York single life.

This year everyone was excited to think that next year the baby would be crawling around. At some point, I should confide in my mom and sisters, well, maybe just Nevie and Josie. Mom would bring it up under her breath every opportunity she got. I'm afraid to ask Kurt if it's okay to tell them. I need them.

Kurt went over the top with gifts for me this year. It started with perfume, clothes, the most beautiful and expensive crib/bedroom set for the baby, and even a brand new Infiniti QX 56 in the garage with a bow on it. I think he is trying too hard to love me, to gift me, to make everything okay when it's not.

We haven't fought, and we don't mention the names of Marcus or Marissa. He's acting as if this is his baby and everything is just dandy. I should be grateful. Instead, I'm freaking out, paranoid he will wake up one day and want out.

I feel so bottled up, and I know he does too, but he refuses to show it. I see it in his eyes when he looks at me. I feel it in the way he touches me. Everything is NOT okay. I want him to yell and scream at me. I want him to get it out of his system and tell me how hurt and angry he is, because I know he is.

Both Sadie and Jayna said this was the best Christmas they ever had. They say that every year.

Maybe faking that your life is wonderful and perfect will eventually make it so. Maybe that's what Kurt is trying to do? Fake it until he believes it! Fake it until it becomes reality.

December 31, 2009

Sadie and Jayna have both asked why we haven't been hanging around with Paige and Marissa. Once school started, it was easy to make excuses. Then I told them about Marissa and Marcus getting a divorce and that Marissa was too sad and stays home a lot. Or I've said that Marissa and I get together during school days, but now they are really starting to question me.

We have spent New Year's Eve with Marissa and Marcus since college. They keep asking when Marissa and Paige will be over, and of course, I have made up another excuse, saying they are visiting family. Basically, I'm a liar now too.

I just booked us a room at the hotel across town that has an indoor pool with a slide. Hopefully, a night swimming will distract them enough so that they at least stop asking why we aren't having our annual party.

Kurt is in the pool house, helping the girls find their goggles and squirt guns. I promised them we'd order pizza and watch the ball drop in our room and have the best party ever. I've decided to stop at the grocery store on the way and let them pick out every junk food item I usually ban from their diet. If they want pop, they can have that too.

Tomorrow seems like a good day to bring up marriage counseling to Kurt. This is going to be a year to put our marriage to the test! I need to hear what Kurt is really thinking, because I know he is biting his tongue, and I want and need to hear him get it off his chest. I think if we were in counseling together he might open up.

I'm craving for him to spit some nasty words at me. I believe I deserve it.

Sadie looked up from the diary and remembered the very night she was reading about. She remembered going to the hotel and eating pizza by the pool. Crazy as it seemed, she remembered her mom letting them drink orange and grape pop and eat sour cream and onion potato chips loaded with dip, and sweets too—sugar cookies thick with frosting and sprinkles, gummy worms, Twinkies, and donuts and hot chocolate for breakfast the next morning.

She remembered it so well because they were *never* allowed to eat like that, and they talked about it for months afterward—especially whenever Sadie and Jayna went to the grocery store with their mom and begged for more of the same junk and always got turned down.

It was after New Year's that Sadie remembered not really asking about Paige and Marissa anymore because she knew her mom was getting upset about it. Sadie and Paige were not in the same classroom at school, and they didn't really seek each other out at recess anymore.

Sadie was deep in thought when she heard the pitter-patter of little feet run across the kitchen tile above her. She quickly tossed the diary back in the tub. Before she sealed the lid and stored it back on the shelf, she grabbed the next diary, labeled Winter 2010. She quietly snuck up to the main floor and then cut through the foyer and used the front steps to go upstairs to her bedroom.

Locking her door, she made herself cozy on the window bed. She saw her dad and Marissa sitting in the golf cart and then Nicholas shooting out the back door, running towards them with his hat and gloves in hand. It was a chilly fall evening.

Sadie pulled a blanket around her, determined to read this diary cover to cover tonight. She knew that it went through April, well past the birth of Nicholas in February. She wondered if her mother was with her now, knowing what she was about to do. She wondered if her mom would be upset. Sadie justified it, thinking it would help her understand the situation between her mom and dad, and also with Marissa.

Down below, Nicholas snuggled himself between Kurt and Marissa in the front seat of the golf cart, and they took off for a ride around the neighborhood. Every time Sadie watched Nicholas with Marissa, she could tell his love for her was getting deeper, like her dad's, she supposed. Sadie realized she no longer felt irritated.

January 3, 2010

We had our first counseling session today, and I think it went pretty well, even though I was the one crying my eyes out while Kurt sat there dry-eyed. Did I expect any different? Not really. It was surprisingly easy to get him there. I brought it up lying in bed, in the dark, at the end of New Year's Day (I couldn't look at him when I suggested it). I took the cowardly approach, which I might add has become customary to me. Anyway, he agreed, saying it was a good idea for us to be able to talk through our problems with someone we can trust.

We have no one but each other to talk to at this point. We haven't discussed whether we will confide in select family members at some point. As of now, I'm too ashamed to even think about it.

Our counselor was a referral from my doctor who prescribes my medication. Not taking any anxiety pills during this pregnancy has been tough, but incredibly liberating. Dealing with my emotions instead of always coating them is giving me a healthy satisfaction.

We spent two hours in therapy today—forty-five minutes individually with Trisha and then thirty minutes together with her at the end.

I basically told her our situation from my point of view, and Kurt told it to her from his. I wish I could have been a fly on the wall during their session. I was speaking so fast during mine, trying to get everything out in the open in our forty-five minutes, that she probably thinks I'm a nut case. I was sobbing and shaking uncontrollably.

I told Trisha that one of my biggest fears is that Kurt is bottling his anger towards me and that, soon, after the baby is born, he'll resent us both so badly that he will leave. I explained that I play these scenes over and over in my head that Kurt takes me to court for custody of the girls and I'm left divorced and alone with this baby to raise.

My fears, about the intimacy that a husband and a wife usually share in the delivery room while a child is being born, are mounting to a near panic as each day passes. I confided that I am also mourning the loss of my best friend. I miss Marissa so much it hurts. What I did to her is the worst possible thing a friend could do. I need to talk to someone about it, and I don't dare mention to Kurt how bad I'm hurting.

Trisha already brought up my concerns about Kurt not expressing his feelings openly. She used words like, "Lydia feels like you may be carrying around a tremendous amount of anger that you aren't discussing with her." She then looked from Kurt to me and back to Kurt as she patiently waited for him to respond.

Trisha looked me in the eye and stated, "Kurt is having a hard time figuring out your feelings toward the baby. He's nervous that you aren't going to create a bond with the baby. He feels you think he doesn't want you to love the baby."

I was crying so hard I could barely get my words out. I was sweating. I was a mess! Kurt was holding my hand and rubbing my back.

We both agreed we needed to set aside time at night to talk through our anxieties. She suggested that, along with our twice weekly sessions with her, we also set up a weekly session of our own without Trisha. She asked us to write down our topics of discussion before we had our sessions so that we would be thinking ahead about what we needed to get off our chests.

We decided to have date night for our sessions without Trisha. We got a laugh when Trisha reminded us that after the baby is born we aren't going to get much alone time, so take what we can now, even if it's a therapy date.

January 5, 2010

Kurt and I had our first therapy date night together last night. I'm so worn out from it that I dumped Jayna and Sadie off at school this morning (Thank God Christmas break is over) and plopped down on the couch in my robe with a vente half-caff vanilla latte from Starbucks drive-thru. I lost myself in a novel for the entire morning.

We have a session with Trisha at 1:30 this afternoon, and Kurt is picking me up for lunch beforehand. I'm determined not to cry through this session! I'm determined to get as much counseling in as possible in the next six weeks or so before I deliver.

There are so many questions I need to ask him. I wish I could do it alone, without a therapist, but I want Trisha to hear his response, so I can hash it out with her over and over and analyze it in our sessions apart from Kurt.

That is one of the things I miss the most about Marissa—hashing out every little petty thing in our lives together. We could over analyze everything to bits until we were so sick of talking about it that, finally, whatever it was didn't bother us anymore.

At some point, I'd like to talk to Trisha about how to deal with Marissa when I see her at school. Do I smile or say hi? Do I look the other way? Do I just avoid her at all costs? People are starting to notice that we aren't speaking anymore—we've always been inseparable. I see the glances and can't actually hear the whispers, but I'm no fool. Women talk. Would anyone ever speculate anything such as this? I swear, if this secret ever got out, we would leave town.

Sadie heard Nicholas's playful scream from outside her window and saw the golf cart careening left then right. Her dad was driving crazy through the yard, dodging trees, weaving in and out. When he hit the cement, he peeled out, leaving black tire marks. Nicholas was in heaven—he loved golf cart rides. He used to fall asleep and take an entire nap, riding around the neighborhood.

Looking at the clock, Sadie realized Travis was done with football practice. She needed a break from the diaries, so she called him. She didn't mention to Travis what she was reading. She wanted to keep it to herself. She felt the weight of it all, but didn't feel the need to unload it on anyone.

Nicholas's bedroom was in the front of the house, overlooking the driveway. Later, when Sadie walked in to put away a pile of clean clothes, she noticed her dad walking Marissa to her car. Watching them kiss and hug was still weird.

The dormer window in Nicholas's room was open, so Sadie heard her dad tell Marissa he loved her. It both saddened her that he had moved on and relieved her that he had. She heard a mourning dove wind up and sing its cooing song. Sadie sang along with the bird, "You'll be okay, kay, kay . . ."

She felt her heart softening towards Marissa as the weeks went by, but it was still so strange seeing the two of them together. When would it feel normal? Would it ever?

Nicholas came bounding up the steps, screaming Sadie's name, telling her all about the movie, the popcorn, the blue slushy, the box of Nerds Marissa bought him, and the crazy golf cart ride.

Nicholas was so happy after spending time with Marissa, especially since time with her meant more time with Dad. Nicholas didn't ask to look through the photo albums of Mom all that much anymore. He didn't watch the videos as often.

With Marissa in their lives, he wasn't as clingy to Sadie. He hadn't come in her room in the middle of the night, crying. It used to be every other night. He had slowly stopped being Sadie's shadow around the house and had started playing more independently. Maybe it was school? More likely it was Marissa.

Sadie took the time and sat down on his floor and asked him questions about the movie; she gave him her full attention. He was talking a mile a minute, his mouth and lips still blue from the slushy, his shirt and hair smelling faintly of popcorn, butter, and Marissa's perfume.

After the full report, Sadie filled the bath with extra bubbles and pretended to be the bathtub monster. She scooped handfuls of bubbles out and chased him around his room, putting them in his hair and on his nose.

Nicholas was laughing that deep belly laugh that Sadie loved. She cornered him and tickled him until he fell to the floor with laughter. Once she finally got him in the tub, they gave each other beards with the bubbles and shaved them off with fake plastic razors.

When she tucked him in bed, she lay with him until he fell asleep, then went and changed into her own pajamas and snuck back into his bed for the night. She missed him kicking her all night long, hogging the bed by lying sideways and taking all the covers.

CHAPTER 54

Kurt

Kurt held the video camera, and Marissa snapped a variety of pictures. Minutes later, the pictures were uploaded onto Instagram and Facebook.

Sadie looked beautiful in her pink dress. She looked grown up. She looked like her mother. Or maybe she moved like her mother. He wished she could be here.

Kurt and Sadie made eye contact, and he felt Sadie knew exactly what was going through his mind. Sadie winked at him. Lydia had always winked at her husband.

Kurt was far more comfortable sending Sadie off to the dance with Travis than Dylan. The group of eight, including Paige and Cody as well as Myla and Jacob and Kyla and Cameron, posed for the camera and then piled into a gigantic Hummer limo to go pick up another six friends.

"When I went to these dances, I spent the entire day washing and waxing my Mustang. We didn't know of such luxury," said Kurt as they pulled away.

"At least we don't have to worry about them drinking and driving," added Marissa, kissing Kurt.

"No, but those kids can get into plenty of trouble in that thing."

Marissa swatted Kurt. "Stop worrying. Let's go. Our reservations are in half an hour."

CHAPTER 55

Sadie

Thanksgiving break meant a five-day weekend. Sadie's school was off from Wednesday thru Sunday, but Travis wasn't off until Thursday, so Wednesday was going to be a girls' day. Paige had spent the night, and they slept late and were loafing on the couch with Jayna, Chrissie, and Nicholas watching *Polar Express* (Nicholas's pick). He was definitely getting a jump on the holidays. He voted to watch *A Christmas Carol* next.

Marissa was coming over shortly, as well as Myla and Kyla, and they were going to spend the afternoon baking pumpkin and apple pies, preparing the stuffing, peeling the potatoes, and making homemade bread.

The first thing Marissa made was a batch of pumpkin cookies to be eaten as they baked. For some reason, it made Sadie think of her mom's brownies. She hadn't eaten a brownie in a year and a half.

Before she knew it, she was grabbing the ingredients. She had watched her mom make them so often that she hadn't any need for a recipe; although she knew her mom had written it down and taped it inside the door of the spice cupboard.

Marissa said they tasted like heaven when she bit into the gooey brownie. Sadie loved it when Marissa said, "Lydia is probably eating one with us right now." Tears pricked their eyes as they gripped each other in hugs. It was a really cool moment.

Myla showed up with black aprons for everyone, each personalized on the front with white embroidered letters. Myla's mom had her own little sewing company she ran from home. She hemmed, stitched, embroidered, and could create anything from a simple scarf, to an elegant gown, to a baby blanket.

The black aprons were soon white, covered in flour. The house smelled amazing and sounded full and happy with a kitchen of women; even Jayna and Chrissie were helping, more eating than baking, but trying, nonetheless. Nicholas was bouncing off the walls from sugar, and Marissa kept handing him spoonfuls of brownie batter, cookie dough, and mugs of hot chocolate piled with whipped cream. He was so in love with her.

Thanksgiving dinner included Marissa and Paige, Andrea, Benton, Travis, and his sister Bella, and of course, the sly mouth of Jayna, and entertainment provided by Nicholas. It was the first Thanksgiving that they didn't spend with grandparents, cousins, Aunt Stacy, or even Aunt Nevie and Aunt Josie. Very non-traditional, but Sadie was okay with it.

Marissa had spent the night for the first time so she could put the turkey in the oven first thing in the morning. She had personally asked permission from Sadie. Marissa hugged Sadie, which she had started doing a lot now. Sadie found it comforting.

The Lions won the game, crushing the Bears with a score of 34-17, so the house sounded like fifty people were inside, hooting and hollering. Everyone was full and content. Sadie was truly thankful.

The rest of the weekend was low key and relaxing. Even though Sadie had finished several of her mother's diaries over the past few months, she went back and reread the one around Nicholas's birth over the span of the weekend.

January 28, 2010

Approximately three weeks until I hold this baby in my arms. Some days the anxiety is overwhelming; other days I am so at peace with it that I forget the circumstances of it all.

I had a horrible dream last night. We were in the birthing room, and when the doctor handed Kurt the scissors to cut the cord, he stabbed me in the throat with them! Luckily, my eyes popped open and that was the end of the dream. I swallowed hard, rolled over, and watched him sleep peacefully for the next hour.

Our counseling sessions are going well. I think it's really helping us both to get everything off our chests. Kurt admitted that this baby isn't being born under ideal conditions, but that he would love the child as if it were his own blood.

Sadie skimmed over an entry talking about her parents' sex life, ew. She quickly scanned over Lydia's words about how awkward it was having sex with her husband while being pregnant with someone else's child. Her mom stressed that not having sex would be worse because it would put a divider between the two of them, but she felt such shame whenever they were intimate.

Lydia felt she wanted to initiate, but feared she would repulse Kurt and get turned down. Kurt felt he wanted to remain intimate with his wife, but never knew how to read her, whether it was the right time.

Sadie felt guilty reading it, but as weird as it was, she was curious, and she had thought about it a lot since she first read it weeks ago.

Anyway, through a nudge per their counselor, she urged them to stay as intimate as possible. She had suggested many ways other than just sex to remain close through the pregnancy. It sounded as if they took a lot of baths together and gave each other a lot of massages. Luckily, Lydia didn't go into great detail. Ew again.

February 2, 2010

Today in our session I asked Kurt how he responded when people came up to him and asked about me and the baby. Does he say we are all great? We are so excited? We tried and tried? Or does he say it was an "oops" baby? I mean I wonder what goes through his head.

At first, he seemed taken aback at my question. I couldn't tell if he was upset or relieved that he was about to get something off his chest. His answer was simple.

"I tell people it was definitely a surprise. I also say that I would never regret having another child."

We left it at that.

February 5, 2010

I saw Marissa today. I was walking out of the post office, and we met face to face on the stairs. I was going down and she was coming up. We looked at each other, and I saw her eyes shift down to my protruding belly.

I had been so hot in the car that I took my coat off. I only had a fitted cotton maternity shirt on with a scarf around my neck, showing my belly off in its enormity.

I managed a smile, but couldn't even get the word "hey" out. I just about tripped on the steps. As quickly as Marissa looked at my face, and then at my belly, she looked past me as if I weren't even there.

It would have hurt less if she had spat obscenities in my face. I almost wish she had.

In the car, I cried all the way home and have been a wreck all evening. I confided to Kurt that I feel like I need to be punished. I want to be punished. I want to show both of them that I take the blame and that I'm sorry.

Kurt said being punished was ridiculous. I can't help but wonder if he wants me to feel this remorseful.

February 8, 2010

The doctor said I was dilated three centimeters today. She also said this baby will come a lot quicker than Sadie and Jayna had.

Kurt called and asked me to meet him for lunch today. The first words out of his mouth were, "Nicole if it's a girl and Nicholas if it's a boy." I had suggested Ginger or Gabe earlier, but that all went out the window when I saw his face. He was excited!

I said one word: "perfect!"

He said that was good, because he already bought the wooden letters to be painted and hung in the nursery. I asked what we will do with the remaining h-a-s if it's a little Nicole, since you can't take painted letters back. His response was her middle name could be Ash. "Hmm" was all I could say to that!

February 14, 2010

I thought for sure I would run into Marissa at school today for the Valentine's parties, but I escaped. I arrived early to help set up Jayna's classroom, and I stayed late to help tear down in Sadie's room. Luckily, there were no hallway run-ins.

Pregnant women get so much attention. Everyone is always asking how you're feeling, how you're sleeping, and whether you're swollen or not. Not to mention, everyone decides to tell you one of their own pregnancy/birth stories. I swear I don't do this. Or if I have, I won't ever again!

Anyway, I can't deny the slight anxiousness that has settled into my stomach that will no doubt stay there until I deliver. Even though Kurt and I are doing fairly well inside counseling and out, I wouldn't be human if I weren't slightly panicked.

Funny, the night he came home with Chinese, I thought our marriage was going to survive. Now I know there are so many different levels to base a marriage on. Living in the same household does not constitute a marriage. Having sex doesn't constitute a marriage, nor does eating meals together, or discussing the children or finances. Those things are small parts; there is so much more. It's a feeling, a deeper bond of respect and trust, a true selfless love.

I broke the trust and have to earn that back. In my eyes, infidelity is one of the most selfish acts a person can ever commit. It's about so many other people than the two involved. It affects other spouses, children, usually friends, sometimes co-workers—the list can go on and on.

Realizing what I have done and the mess I have created kills me, but I know how much worse the damage could have been if Kurt weren't so level-headed and willing to love me fully in the biggest fault of my life. I'd say I dodged a bullet headed straight for my heart.

Actually, I need to be thankful that Marissa has chosen to hate me in silence. Losing her as my best friend has been torture, but she could have chosen to make my life really, really miserable. She could have let the painful, embarrassing truth fly, she could make a scene when we run into each other, and she could easily turn the women at the tennis club away from me. The other mothers at school would despise me if they knew the truth, and so would the faculty. The whispers and stares would follow me like the plague. I hate to think about how my girls would be affected.

The months and years to come won't be without challenges, but I count my lucky stars.

February 19, 2010

Trisha started off today prompting Kurt. "Kurt has something he wants to say to you, Lydia," she said, crossing her legs, grinning at me.

"I forgive you, Lydia," Kurt said. "I think there has been a part of me that has been really angry . . . okay, pissed. It's done. I've let it all go. I love you. I love this baby. I forgive you. Will you forgive yourself? For me? For us? For the baby?"

I cried as we hugged, no surprise there, but Kurt cried too. I've only seen Kurt cry one other time, when his grandfather passed away.

My contractions started after that, as if on cue, and got stronger throughout the day. I really hope I make it through the night. I do not want to go into the hospital at 3:00 a.m.

Sadie and Jayna were keeping track of my contractions after school until they went to bed. They asked if they could skip school and go to the hospital with us, but I told them they would have to wait until after the baby was born.

I already know this is the last night I will go to bed with this baby inside me. Our household will forever be changed. I pray to God that he takes good care of us all. Contractions are about twenty minutes apart.

Kurt is outside, plowing the driveway after four inches of fresh snow fell today. We are all preparing! I'm (hopefully) going to get my last night of restful sleep before being a slave to the demands of hungry cries and wet diapers.

CHAPTER 56

Sadie

Marissa and Paige were now at the Booker household more often than not. Sometimes they would go to Marissa's for dinner, but Marissa spent a lot of time in "Sadie's" kitchen. Sadie couldn't complain, since Marissa was always cooking meals, leaving leftovers, and getting everyone involved in the clean-up so the burden didn't always fall on Sadie.

Once, Sadie came home from a night at the movies with Travis to find all the laundry caught up. Marissa had explained that Nicholas had picked out two horrible movies, giving her an excuse to get off the couch and switch up loads and fold.

Marissa seemed to be careful about overstepping her boundaries; she was always consulting Sadie and asking her if it was okay if she did this or that. The relationship wasn't without flaws, and Sadie had her moments, but it had come a really long way. Most of all, Sadie felt respected by Marissa, and she was trying hard to respect her as well.

Marissa had urged Sadie and Jayna to get out every single box of Christmas decorations, and with her help, they managed to create a festive Christmas atmosphere, similar to the one Lydia had created year after year.

On the bright side, with Marissa around, Sadie had been able to be more of a teenager. She still did most of the laundry and cleaning, but since Marissa would come over a couple of times a week and make dinner, she not only stocked the fridge with extra meals, she would tidy up and run the vacuum or empty the dishwasher. The nights she was over, Nicholas usually clung to her and Kurt, so Sadie felt more like a sister and less like a mother.

Sadie didn't feel guilty spending time with her friends and Travis, knowing Nicholas was getting so much attention from Marissa. It had become customary for Nicholas to ask their dad every morning at breakfast if Marissa was coming over that evening.

So far, Marissa had not spent the night again since the night before Thanksgiving. Thank God they also escaped a marriage proposal at Christmas. Sadie had been nervous. She had hoped her dad would bring it up beforehand if he was thinking of popping the question, but she was still on pins and needles Christmas Day, wondering if he was going to get down on one knee.

The holidays came and went fast. Each one they celebrated without their mother got both easier and more difficult, if that were possible. It was easier in a sense that they were getting used to it. It was harder because the traditions and special touches that she put into every holiday were things of the past, nothing but memories, and for Nicholas, the memories faded, only upheld through videos and pictures.

Every once in a while, Sadie and Jayna would make their mother's famous brownies and watch the home movies. They both read Lydia's diaries. They often snuck down to the basement and dug through the bins, hiding a few diaries in their rooms as they read them, and then snuck back down to put them in their respective bins. They suspected their dad knew they read them, but he hadn't said anything and they didn't talk to him about it.

Sometimes they read their mother's diaries together, and other times they weren't even reading from the same year. Sadie and Jayna had grown closer over the past several months. A shared love for reading and discussing the diaries together helped, but also, Jayna had done a lot of growing up.

Sadie and Jayna shared many laughs and tears as they relived many of their childhood stories, achievements, and milestones in their mother's handwriting.

After Sadie finished reading the diaries of 2009 and 2010 that covered Lydia's pregnancy and the birth of Nicholas, she hid the box on the top shelf, way in the back of the storage room. She knew her dad had shuffled around through it, which made Sadie glad, because after reading through those months, she wanted to tell her dad herself what she was reading. They never discussed it, but Sadie thought those diaries were very healing for both of them.

Early spring arrived, and Sadie was packing up her bag after tennis practice. Paige was supposed to give her a ride home because Kurt was getting the tires rotated and the oil changed on her Infiniti, but Paige wasn't anywhere in sight. She hadn't shown up for practice.

Just as Sadie was about to text Paige, she heard Marissa yell her name. Marissa explained that Paige had gone home sick during last period and had left school in such a hurry she had forgotten her cell in her locker, so she couldn't text Sadie to let her know where she was.

After Sadie helped Marissa break into Paige's locker and retrieve her cell, Marissa suggested they stop by Party Central and stock up on some items for Sadie's 17th birthday party. Sadie had a flashback of her sweet sixteen party last year when Marissa showed up to help her dad chaperone.

Sadie thought of two things. One, where had the year gone? She was turning seventeen in two days! Two, her dad and Marissa had basically been seeing each other for a year! Sadie was more excited about this year's garage party than she was for her sixteenth. She wasn't as sad and broken, and she had Travis, who made her feel real and confident and loved. Last year seemed like a world away.

On their way home, Marissa pulled into the small quaint French diner with killer food. She suggested they have a quiet dinner together to celebrate Sadie's birthday. Marissa quickly called Kurt and told him what they were up to as she gathered her purse and shot out of the car into the cool spring air.

Sadie and Marissa found a small table by the window. The signs of spring were blooming. The pear and crab trees were full of beautiful white and dark pink flowers, and green buds swayed in the wind on the maple trees.

As soon as the waiter took their order, Marissa began speaking. "I know it's been months since you found out what happened between your mom and Marcus, and we've kind of swept it under the rug and moved on, but I want you to know that I don't blame Lydia for what happened, Sadie.

"Marcus was slime. He had been cheating on me for a long time. He took advantage of your mother. Between the alcohol and her medication, she had no idea what she had done. I believe that with all my heart."

Sadie knew all of this, but hearing Marissa speak it, like she truly believed it, was comforting.

"In fact, I never really blamed her from the beginning. I was devastated that my marriage was over, I was devastated that I had lost my best friend, and I was really angry that Lydia was having a baby when I had so desperately wanted another one and Marcus refused."

Sadie watched Marissa as a tear rolled down her cheek.

"I missed your mother every single day, but how do you keep a friendship under those circumstances? Where do you begin, you know?"

"She was pregnant with your husband's child. I can't imagine," said Sadie, appalled at what came out of her mouth.

"I knew your mother inside and out, Sadie. There was no way, in her right mind, she ever would have been capable of such an act, but I still couldn't bring myself to tell her that, forgive her, and move on."

Marissa looked out the window, wiping a tear away. Sadie was beginning to understand how difficult the situation was for Marissa.

"It was easiest for me to completely remove her from my life. Those were the loneliest years. I would see her and Nicholas or bump into all of you as a family, and I wanted to be a part of your lives again, but I just couldn't. I just couldn't," she repeated. "It hurt too badly. I was angry and jealous."

Sadie remembered digging through Lydia's diary until she finally discovered how Marissa found out about what happened on the boat. Marissa had no idea that Sadie knew. Lydia had agreed to a day at the beach. She agreed to tennis matches, lunches, pedicures, and play dates for almost two weeks before Kurt finally forced her to fess up or risk Marissa hearing it from Marcus.

Lydia had finally gone to Marissa's house just before midnight. She pulled Marissa out on the front porch under a warm, starry summer night and told her she was pregnant. At first, Marissa congratulated Lydia and hugged her.

Lydia pulled away from Marissa and stood up from the wicker couch. She was immediately crying. She told Marissa it wasn't Kurt's baby. She told her she had no recollection of the sexual encounter because she was very drunk and medicated. Finally, she confessed that it had happened on Marcus's boat.

Marissa hadn't even screamed at Lydia. She had thrown her hands over her mouth and stared at Lydia in horror as Lydia scrambled for words, excuses, pleading, anything. Marissa had finally told Lydia to just go, go and don't ever come back, and never speak to her again.

Sadie looked into Marissa's eyes. "So how can you be so"—Sadie searched for the right word— "so tolerant of

Nicholas now? I mean which came first? Your feelings for Nicholas or feelings for my dad?"

"Nicholas." Marissa didn't hesitate one bit. "The day I found out about your mom's cancer, I called her. We cried on the phone for hours. We apologized, we forgave, and we tried to forget as best as we could. I went to your house the next day and hung out with her and Nicholas from the moment you girls were at school until she had to pick you up.

"I fell in love with Nicholas instantly. We made up for a ton of lost time while your mom was sick. We hung out almost daily while you girls were at school. I held your mom's hair back after chemo so your dad could have a break and go to work. I played with Nicholas while your mom took naps. I ran to the store for her and helped make meals.

"It was good for both of us. I guess you could say it humbled us; we both had to swallow our pride. For me, I needed to show her that I loved her, that I knew she wasn't at fault. For Lydia, it took everything in her to accept my help and forgive herself.

"As for your father, that truly only came about a year ago. I would call and check up on him. Sometimes we would meet for coffee. We would sit together at your tennis matches and talk. It slowly evolved."

Sadie and Marissa both wiped back tears. Thank goodness their food hadn't been delivered yet.

Marissa went on to tell Sadie that over the next several months she and Lydia had slowly reconciled their relationship. They had talked for hours until they worked through the hurt.

"Your mom asked me to take care of him, Sadie. One morning when we were having coffee, she asked me if I would help Kurt after she passed. She asked if I would watch over all of you."

"I don't get it. Then why did you two keep it a secret that you reconnected?"

"The risk of anyone finding out that Marcus was Nicholas's father was too great. You and Paige were older, and we didn't want you two to start asking questions about what we fought over in the first place. Your mom and I enjoyed our alone time together mending our friendship while you kids were at school. I don't know if it was necessarily the right thing to do, but we knew there wasn't much time left."

Sadie understood. She only wished she had known this all along. She wouldn't have accused Marissa the way she had. "Why did you take the blame? I mean for the past year or for however long you and Dad have been seeing each other, why didn't you just blurt out that it wasn't your fault? I had always thought you'd done something horrible to my mom."

Marissa's lip trembled. "Your mother was an amazing woman. I didn't want you to see her in any other way. If you hadn't read her diary, I would still gladly be taking the blame."

Sadie lost it. How could she hate a woman like that? The tears came pouring out just as the waiter brought their food. The poor guy was caught off guard and had no idea how to react. He plopped the food down like it was going to bite him and asked if everything was okay as he was already backing away. Sadie and Marissa both shook their heads and he vanished.

"As much as I could have dug a grave for Marcus, I couldn't do that to Paige, either. He's her father. She would have hated me if I told her the truth back then; she wouldn't have accepted it. I think it's still hard for her."

They both played with their food more than they ate, and the waiter never came to check on them until they had both set their forks down. He had the check in hand as he cleared their plates. They giggled as he walked away. "We've scared him!" said Sadie.

"Someday, when you're a parent, Sadie, you'll understand. You will do anything to protect your children from harm."

Sadie thought of Nicholas, thought of how they would be protecting him from the truth about his real father for several years. "I think I'm already getting it." She smiled.

They left the French restaurant still hungry, so they decided to walk the streets of town with an ice cream cone. Sadie felt like she was reconnecting with Marissa, her second mother from childhood. Marissa confessed she never in her wildest dreams had ever pictured her and Kurt together.

They rounded the corner and started walking toward the river when Sadie heard the familiar cooing of a mourning dove. She turned around, and sure enough the bird was sitting on the roof top behind her. "I think Mom would be okay with it." Sadie had no idea if this was true, but it came out before she knew what she had said.

Marissa joked, "I promised your mom I would look after Nicholas. I promised I would keep an eye on all of you, but I never imagined like this."

CHAPTER 57

Sadie

This year when Sadie walked downstairs on her birthday, it felt like years had gone by. Seventeen! She could hardly believe it herself. She woke up to a text message from Travis, wishing her happy birthday.

The kitchen smelled amazing, scented heavily of cinnamon. Her dad had the paper in front of his face, but it was curled down at the top so he could watch something on the *Today Show*.

"Are you seriously making cinnamon rolls?"

"I'm seriously *baking* cinnamon rolls," he answered with a wink. "Marissa dropped them off last night, but I *did* turn the oven on by myself and sprinkled some crumbled topping from a Ziploc bag on them."

Sadie peered at the gooey rolls through the oven window. They looked done. "How much longer?"

Kurt looked surprised by Sadie's question and looked at his watch. "Uh, I guess I forgot to set the timer."

Sadie laughed as she pulled on the oven mitts and warmed her face with the hot aroma rolling out of the oven. She pulled them out and wondered if her dad would have thought to check on the rolls or if they would have burnt to a crisp if Sadie hadn't come downstairs.

Her dad came up from behind Sadie. "They're perfect, just like my little girl. Happy Birthday, sweetie." He gave Sadie a kiss on the cheek and she hugged him. "I'm too young to have a seventeen-year-old!"

Jayna and Nicholas must have smelled the rolls because they both came downstairs, asking what smelled so good. Jayna never got out of bed with ease before school. Usually, Sadie threatened to leave without her, and she scurried around the house getting her things together so she didn't have to take the bus.

Kurt walked out of the room and came back in with an enormous bouquet of balloons. "I picked those out," cheered Nicholas.

"Oh yeah, Happy Birthday, Sadie," said Jayna through a yawn, already getting herself a plate.

"Why don't we put a candle in the cinnamon rolls and sing to your sister first," suggested Kurt.

Sadie flipped the cinnamon rolls onto a plate from the Bundt pan and they all admired the buttery goo before them. They lit the candles (a giant 17) and took a picture that Sadie sent in a text to Marissa, thanking her.

Before leaving for school, Sadie sat on her window seat and opened a letter from her mom, reserved for her seventeenth birthday. Sadie had birthday letters to open until she was twenty-five.

Dear Sadie,

Happy 17th birthday, my lovely Sadie!!!

I can only imagine the beautiful young woman you are turning into. My guess is you look more like your aunts and your dad than you will ever look like me. You may favor your father's side of the family when it comes to looks, like eye and hair color and face structure, but you'd have to be blind not to see you inherited my mannerisms, posture, and build.

I know I'm constantly telling you in these letters that I am with you, but, Sadie, I am, I promise. Quiet yourself and you will feel it.

Whatever your day brings forth, be happy and always stay true to yourself. Remember, it's a choice!

Please have a great big party. Every day God has given you is a day to celebrate.

Your dad and I were clueless the day we brought you home from the hospital. The only thing we were certain about was that we loved you. You're an amazing girl, Sadie! Happy Birthday!

Love, Mom

Sadie's party was huge! Scary huge! When she added in all of her friends, Travis and his friends and their girlfriends, the garage was packed. Jayna had talked her way into staying home for the party this year. Kurt threatened Jayna that she and Chrissie were going to be watched like hawks.

This year, Sadie was grateful for Marissa's help. Along with Myla, Kyla, and Paige, they had decorated the garage to look more like a club. Kurt had cleaned out the winter clutter, scraped off the cobwebs, and swept the floor until it shined.

The girls hung strings of twinkling lights, plugged in the disco balls from their bedrooms, blew up balloons, twisted streamers, and set up a table for drinks, pizza, and munchies. Marissa brought over her chocolate fountain and a cotton candy machine she had borrowed from a co-worker.

Kurt tweaked the speakers to make sure the music would be thumping and booming. It was a good thing their neighbors weren't too close.

It took most of Saturday afternoon to get the look they wanted, but at last it was achieved. The girls weren't wearing formal gowns, but they acted as if they were getting ready for the prom. Sadie's bedroom smelled of nail polish, perfume, hairspray, and lotions. The blow dryer was going, and the curling irons and flat irons had already blown a fuse.

Clothes were strewn all over the floor and bed, and it seemed they each had everyone else's clothes on but their own. Finally, after a good two hours, they had all primped to exhaustion.

When they came downstairs, Travis and Cody were in the kitchen hanging out with Kurt, Marissa, Andrea, and Benton.

Andrea gave Sadie a hug. "I hope you don't mind us crashing your party. We promise to stay inside and leave you kids alone."

Sadie had to hand it to herself; she knew how to throw a party. Probably the best advantage was that she could fit a lot of people in her garage, and she didn't have to be on pins and needles about anything getting destroyed. Kurt was strict about taking keys and doing breath checks before anyone was allowed to leave.

Travis came up from behind Sadie and wrapped his arms around her waist, nuzzling her neck. "Can I dance with the birthday girl?"

Sadie turned into him, and they danced to Pitbull and Flo Rida. Somehow they found their rhythm. She felt like she was on *Dancing with the Stars*. Sadie felt alive and free and completely in love with Travis.

She could feel the crowd parting around them, giving them room to dance. Everyone was yelling and cheering them on. Sadie wasn't the least bit embarrassed—she was having the time of her life, soaking up every moment of her night.

When the song was over, Travis dipped and kissed her. Everyone clapped, so Sadie ate it up and bowed. After that, it seemed everyone let loose and danced the night away.

It was 3:00 a.m. when Sadie stumbled, exhausted, into her bedroom. She found a spot on the floor, since her bed was already taken, and curled up next to Myla.

Travis and Cody were sleeping on the pullout couch in the basement. *Crazy*, thought Sadie. Never in a million years would her dad have been okay with Dylan staying over at their house. Sadie couldn't help but wonder if Dylan had thought about her at all on her birthday.

Dylan would have tried sneaking upstairs to Sadie's room. Sadie was glad she didn't have to worry about that with Travis. She wanted to wait for a physical relationship with Travis, and he was a gentleman about it.

Her eyes were so heavy she didn't have the energy to ponder it. She jumped when her cell chirped with a text. Sadie smiled when she saw it was Travis from the basement saying "I love you" and "Goodnight."

CHAPTER 58

Kurt

Kurt woke up feeling anything but well rested. Something smelled really good though, bacon? He took a quick shower, threw a T-shirt and shorts on, and followed his nose to the kitchen.

He found Jayna standing over the griddle, frying bacon, Sadie was adding cheese, ham, and veggies to the egg mixture in the omelet maker, and even Nicholas was helping load the toaster with English muffins.

Kurt helped himself to a cup of coffee. He preferred the way Sadie made it over himself, and took a big gulp. "You look like hell," said Jayna.

"Watch your language," he said, scowling at her. Her mouth was getting bad. "And jeez, thanks for noticing." Kurt made the rounds to each of his kids, kissed their foreheads, and told them good morning.

He didn't have to ask what the occasion was. It really wasn't an occasion anyway, more like an honoring. Kurt was glad the two-year anniversary of Lydia's passing was on a Saturday. He hadn't slept more than a couple of hours last night. He had woken up around two o'clock and couldn't fall back to sleep.

When Kurt woke up and saw the full moon out his window, he immediately thought of Lydia; he wondered if it had been her that woke him. He wondered if her spirit was always with him. Did she know what he thought and felt? He wondered what heaven was really like. He touched her side of the bed. It had been empty for two years!

For the past several weeks, Kurt had been thinking about the next step with Marissa. He thought about suggesting she prep her house to sell, maybe even go ahead and list it, but did that mean he would be asking her to move in with him, or did that need to be followed with a proposal? Was he ready for that? Were the kids ready for that? But really, what were they waiting for? Was timing everything? Or was there never really the *perfect* time for anything?

All in all, both things were enough to keep him awake for most of the night. The coffee was starting to kick in and the laughter over the mutilated English muffins, a la Nicholas, was bringing him around. In the process of buttering the bread, Nicholas had managed to tear it apart and litter it with holes. He hadn't quite mastered the art of spreading yet. Kurt had to admit it was still pretty darn good (due to the butter dripping off the sides).

Nicholas was very proud of his perfectly skewered watermelon. He'd been obsessed with fruit kabobs ever since Marissa had made him some to try to get him to eat more fruit. Now every piece of fruit that passed his lips had to come from a skewer.

They made a small toast to Lydia without letting the sadness of the day overcome them. Sadie had cut handfuls of lilacs and scattered them in vases around the house—exactly what her mother always had done the entire month of May.

After breakfast, Kurt found himself looking over the Sunday paper, observing his daughters cleaning up the kitchen, with Nicholas on the floor playing with modeling clay. Lydia would be so proud—he was so proud. He remembered thinking to himself, praying, that if they could make it through the first two years, they would be okay. They'd made it. They *were* okay. Actually, they were good.

Marissa came over that afternoon with gifts for the kids. Nicholas was thrilled with his first pair of rollerblades, especially since Marissa was the only other person who had a pair, which meant he was going to have her all to himself on occasion.

Sadie and Jayna were given something much more sentimental. Marissa explained that when she and Lydia were in college, they had been out shopping, and as sort of a joke, they bought the classic best friends necklace shaped like a heart with a jagged split down the middle. The girls would wear them from time to time and would even sport them in adulthood when they wanted to have a laugh.

They had both kept them, even during their rough period. Lydia had given Marissa her half when she was sick. She had wrapped it up as a gift and given it to her to keep. Marissa wanted Sadie and Jayna to have them. They bickered and fought and were always annoyed with each other, but at the end of the day, they were best friends and loved each other dearly.

CHAPTER 59

Sadie

Travis discreetly swatted Sadie's butt as he passed the table she was taking orders from. She tried to keep a straight face as she took the order from the elderly couple she was waiting on.

It was quite ironic how the entire gang all got jobs at Snug Harbor for the summer. Sadie, Travis, Cody, Paige, Myla, and Kyla were all hanging at the beach in early June when Sadie came up with the idea that they all apply.

Travis had applied at a local car wash and hadn't heard anything yet. Sadie was in charge of Nicholas only two days each week, and Jayna two, which freed up Sadie's schedule.

Kyla was scooping ice cream but wasn't getting enough hours to even pay for gas. Paige and Myla hadn't given a job much thought. They were always so busy with academics and getting their college portfolios polished, but Sadie convinced them it would be fun and an added bonus on their college applications.

On the way home from the beach, they filled out their applications. It just so happened that the mother of a girl Sadie and Paige had hung out with at tennis camp the past several years was the manager at the restaurant.

She was hesitant to hire a bunch of high-school kids, but she was always losing the college kids halfway through August. They promised they would be available through Labor Day, and the jobs were theirs.

Travis and Cody were freaking out because they had never waited on anyone but themselves their entire lives, okay, except for the occasional Mother's Day breakfast or a generous offer to a grandparent. They were soon enthusiastic when they were told about the potential to make a killing in tips.

Sadie and Paige were also hired as servers, and Myla and Kyla were hosts. They were having the time of their lives this summer. Most days went like this: carpool and hang out at the beach all day, shower and get ready in the beach pavilion showers (disgusting, but worth it), and work in the restaurant at night.

Fourth of July came in with a bang. After working the dinner rush at the restaurant, the gang stayed in Grand Haven for the fireworks. Myla was casually seeing a kid named Brad, who also worked at the restaurant and lived in Grand Haven. He had started hanging with them at the beach sometimes and invited all of them over to his house after the fireworks.

Sadie was sitting on Travis's lap when the call on her cell came through. The screen displayed Andrea Sutherland. "Your mom is calling me," said Sadie to Travis.

"Why is she calling you and not me?" asked Travis, checking his phone to make sure the ringer hadn't accidentally been bumped off.

Sadie answered, and her face instantly fell flat. She gasped at Andrea's quick and desperate words.

"Sadie, your dad, Marissa, Nicholas, Jayna, and Chrissie have been in a car accident. You kids need to head home now! Drive straight to Spectrum Hospital."

Instantly, Sadie was in tears and on her feet, frantically trying to find Paige while listening to Andrea's instructions at the same time. The car ride from Grand Haven to Grand

Rapids seemed to take forever, even though Sadie knew Travis was pushing eighty mph.

Andrea explained that she and Benton had been driving behind Kurt on their way home from watching fireworks when a car ran a red light and T-boned Sadie's entire family, including Marissa. They were hit on the passenger side, Marissa and Nicholas's side.

When Andrea had first called Sadie, they were following the ambulance to the hospital. All Andrea kept saying was that they were in good hands and it happened only five miles from the hospital, so they would be getting care fast.

Paige was in the backseat with her head buried in Cody's chest, crying. Sadie suddenly found herself too scared for tears. Andrea had said very little on the phone. Maybe she didn't know. Maybe she didn't want to say how bad they really were. Maybe she didn't want to give false hope. Maybe they wouldn't make it.

Sadie felt numb as Travis held her hand. She felt him looking at her, but she couldn't turn her face toward him. Instead, she stared out the passenger window. She was glad he wasn't asking her if she was okay or saying everything would be okay. Sadie knew all too well that was not always true and hated those statements.

Andrea met them in the lobby and escorted them to the ICU floor. Sadie knew that was not good. Benton, Chrissie's parents, and two doctors were there, huddled in a circle. She got full reports, but honestly, all Sadie heard were things like internal bleeding, head trauma, broken ribs, fractured pelvis, and ruptured spleen. The list seemed endless, and she had no idea who suffered from what because she couldn't concentrate.

Her thoughts were spinning wildly out of control. Control. Sadie realized one thing was for certain. She hated not being in control. Possibly she had always been this way; possibly since her mom was diagnosed. Whichever, she hated the fact that she had no control over her family's fate.

All Sadie cared to know was if everyone would live. She could deal with the rest of the stuff later. Luckily, Paige interrupted the doctor and asked if they were all going to survive.

"We're doing our best to treat their injuries. Nicholas is in critical condition, and we have stabilized Marissa and Chrissie. Kurt and Jayna have several broken bones that we're treating."

Before walking away, the doctor said they could see both Kurt and Jayna shortly. Kurt had three broken ribs and a torn rotator cuff. Jayna had a broken femur and . . . Sadie honestly couldn't remember, just that they were in the best shape.

Sadie and Paige both crumpled to the stiff, pale blue couch in the family waiting area and cried in each other's arms. "Nicholas, not Nicholas, and your mom, I'm so sorry Paige."

It was then that Sadie realized something. She loved Marissa. She couldn't bear to lose Marissa. She was over it. She didn't care that her dad and Marissa were dating. In fact, she was glad. They were a perfect match, and she was incredibly lucky that Marissa and Paige were back in their lives. Why? Why, God, did it take a car accident for it to sink in?

The next hour seemed endless. Sadie's head was pounding, her eyes and face were a red, blotchy mess, and she was sweating from nerves and anxiousness. When the doctor came into the waiting room, Sadie felt a huge weight being lifted off her shoulders. The look on the doctor's face told Sadie everything. She had a lot of practice reading the faces of doctors over the course of her mother's illness.

Even though Sadie, Paige, and everyone else in the room jumped to their feet at the sight of her, Dr. Kenshaw sat down and gestured for them to do so as well. She reported that Nicholas had been upgraded from critical condition to stable. His spleen had ruptured from the trauma of the accident and was causing internal bleeding into the abdominal cavity. They had to do an emergency surgery called a partial splenectomy, where they removed part of the spleen and sutured it back up.

The doctor said that Nicholas should improve quickly over the next several days. He also had several broken bones in his right arm and hand, but his life-threatening injuries were no longer life-threatening—that was all Sadie cared about.

Marissa was now in fair condition. Luckily, she didn't have any internal bleeding or organ damage, which was a concern with a forceful blow to the pelvis. She had a stable pelvic fracture. Dr. Kenshaw had attached a device called an external fixator on Marissa. It had long screws that inserted into the bones on each side and connected to a frame outside the body, helping to stabilize the pelvic area so it could heal.

Dr. Kenshaw said she wasn't sure how badly Marissa's muscles were damaged because of the severe swelling, and that she might walk with a limp for several months after she healed.

"Will she ever be able to play tennis again?" asked Paige.

Dr. Kenshaw smiled. "Give your mom a few months, and she'll be back on the courts." She grabbed one of Paige's hands and one of Sadie's. "If you have any other questions, don't hesitate to hunt me down." She handed them a card with a pager number on it and gave them each a hug.

Another doctor had simultaneously been speaking with Chrissie's parents and she was doing well. Chrissie was being treated for two broken ribs, a punctured lung, and a broken radius and ulna in her arm. Her stay in the hospital would be a couple of weeks, but she would make a full recovery. A huge collective sigh of relief filled the room as the doctors left.

CHAPTER 60

Sadie

The rest of the summer was all out of whack, but the summer of recovering injuries definitely didn't put a damper on anything. Sadie was once again primary caregiver and had to back off her hours a bit at the restaurant, but she was still ranking it an awesome summer, hanging with Travis and her friends.

Jayna and her dad were treated and released in slings and casts after a few days. Nicholas, Marissa, and Chrissie all put in a few weeks at the hospital, but were breezing through therapy and mending well.

By the middle of August, talk of Pentwater was still a go. Everyone was ready to get away, and Marissa and Paige were staying at the cottage the full two weeks with them. Sadie was beyond excited. She and Paige had grown extremely close. They were always together because of Travis and Cody, work, tennis practice, and camp, and something about the accident formed an even tighter bond between the two of them.

Paige was spending more and more time at Sadie's house, creating relationships with all of them, but she took a lot of interest in her half-brother. Anyone that Nicholas could get to play swords for an hour at a time was instantly his best friend. Paige would squirt water guns in the pool and watch hundreds of Nicholas's dives and cannonballs, loving every minute of it. She had a half-brother, and she was getting a chance at being a big sister for the first time in her life, even if Nicholas had no idea.

The week before Pentwater was miracle week for everyone. Casts were removed, crutches were tossed, and the okay was given to be active (in moderation). Bike rides and climbing dunes would most likely be limited, but hanging on the beach, fishing, campfires, mini golf, and serious ice cream indulgences were all highly attainable.

Nicholas recovered like a champ, with no tell-tale signs that he was even injured. He breezed through physical therapy, and his right arm and hand were completely healed. Thank goodness he remembered nothing of the accident and hadn't had a single nightmare. Kurt was still sore and couldn't play football on the beach with Nicholas, but thankfully Travis and Cody were willing to fill in.

Jayna's leg had healed well. She was supposed to be wearing an air cast for the first week of Pentwater, but she "forgot" it at home. "How convenient of you," Sadie had remarked.

Kurt only said, "That's our Jayna." Those two comments had sent Jayna in a rage about how everyone was always ganging up on her.

Sadie rolled her eyes. "Like Dad said, that's our Jayna!"

Pentwater was still the highlight of the summer. The cottage was a bit cramped with Marissa, Paige, and Chrissie also staying for the first week. Chrissie's parents surprisingly didn't bat an eye about letting her stay, not that the accident had been Kurt's fault.

Cody had joked to Paige about her chasing Travis last summer, and they all teased Cody about his fling with Liz. *Crazy how things end up!*

Liz was staying with her grandparents, so Jayna and Chrissie were usually off chasing boys with her. Sadie was thankful for Chrissie—she was the brains and rule-follower of the trio.

Sadie still went for several walks with Andrea. How different their walks were this year from last! She was very lucky to be so close to her boyfriend's mom, she knew that. Paige accompanied them a couple of times, but usually Sadie and Andrea ventured off alone. Marissa still had plenty of healing to do before she was able to walk the beach.

Sadie and Andrea talked about school, the excitement of senior year, Sadie's feelings for Marissa, how Sadie had a new level of respect for Marissa, and how happy her dad was.

Lydia's presence could still be felt in Pentwater. Sadie knew how much her mother had loved being there, but she found it comforting to talk to Andrea about her when they were walking. Sadie could feel how much more she had healed since their walks last year, and she was thankful for that.

In comparison, Pentwater was boring this summer. Last year, Sadie felt like her world was crashing in around her with the Dylan and Travis saga, the torment over Marissa and Paige, uncovering the truth in her mother's diary, and still feeling a tremendous amount of pain over her mother's death. Sadie loved boring! Boring was awesome!

CHAPTER 61

Marissa

Marissa closed her eyes, leaned her head back on the pillow of her beach chair, and soaked up the sun. Life was good. Kurt and Benton were carrying on a conversation about boats and motors and what they had discovered from their on-line search thus far.

The two couples decided they were purchasing boats over the winter so they would be ready to embark on a boating life next summer. Marissa and Andrea decided to let the guys do all the research on-line and they would enter the hunt when it was time to tour the boats.

The fun part was that it sounded as if they would be traveling to Florida, South Carolina, Massachusetts, and possibly California. Really? Did they need to go to such lengths? Benton insisted yes, and since he was a pilot for a local steel company, he assured them that he would be able to use the Learjet 60XR to travel to the boat shop. The president of the company he flew for owned a 70ft. Hatteras himself and said he would love to escort them on their trip.

Marissa and Andrea laughed that Mr. Spooler would have no interest in shopping for dinghies with them, but Benton insisted he was a down-to-earth man who would be honored to show them the ropes of the boating world. Spooler spent more time on his boat than in the office these days, and he had urged Benton in the past to buy a boat. From time to time, he would text Benton pictures of different boats for sale.

So while Kurt and Benton threw around facts and opinions about Sunseekers, Carvers, Tiaras, Sundancers, Ferretis, and a Mondomarine M60, Marissa and Andrea soaked up the sun and talked about books they had recently read and which were good enough to exchange.

Contentment. That was what Marissa was feeling. She was happy to be alive. The accident had rocked her world. She and Kurt were talking marriage. As if Lydia's death hadn't been a constant reminder to all of them about how short and precious life is, the accident was.

The kids were all getting along, and her relationship with Sadie and Jayna was what it once was, even better. Nicholas, well, Marissa loved him with every ounce of her being. She and Andrea had become great friends, and the two couples hung out often. Marissa wasn't sappy, but every now and again she had to pinch herself because just like that her life had done a one eighty, and she felt she was the luckiest, most blessed woman on the planet.

When Marissa really thought about it, she realized this was the happiest she'd been in nearly a decade. Her marriage had been rocky for a solid two to three years before the divorce. Then came Lydia's pregnancy, her illness, her death, and the struggles that came after . . .

She shifted her weight in the beach chair and leaned forward to stretch her hip. Physical therapy had gone well, especially since they were all encouraging each other through it. If the saying was true—that tragedy comes in threes—she was glad it was behind her: her divorce, Lydia's death, and the car accident. Done. Nothing but bliss from here on out, please.

Paige, Cody, Sadie, and Travis were playing Frisbee in the water with Nicholas while Jayna, Chrissie, and Liz were off, hopefully not getting into too much trouble, in town. Jayna was a bit on the wild side, but nothing Marissa couldn't handle. She often laughed at the stunts Jayna pulled: the sneaking out, getting caught downloading papers on-line, grabbing a car's bumper while riding her rip stick, "misplacing" her phone when Kurt sent texts that she needed to head home, and just being an adventurous daredevil. She reminded Marissa of Lydia, especially during their college days. She had no fear and very few boundaries and limits.

So, yes, Marissa could tolerate Jayna's sometimes erratic behavior and drama. She had the patience and love for Jayna to reel her back in when necessary. When Kurt felt helpless and was ready to give up and Sadie screamed at Jayna, calling her reckless and immature, Marissa would intervene. She knew how to relate to Jayna in a way her dad and sister didn't. She knew it was how Lydia would have handled her wild child.

She loved seeing her best friend's mannerisms, looks, and personalities through her children. Sadie's and Jayna's voices resembled Lydia's so much that sometimes Marissa would be caught off guard, thinking Lydia was speaking to her, only to turn and see her replicas, especially in Jayna.

Nicholas definitely resembled Marcus, but thankfully, there was nothing about his personality that was his father. Kurt had molded him into a caring and polite little guy. He looked a lot like Lydia and Paige. The two of them were no doubt blood-related. Paige often commented on this, and Marissa reveled in how Paige gloated over it.

Even though Kurt hadn't asked Marissa to marry him yet, they had talked not about if, but when. When they finally got around to marriage, they would buy that boat and remodel the basement. Marissa would need to list her house, and they decided Marissa would legally adopt Nicholas, and give Sadie and Jayna the option, as well. As of now, it was about enjoying the rest of the summer and the parting of so many dark clouds.

CHAPTER 62

Kurt

On an unusually hot Saturday in the middle of September, Kurt woke up and decided today was the day. He was going to propose to Marissa. He took a cup of coffee and sat out by the pool and watched the birds. He just sat and thought quietly, listening to nature, the sprinklers, the hum of the pool heater, and the roar of the air conditioner on the side of the house—that really needed service. But, in all of that, he felt incredibly sure that the time was right.

He had bought the ring three weeks ago. What was he waiting for? This, he guessed. Waking up one morning and *feeling* it, *really* feeling like today was the day.

He saw movement inside, Nicholas wandering aimlessly, most likely looking for someone to make him breakfast. Kurt and Nicholas went to wake Jayna first, since she took the longest to rouse, and found her room empty.

"Check Sadie's room, Dad," suggested Nicholas. He was thrilled to be waking up his sisters!

Jayna was sleeping on the window bed, and Sadie and Paige were in Sadie's bed. Kurt forgot Paige had slept over and thought twice about telling the girls his plan with her there. He quickly decided the time was perfect to talk to them all at once.

Kurt didn't have any fancy way of dropping it on them; he just knew *now* was the time. Without any preparation, Kurt just blurted, "What do you think about me asking Marissa to marry me?"

Silence ensued for a second as the girls all sat up and looked from one another to Kurt. Nicholas shouted, "Do it, Dad. Do it!"

"My mom?" asked Paige.

"Yes, Paige, Marissa, your mom."

"Seriously?" asked Jayna, stunned.

"Seriously," said Kurt, looking to Sadie and Paige. "That is, if I get everyone's approval and blessing."

Sadie and Paige looked at each other, and both broke into smiles. "Go for it." Paige giggled.

"Do it, Dad," blurted Nicholas again.

"Yeah, Dad, just do it!" Sadie said, mimicking Nicholas, with a wide smile spread across her face.

"Oh, Sis," Paige teased, as she hugged Sadie, falling back to their pillows.

"What about me?" screeched Jayna, as she hurdled toward the bed, landing on the two of them.

Nicholas jumped on top. "We're having a wedding. We're having a wedding," he chanted as he jumped and pumped his fists to the ceiling.

Sadie

Marissa was expected around lunch time, so they had a lot to do. The girls, along with Nicholas, piled in Sadie's Infiniti to shop for supplies. Their list was growing as they drove. Jayna was jotting down items like poster board, markers, stakes, balloons, can confetti, a headband and material to make a mock veil, flowers, sparkling juice, plastic champagne cups, and, at the request of Nicholas, cupcakes.

Once they returned, it was crunch time. They showed Kurt what they were doing, and he handed the baton over, giving them the okay to follow through with their plan. Since he had little to do but follow their instructions, he went outside to mow the lawn.

It took about two hours to complete their projects and set everything up. Now it was time to do some research. Kurt came inside to shower and was summoned over to the computer. Sadie and Paige were huddled over Sadie's laptop, and Jayna was punching away on her dad's iPad. Nicholas had long lost interest and was off playing.

Kurt saw both screens revealed upscale hotels on white sandy beaches with turquoise water and blowing palm trees. "What are you up to now?"

Jayna spoke up first. "Planning the wedding. We think it should be a destination wedding, and it *must* be some place tropical."

"Yeah, it could be a wedding and honeymoon all rolled into one!" agreed Sadie.

"I think my mom would looove it!" exclaimed Paige.

Kurt

"I haven't even asked Marissa to marry me yet, and you girls already have the wedding and honeymoon planned!?! What date have you chosen for us? Assuming she says yes. Or assuming I don't get cold feet and back out!"

That got their attention. They all looked to Kurt, wide-eyed.

"I'm kidding, but maybe we want to be alone on our honeymoon."

This got an even stranger look, as in, *why would you want that?*

Sadie spoke up, "Nonsense! We thought over Thanksgiving break would be a perfect time. We would be off school. It would be cold here, so we could go someplace warm, you know, make a vacation out of it too."

"That's in two months, girls!"

They ignored Kurt and went back to their computer screens. "I like this place in Tortola, British Virgin Islands, Peter Island Resort. It's the bomb." Jayna pointed at her screen.

"Turks and Caicos or Barbados gets my vote," said Paige.

"What about Fiji, or Belize, or even the Galapagos Islands?" Sadie sighed. "There are so many cool places, how are we ever going to pick?"

Kurt ran his fingers through his hair, announced he was going to take a shower, and declared no one was allowed to book anything.

When Marissa pulled in the driveway, her car screeched to a halt at the top so she could take in the large signs staked in the yard. "Do you think she'll throw it in reverse and back out?" whispered Kurt with a laugh. They were hiding behind the wide square pillars on the front porch.

There were five signs lining the driveway, one for each word, written in large block, multi-color letters, "WILL YOU MARRY ME, MARISSA?"

Thirty long seconds went by before Marissa slowly crept down the driveway. She parked in the circle and got out slowly, as if she was expecting what was about to happen. Sure enough, she still jumped, letting out a scream as everyone popped out from behind the pillars, chanting, "Say yes, say yes," while spraying neon colored confetti at her from aerosol cans.

Kurt made his way up the front walk, meeting her halfway. He got down on his knee and opened up the little velvet box. "Say yes," he pleaded with a grin.

Marissa's hands went up to her mouth as she looked around at the signs, balloons, the four kids, and back down at Kurt. Tears were streaming down her cheeks. "Yes! Absolutely! Positively!"

Nicholas ran to Marissa and gave her the bouquet of flowers, getting the first hug from her. Paige placed the homemade veil on her head, and one by one, they gave her hugs. Kurt, pushed aside, was last. Marissa and Sadie lingered in their embrace, and Sadie whispered in Marissa's ear. Marissa mouthed, "I love you" back in Sadie's ear.

Kurt swept Marissa up and carried her inside, where they poured sparkling juice into the plastic champagne glasses and ate gourmet cupcakes (as big as their heads) in flavors like peanut butter cup, red velvet, chocolate lava, cappuccino, vanilla butter cream, and even bubble gum goo for Nicholas. His entire face and tongue were blue in no time. "I love wedding cupcakes," he said.

They barely got into their first bites when Paige shared the idea of the destination wedding. Kurt crumpled to the couch in defeat as they each chimed in one by one with their ideas. The girls had researched hotels, airline tickets, and wedding packages right down to the flowers, photographer, and cake.

"If these girls had another hour, your dress would have been ordered online and already proceeding through shipping. I swear I just told them this morning." Kurt looked at his watch. "Literally not even four hours ago."

"What was your idea?" asked Marissa.

"My idea? Ha! I was out mowing the lawn."

Within seconds, Marissa was staring at two screens, set up side by side, looking at breathtaking resorts fit for royalty. "Did you girls remember that it actually costs money, a lot of money, to fly and stay at these places?"

"Are you serious, Mom? This is your wedding; splurge a little." Paige looked at Kurt and shrugged, giving him a wink. "Sorry."

Kurt snickered. "Yeah, I can tell."

"Aren't you going to sell your house anyway, Marissa?" asked Jayna.

That got a laugh from both Kurt and Marissa. "These kids have all the answers! Sell the house and we'll be rolling in money."

The rest of the afternoon was spent by the pool with just Kurt, Marissa, and the kids. He enjoyed it when the pool was full of company, but it was nice to have his family all to himself for a change. They were going to be a family of six!

Kurt threw his arms up in the air and told Marissa and the kids to book whatever and wherever they wanted. "Not that it will probably make a bit of difference, but I liked the sound of Tortola, that Peter Island place."

"I picked that place," Jayna said proudly.

Dear Sadie,

Some day you may acquire a wicked stepmother! Kidding! But I'm sure your dad will re-marry. He can't be alone the rest of his life, honey. I gave him my blessing. I want him to be happy.

Try your hardest to embrace her, but between us, look out for Dad. Don't let him end up with some floozy, fifteen years younger, or some mean hag that doesn't give Nicholas affection. He's still little and I want to make sure he doesn't grow up not knowing how to be loved.

It breaks my heart that I can't see you through life, the big events, and the ordinary everyday stuff. What I would give to be able to spend a day with you and your future family at the park or planting flowers or being there at the bus stop as you send your firstborn to kindergarten.

I guess what I'm trying to say is that since you won't have me, it doesn't mean that you can't have anybody. I really hope you can form a motherly bond and your kids can form a grandmotherly bond with someone who will love your father.

I love you,

Mom

CHAPTER 63

Sadie

The night before they were leaving for Tortola, Sadie had a million things to do. She was always a last-minute packer, and she wished she had prepped days ago. Packing for ten days took time, especially since she was also packing Nicholas's suitcase and stopping to help Jayna every other minute.

Travis kept distracting her with Bitmojis of him with a giant heart on his back that read, *I LOVE YOU MORE*, and, *CAN'T WAIT TO SEE YOU!* She playfully reprimanded him that she had a to-do list a mile long.

Sadie still had to finish a written chemistry lab report and email it to her teacher tonight, and it was nearing ten o'clock. Their flight left at 6:00 a.m., which meant they had to leave at 4:00 a.m. for the airport, which in turn meant Sadie had to get up no later than 3:15 a.m.! She was starting to panic. Travis, Andrea, and Benton were accompanying them on the trip. Sadie was ecstatic, while Paige was bummed that Cody would be back home. No other family members were able to make the trip, which was actually okay with Sadie and, from what she could tell, her dad too. Sometimes it just added more drama.

Kurt and Marissa had grown very close with Andrea and Benton over the past year. Thank God Sadie loved Travis's parents, because having her parents and her boyfriend's parents as close friends could have been difficult.

She quickly abandoned the neat folding she was doing to save space and just started shoving swimsuits, sundresses, cutoffs, and sandals in her suitcase. Besides the wedding, she would be living in her swimsuit most of the time anyway.

Sadie thought of her mother. "Whatever you forgot, you buy new" was her motto when they went on vacation. With that, Sadie zipped her bag and hauled it downstairs to the mudroom next to Nicholas's.

By midnight, she had sent her mediocre paper to her least favorite teacher. He was obviously annoyed that Sadie was missing school during her senior year at the same time she was getting college applications ready—even if it was for her father's wedding and half of the vacation was over Thanksgiving break anyway. Jerk.

When Sadie finally turned her light out, she said her prayers half to God and half to her mom. When they returned home from Tortola, Marissa and Paige would be living with them. Most of their stuff had already been moved over, but Marissa was adamant that they not move in officially until the day they returned from their wedding/honeymoon.

This was the last night it would be just the four Bookers. She prayed to God that he would keep them safe when they traveled, that the wedding would go smoothly and be beautiful. She prayed that He would bless their marriage and their new family. She prayed that her mother was okay with it, that her mom was happy that they were happy. She told her mom that no one could ever replace her, but she was so thankful that decades ago her mom had befriended Marissa.

At seventeen, Sadie was well beyond her years, but she still needed a mom, and lying there in bed, she knew there was no one else she would rather have as her mom than Marissa. It had taken a long time, well over a year, but her guard was finally down. She not only accepted Marissa; she loved her too. She was ready to have a mom again.

When her alarm went off, she hadn't remembered falling asleep. Sadie showered in under three minutes, threw her comfy travel clothes on, and her hair went up in a bun. She packed her travel-sized toiletries in her carry on and zipped up the garment bag containing Nicholas's and her dad's wedding attire and her and Jayna's own dresses for the wedding. They were out the door in record speed to pick up Marissa and Paige.

They barely had the Denali in park when Paige flew out the door with a robe on and her hands over her face like she was crying. "Uh oh," said Jayna.

"She's a wreck, you guys. My mom has been up all night crying, saying she isn't ready to get married. I've tried everything. I told her to just get on the plane, that she didn't have to go through with the wedding, but she's refusing to go." Paige was very dramatic, flinging her arms and fumbling for words.

"You kids stay here. I'm going to go talk to her," said Kurt, getting out.

"No! She doesn't want to see you. She feels horrible. I think it's too soon. It all happened way too fast. She's just not ready to marry you yet."

Sadie's heart sank into her stomach as she looked at her dad's face. Maybe she should go talk to Marissa. How could she do this? Yesterday, Marissa had stopped by and dropped off a few more boxes. She and Jayna had even put up a few decorations together around the house. Marissa cleaned out the fridge and scrubbed the floors and bathrooms, saying she loved coming home from vacation to a clean house. She seemed so excited and happy. Sadie totally did not see this coming.

Kurt

Kurt got out of the car, pushed past Paige, and headed for the front door. Paige was running behind him. "Seriously, Kurt, she wants to be left alone! I wouldn't go in there!"

He flung the door open and found Marissa sitting on top of her suitcase, nervously looking at her watch. "Isn't she hilarious? She has been begging me for days to do this to you!" Marissa threw her arms around Kurt. "She's a real peach, isn't she? You can scream at your future stepdaughter all you want. Let's go get married!"

Kurt let out a huge sigh and eyed Paige. She was still giggling as she shed her robe, wheeled her suitcase around them and outside into the cold November morning. He and Marissa lingered inside over a kiss as the kids started honking the horn and yelling out the window that the plane was going to leave without them.

Sadie

The Villa Estates was luxury at its finest. Sadie instantly knew that her father had spared no expense on this trip. As soon as her toes curled around the white powdery sand, Sadie knew she never wanted to leave.

Scuba diving, deep-sea fishing, tennis, snorkeling, wave running, parasailing, zip lining, the list was endless and they were determined to do every bit of it and a whole lot of nothing too. The first three days were spent doing just that, playing and loafing by the pool and on the beach.

To Sadie's surprise, Kurt allowed her and Travis to go parasailing together. It was amazing. Sadie was in heaven. The views were breathtaking and she was beside her boyfriend.

The fourth day was the wedding day. It was weird, getting ready for her dad's wedding. Sadie was jittery, anxious, nervous, happy, and a bit sad, all rolled into one.

Andrea must have sensed it and asked her to go for a walk on the beach an hour before they were to report to the spa to get glamorous.

Andrea always knew what to say and, even better, what *not* to say. She was the best listener. Sadie thanked Andrea for being there for her and giving her advice, but mostly for allowing her to figure things out on her own and helping keep her mom's memory alive.

Before getting their hair and makeup done, all the girls had the works: massages, facials, pedicures, and manicures. The long and glorious morning in the spa was the most pampering Sadie had ever received in her life.

The ladies were in one villa and the guys in another. They helped each other with the last-minute details of dressing and jewelry. Marissa looked stunning in her fitted strapless wedding gown that had a sheer layer of silk showing off her petite figure. The simple, elegant Vera Wang gown was perfect for a beach wedding amidst the turquoise water.

Sadie, Jayna, Paige, and even Andrea all had matching dresses. They were the most beautiful coral color Sadie had ever seen. She joked that she matched the geraniums they potted around the pool every summer, but had to admit they looked stunning against their bronzed bodies and French manicures. The deep plunge that bared their backs kept them cool in the humid tropical air.

The guys all wore Armani, white linen pants and black linen short-sleeved shirts with loafers. The look among the group definitely turned heads. Marissa was carrying a dozen coral roses and the girls a handful of long-stemmed white calla lilies. The guys all had a single white calla lily pinned to their shirt. The look was something straight from a bridal magazine.

Just before they left the room, the girls showered Marissa with gifts. Paige went first. She was giving her mother something old she had found while packing for the move to their new house. Paige's baby blanket, once a beautiful cream-colored chenille blanket, was now a grayish knotted mess. Paige had cut a hunk off for Marissa to tuck under her bra, the only place she could find to stuff it.

Andrea went next, giving Marissa a gorgeous tennis bracelet to borrow. The diamonds would no doubt sparkle beautifully in the sunlight. Jayna was in charge of something blue. Marissa blushed when she opened the sexy and skimpy but tasteful cobalt blue lingerie. "Please don't ever let me see you in it," teased Jayna.

Something new was Sadie's creation. She had a necklace specially made for Marissa that had four rectangular plates with each of the kid's names stamped on a plate. Sadie's gift brought all of them to tears, but they quickly decided they couldn't get sappy or they would ruin their makeup.

Sadie hugged Marissa. "There is no one else I would rather have as a stepmother. Thanks for being patient with me."

Marissa squeezed Sadie tightly. "I've never stopped loving you from the first time I held you in the hospital and you were only hours old. Thank you for accepting me."

Paige gave Sadie and Jayna both hugs and told them how excited she was to have stepsisters, that it was a dream come true.

"I thought we were through with all this sappy crap!" Jayna blurted, dabbing at her eyes with a tissue.

"We have a wedding to get to," reminded Andrea. "The guys are probably all standing at the altar, waiting for us."

As Sadie stood under the pergola adorned with lush greens and exotic flowers, she first checked out how hot Travis looked. She couldn't help but pretend that it was their wedding day. *Maybe someday*, she thought. He blew her a kiss with his lips, and she mouthed "sexy" back to him, and they both giggled.

Next she caught her dad's eye, her dad's nervous eye. He looked happy, really happy, but there was no doubt in

Sadie's mind that entering a new marriage meant letting another piece of Lydia go, his college sweetheart, the mother of his children, the woman he grew into a man with.

Sadie slipped her dad a reassuring smile that she knew he desperately needed from her. He mouthed, "I love you, sweetie," back to her.

"I love you too," whispered Sadie. He sent her a wink as the harp started, and Nicholas dropped sea shells down the aisle as he made his way to stand next to his father.

Like a gentle breeze, a mourning dove fluttered down and found its place on the pergola and cooed along with the harp. It seemed to catch Marissa's attention and her eyes both brightened and glistened at the sight of the bird.

Marissa floated down the aisle in a glow of her own. Sadie saw her dad's and Marissa's eyes lock, and they both broke out in huge smiles.

A chill ran through Sadie as she thought of her mom, hoping she was okay with this. A light breeze blew off the ocean, sending a large purple flower from above Sadie's head down to her shoulder. The cool flower tickled Sadie's bare skin. She felt the soft petals and brought it to her nose, inhaling deeply.

Whether it was a trick of her nose or not—Sadie didn't care. It smelled just like her mother, light and sweet.

THE FABULOUS END

ACKNOWLEDGMENTS

Writing can be a solitary venture, but I give credit to many people for making this book possible.

To my family, Jason, thank you for always providing me with endless love, helping me develop thick skin, modeling perseverance, and not getting too annoyed with my technological deficiencies. Alex, Tori, Cole, and Miya, my love for you is unconditional, and without knowing it, you've all inspired my writing in countless ways. The fun, frantic, and fierce moments—you make it worth every second. I love you to every beach and back!

To my mom, Karen, for being my first reader ever and helping me get past the initial stage fright of letting people actually read my words. Also, to both you and Denny for being the dedicated grandparents you are. It is with your help, that I can concentrate and savor a few moments of peace to articulate a coherent sentence.

Thank you to all my readers, especially Jill MacLaren and Rachel Devereaux for your time, dedication, honesty, and enthusiasm. Jill, your valuable input and guidance helped me navigate telling a story from many different points of view and reach out to a larger audience. Rachel, your attention to detail and love for my characters is so encouraging, and thanks for the extra kick of confidence! You both gave me that fresh set of eyes I so desperately needed.

Sarah Hansen at Okay Creations, for bringing Sadie to life and creating the exact feeling I was looking for, your talent amazes me.

To my editor, Theresa Wegand, thank you for taking on a newbie and guiding me through all these firsts. I've learned so much along the way. Your professionalism, sense of detail, and insight are deeply appreciated.

Thank you God for your scripture. Without it, I would have given up long ago.

ABOUT THE AUTHOR

Jamie Berris is a graduate of Grand Valley State University with a degree in Health Science. After working in the health and wellness industry for nearly fifteen years, she embarked on a writing career.

Her hobbies include running, reading, writing, boating, camping on the shores of Lake Michigan, and traveling with her family.

She resides in West Michigan with her husband and four children. Whispering Waves is her debut novel.

Visit her Facebook page, facebook.com/Jamie Berris

Instagram: JamieBerris